What people are saying about

Safe at Home

"A moving and, at times, heart-breaking story of a small Southern town stubbornly resisting change in the 1950s and a minor league ballplayer caught in the crossfire. The baseball scenes ring with authenticity, and so does Doster's portrait of a small Southern town of the 1950s. After reading *Safe at Home,* you will come away with a better understanding of what black players truly experienced when the color barriers in baseball began to fall."

—PETE VAN WIEREN, ATLANTA BRAVES BROADCASTER

"Richard Doster uses the universal language of sports to illustrate lessons about life in his thought-provoking and gripping novel, *Safe at Home*. The pages are packed with the edge-of-your-seat tension found in a World Series game tied at the bottom of the ninth. It is well worth reading."

—CANDEE FICK, AUTHOR OF *PIGSKIN PARABLES: REFLECTIONS OF A FOOTBALL WIDOW*

"*Safe at Home* provides a vivid look at the culture of the American South a dozen years or more before the Civil Rights movement erupted onto the nation's conscience. This fast-paced read couched amidst a summer of baseball nails the mood of the people—both white and black—in the early 1950s, and reminds us that there were no winners in segregation, just victims, and that includes the nation itself. I eagerly await a director of Stephen Spielberg's caliber bringing this compelling tale to the big screen. It's got *blockbuster* written all over it."

—KAREN L. WILLOUGHBY, MANAGING EDITOR, *LOUISIANA BAPTIST MESSAGE*

"I could say that Dick Doster 'hit one outta the park,' but that might imply *Safe at Home* is only about baseball. Nothing could be further from the truth. *Safe at Home* is about 1950s southern folks struggling with one of America's toughest issues: racial equality. Yet it's not only an issue book or a study of the best and worst in human nature disguised as a novel. Through deft plotting and nuanced characters, Doster makes readers understand—no, care about—people on his pages and their relationships with each other. Plus, he nails small-town southern life so accurately you long for a porch swing and a pitcher of sweet tea. I hated for the book to end and beg for a sequel."

—CAROLYN CURTIS, AUTHOR, WRITER, SPEAKER, AND FOUNDING EDITOR OF *ON MISSION* MAGAZINE

"This is a warm and challenging story about a teenage baseball player and a committed sports writer. It is about talent, grace, redemption, and two people who deeply love the game of baseball. It's about overcoming the culture of the times in the Deep South ... to enjoy the game. Doster writes so cleanly and passionately, I felt like I was right there in the bleachers. I got goose bumps when the crowd sang 'Swing Low, Sweet Chariot'!"

—RALPH N. STEWART, FORMER PLAYER AND COACH,
REGIONAL DIRECTOR FOR THE FELLOWSHIP OF CHRISTIAN ATHLETES

"Richard Doster's *Safe at Home* is a story told with expected conflicts and resolutions, yet it has an underbelly of such poignant truth that it offers the reader a compelling review of our social history that was both magnified and codified by the game of baseball and the breaking of the color barrier. In the end, there's healing in this story and that matters."

—Terry Kay, author of *To Dance with the White Dog* and *The Book of Marie*

"While you're reading *Safe at Home,* it becomes obvious that Richard Doster loves baseball. But this is far more than a baseball book. It's a history lesson and a social commentary. It's about doing the right thing in the face of brutal consequences; it's about courage overcoming the ignorance of racism; it's about using your God-given talents whether you're playing the game or writing about the players who do. Yeah, this book's about baseball, but when you really get down to it, it's about the soul."

—Ernie Johnson, sportscaster, TNT and TBS

"If you appreciate baseball, history, and Southern fiction, *Safe at Home* is an excellent blend. With a vivid style, Richard Doster creates empathy with the struggle of black ballplayers in the era of Jackie Robinson. And with his lucid descriptions of the Jim Crow South, he compels you to imagine Percy's struggle in light of what we know of Robinson's."

—Willy Daunic, host of *Sports Zone* on Nashville's 104.5, former minor league player for the Toronto Blue Jays

"If you've loved baseball your whole life as I have, you've always believed that the game is a true reflection of American society. Richard Doster's book, *Safe at Home,* is a celebration of that belief. Using the backdrop of the racially torn South in the 1950s, Doster rewards the reader with a great baseball story and a fascinating study of the sociology of the times. There's something in this book for the diehard baseball fan and for the reader who never watches the game."

—Jamie Samuelsen, sports radio host, WDFN Detroit

"This story pulls at your heartstrings as you read about how the simple game of baseball has changed the hearts and minds of so many in our country. This is a reminder of how far we have come over the years, and how courage, dreams, and a love for a game can move mountains. I enjoyed the journey through the pages of *Safe at Home,* and I know you will too."

—Brett Butler, former Major League player, former manager of the Mobile BayBears

Safe at Home

A NOVEL

Safe at Home

A NOVEL

Richard Doster

SAFE AT HOME
Published by David C. Cook
4050 Lee Vance View
Colorado Springs, CO 80918 U.S.A.

David C. Cook Distribution Canada
55 Woodslee Avenue, Paris, Ontario, Canada N3L 3E5

David C. Cook U.K., Kingsway Communications
Eastbourne, East Sussex BN23 6NT, England

LCCN 2007939849
ISBN 978-1-4347-0010-0

Published in association with the literary agency of Alive Communications, Inc,
7680 Goddard St., Suite 200, Colorado Springs, CO 80920

The Team: Don Pape, Steve Parolini, Jaci Schneider, Susan Vannaman
Cover/Interior Design: The DesignWorks Group
Cover Photo: © Masterfile Royalty-Free / Masterfile

Printed in the United States of America
First Edition 2008

1 2 3 4 5 6 7 8 9 10

121807

To Sally, who makes every moment worthwhile.
To Ted, for his faithfulness.
To Rob and Angie, for their courage.

And to Pete Van Wieren, Don Sutton, Skip Caray,
and Joe Simpson—who brought a great game to life.

Author's Note and Acknowledgments

This is a work of fiction. The characters in this book and the events of their lives are products of my imagination. But they're inspired by the flesh-and-blood South of the 1950s—a time and place that came to life in my mind through the meticulous work of many others. I'm grateful to Hank Aaron who recorded his experiences in *I Had a Hammer: The Hank Aaron Story* (HarperCollins, 1991). Joseph Thomas Moore's book, *Pride Against Prejudice: The Biography of Larry Doby* (Praeger, 1988) provided context and background. *Local People: The Struggle for Civil Rights in Mississippi* by John Dittmer (University of Illinois Press, 1995) and *My Soul is Rested: The Story of the Civil Rights Movement in the Deep South* by Howell Raines (Penguin Books, 1977) are among many books that provided vivid images of the era. I'm especially indebted to Bruce Adelson for his work *Brushing Back Jim Crow: The Integration of Minor-League Baseball in the American South* (University Press of Virginia, 1999). And I owe thanks to librarians at Emory University and Georgia State University for directing me to newspaper and magazine archives, primary sources that shed light on this troubling time.

Thanks also to Bill Hollberg, one of the few men I know who's willing to do the hard work of being a good friend. And to Lee Hough, a literary agent with a keen eye and persevering heart. And to Stephen Parolini and Jaci Schneider, editors who trimmed deftly and refined beautifully.

OCTOBER 1954

Four events have molded the world to its current form.

At the beginning of time Eve ate forbidden fruit, and as its juice trickled down her chin, mankind's heart began to pump selfishness, envy, and arrogance through his veins—and ever since, we have been a hard lot to live with.

Later, in Midian, God flamed before Moses and commanded him to lead an oppressed people into a land of freedom and fulfillment, forever inspiring hope among the persecuted and callusing the hearts of their oppressors.

Long after that our own country was conceived in liberty and dedicated to, of all things, the proposition that all men were created equal.

And the fourth event—is this: On April 10, 1947, Jackie Robinson became a Brooklyn Dodger.

Sitting where I sit today, and seeing the things I've seen, it seems as though Robinson shook the world harder than Jefferson or Lincoln—and nearly as much as Moses. Who would've thought that a colored infielder could've churned the South into such a frenzy? And who would have believed that a second baseman would have so thoroughly roused the sleepy towns that dot Dixie? But from that day to this one, baseball has been the world's window into the relations of men and races. And ballplayers have been God's chosen tool to melt—or harden—men's hearts.

Whitney is no different from a hundred other towns below the Mason-Dixon Line. City Hall dominates a main square, and side streets spoke off in the principal directions of the compass. The post office, Magnolia Diner, Piggly Wiggly, and three churches—Baptist, Presbyterian, and Methodist—are the main spots where people gather. Life is settled here, predictable, and one day flows easily into the next. Folks are born here and they die here. And in between times they gossip about their neighbors, brag about their kids, complain about the weather, glory in the home teams' victories, and suffer in their defeats.

I've been the sportswriter here since the end of World War II. And since Whitney's never been bigger than a 12-point dot on any map I've ever seen, I follow Stonewall Jackson High School closer than the *Times* covers the Yankees. The state college is in the capital, just eighty-five miles north, and a lot of our folks follow the Raiders closer than grain prices and weather reports. But the team that has taken hold of my neighbors' hearts is our Class C farm team, the Bobcats. Through the summers, and into the fall, this is the team that keeps the town talking. The Bobcats've been Sunshine Circuit champions three times since I've been here, and never finished worse than third. They've sent five kids to the big leagues, and we've been proud to call each one our own.

For as long as anyone can remember, Charley Baxter has run the team. In his playing days Charley spent seven run-of-the-mill seasons in the big leagues; his lifetime batting average was somewhere around .225. He had a decent enough glove but was slower than biscuit gravy. Still, Charley had a flair for coming through in the clutch, and that kept him around the National League longer than anybody expected, including Charley. Since then he's crisscrossed the South on every bus that bears the Trailways name. And on dusty diamonds in no-name towns, he's transformed farm boys and factory workers into fielders, pitchers, and hitters. Charley has always been a by-the-book tactician and a gruff but kind soul who hates to lose. Baseball oozes through the man's pores like sweat through a roofer's. He grasps his game like Beethoven mastered music. And he marshals his team around a diamond better than Lee ran the Army of Virginia during the Peninsula Campaign. The only part of the newspaper Charley reads is the part I write, and that makes us friends, most of the time. Charley has been at home here, and at peace. He, the team, and the town have patched themselves together into a warm, familiar quilt that covers us all.

Up north and out west, the world heaved and pulled and changed course. But here, it had been kind enough to stand still—until 1946. Then it began to stir. In the early '50s nobody knew precisely where it was headed. Nobody knows now. But by the end of 1954, Charley and I stood square in its path.

Part 1

Spring 1953

Chapter 1

We live in a two-story brick house skirted by a wide porch where four wicker rockers, two on either side of a bright red door, beckon our neighbors to visit. At the south end of the porch a matching swing creaks in the warm breeze. And potted plants, whose contents change with Rose Marie's whims, are scattered everywhere. In the front yard a gnarled magnolia takes an imposing stance, transforming an ordinary lawn into something regal. Small flowerbeds lay beside the steps that lead to the porch. Pansies add color there in the winter, but now a fresh crop of impatiens is the ornament of choice.

This is the home where I brought Rose Marie about a decade ago. This is where we've cobbled out most of our life together, where the two of us—day by day, joy by joy, and chore by chore—have grown together, inseparable, and into one flesh. Let me tell you about Rose Marie: She is breathtaking. Her hair is long and thick and the color of maple syrup. Her eyes are darker than ink; they're lively, alert, and always eager. She's childlike and wise; frugal and generous; honest and kind. To anyone who's in her presence, she is effortless company, and she grows prettier, happier, and more captivating by the day.

Our son, Christopher, joined us two years into the marriage. He's a mess almost all the time. At twelve years old, he's a boy's boy who, at the end of the school day, is jumpier than a thoroughbred in the starting gate—waiting for the bell that will set him free. He is forever enthralled by the wonders a drainage ditch offers, and he explores the banks of the Cherokee River as if he were Lewis or Clark, never failing to find some extraordinary new treasure. Often, he and his friends play baseball or football or some other contest they concoct that demands sliding, falling, or plunging into an appreciable amount of mud. From the moment he kicked his way into the world, Christopher gave new meaning to Rose Marie's life, and nothing kindles warmth within me like the sight of my wife mothering our son.

Every morning Rose Marie is up before most of the milkmen in town, and before I can form a coherent thought, she's filled the house with smells that make me love home: frying bacon, percolating coffee, simmering grits. I know I'll cherish the memory of these smells when I'm bent and frail. So I savor them now, strongly suspecting that they're the secret ingredients that transform common houses into the homes that families share. Smells of food, or clothing, or of one another are a part of what binds Rose Marie, Christopher, and me together. And when I smell the bacon and coffee, I'm grateful for the new day. For her. For Christopher. For the life we've been given. And for the place where we live.

Like most mornings, I find her on the porch, coffee in hand and resting on the arm of her rocker. A copy of the *Herald* sits on her lap, open to the sports page and to whatever I happened to write the day before. Sounds from the radio drift out from the kitchen; instead of the usual weather report or latest commodity prices, the voice of Nat King Cole serenades the morning. Sipping my own coffee, I lean into the doorframe, shove my free hand into my bathrobe pocket, watch her, and wait for the morning's verdict.

"Well?" I finally ask. She doesn't look up, just continues to read as if she's studying for a college final. Then she begins to nod purposefully.

"This isn't bad, Hall … in fact, it's good."

I slide into the rocker beside her. "Gee, thanks."

"No kidding," she goes on, "I like this right here:

> "In the bottom of the seventh with two outs and with Andrews on second, Taylor waited on a changeup and drove it deep to the right-center gap. Andrews broke on contact, rounded third, and with no hesitation barreled home. The

> relay was late and strayed up the first-base line. Andrews was safe standing. The run held and gave the Bobcats a 3-2 win, and a three game lead in the standings.

"Very nice." She folded the paper in half, stood, and headed for the door, slapping the paper against my shoulder as she passed. "Good work, Hall, I'm proud of you." Then she reached around me, bent down, and kissed me on the ear. "Chris about ready?"

"Yeah," I said, tilting my head back to meet hers. "He'll be down in a second."

She kissed me again. "Well, breakfast is all set, I'll get it on the table."

I sat awhile longer, letting the coffee have its effect, and basking in the approval of the only critic I really care about. Then I headed for the kitchen too. Chris sat before a heap of eggs and bacon, spreading apple jelly onto a biscuit that leaked butter over its sides. I mussed his hair as I passed. "Ready for school, pal?"

"Yep," he said. "I guess." He wore a blue-striped pullover shirt that was, for the moment, tucked into faded blue jeans. Clay-stained Keds had been pulled over white socks rimmed by a pair of red stripes. His hair, close-cropped and two shades lighter than his mother's, fell evenly across his forehead, banglike, just above thin, honey-colored eyebrows.

"Gonna learn anything special today?" I asked.

"Naw," he answered. Then he looked up and grinned. "Probably just review."

"Review" was the answer he always gave to end any investigation into his schoolwork. I took the hint and moved on to more interesting matters.

"So what's up later?" I asked. "You got baseball practice today?"

His cheeks were puffed full of biscuit and he shook his head no. Then he mumbled, "Building a fort." The response was matter-of-fact, like that of a thirty-year-old man describing an eight-to-five job. "…in the woods," he continued, "down by the river."

"Yeah, well, you guys be careful down there. Don't let any animals eat you, you hear?"

He lifted his eyebrows with waggish gravity. "We all got slingshots," he said. "A bear or snake gets close to us … well, he'll wish he hadn't. And besides, I'd sick Slugger on 'em." At the sound of his name our big brown and gray mutt slapped the table leg with his tail and nosed Chris's hand, prodding him into some overt act of affection.

"What about you?" Rose Marie interrupted. "What's going on with you today, Hall?"

I chased a mouthful of eggs with a gulp of barely warm coffee. "Got an interview with State's baseball coach this morning," I answered, "one he's not looking forward to, I'm afraid. Then I thought I might ride out to South City High, take a look at those kids … just see what's happening out there."

Rose Marie turned, her eyes rounded wide. "South City? Since when does the *Herald* report on South City High? And since when do you care about what goes on out there?"

"Don't really," I answered, "but they're winning. And William—you remember William, the janitor down at the paper—his boy's on the team. He says they got a few kids who can play. I got some time." I shrugged. "Thought it'd be nice to stop by."

Rose Marie rinsed off a plate. "Think you'll spot the next Jackie Robinson?" She tossed me a sly look. "Is that it?"

I grinned back at her. "You never know. Jackie was a Georgia boy before he moved west; stranger things have happened."

"Well," Rose Marie drawled, "I suspect Jackie's momma moved west for good reason."

◆ ◆ ◆ ◆

I had been in this town for years, but never to the colored high school. Cresting Mason's Mill Road, I spotted it nestled at the end of the dusty street, maybe nine or ten miles south of the town square. I swung into the parking lot and watched the kids amble here and there, joking and jostling with one another, finding excuses to avoid the after-school work that I suspected most of them had. I made my way to the main entrance feeling more conspicuous than a red cape in a sold-out bullring. Pulling one of the double doors open, I felt suspicious glances follow me. And whenever anyone met my eyes, I saw the faint signs of trepidation that the presence of a white man brings to this part of town.

I stepped into the main hall and the kids parted before me, clearing a wide path. But as I rounded the first corner, a Joe Louis-sized teacher stomped out of a classroom. We crashed together—his chest to my head—and I stumbled. I groped for a locker or the wall. I touched a hand to the floor to keep from falling. Fear flashed across his face. He scolded a handful of stunned students and then quickly turned to me. "I-I-I'm sorry," he stammered gently, "very, very sorry." He held out a steadying hand. "Please, sir, what can we do to help you?"

I took his hand and shook it. "Jack Hall."

"Yes, sir," he sputtered. "What can I do for you, Mr. Hall?"

"I'm looking for the baseball field." I glanced toward the back of the school. "It's back this way, I guess?"

"Yes, sir." He pointed vaguely in the same direction, "straight ahead and then to your right." He looked puzzled. "You know, we don't get a lot of white folks out to our games."

"No, don't guess you do," I answered. "I work for the *Herald*. Write sports and some other things. Heard your team's pretty good this year. I just came to have a look."

The tension suddenly turned him loose, and a sparkle wriggled its way into his eyes. "Oh, they're better'n good." He grinned. "This bunch … I tell you what, they got magic."

From his tone, his stance, and his smile, I knew that I'd come across a fellow traveler, one who's rightly warmed by the beauty of a well-timed hit-and-run; who marvels at a perfectly thrown changeup when everybody in the stadium's looking for a fastball; who envies the instincts of an outfielder who can hit the cutoff man from the warning track. I returned the involuntary smile that you give a kindred spirit and feebly replied, "You like baseball?"

The smile widened into an *are-you-kidding-me* grin. "Yes, sir, I do." A pause hung between us, and then he said, "Why don't you stay right here for just one second. I'll show you where the field is myself." He disappeared into his classroom.

"I didn't catch your name," I hollered after him.

He reappeared, pulling a well-worn driving cap onto his head. "Walter," he said, squaring the cap in place, "Walter Jackson."

Trailing in Walter Jackson's wake, I passed a dirt basketball court; the chain net on one goal dangled limply from the rim. The other goal was bare and rusty-orange. There was no half-court line, no foul lines, baselines, or sidelines. As we came closer to the baseball field, I could see that a pale red-clay circle was shaped into a diamond by three cloth bases and a hard-rubber home plate. The outfield was a patchwork of green and brown grass speckled by dandelions and other anonymous weeds. There was no fence or lights. A sun-bleached scoreboard wobbled in right field, maybe 350 feet from home plate. In left field a billowing willow stood, the most resplendent foul pole in all of baseball. And in right a humbler pine performed the same duty. Forty or fifty fans sat on a battered grandstand behind home plate: kids mostly, and a handful of parents. Instead of dugouts, each team occupied a bench halfway down either baseline, open to the elements, and defenseless against slashing foul balls.

A couple of spots were open on the second row of the rickety bleachers.

"Here we go." I motioned to Walter and slid down to make room for him. He stopped. He stood there, flustered—as if he'd been stumped by a problem that was too ticklish to even mention.

Then Walter held up both hands. "You wait right here," he said. He rushed over to a couple of men sitting nearby, farmhands or sharecroppers who sat in tattered, rust-eaten lawn chairs along the first-base line. While I watched Walter, the man beside me—a plant worker I guessed from the smell—rubbed his hands together. He shuffled his feet. His eyes darted back and forth, first at me, then quickly away. He crossed his arms, then uncrossed them. Scratched his head, and his arm. Then he shot up from his seat and rushed to the backstop. And he stood there, staring straight ahead with his fingers laced through the chain-link fence.

Walter returned with one of the lawn chairs, its former occupant straggling behind. He set it down beside the bleachers and said, "Why don't you sit here. And Horace," he motioned to the chair's owner, "he'll take that seat."

I looked at Walter and then at Horace. Then, slowly, I nodded my agreement. "Sorry," I mumbled. "Guess I wasn't thinking. Thanks, Horace."

"Yes, sir," Horace answered, "it ain't no problem at all." He climbed into the grandstand, and I took his chair—a makeshift "white section" at South City High.

South City's coach stood a few feet in front of home plate. He wore khaki work pants, a sweat-soaked T-shirt, and a bright red South City cap pulled low to shade his eyes from the sun. He motioned toward third. "Get one," he barked, as he stroked a routine ground ball down the baseline.

Walter leaned forward, resting his arms on his knees. He backhanded my leg and motioned toward third. "He's the most magic of all," he said. Walter's eyes traced every motion as the shortstop, second baseman, and first baseman all took a turn scooping up soft grounders. I don't believe I've ever seen anyone so entranced by infield practice.

The coach turned his attention back to third, and this time yelled, "Get two." Walter watched the kid glide to his left, and in a single smooth motion accept the ball into his glove and throw across his body, leading the second baseman perfectly in the first half of an imaginary double play. I studied the kid for a minute—the shape of his nose and mouth, the way he was built—then I looked back to Walter and laughed. "That's your boy, isn't it?"

Walter's head bobbed. "Yes, sir," he said, "and I'll tell you what, that kid can play. Just watch him … boy's smooth as silk."

"What's his name?" I asked.

"Percy." Walter gleamed, his eyes never leaving the field. "Named after his grandfather."

Percy Jackson was seventeen, and a junior. His legs and arms were too long for his body, but they were synchronized like pistons in a just-tuned V-8. When he wasn't playing third, he pitched: fastballs and changeups mostly, nothing fancy. He was hitting .364 the day I first saw him, and he had a swing that brought Stan Musial to mind. He was a slow-moving kid who ambled from one place to the next, shiftless and lazy-looking—until a ground ball violated his territory. Then he pounced like a cheetah who'd just spotted dinner.

Chapter 2

Memorial Stadium is the home of the Whitney Bobcats. It stands on a rise near the banks of the Cherokee River, three and a half miles from the center of town. As you come up the hill toward it, you round a leftward bend where the red-clay road traces a thick forest of pines and poplars, all draped in a thick curtain of kudzu. When the road restraightens, the stadium flashes into view and stands like a fortress: deep red brick against the infinite blue sky, perched high, and protected by a wide ribbon of blue-black water.

Closer, the road forks into a pair of dirt parking lots where a handful of Bobcat-hatted attendants hustle from one row to the next, directing Chevys, Buicks, and Fords to their places. As fans emerge from their cars, they're baptized by the glow of stadium lights and dusk filtered sunshine. The air is tinged with anticipation, and the just-cut grass, boiling hot dogs, and roasting peanuts are perfume that sends a shiver down every baseball lover's spine.

The stadium's brick façade houses a two-window box office. And ushers, who consider the task of tearing tickets a solemn duty, herd fans through four turnstiles. When it's filled to capacity, the stadium seats five thousand five hundred.

The press box is small but comfortable. It's perched at the highest point inside the stadium, behind the last row of seats, slightly off-center to the first-base side. Inside, there's room for a half-dozen reporters, but no more than three or four ever show. That night it was me; Jeff Harrison, a reporter-announcer-advertising salesman from WHTY, our local radio station; and Hank Wheeler, the reporter from Madison.

I've crossed paths with Hank for the ten years or so I've been here. He went to the University of Alabama, and from what I hear, his desk is a shrine to the Crimson Tide. He's a good baseball man, likes basketball well enough, tolerates golf, and worships college football. A Lucky Strike is a permanent appendage to the man's lower lip. And a paper cup, two fingers full of Jack Daniels, ordinarily rests within arm's reach after sunset. Hank's been covering sports for twenty-five years, and I believe, with a few likely exceptions in the Auburn area, he is the most trusted man in Alabama.

Jeff Harrison is a thin, shy man, and a bona fide public servant. He believes with all his heart that he's been sent into the world to love his neighbors—to provide them with local news, weather reports, and grain and cotton prices. Jeff loves baseball, and he loves hanging out in the press box where the air's filled with the smell of cheap cigars, where he can knock back a beer with the guys, and where he can talk earnestly and forever about batting averages, ERAs, and RBIs.

For the three of us, being here is a high and holy privilege.

Whitney and Madison were both expected to finish near the top of the standings. Both had a handful of kids with a shot at the big leagues. And, at that point, Madison was two and a half games behind us. When I walked into the press box, Hank was settled into the seat nearest the door, scribbling notes on a pad. He shot a quick wave my way and continued transferring thoughts from mind to paper. From the top of the stadium we heard bats cracking and mitts popping; we smelled the fresh-cut grass and just-laid chalk.

Fans were packed tight behind home plate, but just a smattering of dark blue caps dotted the bleachers. And in the colored section out toward left field, no more than a hundred fans were settled in for the night's game.

"Well," I said, "how are things looking for your guys tonight?"

Hank jotted down another few words and then tossed his pen on top of the pad. "Pretty fair. Nichol's pitching, his ERA's under three. Patterson's on a five-game hitting streak, team hasn't made an error in a while." He shrugged. "If we keep that up, it oughtta be a game."

"Yeah," I said, "I expect so." I began to make myself comfortable near the center of the room, arranging a legal pad, the ten perfectly sharpened pencils I always bring, along with a half-eaten hot dog and a sweaty cup of Schlitz. At the other end of the room Jim Holby, the PA announcer, fumbled through stacks of files and folders searching for the National Anthem. He cued up the forty-five on the record player behind him. "Well, Jack," he said, "looks like you're 'bout set for one more night of baseball."

"Yeah," I replied, stretching the word to three syllables, "I'm just about there."

He glanced at the clock on the back wall. "Well, it's that time." He flipped a switch on his microphone, and with proper reverence announced, "Ladies and gentlemen, please rise for the National Anthem." We all obeyed, and the ancient recording blared through the stadium's speakers. Jim glanced at his watch; he rushed to the door, scanning the crowd nervously, and then hurried back, shaking his head. "Pastor Green doesn't show up here in about forty-two seconds, you're giving the invocation," he declared, his eyes on me.

I went on mouthing the words to the Anthem and shook my head: "No way." But just as the crowd proclaimed this to be "the land of the free," Daniel Green strolled in, calm and perfectly composed. He plopped into the seat beside Jim and placed both hands around the mike. And after the two thousand fans had concluded once again that America was "the home of the brave," Green said, "Ladies and gentlemen, please bow your heads. Let's pray." The crowd solemnly complied, and the pastor asked God for a safe night and good sportsmanship.

Hank, Jeff, and I spent the evening making notes. We criticized the moves both managers made and passed judgment on each player as he stepped to the plate. In the top of the eighth the Bobcats were ahead by two, and Jim Cook, a decent reliever, was on the mound facing the bottom of Madison's order. Rick Dolan, the owner of the Bobcats, wandered into the booth, a foam-topped beer in hand, and the stub of an unlit cigar dangling from his lips. He raised his glass in a mock toast. "Boys," he said, and then slumped into the chair beside me.

"You're looking a little low for a man who's got a two-run lead," I cracked.

He took a long swallow through the foam. "Yeah," he said, "maybe so."

Jeff and I exchanged a cautious glance. "What's going on?" Jeff asked. "Your dog just die?"

In a tone that was meant to betray the words, Rick slurred, "Ah, it's nothing."

"You wouldn't be up here if it was nothing," I shot back. "Come on, tell us what's going on."

He didn't reply. Instead, he turned to Hank. "How you guys doing down in Madison?" he asked.

Hank stared into his own cup and swirled the watered-down bourbon a time or two. "What are you getting at?" he asked. "You know how we're doing." He gestured toward the field. "We're two and a half games behind you guys; 'bout to be three and a half. But hey, it's a long season … some of our guys get their rhythm back and we get everybody healthy, we'll be hanging around come fall."

"Yeah, I suspect you will." Rick stared out toward the field, then looked to Hank again. "How's the crowd down there, folks coming out to the ballpark?"

Hank took a swig of the thinned bourbon. "Okay," he said, "I see what you're getting at." He paused for a second or two and then sat back in his chair. "It's about like this," he said, waving his cup over the grandstand. "It's down; quite a bit down."

"It's like this all over the place," Rick said. "You guys have seen it; the whole league's down the toilet and nobody knows why." He sipped from the beer again. "What in the world are people doing now they weren't doing a year ago …" he wondered, mostly to himself, "… or two years ago?"

Hank, Jeff, and I traded awkward glances. And Rick just sat there, twisting his cup slowly, gazing out toward the field.

Four, maybe five seconds passed. "They're staying home," Jeff finally said. He was sitting on the ledge, his arms folded across his chest. "I don't think they're going anywhere else. I believe they're just staying home."

"But why?" Rick moaned. "We're putting some good teams on the field. We've got three prospects out there right now … guys who could be called up any day. Madison's got at least two, maybe three. And Charley's doing a hell of a job down there." He glanced up at Jeff. "So why would anybody want to stay home?"

"Because it's cool," Jeff said.

Rick turned his palms to the ceiling. He gaped at Hank and me, eyes begging for an explanation. Then he turned back to Jeff. "What are you getting at? What do you mean, 'it's cool'?"

Jeff pushed himself off the ledge. He laced his fingers on top of his head and said, "I was making a sales call at Fred's last week, you know, the appliance store. Ended up selling him four spots a day for the next four weeks; biggest schedule he's ever bought. And every spot's about air conditioners." He dropped his arms and began rubbing his chin, mulling the thing over. "This used to be the best place in the world to spend a summer night. You could catch a break from the heat, see a ball game, buy a cheap beer. But now—"

I rested my chin on the back of the chair in front of me. "You know, that makes sense," I said. "Jeff might be on to something."

Rick rubbed his eyes, tired and worn through the tread. "So people came to the ballpark to get cool, is that what you're telling me?"

Jeff shrugged. "Could be."

Rick crossed his feet on the ledge. "Well, there's not a lot I can do about that, now is there? I can't air-condition the stadium. But, gentlemen," he struck a match and set the half-smoked cigar glowing, "I gotta figure something out. Everybody in the dad-gum league had best figure something out—and fast." He turned to Hank and me. "'Cause this can't go on, fellas. This cannot go on."

Chapter 3

I cannot think of the thing that would soothe a man more than warm spring nights in Whitney. The far-off barks of lonely dogs, the groans of tree limbs strained by a light wind, and the rush of the breeze passing through town.... Calmed for the moment by these charms, I arrived home after the game.

The porch light was on, but inside the house was dark. I felt my way to the stairs, climbed them as lightly as I could, and peeked into Chris's room. By the dim glow of a night-light I watched him enjoy the well-earned rest of a hard-playing boy, then I eased into my own room. I heard the deep breaths of Rose Marie's sleep. In the dark I washed and brushed and flossed, I hung my clothes over the back of Rose Marie's chair, and slid into bed beside her. Her leg lazily reached over and brushed mine. In reply I touched her shoulder, and she, not quite conscious, touched the top of my hand ... and then drifted back to her dreams.

The conversation with Rick began to prowl in my mind. I've been around long enough to know that when a rich man's troubled, there's plenty for humbler men to fear. At one a.m. and three and again at five, I stared at the clock, wide-eyed and restless—a pack of troublesome thoughts plaguing me. Through the night I argued with myself, as persuasively as I'm able, that the Bobcats were as permanent as the Cherokee River. I reminded myself, again and again, that the team was fully braided into the fabric of the town, that they, along with the diner, the Ladies Study Club, and the churches were a part of the recipe that gave the town its flavor; take away a single ingredient and the formula changed. We'd become some mutated form of our old selves—something different and unknown.

The next morning I was up before Rose Marie. I told her I had to go down to the diner.

◆ ◆ ◆ ◆

While the morning is still gray and damp, the diner bustles. Plates clank, silverware clatters, and by six thirty the voices of hardworking folks, all talking at the same time, have jumbled together into an indecipherable hum. White-aproned waitresses, clad in blue-check dresses, squeeze past one another in narrow aisles, holding coffeepots high overhead and barking out orders to invisible cooks who fry, flip, and toast behind the bright yellow wall.

I settled on a stool at the counter where Helen, a slight, fifty-ish woman made to brighten early mornings, flipped the blue cup on the place mat and gave me the day's first dose of hot caffeine.

"So, Rose Marie kick you out of the house again?" she said with a grin.

"Shows, doesn't it?" I said.

She took my order, winked, and patted the top of my hand. "That'll be right up, hon."

I spun around on the stool, sipped coffee, and tasted once more the peculiar flavor of my hometown: farmers sitting sideways worrying to one another about the heat and rain; salesgirls leaning halfway across their tables, garnishing rumors of unrequited love; businessmen haggling over prices.

Luther Smith, a foreman at the chicken plant, walked past on his way to settle up, a toothpick perched on his lower lip, a John Deere cap pulled down to his eyebrows. He thumped me on the shoulder. "How 'bout those Bobcats? They're looking good, aren't they?"

"Did last night," I replied. "You see the game?"

"Naw," he said. "You know, I don't think I've been to three games all year. I gotta get out there more often."

"Yeah, you do," I said. "Where you been anyway?"

"To tell you the truth, I don't really know. But hey," he said, changing the subject, "the Cardinals might make a run this year, you think?"

"Could," I said skeptically, "but I wouldn't bet the farm on it."

"Well ..." he pulled the toothpick from his mouth, "you're right about that. I watched 'em last Saturday and old Stan the Man, he went 2 for 3, hit a sac fly in the eighth—"

"And then Mizell blew it." I shook my head. "Man had a lead going into the eighth and couldn't hold it."

"Like you said, can't bet the farm." Luther placed the toothpick back on his lip. "Well, I best be going."

I slapped his shoulder. "We'll see you later—and you get out to the ballpark, you hear?"

I looked around for another familiar face, and strolled over to Mike Warren, a banker friend from church. "You been doing all right?" I asked.

"I'd be doing better," he said sourly, "if it weren't for this." He had the paper spread in front of him and stabbed at it with his index finger. "You ripped the Raiders to shreds here, Jack."

"Yeah, and I'm real sorry about that," I teased, "but you know, they are 3 and 10; team batting average just soared to about .235 ... to tell you the truth, I thought I went pretty easy on them."

"Yeah, maybe so," Mike whined, "but still—"

"Hey, Mike," I interrupted, "mind if I ask you something?"

He held a fork full of grits in midair. "Probably not, what's on your mind?"

"What'd you do last night? After you got home from work, after dinner—what'd ya'll do?"

"Well," he said, the fork still poised in the air, "I helped Bo with some homework I guess, finished reading the paper, and then Margaret and I watched *I Love Lucy.*" He raised his eyebrows at me. "She loves that show."

"She's not alone there," I assured him. "And how 'bout the night before," I asked, "you stay home then, too?"

"Yeah. I left the office a little early; Bo needed help with a science project and we had the Thompsons over for dinner."

"Ah, he's a great guy," I said. "You must've had a good time."

Mike curled a lip. "To you, he's a friend. To me, he's a customer. But yeah, it was nice."

I put a hand on Mike's shoulder and got up to leave. "Thanks," I said, "appreciate the help."

"Sure," he answered, "no problem."

I wandered back toward my seat, dodging a waitress along the way. I was nearly there when Mike called, "Hey, Jack."

I turned.

"After dinner the four of us watched *The Colgate Comedy Hour*—if you were wondering."

"I'll make a note of it." I laughed and went back to my seat.

Helen banged breakfast down in front of me and topped off my coffee. "You set the world right with those boys?" she asked.

"Yes, ma'am, I believe we got it all worked out." I spread the napkin across my lap. "Hey, Helen, let me ask you something: You and Ed, ya'll ever get out to see the Bobcats play?"

"Sure, he drags me out there every once in a while," she said. "Why?"

"Taking a scientific poll," I answered. "You like going out there?"

"Yeah," she said, "he doesn't have to drag too hard. It's nice gettin' out of the house. You see a few friends, have a cold beer and a warm hot dog."

"Doesn't get better than that," I said.

"Well, if Ed can see the Bobcats every now and then, and if the Braves come on TV once in a while, he's got everything he needs. And if he's happy, well then, I got a marriage made in heaven …" she winked slyly "… or someplace thereabouts."

◆ ◆ ◆ ◆

I have found that big-city people fiercely cling to false notions of what life is like in a small town. They believe, for one thing, that the bonds of our friendships are more deeply rooted than their own; that small-town folks deeply care for one another, and look past things like prominence and possessions. They believe this, I've concluded, to compensate for the guilt that springs from their own devotion to big money, fine houses, and fancy cars. Surely, they hope, there's an Eden where the sins of unconcealed selfishness have yet to intrude—a peaceful place, like Whitney. In their more reflective moments, when they quietly sip brand-name bourbon, they dream of rocking on the front porch past dark with neighbors who relish good times together, and who share a bond that is untouched by covetous ambition.

They are wrong, of course. The ties that bind small-town people are often the most fragile. After all, there is so little here, other than the faults of our friends, to occupy our attention. Towns like ours are fertile ground, where jealousies ripen into bitter fruit—more sour than anything any Atlantan has ever tasted.

But we have one thing big cities don't. Only small towns have small-town papers, and the *Whitney Herald* is among the things that help hold us together. Every day the whole town gathers at the paper. When we open each day's edition, we never read about some distant "they"; we catch up on friends and neighbors, and read about places we've known and loved for a lifetime.

Joe Anderson owns and publishes the paper. He is a grouch if there ever was one, a nonstop complainer, and a hothead who's never been happy for five consecutive minutes in his entire life. He's bald on top and forever rubbing his smooth dome, often with both hands, and usually in disbelief at somebody else's impossible stupidity. He rants and raves constantly. He's stingier with a compliment than Jack Benny is with cold, hard cash. And he is, for reasons I don't entirely understand, adored by everybody who's ever lived here.

From its first day the paper's been in his family. Old man Anderson, Joe's dad, still stalks the halls once a week, grumbling about how the place is rushing toward hell in a handbasket. But this is Joe's paper now, there's no confusion about that. Joe is to newspapering what Robin Roberts is to pitching. It's more instinct than effort; an undiluted expression of the way the man is made. He loves the influence he wields on politics and business, he'd rather write than eat, and he reveres the role of the press, especially in small towns. He inspires great trust, but also great fear. They all know—the politicians and businessmen—that Joe will nail them, mercilessly and without hesitation, should they ever betray the trust of his town. The man's got no axe to grind, no grudge, or any particular agenda. He is, simply, the self-appointed and undisputed guardian of the virtues that make Whitney the only place he's ever wanted to live.

One of his few close friends is Rick Dolan. The two started school together when they were six, and kept at it until they were twenty-two. Their families often keep company at the country club, and Rick and Joe play golf together, maybe once or twice a month. If there were more to the Bobcats' problems, Joe would know.

I rapped on the open door of his office. Inside, he was hunched over his desk where today's edition crowned a mountain-high pile of who-knows-what beneath it. "Got a minute?" I asked. He peered over the top of his glasses and waved me in.

"Main News looks decent," he said, looking back at the paper. "But I don't know what's wrong with State and Local … lead story's about a couple of new fire hydrants … must be all of fifteen people who give a rip…." He frowned and rubbed his head, then tossed the paper aside. "What's on your mind, Jack?"

I told him about Rick and replayed the conversation as precisely as I could. About halfway through Joe slumped into his chair and looked away, someplace off in the distance. I got to the end and said, "So what do you think? What's going on?"

"I don't know much more than that." He took a gulp from a handy bottle of Coca-Cola, and began stroking his head again. "To tell you the truth, I'm surprised he told you. Baring one's soul to a reporter like that, even a friendly one …" he shook his head "… not usually a good idea."

"Maybe not," I said, "but I think he's just looking for help." I got up and paced in front of the tall bookcases along the back wall. "You know," I said, "we could give 'em more coverage, help him with some promotional ideas…."

"Yeah," Joe said, "might help."

"… Problem's television," I added.

He scowled. "What are you talking about? What's television got to do with anything?"

"I just talked to a half-dozen people over at the diner—every one of them likes baseball, and every one of them watches television. They look at it every night. The Bobcats are fun to watch, don't get me wrong, but why would anybody pay to see them when you can stay home and watch Musial or Erskine? And think about it, Joe, how're guys like you and me going to talk our wives into spending three hours at a ballpark when they can stay home and watch *I Love Lucy* or Dinah Shore or Arthur Godfrey? And Jeff was right too," I muttered.

"Jeff?" My boss looked puzzled.

"Yeah, Jeff Harrison, over at the radio station. He was telling us about how Fred's selling every air conditioner he can get his hands on. Makes staying home pretty tempting."

Joe grunted. We sat there quietly, neither of us knowing what to do next. Finally, I asked, "What's he gonna do, Joe?"

William, the janitor, marched by the office carrying a broom and dustpan. "Hey, William," Joe called, "how 'bout bringing me another Coke, could you do that?"

William returned a compliant grin. "Sure thing, Mr. Joe," he said and disappeared down the hall.

"I don't know," Joe said. "But if you figure something out, don't keep it a secret. He's looking for an answer, and I don't have one."

I drifted back to my desk, thinking that somebody, somewhere, must have a solution. This was baseball, the sport of Ruth, DiMaggio, and Williams—the dad-gum national pastime. Why, every twelve-year-old in Whitney could rattle off Musial's batting average and Spahn's ERA … this was baseball.

I got Hank Wheeler on the phone. Attendance for every team was down, Hank told me, and they were all struggling. I talked to other reporters from around the league, and their stories were the same. They had all hit a snag, and everybody was beginning to wonder what would happen.

I called Hank back. "What about other leagues?" I asked. "They down too?"

There was a jittery pause, then a curt, "No." I drummed a pencil against the desk, waiting. "Some are having real good years," Hank added.

Then it dawned on me. "Dallas?" I asked.

"Doing fine," Hank answered.

"And Jacksonville?"

"I believe they're doing better this year than last year."

I hung on the line for a moment or two without saying a word. "The Triple I league's doing pretty well, I bet?"

"You'd be betting right."

"Where have we been?" I finally asked. "We haven't been paying attention."

"Oh no," Hank shot back, "that's where you wrong, Jack. Maybe *you* haven't been paying attention, but there're plenty of people who have. And let me tell you something, Rick Dolan and every other owner in our league—they know what's going on. But they don't want to talk about it; nobody in the Sunshine Circuit is willing to say it out loud. And Jack—?"

"Yeah?"

"You do not want to be the first."

◆ ◆ ◆ ◆

Burt Reeves was one year into his second term as mayor. He was perfectly cast for the role: six foot three, with straight black hair parted precisely on the left side, trim and athletic, and graced with a pair of earnest brown eyes that hound dogs envy. He wears a blue or gray suit every day. The knot of his tie is perpetually tugged an inch below an open collar, and by nine thirty the sleeves of his crisp white shirt are rolled halfway to the elbow. Wherever he goes, Burt walks like a man on a mission. And by his presence alone he makes people feel content and secure. In return they give him the power he craves.

Like few others, Burt understands the ebb and flow of life in Whitney. As a boy he'd seen the cruel flux of an agricultural economy. His father was Richard—the "Reeves" of Reeves General Store—and he had, in the lean years of the late twenties and early thirties, shown great kindness to his neighbors, even at considerable costs to himself. So many people simply couldn't pay, and Richard Reeves couldn't bear to watch them do without. A generous credit policy evolved into outright charity, and the Reeves suffered along with their friends. They managed to scrape by, to hold on to the store, and to eat every day—though Burt always suspected his parents had missed more than a few meals. Burt had learned from his father that it wasn't always easy to love your neighbor—that it sometimes required great strength, and often involved considerable costs.

His father became mayor in 1936, and grudgingly embraced the New Deal. He hated the bureaucracy of it. And he gagged on the cold, technical precision that had taken hold of his beloved party. But his friends were in pain, so Richard Reeves would abide some things that were hard to swallow. He ran his business and his town until 1948. Then his oldest son, Dick, took over the store, and Burt took over the town. The people transferred the title willingly; Burt ran unopposed in '48 and '52. By then prosperity prevailed, and no one could see any reason to change.

Burt graduated from the state college where he'd been a better-than-average halfback on a 6-4 football team. He married Jean Smathers, a pretty girl from a good family. He became a deacon at the Baptist church, joined civic groups and clubs, and showed a knack for getting involved in small things that changed people's lives. He befriended those who had problems, whether they were big-shot businessmen, or small-potatoes clerks, and he always did what he could to help. Burt had gotten half the town their home loans. He'd helped every farmer within seventy-five miles buy land or equipment. And he'd helped Rick Dolan expand the chicken plant at least three times. A good part of the town was, in one way or another, obliged to Burt Reeves. And nobody begrudged the debt.

Just before lunch I stopped at the bank, thinking I might catch Burt before he made his way to City Hall. Margaret, his secretary, was stationed in front of his office, typing diligently and tending to the bank's business. "Hey, Margaret," I said, "you suppose Burt's got a second?"

She twisted around to face me and smiled. "I bet we can squeeze you in, hang on for one second." She stood and smoothed her skirt, then rapped on the door and stepped inside. A minute later she returned, with Burt trailing behind her.

"Jack!" Burt reached for my hand. "Come on, walk with me, will you? I'm just heading over to City Hall, gonna grab a sandwich on the way."

We walked into the noontime sun and the busy square. "So, Jack," Burt started, "what're we going to do about the teams around here? The Raiders ain't much better'n Little Leaguers. There ain't a kid on Jackson's team who could get a hit during batting practice. The Cardinals are in third place … if it weren't for the Bobcats, we wouldn't have a dad-gum thing to cheer about."

"No," I said, "I don't guess we would. But the Bobcats are solid, not a weak spot in the lineup; I wouldn't be surprised to see them win it all."

We came to the diner. "Let's stop in here," Burt said. We picked up a sandwich and a bag of chips, and then made our way to City Hall.

The mayor's office might be bigger than the living room, dining room, and kitchen of my house—all combined. A sitting area is against the west wall—two facing couches with a cherrywood coffee table in between, and a pair of chairs facing one another from each end. Two red-leather wing-backs sit in front of his desk with an accent table beside each one.

We tossed our bags on the coffee table and took a seat, Burt on the couch and me in the chair beside him. I shook the chips onto the white deli paper and told Burt about the talks I'd had with Rick and Joe. I popped a chip into my mouth and said, "What else can you tell me about this? And what's the city planning to do?"

Burt took a bite of ham and cheese on rye. He dragged a paper napkin across his mouth. "Now, Jack, you're a good friend, but you're a reporter, too … we talking on or off the record here?"

"Any way you want," I said.

He nodded stiffly. "Off." Then he launched an hour-long explanation about how the Bobcats owed the city back rent on the stadium. The city council, he said, was willing to foot the bill, at least for now, but things didn't look good. Rick owed the Trailways Bus Company and the Quick Cleaners, too.

"But there's a plan, isn't there? For next year?"

Burt swigged from a bottle of Coke and sat back on the couch. "Jack, I just don't know what kind of plan there could be. People just don't seem interested." He shrugged, looking like he'd said all there was to say.

"So what're you going to do?" I asked.

"Right now, Jack, to tell you the honest-to-goodness truth, none of us knows what to do."

"But we're going to do something. I mean, they've got to be here, you wouldn't just let them fold?"

"I'm going to do whatever I can," Burt said. "But it's going to take more than me. People got to get out to the games, Jack. They got to buy tickets, that's the bottom line here … folks don't do that, there's not a heck of a lot any of us can do."

Chapter 4

Toward the end of the day the clatter quiets down to a friendlier form of chaos. The sunrays that slant in from the west windows are long and kindly. The bells ring more gently, and the voices, at least in my corner of the world, have grown calm.

William had begun emptying cans and sweeping floors, and I was on the phone with Charley talking about subjects we never grow tired of: pitching and hitting, fielding and throwing, hot streaks and slumps. One of the copyboys strolled up to my desk looking like the bearer of news I didn't need. I swiveled to avoid him, but the effort just provoked more pronounced pacing and sighing. And so, at the risk of shattering the calm, I surrendered. I dropped the phone to my lap and aimed a peeved glare right between his eyes. Unfazed, he made a hitchhiker's motion toward the back of the building. "Couple of colored guys asked to see you," he mumbled. "They're waitin' out back, you want me to tell 'em anything?"

"You know who they are or what they want?" The kid shook his head no. "All right." I waved him away. "Just tell 'em I'll be there in a few minutes." I finished up with Charley, scribbled down a few notes, and then drifted back to the place where deliveries and Negroes enter the building.

Walter and Percy Jackson sat in a pair of red vinyl chairs that had once been in the main reception area, but were now slit open with the foam rubber stuffing erupting through the gashes. The sight of Walter brightened the afternoon. He held out his hand to take mine and flashed a warm smile; then he looked down and shuffled his feet.

"What can I do for you?" I asked Walter.

He glanced up for a moment, and then looked back down. "Well, Mr. Hall, Percy's playing tomorrow and if they win they go on to the state playoffs." He toed the floor and shoved his hands into his pockets. "Now, Mr. Hall, I don't mean to presume, you understand. I-I-I truly don't. But I was just thinking you might like to come out, maybe write a little something about the game." He looked up, his eyes hopeful.

To the *Herald's* readers, Walter's world was some fog-shrouded place on the edge of town, a place that barely existed, and surely didn't matter. "I don't know, Walter. If I can, I'd like to see 'em play again." I turned to Percy. "When I was out there a couple of weeks ago, you boys looked real good," I said, "and you made some nice plays."

Like his father, Percy studied the floor; he buried both hands in his pockets, and stayed mute. I looked back to Walter. "What time's the game?"

"Starts at four; boys'll take infield about three fifteen I suspect."

I nodded, and then tried Percy again. "You boys got a chance?" I asked.

"Yessir," he mumbled, head still bowed.

"You going to play third again?"

He shrugged, still not looking up. "S'pose," he mumbled.

"You're a pitcher, too, right?"

"Yessir."

I turned back to Walter. "Well," I said, "I'll stop by if I can."

Walter pumped my hand like a parched man at a dry well. "Yes, sir, that'd be good, real good, Mr. Hall. We 'preciate it."

◆ ◆ ◆ ◆

Some mysterious force drew me to Walter Jackson; it was an attraction I could neither explain nor oppose, and the next day I yielded to it. I arrived in the top of the third inning. Eighty or ninety people sat in the stands, stood behind the backstop, or lined the base paths. And while the crowd was small, the mood was tense, and every eye was glued to the action. The score was tied, there was one out, and South City's shortstop was at bat. A fastball blazed toward the middle of the strike zone, and the batter lined a rocket over the second baseman's head—a solid single. The next kid rolled a soft grounder to the third baseman, who threw to second, forcing out the lead runner, and leaving a man on first with two outs.

Percy stepped to the plate. I looked at Walter. I observed every gesture and movement. He paced and clapped. He chattered ceaselessly, and while I couldn't make out his words, I could tell he was coaching his kid the same way I coached mine: standing sideways, holding his hands as if he were gripping a bat, and moving his feet like a hitter striding into the pitch.

Percy gave him an indistinct nod and then faced the mound. The first pitch was a fastball, high and inside. Percy stepped out of the box, knocked dirt from his cleats, and looked toward third—to his coach—for signs. The next pitch was another fastball, belt high but inside again: ball two. More instructions from father and coach, another nervous tap at the spikes. This time I could hear Walter. "You're ahead of him now, he's got to come to you." A third fastball, just above the belt. The umpire yelled, "Strike," and the count was two and one. The pitcher went into his stretch for the fourth time; he looked toward first, then came home with a curveball. Percy cocked his right elbow, then quickly checked his swing. The pitch swept outside for ball three. Walter clapped his hands and then paced back and forth. He clapped again. "Here's your pitch," he said. "He's gotta come to you now." The pitcher tossed the ball to first, more to calm his own nerves than to hold the runner. Then he went into his stretch, and this time threw a letter high fastball down the center of the plate.

Percy stepped into the pitch, a flawless imitation of what his father had just shown him. The bat cracked like a gunshot, and the crowd shot to their feet. Ninety black men craned their necks, following the flight of Percy's line drive.

It screamed over the third baseman's head and landed fifty feet behind him, no more than a foot inside the foul line. The ball kicked left, running faster than a spooked rabbit.

The left fielder chased it down, while Percy's coach windmilled frantically, yelling for the kid on first to run harder.

The left fielder caught up to the ball; he whirled and threw.

Percy's teammate churned around third.

The ball bounced ten feet in front of home—a perfect one-hop throw.

The runner slid, cleats flaring in the sunlight, and buried his right shoe deep into the catcher's bright orange chest protector.

The ball grazed his mitt and skittered away.

The umpire, crouching low, yelled, "Safe!"

Percy stood at third with an RBI triple; South City had an early one-run lead.

Walter Jackson shook a victorious fist. The men around him slapped his back; they shouldered him playfully, elbowing him in the ribs, the whole gang of them laughing in celebration.

"That's clutch hitting right there," I said, walking up beside him.

Walter's eyes were damp, and his smile lingered. "You saw it?" he asked.

"Oh yeah," I answered, "the whole thing. He worked that pitcher like a pro."

"This kid can play, Mr. Hall, I'm telling you … he can play."

I stood with Walter for the next four innings. In the bottom of the seventh South City clung to the one-run edge. Their pitcher walked the first batter. The next man bunted him over to second. The third batter dribbled a soft grounder down the third baseline. Percy barehanded the ball and rifled it to first for the second out. But the tying run was now at third. The next man walked on four pitches, and South City's coach had seen enough. He brought the left fielder in to play third, sent the pitcher to left field, and brought Percy to the mound.

After a few warm-up tosses, Percy looked in for the sign. His first pitch was a fastball right down the middle. It hit the catcher's mitt, sounding more like a detonation than a pop, and I thought to myself: *That wasn't a pitch; it was a dare.* Second pitch, another fastball, fouled straight into the backstop: strike two. Third pitch, third fastball—grounded weakly to the right side. The second baseman fielded the ball easily and tossed it to first for the final out.

Walter Jackson rushed onto the field. He embraced his son, rubbing the top of his head and slapping him on the back. Other players and parents crowded around and paid homage to the awkward boy who hit and threw and fielded baseballs with extravagant grace. Percy finished the game with two hits, the game's decisive RBI, and four putouts. And he had successfully closed the game, getting the final out with three pitches.

For the next day's paper I wrote a few lines in "Other News," a collection of tidbits we put on a page-three sidebar. I concluded this way: *Percy Jackson might be the best third baseman in the state. And he's surely one of the five best players around. South City goes into the first playoff game at home next Tuesday. First pitch is four o'clock.*

◆ ◆ ◆ ◆

The next morning Rose Marie gently rocked in her usual place, coffee in hand, the paper open in her lap. When I stepped out to the porch, she glanced up, squinting in the sun, puzzled. "What are you doing here, Hall?" She gestured vaguely toward the paper.

"What do you mean?"

"Well, I'm not really sure you want to go around telling people some colored kid's one of the five best players around." Her tone was light, but I could hear the hesitation behind it. "Some people may not take it too well."

"Oh, I think it'll be fine," I said. "This kid's good, Rose, there's not a player on Jackson's team that comes close to this guy."

"That may be," she said, "but it's not really any of our business, is it?" She cut me a quick glance. "And it surely doesn't belong in our paper."

I frowned, trying to be nonchalant. "They read about Jackie Robinson all the time," I said. "And just a couple of days ago, down at the diner, everybody in the place was oohing and aahing about a home run Campanella crushed in the seventh. They'd all seen it on television, and—"

"Well, I guess that's my point," Rose Marie cut in, "when Negroes play baseball, they do it on television. They play up north...." Her rocker creaked, and she looked at me, eyes narrowed, lips clamped tight. "We're not all that concerned with the colored boys who play around here." She leaned closer, leaned over the arm of her chair. "And if for some reason we are, let's not compare 'em to the white boys, okay?" Rose held my eye—two, three, four seconds long. Then she rounded her eyes, asking if I'd understood what she was trying to say.

I put my hand on her arm, my eyes stayed steady on hers, and I said, "There's nothing to worry about, Rose. It's just three lines in a sidebar nobody reads. I saw a colored kid play some good ball, that's all. He's a nice kid. And his old man's a decent guy. That's all there is to this."

She bit her lower lip and cocked her head to the side. She stood, folded the paper in half, and started toward the kitchen, dragging her hand over my shoulder as she passed. "All right," she said, "but from now on, it might be better if we just left them alone."

◆ ◆ ◆ ◆

After breakfast I drove to the stadium to visit Charley. His office is small and irregular. A long, narrow window stretches across the top of the back wall. The floor is black-and-white tile, and the walls are covered with team pictures. From a distance they all look the same. Some are from Charley's days with the Cubs and Dodgers, but most are of the Bobcats teams Charley's managed for the past thirteen years. They line the wall in perfect chronological order. Charley can name every kid on every team, and he can tell you exactly what each one is doing today.

Charley sits behind a beat-up wooden desk that's losing its war with time. A black phone rests within arm's reach, and an *Old Style* beer mug, a relic from Chicago, holds a dozen half-eaten pens and pencils. Three weeks' worth of scorebooks are scattered across the top along with a heap of scouting reports. But the most striking thing about Charley's office is the enormous chair behind his desk. The fabric on every corner is frayed. The springs, battered and abused for who-knows-how-long, squeal for mercy whenever Charley moves. And the whole contraption lilts to the right, crippled by old age and a hard life. Charley's had it as long as I've known him; it's the symbol of an era, he says, and he isn't about to make a change.

I sat down in a folding metal chair, took out a pad and pencil, and began the routine we've perfected over the past seven seasons. Charley enjoys the ritual as much as I do—glad for the attention, and pleased that someone cares about his work. He answered the same questions with the stock answers fans expect. He dutifully went through the motions, but this morning I could tell he was preoccupied with other matters. Outside, a few guys strolled into the dressing room. Locker doors creaked open and slammed shut … players came in to take batting practice; pitchers to throw; infielders and outfielders to play catch or just hang around because this is the place that feels most like home.

Our business was done for the day and I got up to go. But when I reached the doorway, Charley called, "Hey, Jack."

"Yeah."

"How good is he?"

I returned a blank stare. "How good's who?"

Charley picked up the morning paper. "The colored kid."

I took a step back inside. "Why do you want to know?"

Charley shrugged, a little thrown by the challenge. "Just curious, that's all. I like baseball, same as you."

I ran a hand over my mouth and chin and looked around to make sure nobody was within earshot. "He's better than anybody we've seen in a long time."

"You going out there again?" he asked.

"I don't know, I'm thinking about it."

"Tuesday at four, huh?"

"Yeah."

"We got an off day Tuesday," Charley said, "maybe I'll ride out there with you."

◆ ◆ ◆ ◆

I headed back to the office, weaving my way through traffic and pondering the work that waited: recruiting updates for college football, State's search for a new defensive coach, rumors about other coaching changes. And there was more baseball news, too. I felt an itch to write about the

Cardinals and Braves. And I wanted some time to think, and to figure out what I could do to solve the Bobcats' problems.

I breezed through the front door. Louise, the receptionist, was busy, answering calls. William was there, cleaning ashtrays and straightening magazines in the lobby.

"Morning, everybody."

William perked up when he saw me. "I read what you wrote …" he said, "… about Percy."

"Oh?" It had never occurred to me that William might read something I wrote. "Well … good, glad you saw it."

"That was real nice," William continued. "I never read anything about our school in the paper before."

"It was a good game," I said, heading back to my desk, "and your boy looked good out there too."

The day was still young, but typewriter keys were already pounding paper and carriage returns rang, blending with the bells from a half-dozen phones.

I fumbled at my desk for a minute, shuffling through papers, looking for phone numbers. Somewhere in the distance, through the din, I detected a dull thump, but I was too absorbed to pay it much mind. It persisted and became more determined. But so did I, floundering through the mess I'd made, looking for the things I needed. Matt Dillman, the reporter who sat behind me, finally said, "Hey, Jack, it's for you."

I turned. "What?" I asked. "What's for me?"

Matt glanced down the aisle. "Joe," he answered.

Our boss was leaning out of his office. He was rapping on the door and waving at me.

I lifted a finger to the air and rushed in his direction.

"Come on in," he said. Joe held up his watch, studied it, and then turned it toward me. "It's ten forty-five," he said, motioning for me to sit down. "Most people have had their paper for what … four, maybe five hours? And it's a small town," he went on, "it's not like we live in Atlanta or New Orleans."

"What are you getting at?" I asked

"I'm getting at this: We're a small town, but in the past three hours we've had … oh, I don't know, maybe fifty, sixty phone calls—most of them from loyal subscribers wanting to know why the hell we're writing about a colored kid and why we think he's the best player for a hundred miles around."

"You gotta be kidding," I said.

Joe curled his lips. "Does it look to you like I'm kidding?"

"It's not a story, Joe. It's not even a sidebar. Shoot, it's not even filler, it's just a couple of lines."

"For crying out loud, Jack, you've been in this business a long time. If it's in the paper, it's a dad-gum story. And you just told the entire town, all of our good subscribers, that some nigger—some boy whose old man's a sharecropper—is a better ballplayer than their kids."

"His old man's a schoolteacher," I said, "and he *is* better than their kids."

Joe peered over the top of his glasses: "You might be missing my point here."

"No," I grumbled, "I get your point. I just can't believe it."

◆ ◆ ◆ ◆

When I pulled into the driveway, Rose Marie was sitting on the front porch, rocking, engrossed in a thick novel, and sipping from a tall, moist glass. The radio played in the background, louder than usual, and my wife looked to be a woman of leisure.

I parked the car halfway up the driveway. "What are you doing?" I asked through the open window.

She peered up from the book. She looked right then left—to see if there might be some reason for my confusion—then she smiled and said, "Well, I'm reading."

"Yeah, so I see. Good story?" I prodded.

"Oh yeah, can't put it down." She closed the book, marking her place with a finger. "Probably will in a few minutes, though, when you take us out to dinner." She rocked back and forth slowly, her face was bright and her voice playful. "That's assuming of course that we find a restaurant that'll serve us."

I dropped into the chair beside her. "I'm guessing something about your day was out of the ordinary."

"It wasn't bad, Jack." She ran her fingers through her hair. "Oh, except for the phone."

"The phone?"

"Yeah," she said, "the calls for you. All thirty-seven of them; the ones that started right after you left…."

On cue the phone rang. Rose Marie lifted her chin, smiling. "… and haven't stopped since."

"You talk to many of the folks who called?" I asked.

"Yeah, I talked to some this morning. I quit answering around ten. Thankfully, most were from people we know … just wanting to pull your leg, curious about when you became such a fan of the Negro league."

"But not all?" I said.

"Well …" she stretched the word long past its natural borders, "there were one or two who had some questions about your ancestry; made some interesting comments about your mother."

"Just one or two?"

"Yeah." She reached over and touched my arm. "They haven't been bad, just persistent. And they've died down now." She threw her head back toward the house. "That's the first one we've had in an hour. I suppose everybody who's got a mind to call has done it by now. But I had to get out of the house. So if you want dinner, let's go down to the Magnolia, okay?"

"Sure," I said. Then I took her hand and squeezed it. "I'm sorry about this; I'd have never guessed in a million years that people would get worked up over a few lines at the bottom of page three."

She squeezed back. "Well, now you know. So let's just leave the colored folks to themselves and tend to our own business. Everybody'll forget about this in a day or two."

I was about to ask if Chris was home when he and Slugger trudged up the driveway. His cap was pulled low, his mitt hung from his left hand,

and a twenty-eight-ounce Louisville Slugger rested on his right shoulder. "Hey there, pal," I called, "how was practice?"

"Good," he said.

"You get some decent hits?"

"Oh yeah, I put some good wood on the ball."

He climbed the porch steps, plopped down, and sat cross-legged between us. Slugger moseyed my way, panting, and forcing his muzzle under my hand, begging for affection. We talked a minute more, then I asked Chris to put his things away and wash up. I told him we'd go to the diner for supper, and then watched as his full-faced grin revealed dreams of grilled cheese sandwiches, thickly buttered and toasted the diner's special way.

We piled into the car—a man, a woman, and a boy who had all the things most people want out of life. We got to the bottom of the driveway; I shifted into drive and began to pull forward when, from the backseat, Chris calmly said: "Hey, Dad, are we nigger lovers?"

Chapter 5

I was eight years old when words in a newspaper captivated me with the sights, sounds, and smells of big-league baseball. Through words on a page I'd met Gehrig and DiMaggio. Stories from the big-city stadiums brought me face-to-face with Al Lopez and Enos Slaughter. And first-hand reports from faraway cities made me eager each morning to check the stats for Mel Ott and Jo-Jo Moore.

And now I prayed that words in a newspaper could bring baseball back to life in Whitney, that the right words would rekindle fans' love for the game and stir new dreams of agile athletes doing extraordinary things with bats, balls, and gloves.

The next afternoon, brimming with hope and determination, I began composing a two-page spread for Friday's paper. I imagined in-depth articles, photos, and the endless charts that feed statistics-hungry fans with the facts they gorge on. The upcoming series with Dittmer was of no particular consequence, but I'd treat it like the World Series, and by the time I was through, readers would think that half the players on both teams were destined for Cooperstown.

The schedule worked in our favor. On Friday, Dittmer would send Mike Riggs to the mound. This guy was a legitimate prospect. His ERA rarely peeked above three, and his fastball never looked bigger than a BB. He'd made a trip or two to the big leagues already, and in the few weeks he'd spent there, he had struck out Aaron and Mays. To quell my new critics, I'd run wire service photos of the Negro stars, and highlight each with a caustic caption: *Riggs to Aaron: "Have a seat, Henry,"* and, *"Riggs Says So Long to Say Hey Kid."* With articles and anecdotes I'd turn Mike Riggs into an ogre, and make readers believe he was the next Carl Erskine.

Jeff Harrison and the radio station pitched in too. WHTY ran promotions all week. They staged live remotes from department stores and car dealerships. Parents swarmed each location, where kids collected autographs and had their pictures snapped with bigger-than-life stars.

The coverage sent a charge through town, and on Friday night the crowd jolted Memorial Stadium back to life. Anticipation filled the eyes of young boys towed into the stands by eager dads. The red-clay road leading to the field was stacked with family sedans and farmers' pickups. The box-office line snaked around itself three or four times as fans slithered into the stadium. And the concession stands pumped out hot dogs as fast as they'd boil.

Mike Riggs lived up to every expectation I'd created. He tossed a three-hitter, struck out eight Bobcats, and gave up a solitary, unearned run. Dittmer took the first game, 3-1. More than five thousand fans thoroughly enjoyed the loss, and Charley, Rick, and Burt were the happiest bunch of losers I'd ever laid eyes on. On Saturday our own ace, Sam Fowler, put on a big-league show that rivaled Riggs', giving up four hits over eight innings, and only a pair of runs. The home team bounced back, 4-2, and the crowd held at about four thousand seven hundred. On Sunday, close to four thousand two hundred paid to see the home team take the rubber game in a 7-3 win that featured three solo shots from the good guys.

Baseball had been reborn. And life was good again.

◆ ◆ ◆ ◆

Tuesday afternoon I swung by the stadium to pick up Charley. I found him in the locker room, alone, standing in front of a full-length mirror. He wore faded blue jeans, a red-checked shirt, a wide-brimmed hat Captain Kangaroo would've envied, and a pair of sunglasses that made him look like a beatnik in the throes of a midlife crisis.

"Date for Halloween change?" I asked.

Charley frowned. "Nah." He made a quarter turn, looking into the mirror. "I was just hoping nobody'd recognize me, that's all … last thing I need is people wondering what I'm doing at some colored kids' game."

"Charley," I said, "there's going to be two white guys there—you and me. There's a real good chance somebody's going to notice. And if they want to know who you are, it ain't gonna take a call to Dick Tracy. They'll reckon one of two things: You're there trying to hide under a stupid hat—which will make them all the more suspicious. Or, that you like baseball and you're watching the only game in town."

Charley scowled. "You don't think people will wonder why I'm there? I don't want any rumors, Jack ... people getting all worked up over nothing these days—you already found that out."

"Exactly who do you think you're going to see out there?"

Charley gnawed his lower lip, still gawking in the mirror.

"Get rid of that nonsense," I said, "and let's go."

The air was choked full of humidity, the anxious chatter of players and coaches, and the pops, cracks, and claps of two teams warming up for a big game. The faces around us were dark and strange, but the sounds were as cordial as a high-school pal.

Charley and I wandered over to the makeshift batting cage where the South City coach lobbed strikes and parceled out advice about stance and stride. Infield practice followed, and we stood along the third-base line watching Percy glide to one ground ball after another, then rifle each throw to a small target on the opposite side of the field. Walter joined us, and I introduced him to Charley. A nostalgic grin eased across the schoolteacher's face; he swayed back and forth. "Oh, I know Mr. Baxter. We go back a ways, he and I." Charley crinkled up his face in surprise. Walter stared down; he started pushing dirt around with his toe, and stabbed both hands into his pockets. "I played a game or two for the Kansas City Monarchs," he began. "I wasn't a regular ... just played when they needed somebody to fill in ... you know, played when I could get off work. The Cubs came barnstorming through town one time and I was in the lineup that day."

Charley fished a handkerchief from his pocket and mopped his brow. "No kidding," he said with a grin. "How we'd do?"

Walter stared down again. "Well," he said, shoving more dirt around, "you got the best of us that time. I believe you won, 5-2." Walter chuckled and looked up, staring off into the past. "I was playing first. And early on—maybe the second or third inning—you drew a walk. I was holding you on—though, as I recall, you weren't much of a threat to steal. Old Willie Dutton was on the mound, having a pretty good day, too. You crept off the bag a good ways, and Willie gave me the look. I nodded back, gave him that little tilt of the head that nobody else could see. And bang!" Walter slammed his hands together, and Charley and I jumped. "We got you—we picked you off...." Walter smiled, remembering. "We had you leaning and bang!" He clapped again. "Just like that, I put the tag down and got you. I think about that every time I read your name in the paper, the day old Willie D. and me picked you off in Kansas City."

Charley listened—spellbound—and his face glowed. He clapped Walter on the back. "I remember that," he laughed. Then Charley looked at me. "Gabby Hartnett was our manager. I jogged back to the dugout and he was waiting for me on the top step of the dugout. I ran to the other end trying to stay clear, but he chased me down and chewed my butt up one side and down the other. We were up 1-0, and we needed base runners. Gabby couldn't believe I'd gotten that far off first. He was spitting nails, and I believe he challenged my manhood that day."

As old rivals do, Charley and Walter basked in the memory of an old battle, and the three of us stood behind the home-team bench, eager to watch the game we all loved.

And on this day Percy Jackson played on the edge of perfection. He went 3 for 4 at the plate, fielded three ground balls, caught a pop fly in foul territory, and scored two runs. On the way home Charley and I rode quietly, though at times I believed I could hear his mind churning. As we neared the stadium, I asked, "Thinking about the series with Clayton?"

He shifted a little in his seat. "Naw," he said, "not really ... mind's just wandering—that's all." He smiled, and we were content to stay quiet.

I pulled into the parking lot near his office. "All right," I said, "I'll catch up with you tomorrow."

"Yeah," Charley answered, "thanks for the lift."

The door squeaked open and Charley headed toward the locker room. "Hey, Charley," I called through the open window, "what'd you think?" He turned, his blank stare demanding an explanation. "… about South City. What'd you think about the game?"

"Oh, it was good," he said. "There're some kids out there who can play; surprised me, to tell you the truth."

"That Jackson kid's for real, don't you think?"

Charley nodded. "Could be," he said. Then he disappeared.

◆ ◆ ◆ ◆

Wednesday, fewer than two thousand seven hundred cranked through the Memorial Stadium turnstiles. Thursday, the crowd thinned further, and on Friday, the first night of a perfect weekend, no more than two thousand five hundred paid to see the Sunshine Circuit's best team. Things settled back to where they had been, and the press box felt like a locker room after a hard-fought loss.

Jeff Harrison and I surveyed the damage, and we accepted a truth neither of us could have conceived six months earlier: Lucille Ball and *My Little Margie* had become more popular than ballplayers. Monochromatic actors who performed in a fifteen-inch box had become more enchanting than life-size athletes who played their parts on a dirt and grass stage that stretched more than four hundred feet under the moon and a million stars, in a theater filled with fresh air, where peanuts and popcorn were never more than a few steps away.

Jeff was perched on the top row, leaning forward and resting elbows on knees. "Dang it," he moaned, "maybe we could use some kind of big promotion … a raffle, or contest … something like that." Another moment of dejected silence passed, then Jeff thumped me on the shoulder. "You know what," he said, "I bet Good Buy Bob Bodine would donate a used car we could give away. What would you think about something like that?"

"I don't know." I shrugged. "… might work, once. But what do we do after that? How many cars you s'pose Good Buy's gonna give us?"

"I don't know," Jeff groaned, "but we gotta do something—something that makes coming out to the ballpark worthwhile, you know what I mean?"

"Yeah," I answered. "You're saying we gotta do something besides play baseball."

◆ ◆ ◆ ◆

Saturday arrived in the usual manner of spring mornings. The sky soared immeasurably high and blue, with white wisps gliding through it. And the temperature felt feverish before breakfast, when the rituals of Little League always begin: a pregame meal with plenty of meat and eggs—and a sizable portion of the mental preparation that begins at the table, with earnest dads asking nervous sons if they're rested and ready.

On most Saturdays I'm as eager as Chris, and we get to the field early. Chris and I need baseball—of any kind, at any level. It is not just a game for us, it's a sustaining force; a thing we breathe the way others inhale air. We thrive on the chatter. And the scream of an umpire pronouncing a player's fate is music that never grows old. At baseball fields the same words of profound advice and encouragement pour forth from every crowd: "good eye," "watch it all the way," "you'll get 'em next time." It comforts me to know that in every corner of the county the same phrases fill the Saturday-afternoon air. This is the language that binds fathers to sons, and that glues neighborhoods together.

When Chris and I approached the field, a handful of older boys were tending it with rakes and shovels. Jim Stanley, Chris's coach, was in the dugout dumping bats and balls from a giant canvas bag. Jim owns a plumbing supply store on the outskirts of town, and he's been a fixture in the league for at least ten years. He wore a dark blue cap, a Stanley Plumbing Supply T-shirt, white shorts, and the deep creases of a man who works hard for a living. But neither time nor the lessons of a hard life had whittled away his infectious good humor. I had known Jim a long time, and I knew, at heart, he was still just a kid who wanted to play.

"Morning, Coach," I called.

Jim stood up straight and grinned at Chris. Then he rested both hands on the boy's shoulders and cheerfully asked, "You ready, buddy? We're gonna need you to come through today, you hear?"

Chris grinned up at the stocky plumber. "I'm ready," he promised.

A couple of the other boys ambled up, and Chris strayed off with them. "Anything I can do to help?" I asked.

"No," the coach replied, "I think I got it." He leaned bats against the chain-link fence in front of the dugout and herded a bunch of loose practice balls together.

"You all right?" I asked. "You're looking a little out of sorts … sure there's nothing I can do?"

"Yeah, Jack, I'm sure." Then Jim measured me with a longer-than-usual stare, and said, "… unless you can find a good colored boy for us. I s'pose we could use one in the infield, what do you think?" He held my eye, just long enough to make me uneasy, then broke into a more hospitable grin.

I played along. "Well, I think you're pretty well set. But if I come across a kid who can help, I'll tell you what, I'll send him your way."

More boys and parents arrived; we greeted them, and then Jim turned back to me and said, "You know, on second thought, why don't you just leave 'em where you find 'em. I don't believe I'll be able to use any colored boys 'round here." Then he called out to Chris and the others and told them to come in out of the sun.

◆ ◆ ◆ ◆

The next morning, as we visited with friends on the church lawn, I spotted Jim. He and Barb and their two boys were rushing in from the parking lot. Matt and Tom sported matching blazers, shirts, and ties—picture perfect, as if they'd been posed for the Sears catalog. Jim Stanley was a marvel. He was a tough-looking guy: thick, muscular, rough around all the edges—the kind of guy you'd want beside you in a dark alley at midnight. But kids perceive traits that are hidden to older eyes, and they were drawn to him like nails to a magnet. Jim graciously gathered them all in, calling every kid by name and dispensing an easy stream of playful words.

Every Sunday, Jim makes sure to visit with the boys on his team—to brag on them, to embellish their play, and to tell them to be on time for Tuesday's practice. Chris and I waited on the church steps, eager to cram in a few quick words. Jim glanced at us, and then quickly looked away. He leaned into Barb and whispered to her. And then placed his hand on her shoulder; he called after his two boys and guided his family through the side door.

Chris looked up at me, his eyes begging for an explanation. "We'll catch up with him after church," I said, mussing his hair cheerfully. He curled his lip, still puzzled, and I prodded him forward, into the sanctuary.

Rose Marie waited in our usual seats, browsing the church bulletin. Chris and I hurried toward her, down the center aisle. As we marched south, the Stanleys came north. As we came to our row, they reached theirs. Chris and I broke to the left, they turned to our right. As Jim pivoted into his pew, our eyes met again—for just a second—but long enough to absorb the full measure of his anger.

I felt hollow, as if I'd been spurned and cast aside, and the notion didn't sit well. Jim Stanley and I had been friends for a decade. We both loved kids and baseball, and I couldn't tell you the number of times we'd made a spectacle of ourselves, laughing together so hard that spectators stopped and stared. And now, sitting in church early Sunday morning, just four rows behind my good friend, it looked as if fifty words—a couple of throwaway lines buried on the bottom of page three—might destroy everything we had together.

My mind strayed to South City High. This had been a diversion, a way to kill some time on a slow day, nothing more than an afternoon's amusement. With a blast from the organ my daydream ended. The congregation stood, and with the choir our collective voices petitioned God, asking him to bind our hearts in Christian love. My eyes lingered on the back of Jim Stanley's head, and I wondered if fifty words could destroy the kinship we had treasured.

◆ ◆ ◆ ◆

Monday morning William was ready to burst with news he could barely contain. And before I could get the cream into my first cup of coffee, I learned that South City had won their state championship. William's own boy had played well. Percy, William told me, had pitched a gem. He had given up just four hits and a couple of runs. At the plate he had gone 2 for 4, including a two-run homer in the fifth. On the south side of Whitney, Sunday was a day of jubilation.

"Jack!" Joe's voice boomed from down the hall.

I hustled down to his office. Mark Adair, the city editor, was already inside.

"Morning," I said, looking at them both. "What's going on?"

Joe rubbed the top of his head. "I was just telling Mark that I want you to go to the city council meeting today. It starts in an hour, and both of you ought to be there." Mark didn't say anything, but I could see that he wasn't any keener on this idea than I was. And, since the city council wasn't a part of my plans for the day, I balked.

"What's going on?" I asked. "Why would I need to be there?" Joe circled behind his desk, glaring over the top of his reading glasses. "At the last minute Bud Parsons put the Bobcats on the agenda," he said. "I don't know what's on his mind, got no idea what he plans to say. But if there's news about the Bobcats, I want you there."

Bud Parsons was a local legend. He had played football and baseball at Stonewall Jackson High, and had always gotten along fine with just about everybody. A week after graduation he married Jane Page, a plain brunette who willingly faded into whatever background was handy. They had a two-bedroom home on Pine Street, a white cinder block with blue shutters, and a postage-stamp lawn where they reared a pair of boys—both Bud look-alikes—and lived, as far as anybody could tell, ordinary and happy lives.

Bud was around five foot eight and maybe 180 pounds. He was thick and fire-pluggish, and his hair was still brushed back in the same crew cut he'd worn since the sixth grade. It wasn't a style that flattered his round, fleshy face, but Bud had a harmless, agreeable look all the same. And if you lived in Whitney, it didn't matter who you were or what you did, sooner or later Bud's path was bound to cross yours. He wasn't a particularly powerful presence, but he did seem to be a persistent one.

Three days after his wedding Bud went to work for the Parks Department. He kept schedules and made sure everything hummed along in good order. In the course of his day he got to know every kid who played on any city playground. He liked them all, even those who were clumsy and slow, and they liked him right back. He coached city-league teams in every sport, and that put him in touch with just about every parent in town. And because their kids liked Bud, parents liked him too. He wasn't polished or sophisticated. He wasn't particularly smart, or especially talented. He was just an ordinary guy who put in an honest day's work. And whatever he lacked in intellect, Bud made it up with grit.

In time he was duly rewarded. Three or four years ago he became head of the Parks and Recreation Department. That not only gave him a spot on the city council, it makes him responsible for Memorial Stadium—for collecting rent, and for hiring, firing, and paying the groundskeepers and ushers. Bud cares for the place like a kid cares for a brand-new bike the day after Christmas. Bud cherishes his job, and every park in town.

Our city council is no different from other small towns'. Members sit in high-backed chairs behind a raised, dark-paneled platform. Burt sits behind the city seal, with four council members flanked on either side. It's as ordinary as government gets. And yet, when you sit in the council room, you become faintly aware of something noble. Democracy dwells here in a plain room in a tiny town where the world takes no notice. In that lies a hint of splendor.

Council members made reports, debated a handful of minor issues, and made all variety of motions—and Mark covered his beat meticulously, making all the notes a good reporter would ever need. After a couple hours of ordinary business the mayor turned to Bud.

"Y-Y-Yes, sir," Bud began," I-I-I want to bring up the situation we're having at the stadium. The Bobcats' attendance is down this year, ya'll know that, and they're having some trouble makin' rent payments. And, Mr. Mayor, the thing is, I'm afraid we're gonna have trouble paying our own people pretty soon. If we don't get that rent money, well, in the next month or two, we may be a little short ourselves, that's the way things are headin'. We just need to figure out what we're gonna do."

"Is there some kind of motion you want to make?" Burt asked.

"No," Bud said, "thought maybe we'd just open it up for discussion today … hear some ideas. I-I-I don't mean to propose an answer just yet."

"All right then." Burt looked to one side of the platform and then the other. "Any discussion?"

Councilors rustled through a few papers. Then Hal Taylor broke the silence. "They payin' anything at all right now?" Bud shook his head no. "Well, it seems to me like we need to be getting something," Hal said. "Maybe instead of a fixed payment, we ought to take a percentage of the gate. That'd be fair for everybody, and even if it's small, it's something. Might be enough to keep our heads above water 'til Rick gets this thing turned around."

Ed King, a council member who runs the Western Auto, chimed in, "Makes sense to me, and maybe we could raise prices on Cokes and hot dogs. Just a penny or two, nothing anybody'd notice."

"Maybe we could charge for parking," someone else suggested. "I don't think folks would mind."

And so the conversation went. Comments and suggestions came from the council, and from the gallery, too. No one made any objections, and Bud seemed happy, jotting down each idea as it was tendered.

A little before five I started gathering what I needed for the game, and I was about to head out when Mark Adair called from across the room.

"Hey," he said, "I know you need to get going but we need to talk."

"Sure. What's on your mind?"

"It won't work, Jack, none of it. All that stuff we heard today, if you add it all up, if every idea got put into place, it's not enough."

"What do you mean?" I said.

"I've done the math," Mark continued. "If the city charged fifty cents for parking, if they raised the price of beer and peanuts by five percent, if they charge fifteen cents more for a ticket—and then took a ten percent cut of everything—it's not enough. Jack, if they do all that, they still need more fans—a lot more."

I sank into the chair beside Mark's desk and closed my eyes.

"I'm working on an article," Mark said, "but I want you to see it first." He cranked up the carriage of his typewriter and read:

"Yesterday the city council heard informal suggestions for making up the financial shortfall at Memorial Stadium. The shortfall comes as a result of poor attendance at Bobcats games this season…."

He went on to detail the team's account with the city, and gave projections for the rest of the year. He mentioned a few of the offered suggestions, and then concluded:

"Today the Bobcats are not financially viable, and if current attendance trends hold, nothing short of a large subsidy can keep the team alive. Without a surge in attendance the Whitney Bobcats could become a part of our town's history."

My head began to pound. "I know you wouldn't write this if you weren't sure," I said. "You've double-checked the numbers? You got the facts absolutely right? You're sure?"

"Jack, it's not even close. Believe it or not, I'm whitewashing this thing. Unless somebody—Rick Dolan or somebody else—foots a big part of the bill, it's over."

"You mentioned this to anybody else?"

Mark shook his head no, then added, "But I suspect this'll be in tomorrow's paper."

"Well, thanks for the heads-up." I called Rose Marie and told her I wouldn't be home for dinner. And then I headed for the stadium.

◆ ◆ ◆ ◆

Charley was in the dugout, posting the night's lineup and talking with Tom Terry, the first-base coach. "Charley, we gotta talk," I said. His head rocked, puzzled at my abruptness. "Okay," he said, dismissing Tom with a glance.

We headed toward right field, and I told him that, unless something drastic happened, the Bobcats wouldn't see another season. He heaved a long and sad sigh. "Never thought I'd see the day," he said. He put his hands to his face, rubbing his eyes and forehead. "Guess we should've seen it coming," he went on. "Just didn't want to face it, didn't want to think this day would actually get here."

He looked out across the field—at the scoreboard and outfield fence—at the bases and pitcher's mound. "I guess we shouldn't complain," he said, "it's been a real good run, and nothing lasts forever." He wouldn't face me, and I could hear his voice quiver.

"Charley," I said, "it doesn't have to be over."

"How you figure?" he answered, still looking away. "I don't think Dolan's got the money. He's plenty rich, I know that, but he's got another business to run. And I don't believe he's gonna prop up this one with money from that one, you know what I mean?"

"Yeah," I said, "and I think you're right about that. But there's another way. We can boost the gate—you and I both know it—and we can do it right now." A couple of players roamed our way and started throwing softly, beginning to warm up. A loose ball rolled nearby and Charley tossed it back where it'd come from. Then he stood in front of me. He planted both feet squarely; he couldn't have been more than a foot away. He fixed his eyes squarely onto mine. "Jack, if you're thinking what I think you're thinking, you're the dumbest reporter this side of Brooklyn."

I met his stare. "You really think so?" I turned and swept my hand out over the field. "You ready to say good-bye to all of this? You ready to leave these kids you been coaching, the dugout, the locker room?"

"If I don't have a choice, I am. For crying out loud, Jack, I didn't think I could walk away from playing 'til nobody'd have me. Do I think I can walk away from this? Losing this team—that'd be like losing my wife. But you know what, I did lose her. Hurt so bad I didn't think I could draw my next breath." Charley stood quietly, composing himself. "But I took one breath and then another," he said, "and then another one after that. No, I don't think I can stand to lose all this. But one way or another, I'll get through it."

"But you don't have to. That's what I'm saying."

"Yeah, I think I do, Jack. And you do too. If we do what you're thinking, things won't be the same. Folks in Whitney … well, things just won't be the same, that's all. No matter how you cut it, we lose."

"You're half-right," I said. "Things won't be the same. But if we keep the team, how do we lose? We might have something to gain."

"You're dumber than I thought," Charley said. "We got a lot to lose. And you get behind something like this, you got plenty to lose."

"Like what?"

"Your friends," Charley said. "Your job. Your reputation. Listen to me, Jack, you do what I think you're gonna do, and you—Jack Hall—you could lose everything."

"Charley, if we lose this team, we lose a piece of the town. We lose a big piece of our lives."

"We do what you're talking about and we lose the town anyway. And if you don't think so … well, then you ain't got the brains God gave a plow horse."

"Charley, I'm going to talk with Dolan after the game, and I want you there with me. I don't want to lose this team."

The grounds crew began to put down new foul lines, and the machine squealed passed us. Charley fixed his gaze on the field again, took in the activity around us, and said, "I don't know, Jack, I'll think about it. Maybe I'll be there, but I ain't promising." Then he turned and looked me in the eye again. "But I'm curious," he said. "What are you going to say? I mean, what exactly are you going to tell the man?"

"Simple," I answered. "I'm going to say, 'Rick, I got a plan to save the team. Sign Percy Jackson.'"

Chapter 6

Rick Dolan leaned back in his seat, feet propped on the tin roof of the home team's dugout. He sat alone, cracking peanuts and chasing them with a beer that was getting warmer by the pitch. A steady stream of fans flowed by to say hi. Friends helped themselves to the seat beside him and chatted for an out or two. And players, as they limbered up near the on-deck circle, gave him their version of how the game was going. Rick looked like a man who was precisely where he belonged. His eyes were glued to the game. He tensed at every crack of the bat. He savored his team's good plays, cringed at the bad ones, and in between swapped notes with whoever was willing to trade them.

Leading into the bottom of the seventh, while the rest of the crowd stretched their legs and hurried to the concession stand, I hustled down the stadium steps and took my turn in the seat beside him. We exchanged updates on our wives and kids, complained about a bad call in our half of the sixth, and admired the good weather. A few minutes eased by; the Madison catcher yelled, "Coming down," and over the loudspeaker Jim announced the first batter. As I stood to go, I asked Rick if he had some time after the game. He shrugged and offered me some peanuts. "Sure," he said. "I'll come up and find you."

The press box had cleared early and I was alone when he arrived. Half the stadium lights had been killed, and the cleaning crew moved through the aisles sweeping, picking, and mopping up after the sparse crowd. Rick carried a pair of fresh-drawn beers, handed one to me, and said, "So what's on your mind, Jack?"

"Your team," I answered, taking the beer and nodding "thanks." Rick fell into a seat and lifted his cup, an invitation for me to go on. "An article's coming out in tomorrow's paper," I began. "It'll be in the city section, and it'll tell anybody who cares to read it that we've been burying our heads in the sand, that nobody around here's facing facts about money."

Rick set his cup on the ledge, put a hand to his face, and pinched at the bridge of his nose. "Oh, jeez," he moaned, "just what I need. All right, what else?"

"It's all pretty factual," I said. "Doesn't blame anybody, doesn't draw any conclusions about what ought to be done; just says that if attendance doesn't go up, the team won't make it."

Rick grabbed the beer and sat back, straining to herd his thoughts into some kind of sensible order. Outside, heavy steps clambered up the stairs. We turned and watched Charley wedge his way into the narrow doorway, a towel draped around his neck, cap pushed back high on his head, his face flushed and haggard.

"Good game tonight," Rick said.

"Yeah," Charley answered, "wasn't bad. Thanks."

"Jack told you about this article?" Rick asked.

"Yeah, he gave me the highlights."

"Don't s'pose it'll do much for morale."

Charley straddled a folding chair sitting backward and crossed his arms over the backrest. "Naw," he said, "it won't be good. These kids are young, they never thought about anything like this … probably cause 'em to worry quite a bit."

"Yeah," Rick echoed, "I s'pose so." Then he looked at me. "Well, thanks, Jack. I don't exactly know what I'm going to do about it, but I appreciate the heads-up." He stood and started for the door.

"Rick," I said, "that's not what I wanted to talk to you about. You got another minute?"

He eyed me curiously. "Yeah," he said, "I s'pose. What else you got?"

"If I had a plan to jack up attendance, you'd be interested, right?"

"Jack, if you knew how to get more people in here, I'd kiss you on the mouth. But with all due respect, I doubt you got something in mind we haven't already thought of."

Charley sat like a statue, transfixed, his eyes fastened on the floor. He sniffed and ran a finger under his nose. Then, almost imperceptibly, he raised his eyes to meet mine. Outside, a stadium worker tramped by, singing like Nat King Cole. I leaned forward and clasped my hands together. "Well, Rick, I think—"

"Rick," Charley barged in, "we need to sign this colored kid out at South City High; kid's name is Percy Jackson. And you oughtta sign him tomorrow."

Rick didn't blink. Or twitch. Or flinch. He just sat stone still. The three of us, we all sat frozen. Finally, when I couldn't stand the silence any longer, I said, "Rick, every team that's making it—they're all playing Negroes: Dallas, Jacksonville ... even Hampton. And they're all gettin' good support, from whites and blacks alike. We're not exactly breaking new ground here."

Charley's thaw continued. "The kid's good, Rick. He can play. And he can help us every way we need help."

Rick took a deep swig. He dragged a sleeve across his mouth, and a smile cracked his clamped lips. Then he chuckled and shook his head in disbelief. "You guys are out of your minds," he said. The smile vanished and Rick's eyes bored into mine. "Anything about Whitney remind you of Dallas?" he asked. He aimed his glare at Charley. "Or maybe you think this is like Florida where half the population's a bunch of snowbirds." Then he looked away. "This is a quiet town," he muttered, "we don't have any trouble here. What in the world you think's gonna happen if we sign a colored kid?"

A few awkward seconds ticked by, and then I said, "Your team will survive, that's one thing."

Rick looked out toward the field. "Don't be too sure," he argued. "This ain't like other cities, Jack. People here ... they ain't gonna put up with that."

Charley rose from his chair, slowly, like a bear who'd been roused after a long winter. "So you gonna fold things up? Is this it, this our last season? I need to know," Charley said. "I got a life. And this team—these boys—they're my family. I got to tell 'em what's going on. And that means you gotta tell me."

Rick dropped back into his chair. "You're right, I need to let you know … need to let all the guys know. The article's right," he went on. "We've just been hoping things would work out, but I guess time's about up."

Near the dugout a switch thumped, and the last of the lights went dark. The three of us sat in shadows thrown by a bright half moon. "Rick," I pleaded, "sign this kid. He can play. And he can bring a crowd."

Rick sat quietly, trying to sort through the things that had turned his carefree life into confusion.

"He's a quiet kid," I added, "comes from a good family. He'll mind his manners."

Rick pinched at the bridge of his nose. "It ain't gonna happen," he declared. "Coloreds and whites on the same field at the same time … in Whitney? We'll see snow in July sooner'n we'll see that. And besides, it's against league rules." He took a last, long swallow of beer and tossed his cup in the trash. "And, boys, I'm not going to be the first guy to test 'em."

◆ ◆ ◆ ◆

The alarm screeched, a rude shove into the day, and for the first time since the tenth grade, when Debbie Clark dumped me faster than I'd dropped algebra, I didn't feel like going. I didn't want to face a single thing that waited. And most of all, I didn't want to puzzle together a picture whose pieces wouldn't fit.

I trudged downstairs, hoping coffee would provide a prayed-for perk. But Rose Marie kicked things off to a gloomy start. She rocked quietly, steam still curling from her cup, and with no prelude or overture, she flatly said, "You keep this up, Hall, and you'll be writin' in a no-horse town pretty soon."

I dropped into the seat beside her. "Well, good morning to you."

She rubbed my arm apologetically. "This article," she said, "a little skimpy, don't you think, for a two-run game?"

"Yeah, probably. I finished late," I told her, "just didn't have time to do much more. Didn't have much inclination, either."

She lowered the paper. "Didn't have the inclination? Good grief, Hall, what's that supposed to mean?"

"You seen the city section?"

"No," she said, "not yet." Her eyes lingered on me. "Jack, what's wrong? You don't look good."

"I was up late talking with Rick and Charley; just find the city section."

Rose Marie fumbled through the paper. "Okay," she said, "I got it. Now what am I looking for?"

"Find an article by Mark Adair, headline probably says something about the city not facing facts, something like that."

She scanned the headlines, flipping to pages two and three. "Yeah, here it is," she said, "page three." Rose Marie read while I rocked and observed "scene one" of a day I didn't look forward to. Everything was just as it had always been, except, for the first time in more than ten years, I felt out of place and ill at ease.

As Rose Marie read, her shoulders slumped under the weight of Adair's words. "This is awful," she said. "Any idea what Rick's going to do?"

"No. Charley and I talked about it. If he wants to keep the team, he's got to draw more people, and if wants to draw more people, there aren't a lot of options." I rested the mug on the arm of my chair. "Other teams, other leagues … they're getting better attendance, but most of them are getting a good-size colored crowd. They're seeing—"

Rose Marie's rocker stopped in mid-creak. She turned and grabbed my arm. "Percy Jackson," she gasped. "That's what you're thinking, isn't it?"

I flinched, stung by the scathing tone. "Well, it's one possibility," I stammered. "Rose, look, we're just trying to come up with a solution, we're trying to figure—"

"Jack, Jack, Jack," she cut me off in mid-sentence, "you've been trailing after this boy for who-knows-how-long. First he was the best player for a million miles around. Now he's the answer to all our problems. Hall, I'm telling you, you've got to put a stop to this."

Rose became quiet. She dropped her head, shaking it back and forth. "You think we've got problems now," she sighed.

And I knew where the memories were going.

"Rose, I'm just trying to get more fans to the ballpark, to find a way for Rick Dolan to pay his bills."

She began to rock again—distractedly—her thoughts drifting back to another time and place.

"I'll tell you what I told Rick." My tone had turned breezy, an attempt to hold on to her, to fight the pull of the past. "This is not a new idea. Other teams are doing it, and it's working out fine."

Her rocker came still again. She closed her eyes. "Jack, this boy's colored. He lives in the colored part of town. That's where he plays, and that's where you need to leave him." Her voice was softer, but no less desperate. "I'm telling you this for your own good, Jack. And for his, too."

She stood and ambled down the length of our porch, raking her fingers through her hair, and searching for words. "This is going to be a disaster, Jack. White people and colored people, they just can't get mixed up like this...." Her hands went to her face and eyes, and then back to her hair. "It makes us do crazy things, Jack—all of us—them and us." She stood beside the porch swing. "You need to leave this boy at South City High. You need to leave him where he belongs."

"Rose, this isn't what you think it is."

"Jack, there are things in this world that aren't meant to be, and this one's near the top of the list."

She tilted her face into the sun. Her memories picked up speed, dragging her back to the one place she dreaded to go. She balled a fist. Slowly, she brought it down to the rail, barely touching it to the wood. "Don't do this, Jack. Kids are calling our son a nigger lover. They're mocking that poor child because of what you've done—because of what you wrote. Their parents have called our house and laughed at us … and this is just the beginning; this is the easy part."

She turned; her eyes were red and damp. "Me and Chris, we're going to pay for this, Jack. You will too. And this colored boy, this Percy Jackson you've been drooling all over, he's going to pay a price you can't imagine."

She sat back down on the edge of the swing, her toes just brushing the floor. The wood and chain groaned softly. She swayed there, gazing backward in time, to an August afternoon nineteen years ago, before Percy Jackson was born. She had just turned seventeen and was about to begin her junior year.

Rose had been going out with Jessie Williams, an outside linebacker on the Poindexter High School football team. They were on their way home from the lake—a bunch of kids had been picnicking—when Williams stopped along a county road for gas. Rose Marie and her friend Peggy Holmes went in search of a restroom. A young colored boy was there, outside the filling station doing chores: sweeping, picking up gum wrappers and bottle caps. Rose Marie wore a pair of white shorts that day, and a black sleeveless shirt. Her calves, knees, and thighs glistened with sweat. Her arms, neck, and cheeks were slick with a thin film of perspiration. And her dark hair clung to her neck and forehead.

Rose has never understood the effect she has on men. When she passed, the colored kid beamed—his black face was transfigured out of dreariness and into a beacon of adolescent delight. He issued a long, low whistle. "Hey there," he called, the reflex of a boy who'd been caught off guard by a pretty girl.

At the sound of the whistle, Williams turned. He looked to his buddy, a lineman named Ramsey Mayberry. They stared at one another, too stunned to speak. Side by side, they marched toward the fourteen-year-old Negro, their faces reddening, their anger heating to a boil. Without a word, with no warning or explanation, Williams slammed the kid into the concrete wall. "What do you think you're doing?" he screamed.

The boy's eyes ballooned with horror. "Nothing," he gasped. "Honest, I ain't doing nothing."

"Jessie, stop it," Rose demanded.

"Lying nigger." Mayberry grabbed the boy by the collar, lifting him to his tiptoes. With teeth bared, he said, "I want you to get on your knees and beg these girls for forgiveness."

"Stop it!" Rose screamed. "You don't need to do this."

The station owner rushed from Williams' car. "All right, settle down," he shrieked, "let's just all settle down here."

"Your nigger's whistling at white women." Williams spat out the words. "And he's about to learn some manners."

Mayberry tightened his grip on the boy. "I want you on your knees," he raged.

The boy began to crouch.

The owner was small and frail, and no threat to either football player. "Look," he pleaded, "this boy's new. I don't believe he meant nothing, really."

The all-county linebacker slapped the colored boy with the back of his hand. He glared down at the cowering form. "Where you from?" he demanded.

The boy raised his hands in the air—in deference and for protection. In a limping whisper he cried, "Ph-Ph-Philadelphia. I came to live with my grandma."

"That how niggers act in Philadelphia?" Mayberry slapped the boy with his open hand. "That how you treat white women up there?"

The boy's eyes flashed to his boss, then to Williams, then to Mayberry. "I'm sorry," the boy said, "I-I-I didn't mean nothing." He looked to Rose Marie, his eyes begging her to intercede. "I didn't mean nothing, ma'am, I swear."

Mayberry yanked the boy to his feet. He held the kid's arms behind his back, and Williams punched him in the gut—a blow that folded the boy in half.

"That's enough," Rose Marie cried. "Let him go, Jessie."

"Get inside, Rose," Jessie flared. "This boy's got a few things to learn about life in the South."

Rage had taken control of Jessie Williams. He cocked his fist and hit the boy again. Blood exploded from his nose. Williams, now enslaved by his own anger, hit him a third time. And then a fourth. The boy's knees turned to jelly, and Mayberry tossed him aside like a sack of wet garbage. He kicked him in the ribs—once, twice, maybe three times—nobody could say for sure. Then he looked at his teammate and said, "I can't think of anything that's sorrier than a Yankee nigger."

Williams took a turn kicking at the coiled and quivering boy. "No," he said, "me neither." He stuck his foot under the boy's shoulder and rolled him faceup. "You going to ever look at a white women again as long as you live?"

Blood trickled from the boy's mouth and nose. His eyes were red and swollen shut. Williams nudged him with his foot. "You hear me, boy?"

Mayberry put his hands on his hips and stared down, disgusted. "You deaf?" he yelled.

Peggy Holmes covered her mouth. "Oh no," she gasped. "Oh God, no."

Rose burst into tears. "That boy's not moving, Jessie."

Williams bent down. He waved a hand over the boy's eyes; he held it over his nose and mouth. He gazed up at Mayberry, and then to the old man. "Call an ambulance," he whispered. "Right now."

Three weeks later Rose Marie was summoned to the Bertram County court. Lawrence Horford, the colored boy, was there, his nose bandaged, his left arm in a cast and held at a forty-five-degree angle in a tattered and dirty sling. His cheeks and eyes were mottled—blue and black—remnants of the terrible beating. He wouldn't look at Rose. His eyes would not come level with hers, for fear of the consequences.

The trial of Jessie Williams and Ramsey Mayberry lasted for five and a half hours. The jury deliberated for less than two. Both boys were declared innocent of the attack on Lawrence Horford.

On the front porch that day, the bloodied face of a young black boy was alive in Rose Marie's mind. And it was the only lens through which she could see Percy Jackson.

"This is different, Rose," I tried to explain. "This isn't anything like what you're thinking."

She looked at me, grieved by the memory that had stuck in her mind. "We don't bring out the best in one another, Jack—colored people and white people, I mean. And if you take this further, if you push this, it won't be about baseball. It'll turn into something we don't want any part of."

◆ ◆ ◆ ◆

A phone message was taped to the back of my chair: "CALL MAYOR'S OFFICE ASAP." I dialed the number. Burt wanted to meet for lunch. Something to do with the Bobcats, and it was urgent. Could I be there?

"Sure," I said. "Tell Burt I'll see him around noon."

Rick, Charley, Joe, and Bud were scattered around the office when I arrived. Burt was enthroned in a red wingback chair, clipboard on his lap, pencil in hand, scribbling notes and oblivious to what was going on around him. Mark Adair strolled in, trailed by a kid who carried a boxful of sack lunches from the diner. He set it down inside, and Margaret closed the door.

Joe pulled out a sack. "Ham on rye!" he called. Rick raised a finger and Joe tossed him the bag. "Roast beef." "Chicken salad." After the last bag was claimed, Burt asked a blessing, and we dug into the food.

With his mouth half full of roast beef, the mayor began. "This is just an informal get-together," he said. "Nothing official … just a few baseball fans who want to make sure a professional team stays in town." He raised his half-eaten sandwich toward Adair. "Mark, you wrote a good piece in today's paper … gave us all a wake-up call, forced us to face some unpleasant facts. You've done some thinking on this, got any idea about what it'll take to keep this thing going?"

Adair was not comfortable in this spotlight. He squirmed, trying to get his mind and mouth together, and then finally said, "People." The room sat still, waiting, and Mark fumbled around for a few more seconds. "It's pretty simple," he finally said, "the figures are in the article. With the crowds you've been drawing, you can't raise prices high enough; you can't charge enough for parking. If you don't get a big bump in attendance, you can't break even."

Mark looked at Rick Dolan. "You're the businessman." He said. "Your figures must show the same thing."

Five heads swiveled toward Rick. "To tell you the truth," he said, "we never ran this like a business … never needed to, never really wanted to. As long as we broke even, I didn't care; wasn't in it for the money. But you're about right," he said. "I've had my guys look at it. If we leave prices where they are, we need to average somewhere around three thousand. Right now we're in the neighborhood of two thousand three hundred.

"Listen," Mark said, "I've gone over all this. If you don't get more fans, you don't make it. Either that, or you need somebody to bankroll it—somebody who doesn't mind taking the hit."

Bud Parsons spoke up. "M-m-might be some folks around town who'd be willing to overpay for advertising," he said. "I-I-I bet we could get some sponsors."

"Yeah," Joe grumbled, "but for how long? They're going to have to put up more next year, and more the year after that. We might be able to stall for a few months, but that's about it."

I looked at Rick warily. "You know," I said, "we're just about the only league having this much trouble. Even if we figure out how to save the Bobcats, I'm not sure it's going to matter. Who they gonna play? Attendance is down everywhere."

Rick glared at me. He cocked his head to the side and bit his lip, warning me: "Don't go there." With the memory of a dejected wife still fresh in my mind, I went for broke. "Gentlemen, I believe we got one choice here," I declared. Then, looking at Rick, I said, "You're going to have to sign some Negro players."

Bud Parsons shot up like a bottle rocket, his chubby face redder'n a ripe apple. "You're loonier'n Clarabelle," he screamed. "I can't believe what I just heard. And you listen to me: That ain't gonna happen. I guaran-dang-tee it." He mustered every ounce of disdain he could gather, and without taking his eyes off mine, declared, "As long as I have any say about anything round here, we will never see a nigger on the same field with white boys."

I turned to Burt. "Listen," I said, "Negroes are coming out to see colored boys play all over the country; there's no reason why they won't do it here."

Joe looked at me as if I'd just called his mother a long string of foul names. And Burt rested his chin on steepled fingers. "Jack," Burt said calmly, "I don't think we're going to do anything like that. We need to come up with an answer, but we need to stay inbounds." He shifted his eyes up to mine. "You hear what I'm saying?"

A breeze drifted in, and Charley began a ponderous stroll around the room. Everybody's eyes trailed him as he ambled up to one of the big open windows. A gust curled the bottom corner of the curtain, and tubes of light slanted in at a steep angle. "Bud," he said softly, "what do you s'pose would happen if we did sign a colored boy? You think Whitney'd fall off the face of the earth?" He slowly turned toward us. "Maybe all the white boys'd catch some sort of disease? What do you think, Burt … think the white boys are gonna all of a sudden get a hankerin' for pig's feet and chitterlings?" Charley searched each man's eyes. He held out his hands, begging for some kind of reply. "I want to know," he said.

A passing cloud cast a brief shadow. Mark squirmed. Bud smoldered. Burt and Joe sat coolly, pondering Charley's questions. The Bobcats manager walked back to the window. He leaned into the sill and quietly said, "Pee Wee Reese's been playing with Jackie Robinson for a while now, ya'll seen anything happen to him? He's been on the same field with Roy Campanella, too; he looks fine to me. So do Duke Snider and Gil Hodges."

He turned to face us again. "Now you all listen to me, I've played with colored boys. I'm the only one in this room who has. Been on the same field with 'em plenty of times. Shared a locker room with 'em too. And I'm here to tell you, it won't hurt anybody. Nothing terrible ever happened to anybody because colored boys and white boys used the same bat or threw the same ball. What's got you boys so scared?"

"It's wrong," Bud exploded. "It ain't got nothing to do with being scared. It's a matter of right and wrong. It's a matter of what the good Lord intended. And, friend, we ain't gonna mix races 'round here. We ain't gonna mix 'em in my ballparks."

Burt's more soothing voice reentered the fray. "Charley," he said, "if we signed a Negro player, I don't s'pose anything would happen to anybody. It's just not what we do here, you know that."

"Yeah, Burt, I know that. But I'm not sure I understand it. Dallas can play colored kids. Jacksonville can. Colored boys play in Lakeland, Florida. Shoot, teams from all over the place are playing Negroes." He looked at Rick. "And they're making money. All of those teams are going to play again next year. Every one of 'em can pay their rent." Charley's gaze traveled from one man to the next. "Do you hear what I'm telling you?"

Joe cleared his throat. Then calmly, and with an air of finality, he said, "Burt's right, Charley. It is not the way we live 'round here. And I don't see that changing."

Chapter 7

Tuesday, the Bobcats played an afternoon game and I made it home in time for supper. Making my way from the car to the house, I faintly heard the laugh-track cheers of a studio audience as they blended with the more familiar clatters that come from our kitchen. I hurried up the back steps, casting a careless glance through the kitchen window—and caught a surprise glimpse of Rose Marie. She stood at the pantry wearing tattered cutoffs and an old work shirt that was paint-stained and torn. As she moved, a pair of well-worn flip-flops made it sound as if a toy motor propelled her from pantry to stove to sink. Her hair was stretched tight into a ponytail that bounced like a schoolgirl's, and her face was free from makeup she didn't need. I've been with her nearly every day for fourteen years, but I've never gotten used to her perfect face, long legs, and flawless curves. And I still gasp when she suddenly comes into view.

Quietly, slowly, and with great deliberation, I eased the door open. Like a cat stalking prey I crept behind the kitchen wall. She flip-flopped back to the refrigerator, and as she reached for the handle, I sprang, throwing my arms around her, and pinning her arms to her sides. She tensed, and I buried my nose into the nape of her neck. "Where is he?" I demanded. "Your husband—is he here?"

We had played the game a thousand times before, and every time Rose Marie had leaned back to meet me, had wriggled a hand free and cupped it around my head. "Don't worry about him," she'd sigh, "he's busy watching baseball." But now she stiffened and squirmed away. She patted the top of my hand, and with a forced, bland smile noted: "You're not at the game."

Everything within me collapsed. I mustered as normal a voice as I could find and said, "Day game today, remember? Just ended."

She forced another limp smile. "Sorry," she said, "… forgot. Hope you don't mind macaroni and cheese."

I sniffed at the cheddary air. "Just what I was hoping for?" I smiled.

"Well, it'll be ready in a minute. You beat Chris home, but he should be right along."

We stood there for a moment, face-to-face, with nothing to say. Then Rose Marie went back to the cupboard. She grabbed three plates and started dealing them around the table.

"Anything I can do to help?"

"Yeah, you can grab some forks and glasses if you want."

Behind us the screen door creaked open. My son and his dopey mutt trudged in, looking bushed and in need of nourishment. I patted the dog's head, and shook it back and forth playfully, then looked at Chris. "Hey, pal, what kind of trouble you get into today?"

Before he could answer, his mother said, "Dinner's ready. You need to go wash up."

Chris glanced from me to her, curious and confused. "Okay, Mom," he said, and scampered up the stairs. I roughed around with Slugger for a second or two more, then retrieved the forks and glasses. Chris bounced back into the room, dragging clean, damp hands across his blue jeans. Rose plunked down a bowl of gooey noodles. After I'd mumbled my way through a distracted prayer, she started the bowl around the table.

Chris's eyes shifted from her to me, then down to his noodles. Quietly, he reached down and stroked his big dog's head, and there found the room's only source of predictable warmth.

After dinner, in an uneasy silence, Rose Marie and I washed and dried the dishes. As I returned the last fork to the drawer, I asked if she wanted to take Slugger for a walk. She toweled off her hands and flung the dishrag over her shoulder, shaking her head no. But before she could speak, the dog began yelping, flashing his brown hopeful eyes and flouncing before the shelf where we keep his leash. His yearning eyes were more persuasive than mine, and Rose Marie relented.

Slugger has never quite understood who's to take whom for the walk. When I placed the leash around his neck, he reached back, took it into his mouth, and frantically pulled forward. He and I stumbled out the front door and down the steps, wrestling for control. Behind us the door slammed. Rose Marie clamped her arms tightly around her chest. She marched toward us, and the three of us walked silently.

Before long, Slugger strained at his leash, vainly hoping to run down a defiant squirrel. Then he rushed from mailbox to power pole to freshly planted flowerbed—in a dogged search for fresh scents. As we got to the end of our street, I said, "Rose, please stop being angry. There's no reason for it."

She lowered her chin and marched on, quietly. After several seconds had passed, she said, "Jack, I'm not angry. It's just that you … you want to change everything, and you act like it's the easiest thing in the world. You want to turn things upside down, and you go on and on saying it's just about baseball. But, Jack, the things you're talking about, they've got nothing to do with baseball."

We walked the length of several more lawns. I ached to make her see things as I saw them, but knew no words that were up to the task. We greeted neighbors who walked their own dogs and pondered their own problems. We watched the sky dim from blue to gray. We listened as birds perched on opposing wires sang and replied. And as we reached the end of the next block, I said, "Rose, if the Bobcats leave, won't that turn everything upside own? If they just disappear, won't that change everything?"

An uncomfortable silence passed, then she replied, "Yes." Her voice was thoughtful and reflective, not angry. She tilted her head back, thinking, searching the stars for some clearer explanation. "I suppose it will," she said. "If the Bobcats aren't here, that would be a big change. And it would be sad, especially for you. But it's not the same, Jack. If the Bobcats aren't here, we'll miss that. But it won't change how we live."

"Rose, that's what I'm trying to make you see. If the Bobcats aren't here—then you, me, and Chris—we won't spend Saturdays at the ballpark ever again. Chris will never sit in the dugout with real ballplayers. He won't play catch with guys who are going to be in the big leagues one day.

You won't lounge around the grandstand wearing shorts and sleeveless shirts getting tan. There'll never be another Friday night when you slip up to the press box and knock back a beer with the guys."

A two-tone Rambler coasted by, while three houses ahead, in the middle of the street, two sisters turned a rope and a third girl skipped it, all of them chanting a familiar rhyme.

"Rose," I pleaded, "if it takes a seventeen-year-old colored kid to keep all that … I don't know, it seems like a small price to pay."

She drew a long breath that made a sad, shuddering sound. Then she reached down and squeezed my hand. She leaned into me, resting her head on my shoulder, and a tidal wave of relief flowed through me. I squeezed her hand in reply. A moment later she turned loose and reached up to brook the tears that had pooled in her eyes.

◆ ◆ ◆ ◆

Mark Adair sat in my chair with his feet propped on top of the desk as he scanned the morning's headlines.

"Comfortable?" I asked.

He lowered the paper. "Not really, but thanks for asking." Then, turning serious, he said, "I got a call late last night from Ed King. He'd just heard about some emergency council meeting—and word is, the whole thing's Bud's doing. I'm headed over there, thought you might want to tag along."

This can't be good, I thought to myself. "Yeah," I said, resting my briefcase on the desk. "What else do you know, anything?"

"Not much," Mark replied, "but I'm guessing Bud wants to get everybody as riled up as he is. And I'll tell you what: If he thinks anybody's even tinkering with the idea of integration, he's gonna fight—and it ain't gonna be pretty."

"Yeah," I said. "Let me give Charley a call, then we'll go."

A handful of council members milled about the auditorium. The anticipation that attends most meetings was absent, and an air of uncertainty hung in its place. Deeper into the room three councilmen—Ed King, Hal Taylor, and Dave Myers—gathered beside a gurgling coffeepot. "Morning, gentlemen," Mark said as they cleared our path to the coffee.

"Good to see members of the press with us this morning," Ed replied.

Mark shoveled sugar into his cup. "Well, it's good to be here." Then he turned to Hal and Dave. "You know, somebody usually let's us know about these meetings a few days ahead of time. Seems like somebody might be wanting to keep this one under their hat?"

Dave shook his head. "Tell you the truth, I don't know what this is about myself. But I don't believe anybody's keeping anything from you boys."

"Just an impromptu thing," Hal offered. "Didn't get word myself until after eleven last night."

Behind us the door barged open, and a shaft of sunlight ushered Burt into the room. His head was bowed, and he looked as though every drop of good cheer had been drained from his body. Without a word or so much as a smile, he tramped to his seat, dumped a batch of files there, and began shuffling through them. I poured an extra cup of coffee. "You look like a man who's carrying an awful burden," I said, "thought maybe you could use this."

He peered up. "Right now," he seethed, "my heaviest burden would be you."

I was stung. "What are you talking about? What did I do?"

Purple veins bulged at his temples and he tossed his pen aside, disgusted and beat. "Back off, will you, Jack? You're a sportswriter, just give us the dad-gum scores."

For the second time in just a couple of days, I had felt the fury of a loved one's wrath. I staggered to a seat in the gallery, wounded and torn, and wanting, more than I wanted anything else, my wife's love and my friend's affection. But I couldn't imagine Whitney without baseball. And somebody had to do something.

Just one kid on one team—that's all I'd suggested. We weren't going to drink from the same water fountains or eat in the same restaurants. We weren't going to do anything that hadn't been done before. I rubbed my eyes hoping to ease the pain, and prayed for some other alternative.

The door flew open again. Bud marched through, and with a briefcase in one hand and a bulging stack of papers in the other, he advanced to the platform. He stood behind his seat for a moment or two, and then peeked up, quickly surveying the battleground. His eyes met mine briefly, then he began placing a neatly prepared packet at each place along the dais. He returned to his seat, nervously stacked meaningless piles of paper, and then folded his hands like a well-behaved schoolboy. Five more minutes ticked by before the other commissioners settled in. Burt pounded his gavel and the room became still. He explained that any three members could call an emergency meeting, and that Bud, Jim Caldwell, and Cale Warren had called this one. With a glance to his right he surrendered the floor.

Bud held up a piece of paper, and fighting off a bad case of nerves, began. "E-E-E-everybody ought to find a mimeographed copy of a proposed ordinance in front of them," he said. "This is something that me and Jim and Cale would like y'all to pass this morning. Y-Y-you can read over it yourself. It's short and to the point. I-I-in a nutshell this'll make it against city law for coloreds and whites to be in the same park at the same time. There's going to be specific days when the parks'll be open to colored folks, and they can use them as they please. Other times, the parks'll be for whites only. That's the gist of it. T-T-take a minute, look it over, and speak up if you got questions."

While the councilors studied silently, Charley slipped into the seat beside me. Coffee continued to perk in the background, and a remnant smell of bacon lingered in the air—courtesy of the diner just across the square. Ed King swiveled around to face Bud. "Bud, I don't suppose I got any problem with what you boys've written here," he said. "I guess I'm just wondering why … you all of a sudden got a bunch of colored folks doing something they ain't supposed to be doing?"

Before Bud could reply, Cale Warren took the floor. "Ed, the thing is we need to get this on books before there's a problem. You look around at what's going on these days, there's some real bad things happening. Over in Birmingham you got coloreds moving into white neighborhoods causing nothing but grief; people burning up houses, fighting with one another.... Over in Chapel Hill, North Carolina, they had a bunch of colored kids trying to get into the college." Cale's eyes settled on me and Charley. "And I got wind the other day that some AA league signed a colored umpire; over in Texas or Oklahoma, I can't remember which." He turned back to Ed. "If we get this on the books right away ... well, we're just hoping we don't have to deal with a big mess later on."

"O-O-other questions?" Bud asked.

"Just curious," I said, "how are the Negroes supposed to know when they can use the parks?"

"All that's going to be spelled out," Cale answered. "The ordinance won't go into effect for a month or so. We'll post signs at all the entrances listing the times. And we're thinking about raising the flag when it's 'colored time.' That way, whenever the flag's up, everbody'll know it's time for the Negroes to be using the parks."

Charley tossed up a hand, claiming the floor. "I want to make sure I understand something," he said. "Let's just say that a white man, for whatever reason, wanted to play catch with a colored kid. If I'm hearing you right, he can't do that. Is that what you're saying?"

"Th-th-that's right," Bud declared. "Blacks and whites won't be mixin' in our parks. White folks will play with white folks; coloreds with coloreds—just the way God intended." Bud looked around the room, inviting the next question.

John Drake, the quietist member of the council, shifted in his seat timidly. "Bud, I'm just wondering what we do when folks come from out of town. Let's say a team from up north comes to play and they got colored boys with 'em. What're we going to do 'bout something like that?"

Jim Caldwell, the third member of the triumvirate, stabbed a finger into the air. "That's exactly what we're talkin' about," he cried. "In Whitney whites play with whites—that'll be the law ... teams like you're talkin' about—if they want to play here, well, they can leave their colored boys at home. Or let 'em sit in the grandstand—in the colored section—that's the choice they got."

John pushed a little further. "So what we're really saying is we won't be having any teams from up north play down here—because I believe just about all of 'em let colored boys play nowadays."

Bud folded his arms. "John," he said, "we hardly ever play anybody from up north. Wh-Wh-when we do, well, like Jim said they're going to have to leave the Negroes at home. And if they got a problem with that, I believe we can get along just fine without 'em."

Burt's patience had expired. Abruptly, he asked, "Is there any more discussion?" And without waiting for a reply he said, "All right then, let's vote. All in favor?"

There was a feeble chorus of "ayes."

"Anybody opposed?"

The Whitney City Council remained silent.

Part 2

January 1954

Chapter 8

Winter is a dreary time for a sportswriter on my side of the Mason-Dixon Line. At the diner and bars around town, people talk more of the football season that's past than the basketball season that's present. No games of consequence take place in the wintertime, no life-and-death battles, no glorious victories or heartbreaking defeats. Marriages and friendships remain unscathed by the outcome of winter games, and life drags on, one dismal day after another. By the middle of February the most exciting thing a sports fan can do is count down the days to spring training, and to opening day of the one season that truly matters.

In Whitney our eagerness was overcast by doubt. Last year the Bobcats finished a half game behind Jeffersonville, who won the league championship. But attendance remained poor, and by the time Rick paid off the cleaners, the Parks Department, and the bus company, he'd lost enough money to make mortal men gasp. And so, in October, Rick stunned the town with a piece of perfectly predictable news: The Bobcats were for sale.

Bud Parsons' park ordinance went into effect as scheduled, quelling the bad-tempered talk about blacks and whites playing together. No rancor or resentment has been visible; black people and white people have gone about their business as they always have—and as most folks suspect they always will. The friction between Burt and me eased, and life with Rose Marie settled back into its affectionate rhythm.

Throughout the fall of '53, William delivered play-by-play reports of Percy Jackson's football feats. He led South City to an 8-2 season, threw for more than a dozen touchdowns, and completed 53 percent of his passes. Nobody on my side of town paid Percy much mind, but folks everywhere, white and black, had formed a murky notion that he was a good kid who could play ball.

As 1953 gave way to the new year, Rick had yet to hear from a serious buyer, which, upon much reflection, wasn't surprising. Anybody who had the means also had the brains to know that every team in our league was losing money. Only the most optimistic fan could entertain the notion that the Sunshine Circuit would survive. We hoped Rick might have a change of heart, but he'd said emphatically and often that he couldn't afford another year like the last two. We all believed him, and no one blamed him.

Charley had begun looking for work, thinking he might catch on in the big leagues as a hitting instructor or dugout coach. He'd been quietly shopping his players around too, hoping to find them a spot on other teams in other leagues. And I was trying to figure out what I'd do without a team to call my own. Baseball fills up the better part of my time for seven months out of the twelve. Without a team, who needs a writer?

Winter is a dreary time, and this was been the bleakest one I'd known. And yet, it was hard for a God-fearing man to completely lose heart. While neither old nor especially wise, one thing I've learned is this: None of us knows what the next minute holds. We can never foresee the stroke of good fortune that's waiting just five minutes into the future. We can't know the ultimate end of tragedy, or fathom how a casual encounter will change our course forever. Looking back, we more clearly see that we are always where we are intended to be. And once in a great while, we find ourselves in the midst of men and events that reshape life's meaning.

Musing over the events of our lives, it is hard to have faith in chance.

As difficult as it was to see at the time—as confusing as it is even now—I know that the next day's episode served some higher purpose. The story is of mundane events and ordinary people, of honest folks just doing their jobs and trying to do the right thing. And yet, by the end of the day, one link at a time, a chain of calamity formed that would change my town forever.

It all began with my Ford coupe. It had been rattling for the past few days and I could feel the vibration through the steering wheel. I dropped it off at the shop and grabbed a bus into town.

Sometime around five or five fifteen I walked to the corner of Main Street and Davis to catch the bus home. A handful of others stood near the transit shelter. Some chatted about the ups and downs of their day, others read their newspapers, and some stood alone, peering south, hoping to catch a glimpse of their coming ride. In due course bus No. 44 eased into the stop. Three or four of us marched up the steps, deposited our dimes, and turned into the aisle to find our seats.

The bus roared into Main Street, and as routinely as the sun travels from east to west, followed its prescribed path, gathering and depositing the men and women who make their way in Whitney. They come and go—at Lee Street, then Magnolia, then River Road—returning to the homes where their stories unfold. The bus turned east, down Poplar Street heading into the residential areas. The homes along here are old, and many are majestic with carpet-like lawns that slope gently to the street. At each of the next few stops we collected three or four Negro women—the maids who tend to the Poplar Street families. Many are wrapped in unfashionable old coats and most wear a weary look. But, like me, they're eager to get home. They, too, deposit their coins; then step outside and make their way to the back entrance of the bus.

Undistracted by stop signs and traffic lights, my mind wandered back to baseball. Every March, early in the month, we do a full center spread: "The Major League Scouting Report." We preview the teams, analyze strengths and weaknesses, and give readers the latest news from spring training. While the passengers around me were occupied with notions of dinner and a good night's rest, I began roughing out this year's Report. The Cardinals, I thought to myself, couldn't lose. They had four guys who could hit .300: Musial, Sarni, Schoendienst, and Moon. The bus chugged along and I could hear Harry Caray reel off the starting lineups, I could see Sportsman's Park brimming with delirious fans, and as the bus spewed foul exhaust into the air, all I could smell was peanuts and Cracker Jacks.

But the spell suddenly broke. The gravelly, merciless voice of a passenger behind me snarled, "You get on outta there, and get back where you belong, you hear!" I noticed the bus driver's eyes dart back. He had one of those long, wide mirrors—the kind that lets him see the entire inside of the bus. His eyes flashed back again, then a third time. I noticed that the front of the bus—the part reserved for white passengers—had just about emptied, while the back of the bus was full. Three or four colored women stood in the rear, hanging on to the overhead straps. But one, Beatrice Washington, sat in the last row reserved for whites. I'd known Beatrice for a long time. She worked for Burt, and she had been a part of his family for longer than I'd known him. The voice from behind lashed out again. "Didn't you hear me, nigger? I said get up and get back where you belong. Get on now!"

A young woman sitting near me softly entered the clash. "She ain't hurtin' nothing," she said, "just let her be."

The bus pulled into the next stop. The driver rose ponderously from his seat and marched down the aisle. He leaned down and spoke to Bea in a quiet, stern voice. "You know you can't be sitting here. Now get on up and move back, you hear?"

The old woman's chin fell, and she sat perfectly still. The driver hovered over her, shifting his weight from one foot to the other, feeling the pressure of all the eyes on him. The angry passenger mocked her, "I don't know, Gus, maybe she's deaf … you think?" Gus ignored him, and then crouched down to talk with Bea, eye-to-eye.

"Listen," he said, "you're gonna have to get up, 'cause I can't move the bus 'til you do—you been riding with me long enough to know that. Now c'mon."

Bea clasped her hands on top of her purse. Softly, and staring straight ahead, she said, "I been on my feet since six thirty this morning; made breakfast, done the laundry, and made up the beds. Then I made lunch and dinner, swept up the walks and driveway after that, and to tell you the honest truth, I'm just too tired to stand."

The woman beside me intruded again. "Gus, let the poor woman sit, and let's go."

Gus spoke to Bea again. "I understand," he told her. "But you can't sit here. You got to be in the colored section, or you got to get off. And you gotta do it right now." The maid's shoulders heaved, and she just sat there. Then she reached behind her, pulled the "Colored Section" sign off her seat, and refastened it to the seat in front of her.

Instantly, Gus snatched up the divider and slammed it back where it had come from. "You can't do that," he snapped. "It goes here. And it stays here. Now move or get off. I'm countin' to three.

"One," he declared. Bea sat still. "Two." The old woman didn't budge. The bus was so still I could hear my watch tick. "Three." Beatrice sat like a statue in Monument Park. Her eyes had welled up with tears, and her lip quivered. Every eye was fixed on Gus. He sighed, and in that troublesome breath I could hear his own sadness. Reluctantly, but decisively, he snatched the old woman from her seat. Bea stumbled in the aisle and slapped at his hand. "Stop it!" she screamed. "You get your hands off me."

Gus dragged her down the aisle. "You're not leaving me any choice here, Bea. You're not giving me any choice at all."

From behind me the callous passenger sneered, "Dad-gum niggers just don't know their place." Gus climbed back aboard, retracted the door, yanked the bus in gear, and pulled away. Without thinking, I tugged the overhead chord, signaling that I wanted to get off.

A bench was inside the bus shelter. "Bea," I said, "why don't you sit down, and I'll find us a way home." She sat silently as I went to the nearest house and used the phone. With two calls I'd found the mayor and asked him to retrieve us. Then I called Rose Marie and told her I'd be late

It was just past seven when Burt dropped me off. By the lamplight I could see Rose Marie and Chris in the living room. I opened the front door and could hear Chris as he spelled "p-r-o-t-e-c-t-i-o-n," and then, with confidence, declare "protection." The screen door slammed shut and Rose Marie rushed out to find me. "Hall," she called, "are you okay?"

"Yeah," I said," hugging her, and tossing my keys on the table. "I'm fine, sorry I couldn't explain."

I told her the story. Rose Marie was grieved. She sympathized, knowing Bea was hardworking and loyal, and that she was a gentle woman who meant no harm.

Chapter 9

I sat at my typewriter lost in the words I had just written, and certain that no man had ever rendered a more perfect picture of Harvey Haddix's fastball. All the everyday noises had retreated to the distance and were powerless to distract me from the portraits I'd drawn of Stan Musial's power and Wally Moon's speed. But we inhabit an imperfect planet, and the spell couldn't last. Louise, the switchboard operator, tapped me on the shoulder, snapping the trance, and forcing me to face the real world. "I've been trying to reach you," she scolded, "Margaret just called." She handed me a slip with Burt's number scrawled on it. "You need to call her back. Right now."

I dialed; Margaret picked up halfway through the first ring, and we made an appointment for noon. She hadn't gotten wind of what was brewing, she said, but Joe had been back and forth like an ambitious ant, and she'd been swamped with calls from glum-sounding councilmen.

The bells from the First Baptist Church told the town that lunchtime had arrived when I rapped on Burt's door. My boss stood at the windows, silhouetted by the bright light outside. His hands were buried deep in his pockets, and from across the room I could see deep rows of worry plowed across his forehead. Burt stood behind his desk, shoulders stooped, with his head bowed. His tie was tugged low, and his shirtsleeves were turned to the elbow. Reluctantly, I slipped inside. Joe made a half turn toward the window and stared outside, where people scurried to diners and burger stands. He rubbed his head, trying to ease whatever pained him, and motioned toward the chairs.

"Jack, we've got a little problem," Burt said.

"Yeah, I gathered."

"… and I was thinking maybe you could help." Burt slumped into the seat beside me. "I want you to see if you can get some of the colored folks to settle down," he said. "I got a feeling there's some trouble brewing. And, well, you've made some friends down there. I was hoping you could talk to somebody, find out what's going on."

"Uh-huh," I mumbled. "Exactly what kind of trouble are we taking about?"

"It's the bus ride," he said.

"Seems Bea told Phil Edwards 'bout the whole dad-burn thing," Joe grumbled, "and from what we can piece together, he's got himself all riled up."

Phillip Edwards was the pastor of New Hope Community Church, the largest congregation on the south side of town. He was a powerful-looking man, thick and built low to the ground. He'd been a linebacker at Grambling and still looked as though he'd love nothing more than to crush a halfback two feet short of a first down. He was smartly dressed all the time: black business suit, crisp white shirt, and a black tie perfectly knotted and held in place by a glistening gold clasp. He was, from everything I'd heard, a bright guy with a vocabulary that would put most of the reporters I know to shame.

"I know Phil," Burt said, "and he's never caused any trouble. He's a good man; I can't imagine he wants to stir things up, but … I don't know, I just got a feeling something bad's going on. Think you can nose around?"

"Yeah," I said, "but if you know him, why don't you just pick up the phone and call him?"

"We got to know what's going on before we can talk to him," Joe growled, both hands now gouging his bloodshot eyes. "If he's up to no-good, it ain't likely he's just going to fess up to the mayor."

"I will call him," Burt added calmly, "but I think it'd be best if I had a little more information. What do think, Jack? Can you dig around?"

"I'll see what I can do."

◆ ◆ ◆ ◆

Rose Marie and I watched as Chris concluded his prayers. She tucked him in and gently kissed his cheek; I smoothed his tousled hair. "Good night, pal."

Then Rose and I headed downstairs. She looked to see what was on TV, and I went to the kitchen and poured us both a drink.

"Want to watch Arthur Godfrey?" she called.

I came into the living room and handed her a glass. "Sure, who's he got on?"

"I don't know." She grinned. "Let's just watch and see."

We nestled into the corner of the couch. Rose pulled a blanket over us, and as TV light shimmered through the room, we sipped and laughed. A few minutes passed before a commercial faded up, and a bubbly brunette unveiled GE's latest refrigerator, marveling at its revolving shelves and automatic defrosting. I filled the time telling Rose Marie about the talk I'd had at noontime. Arthur Godfrey reappeared, and Rose Marie, with her head resting on my shoulder, said, "If there are enough seats, I don't see why there should be a problem at all. Who wouldn't want to make room for somebody like Bea?"

"I can't figure it either," I said, "but tomorrow I might check with Walter Jackson, see if he knows what's going on."

◆ ◆ ◆ ◆

Just three minutes were left in the first half when I straggled into the gym. South City led by four, and Percy was bringing the ball up court, calling out a play and waving a forward to the left baseline. I scanned the crowd, hoping to find Walter, and on my third or fourth pass spotted him, standing on the top row near half-court with Percy's mom—both too nerve-wracked to sit for very long.

I stood in the corner on the visitor's side and kept my eye on him. For the next few minutes the teams swapped buckets, both coaches screamed in last-minute plays, and the home crowd groaned at the refs' bad calls. Time ticked down, the buzzer blared, and the teams retreated for a few minutes of treasured rest.

I crossed the court, keeping my eye on Walter as he made his way to the floor. He had a couple more steps to climb down when his eyes met mine. A smile flashed across his face, and mine, too. "I saw you over there." He grinned. "Our basketball team—they're not all that good—so I'm wondering what brings you out here on a cold night?"

"Good to see you," I said. I shook his hand and grabbed hold of his shoulder. "I'm gonna grab a Coke, you want one?"

He jammed both hands into his back pockets, and tightened his lips. With an uncertain glint in his eye, he glanced up. "Sure," he said, "be happy to." We zipped up our jackets and headed for the concession stand.

"You seen Bea Washington lately?" I asked, handing him a Coke.

"Yes, sir," he said cautiously, "spoke with her just last night. And that was a real nice thing you did for her. Folks 'round here appreciate it too."

"How's anybody know?" I asked. "I wouldn't expect something like that to get around, wasn't that big a deal."

"Was to folks 'round here." Walter peered out from under his cap. "And I believe it's getting to be somewhat bigger."

"What do you mean?"

"Well, some people are just startin' to think it ain't right, that's all."

"What's that?" I prodded.

"Having to stand in the bus, like Bea did—especially after they worked all day." Walter glanced off to the side. He heaved a deep breath. "It's hard, Mr. Hall. My wife," he gestured toward the gym, "she puts in a long day, then she comes home and cooks for Percy and me and his sister. If she's got to stand up all the way home, that ain't right." He took a swig from the Coke and gazed somewhere above the crowd. "It's hard for a man to take, too—when his wife has to stand—you know what I mean?"

A pause hung between us. "Yeah," I said, "I think I do."

Walter held my eye, wondering, I'm sure, how I could possibly know. "Well, anyway," he went on, "I believe some men might visit with the bus company … see if they can work something out."

I pitched my cup in the trash. "Who's that?" I asked.

"Reverend Edwards," Walter replied. "I hear he's putting together some kind of committee to look into things."

Inside, the band struck up the South City fight song, and cheerleaders brought the rested crowd back to life. "Sounds like the second half's about to start," I said. "We better get back inside."

"Yes, sir," Walter replied. "I'm just going to grab a Coke for Roberta."

◆ ◆ ◆ ◆

"It's not really the bus company's problem," Joe said when I reported the news. "They're just doing what the ordinance says. If anybody's going to do anything about this, it'll have to be the city council."

"Well, I guess they'll find out soon enough. And maybe that'll buy Burt some time to figure out what he's going to do."

"Yeah," Joe said, "maybe. So what's the mood like down there? Anybody about to do something stupid?"

"No, I don't think so. They want a place to sit down, that's all."

Joe peered over the top of his glasses; he smirked and said, "Oh, is that all?"

Phil Edwards and his four-man committee had an appointment with the Whitney Transportation Authority, and with Thomas Stone, its general manager. The meeting had been set up a couple days in advance, and Edwards had given William the news, along with an order to pass it on to "his friend at the paper." I passed the word on to Mark Adair.

"Well," Adair said, "if the meeting's at eight, I'll be there by seven forty-five." Then he lifted his chin. "You don't have much to do these days," he said. "I wouldn't mind another set of eyes and ears down there."

Adair and I were waiting when Edwards and his men were directed to the colored waiting room. Ten minutes stretched to fifteen, which wearily wore on to twenty. The preacher began to pace. He checked his watch, frowned, and sighed—and in every visible way made his resentment known. He stewed and steamed, and an hour must have passed before Stone's secretary drifted in. She steered us into a dark-paneled boardroom;

a picture of Eisenhower was on one wall, and photos of Burt and the city council adorned another. Fifteen more minutes boiled away before Stone calmly entered the room, a prim-looking man, hair brushed straight back, wire-rimmed glasses pushed halfway up a protrusive nose, neatly centered beneath dark, thick brows. He offered an apology that was somewhere on the south side of halfhearted, and then abruptly said, "What can I do for you gentlemen?"

Edwards leaned toward him, stretching across the glossy wood table. "Mr. Stone," he began, "for the last few days we've all been doing some counting." He paused, forcing Stone to prod him.

The general manager unclasped his hands, imploring the preacher to continue. "That's interesting," Stone said, "and how does your counting concern the WTA?"

"Glad you asked," Edwards said with a smile. "We've been counting the people who ride your buses. And we've been paying particular attention to how many are Negroes, and how many are whites." He paused again.

The WTA manager, looking a little confused, reclasped his hands. "Yes, Mr. Edwards, again interesting, but I'm busy. Please—what does your counting have to do with us?"

"By our count, Mr. Stone, I'd say that somewhere around 70—maybe 75 percent—of the people who ride your buses are colored."

"The precise figures for last year were 73 percent Negro, and 27 percent white," Stone replied. "I don't mean to be rude—but please—get to the point."

"Isn't it interesting," Edwards said, stretching farther toward Stone, and now jabbing a finger into the air, "that practically all the colored people in this town ride your buses? They pay 73 percent of your fares—and you don't make room for 'em to sit down. Doesn't add up, does it?"

"Mr. Edwards, the seating allocation is set by the city council. If you want to talk about that, you need to take it up with them."

Edwards leaned back, nodding up and down. "Yes, yes," he said, "I understand all that. But here's what I don't understand: If 73 percent of the fares come from colored folks, why don't *you* go to them? Seems to me you'd want to take better care of your best customers."

Stone removed his glasses; with his thumb and forefinger he rubbed both eyes. "Mr. Edwards, if you want to talk about seating, you need to see the city council. I just do what they tell me."

A prankish smile cracked the preacher's lips. He pushed back from the table and bent forward, his elbows on his knees, hands folded, with his index fingers pressed together and pointing. "Now I don't mean any disrespect," he said, "but I don't quite buy that … afraid I don't buy it at all, to tell you the truth. You build new bus stops from time to time. You change routes every now and again, and on occasion you buy a new bus. Now from what I hear, you're the one who does all that. When something needs doing, you go to the city council, they don't come to you. Now I might be wrong of course, that's just what I hear."

Stone replaced his glasses and turned to Edwards. "Yes, we recommend operational changes, and the city council normally goes along—"

"Well," Edwards cut in, "seems like somebody needs to suggest that you make more room for colored people, don't you think?"

"That's more than an operational issue," Stone said. "It's really—"

"If it's not an operational issue," Edwards barged in again, "what is it? I'm afraid I don't understand."

"It's the kind of issue you're going to have to take up with the city council. Now I really have to be going." Stone stood and turned for the door.

"I mean to take it up with you," Edwards said coldly.

Stone turned slowly and faced the preacher. "Mr. Edwards, I've tried to be clear. There's nothing I can do."

Edwards' eyes stayed fixed on Stone's. "Oh, I believe there is," he said. "In fact I'm sure of it. The city council knows you. They trust you. You said so yourself—they go along with all your suggestions. Now we're here representing 73 percent of your customers, and we're counting on you to help us out."

Stone smoldered. With a brusque tilt of the chin, he said, "Good morning, gentlemen," and stepped through the door and into the hall.

"Mr. Stone," Edwards called after him. "If you don't help us, then 73 percent of your customers are going to find another way to get around town." Stone stopped, but didn't turn. "I want to be clear," Edwards hollered. "If you can't make room for us, then we'll be walking right out the bus door."

Stone's chest rose and fell with a huff. Then he disappeared down the hall.

Edwards looked each of his men in the eye. "All right then," he said, "looks like it's time to move. We ready?" Silently, and revealing nothing more than an unyielding spirit, each man conveyed that he was.

◆ ◆ ◆ ◆

New Hope Church sits on a shady patch of land that's no more than a ten-minute walk from South City High. An ancient cemetery surrounds the clapboard building, and gravestones—battered for a hundred years by wind, rain, and sun—push up through the pine trunks and untamed ivy.

Adair and I followed close behind Edwards, his car and ours racing down the dusty driveway, swirling up the "smoke signal" that an anxious crowd had been looking for. Before his car even came to a stop, Edwards leaped from the passenger side. He barely noticed the throng; didn't speak to any of those who reverently approached him. Instead he walked directly to a young man in a brown sweater and tan straw hat. The taller man bent down to listen as Edwards issued a set of crisp orders, punctuated by sharp gestures toward the east and south. When Edwards finished, he slapped him on the back and gave him a light shove—like a coach sending a fresh player into battle. The young man hurried into the crowd where he handpicked three men. They huddled together, sharp nods were exchanged, then they marched away—propelled, I thought, by a kind of doggedness that none of them had ever known.

Edwards went to a second man, and then to a third—repeating the same routine. His committeemen had also dispersed into the crowd, carrying out their prearranged orders.

With his immediate duties done, Edwards relaxed and roamed the church grounds. He spoke warmly now to those who approached him, looked each one in the eye, and gently took their hands into his. He clasped them on the shoulder and hugged them. He treated each one as if they, at that precise moment, were the only person on earth, and they hung on every word he uttered.

But the restful pause wouldn't last. A glistening black Ford barreled into the parking lot and slid across the gravel, coming to rest beside Edwards' Chevy. The driver was a prosperous-looking man in his mid-forties: tall, in a crisply pressed brown suit, and jittery as a sprinter in starting blocks. He burst out of the car, flicking a cigarette to the ground, and hurried toward Edwards. The pastor, catching the sight from the corner of his eye, threw up a hand, halting the man in his tracks. Edwards consoled an old woman who needed one more minute of kindness, patting her hand, gently kissing her cheek.

Then, briskly, he moved toward the Ford. He waved appreciatively to those who had hoped to greet him, promising he'd be back soon. He hopped into the black car, and the two men sped away.

"Who was that?" I asked Mark.

"That," he said, "was Chester LaBarr."

"Well then, I don't guess this is likely to stay quiet."

"No," Mark answered, "I don't believe it is."

Chester LaBarr had come to town four years earlier. And as far as I know, he was the only Negro in the state who owned a radio station. Mark and I hustled back to his car. He turned on the ignition, and then fumbled with the radio until he'd dialed in all three hundred watts of 1340-WHCL. A gospel song was coming to a close; we waited through a funeral-home commercial and a sixty-second pitch for life insurance. Then the announcer said, "Ladies and gentlemen, please stay tuned for a community announcement."

A pause. And then a winded voice said, "This is Chester LaBarr, owner of WHCL Radio. We have a special announcement today for every Negro in Whitney. And here to make it is Reverend Phillip Edwards."

Like the few black preachers I'd heard, Edwards got his crowd warmed up in a hurry. "Ladies and gentlemen," he began, "it is time to stand up for what is right, and to stand against things that are wrong. It is right for all the hardworking men and women of our town to have a seat on every Whitney city bus. And it is therefore time to act. Come to New Hope Church at six o'clock Wednesday evening. Come to stand up for your rights, to stand up for your wives and mothers and daughters, to stand up for your friends and neighbors…."

Edwards' invitation played on the halfhour for the next day and a half. Meanwhile, the brown-sweatered young man, and the others like him, circulated through the colored section of town, street by street and door to door. Word spread faster than a ripe scandal.

Chapter 10

At 6:05 Wednesday night, Edwards emerged from the back of his sanctuary, and the overflow crowd became still. Poorly wired lights hummed above the congregation, while a doddering old heater wheezed. From a wooden lectern that was thirsty for three coats of polish, the preacher studied them, and I am certain that he saw each person face-to-face, Whitney's ill clad and illiterate, the least important people of a nearly anonymous town. He contemplated their place in the world and he saw them, not as a random group of the black and poor, but as the handpicked flock that he'd been given; that he was meant to tend.

Edwards was born to the pulpit, as natural there as Babe Ruth was to a batter's box. But that night he ventured into the uncomfortable unknown, and had no idea of where he was leading. He cleared his throat, hesitated, looked down at notes he didn't have, and cleared his throat again. Then, quietly at first, he began.

"Thomas Stone," he said, "is the manager of the Whitney Transit Authority. Mr. Stone is aptly named." He raised his Bible over his head. "All of you know that Jesus said, 'Blessed are the poor.' But today, my friends, you and I must contend with a stone-hearted man who will not even comfort the poor with a place to sit. Jesus," he continued, his voice beginning to rise, "Jesus said, 'Blessed are the meek,' but in the town of Whitney, a stone-hearted man makes no room for the meek—not in his heart—not even on a city bus. Jesus said, 'Blessed are those who hunger and thirst for righteousness,' but in Whitney, those who are weary are told they must stand."

"That's right," a woman's voice declared from the third row.

"Only a man with a stone heart," Edwards continued, "could look the other way when a good woman like Bea Washington—a woman who pays her full fare—asks for nothing more than a few minutes rest. Only a man with a stone heart," Edwards now thundered, "would refuse to bless those who have blessed him with more than 70 percent of his business.

"And I'm telling you today," the pastor declared, "that Thomas Stone needs a change of heart."

"Yes," someone called. "Amen," shouted another. "Change of heart," echoed a third voice from Edwards' congregation.

The pastor smiled at the affirmation. "It grieves me to tell you that the only way to this man's heart is through his wallet. Mr. Stone and the city council—they have no love for their neighbor. No," he said, shaking his head sadly, "they only love their neighbors' money. And I'm telling you today, they need a change of heart."

A young girl, barefoot in the winter cold and wearing a thin, tattered dress, stood, raised both hands toward heaven, and cried, "A change of heart." She was readily sustained with shouts of "Amen."

"If we are forced to stand, then we gonna stand together," Edwards preached. "If we hope to change men's hearts, we're gonna have to stand side by side."

Another chorus erupted from around the room "Gonna change hearts." "Stand together."

"I need to know," Edwards said, mopping his now-drenched brow. "I need to know, are you willing to stand? Are you willing to suffer to change the hearts of stone-cold men? Are you?"

The powerless people of Whitney erupted with force. "Change their hearts." "Stand together!"

"All right then," Edwards said, "all right. We got a plan. And if we stand together, we will succeed."

From out of nowhere the committee appeared; they streamed down the church's three aisles. "I want you to listen," Edwards said, "as these men explain." The committee sent mimeographed papers down the rows, and one of them made sure that Mark and I had a copy too. On a map of Whitney someone had drawn fifteen, maybe twenty large dots. These, we were told, marked the locations of gas stations, Negro-owned stores, or public places that were near bus stops. From six in the morning until seven at night a stream of cars would flow from dot to dot. Bus riders were to wait there for a ride, and they were not, no matter how dire the need, to set foot in a Whitney city bus.

◆ ◆ ◆ ◆

Early Saturday morning city hall was lonelier than a ghost town, abandoned, except for Mack, the white-haired security guard. With a smile and snappy salute he waved me by, and I bounded up the marble stairs, two at a time, to Burt's office on the third floor.

His feet were propped on his desk, and he looked weighed down by things that were beyond his understanding. Already, Negro-driven cars paraded through town, rehearsing their routes, timing themselves from one "dot" to the next, setting a precise schedule for the boycott that was about to begin. In plain view of the whole town they moved with military precision. And, throughout Whitney, an emptiness we couldn't describe lingered; some hard-to-grasp notion that we had been abandoned by the neighborliness we had always known.

Late Friday, Burt had made calls to the council members, and to no one's surprise, found little consensus. Bud and Cale flatly refused to consider any change. Others balked at the thought of caving in to an ultimatum from the south side of town.

Burt leaned back, searching the ceiling for answers. Joe gulped coffee and rubbed his head fretfully. "We got to give 'em the dad-gum seats and get this thing behind us," he said. "We don't, and we'll be the next dad-gum Birmingham. Got to make this go away, the faster the better."

"Yeah," Burt mumbled, and then he looked at me. "There's a council meeting Tuesday morning. We've been talking, outlining a plan, and Joe's getting something in the paper tomorrow and Monday—maybe again on Tuesday—to spell it out."

"We'll say something about making a very slight adjustment," Joe said, holding his thumb and finger an eighth of an inch apart, "just to let bus drivers move the divider if they need to. That's all, nothing more."

"We got to make sure that everybody understands we're not talking about giving 'white' seats away," Burt said. "And nobody's putting colored folks in the white section." He ran his fingers through his hair. "Jack, I'm going to give Phil Edwards a call; see if I can get him to stop this nonsense. Maybe you can let that Jackson kid's old man know what we're working on, see if he'll spread the word too. Maybe we can keep things settled down."

I cringed at the suggestion. "I don't know," I said, "I don't have any good reason to see him, and I can't be going down there just to be delivering messages. How about I let William know first thing Monday, and make sure he passes word along."

"That'll work," Burt said, "I'll have somebody let the cleaning people around here know too.

"All right," Burt concluded, "I got to get back on the phone and see if I can hustle up some help."

"Yeah," Joe said, "I'm heading to the office." He looked at me. "I could use a little help."

On my way home that evening I passed a half-dozen cars rehearsing their routes, and wondered where this had begun. We had all been content. Then one day a tired woman simply wanted to rest. She acted out of weariness, not rebellion. She acted to keep a seat, not to make a stand. And by her act she unleashed an arsenal of resentment that had been caged—unseen—for God only knows how long. Phil Edwards was, at heart, a peaceful man. And the men and women south of the Norfolk-Southern tracks had never complained. But now—on this day, in my town, and in my life—restlessness was on the loose. In Chevys, Fords, and Chryslers, resentment flowed through the streets, and into the heart of Whitney.

◆ ◆ ◆ ◆

Sunday evening another meeting took place at New Hope Church. The committee gave out final details and handed out precise schedules. The cars, Edwards said, were ready, and the boycott would begin first thing the next morning. On the south side of town fortitude had replaced resignation.

And Thomas Stone was about to take a very rough ride.

Monday arrived just as it had six days before: overcast, cold, and breezy. I hugged a coat tight against my chest, walking into the wind, to the bus stop where I'd catch the No. 44, to see for myself what Phil Edwards had wrought. Ten of us—all white—wound our way through town. At the Esso station near the Main Street stop, two Negro women nervously waited. A little farther along, at the Standard Oil, a lone black man, trying his best to remain invisible, pulled his hat down tight and searched for his ride.

Mark Adair had ridden a bus that morning too. When he boarded the No. 27, one Negro sat in the back, alone and mystified. All told that day, only six of our colored citizens had boarded the town's buses.

Tuesday morning the council members arrived early, with their game faces on and ready to play hardball. Cigar-chewing reporters from a handful of nearby towns bunched together near the back of the room. Phil Edwards, who had arrived at seven thirty, was planted in the middle of the colored section's first row. All twenty seats in the section were gone by seven forty-five, and by eight, fifty or sixty late-arriving Negroes stood two and three deep along the back wall.

The council quickly disposed of tamer business. Then, at 8:35, Burt made a motion that City Ordinance 222 be amended. He wanted to allow bus drivers to expand the colored section on city buses when extra seating was needed, and if—and only if—it was also available. Reading the carefully worded motion, he made it perfectly clear—to the council, to reporters, and to Phil Edwards—that no white person would be deprived of a seat, that no colored person was ever to sit in a seat reserved for white passengers, and that coloreds and whites would not mix in Whitney city buses. John Drake seconded the motion.

Bud objected—flatly and stubbornly. Cale "didn't like it one bit," and knew, "as sure as the Pope was Catholic," that this opened the door to all sorts of things we didn't want any part of. Others, casting a bitter eye toward the back of the room, made it plain that they didn't appreciate being railroaded by those who had no business trying to run the town.

After ninety minutes of broiling debate the vote was called, and Burt's motion passed five to four. Edwards and his disciples left quickly. Bud and Cale sat alone, stewing over Whitney's first slip on the inevitable slide to perdition. Reporters scribbled their final notes. By 10:40 the room had cleared, and the boycott was over.

◆ ◆ ◆ ◆

It was the warmest Saturday we'd seen since September, and winter had kept us cooped up too long. Spurred by warm air and a bright sky, we made spur-of-the-moment plans for a picnic. I made sandwiches and packed potato salad. Chris tossed a jar of homemade cookies into the cooler, and Rose Marie filled a tall thermos with sweet tea. The four of us piled into the Ford and made a quick escape to Cherokee River Park.

The day was a herald of spring, and we spread our blanket under an unblemished sky. We ate and drank together, we played "I spy," and took turns telling well-worn knock-knock jokes. In one of the open grassy fields we tossed a football. And Chris wore Slugger out, throwing an old tennis ball that no self-respecting mutt could possibly ignore.

Soon we were in grave need of rest and cookies and cold tea. While we caught our breath, we lay flat on our backs, our heads touching, and one after the other we described the shapes that were beginning to form in the gathering clouds: a cat's head with a bent ear, a flickering candle, a running Scotty dog....

Rose Marie was first to revive. Filled with a second wind, she declared she'd never seen a better day for a long walk, and that was all we needed to hear. We were up and on our way down the trail that traces the riverbank. Chris and Slugger rushed ahead, chasing balls, hurdling fallen trees, and doing the things that God made boys and dogs to do together. Rose Marie and I lagged behind, walking hand in hand—grateful for an adventurous son and a faithful dog.

"This was a good idea," she said, "I'm glad I thought of it."

"You?" I squeezed her hand. "I was thinking this might've been my idea."

"Oh, sure it was," she replied, "all the good ideas are yours. And those cookies, those must have been your idea too."

"Funny."

Ahead of us Chris called Slugger, who ran to him—tennis ball in mouth—with expectant eyes that begged, "Let's do it again." Rose and I basked in the breeze, watching it ripple the water. She leaned into me and reached over, taking hold of my arm. "So how is it at work?" she asked. "You thought any more about what you want to do?"

"Some," I sighed. "I don't know ... I hate thinking about it."

"I know," Rose said squeezing my hand, "I hate it too, but spring's about here. We need to figure out what we're going to do."

"I've heard from a few other papers. Might be a slot in Hattiesburg; heard about something else in Columbus. But I don't want to go. Joe said there's plenty to do here, and I can tell he wants me to stay. He swears there'll be plenty of baseball to write about ... keeps telling me to just be patient."

"What would you do?" Rose asked.

"I don't know. More on the big leagues, I guess. And I can pitch in on city stuff ... do odds and ends."

"Is that what you want?"

I shook my head. "What I want is to cover the Bobcats. I want to be up in the press box and watch you in the bleachers. I want to watch Chris play catch with Giles and Douglas. I want to talk baseball with Jeff Harrison. I want to interview Charley, I want—"

"Yeah," she said, "I know. I know."

"So I'll write about the Cardinals and the Braves. I'll do stories about the Lady's Club and the Historical Society. And you and I will live here together. We'll raise that boy and that dog." I hugged her tight. "And life will be grand."

◆ ◆ ◆ ◆

Despite all the suspense in my life, only one thought was on my mind Monday morning: Spring training was just a bunt away. Pitchers and catchers reported next week, position players the week after that, and full workouts began in just ten days. The flavorless days of winter were waning, and I was rapt in my final preparations for spring.

"Jack." Louise walked up. "Joe just left for the mayor's office. He wants you to stop by in a couple of hours, said there was something he and Burt need to go over with you."

It was around eleven when Margaret told me to go in. Burt was hunched over his desk, mumbling and sorting through a mess strewn across it. Joe was right beside him. When I walked in, Burt glanced up and Joe turned, but without a word they returned to their work. I just stood near the door. A full minute must have passed. And then another. I cleared my throat and coughed. "Coming," Burt muttered, "coming." But neither man looked much distracted. Thirty more seconds passed—as did three or four muffled phrases between them. I lingered where I was, arms folded, worrying the time away. And then a loud thwack jolted me.

"Done," Burt declared. He again slapped the desk triumphantly. He stood, tossing his glasses aside, and walked around the desk, motioning for me to take a seat.

"You need anything?" Burt asked. "Cup of coffee, Coke?"

"No," I said, " I don't need anything. Come on, Burt, what's going on? What are you two doing?"

He slid into the seat beside me. "It's a long story," he said. "So relax for a minute and trust me. I'm going to tell you what all this is about. But first, I need to tell you a few other things."

He had, he lamented, not had a sound night's sleep since "who-knows-when. The whole boycott thing—that tore me up, honest to goodness, Jack …" he shook his head sadly "… made me sick to my stomach. People here …" he struggled for the right words "… I don't know, they've never been set against one another like that; never been so many people so out of sorts all at the same time."

He couldn't expel the nagging thoughts from his mind, and while the rest of us slept, he struggled to understand Bea Washington and Thomas Stone; he tried to figure out Bud and Phil, and at three and four and five o'clock in the morning, he wondered what it'd take to make Cale and Chester LaBarr both happy.

"Life's always been good here," he said, "and I swear, there's never been a better place on God's good earth to live. For the life of me I don't know what went wrong." He stood up, raking his fingers through his hair, roaming the room, and trying to file new thoughts into some kind of sensible order.

"It seemed that the world had come to a crossroads," he said. "There are things that have been set in motion that nobody can stop … doesn't much matter if we understand 'em or like 'em…." He shook his head and looked down. "I didn't think much about it when Truman mixed blacks and whites in the army. We needed boys to fight, and when a war's going on, I don't s'pose you worry a whole heck of a lot about who's standing beside you so long as he's pointing his gun the same direction you're pointing yours." He paused at the windows and gazed outside. "But then, what's it been, six years since Truman forced a civil rights plank into the platform … didn't feel right then; don't like it any better now." But it was at that moment, Burt believed, that a new course had been fixed. He walked again; thinking about how the past had brought us to the present. "You might remember," he reminisced, "I was at the '48 Convention…. Wildest thing anybody ever saw. Old Strom, he and Wright were in all their glory. And everybody in the delegation—we were right there with 'em—proud as we could be, standing up for what was good—Dixiecrat to the core." He slumped back into the chair. "But the tide had turned, Jack. We got a million votes, won a handful of states, but it was us against the world." And now, Burt mused, there must be six, maybe eight cases in front of one kind of court or the other—colored folks barging their way into white schools. And the Supreme Court, "they put it off last year," Burt said, "but they got to say something this time around." He shook his head glumly. "You look at how things are going, I don't expect we're gonna like what they got to say." He was up again and roaming. He jammed his hands into his pockets. "Shoot, you take a nice little town like ours; we got Phil Edwards—he's sitting down there just waiting to stir things up again; think what it's like in Little Rock or Memphis or Birmingham. I'll tell you what, Jack, I can't go through it again, can't put our people through it. And I ain't about to surrender my town to Phil Edwards. Or to Bud Parsons, either. This is going to be a good place to live, and folks here—they're gonna get along, you hear?"

"Yeah," I said, "and I believe you too. So what're you going to do?"

"We're going to keep the colored folks settled down," Joe said. "Poor old Burt, he's been wracking his brain trying to figure out how to do that without getting everybody else all worked up."

"Yeah," I said, "and …?"

"All right," Burt said, "here's the thing—"

There was a loud knock at the door. Rick Dolan stood there, an east-to-west grin stretching as far across his face as it could reach.

"You ready?" he asked, his eyes shifting from Joe to Burt.

"Yeah," Joe said, "everything's set." Joe reached under the desk and pulled out a camera. "Here," he said, handing it to me, "you're gonna need this."

"What for?" I asked. "What's going on?"

Rick stepped into the office. "You see these two guys?"

"Yeah," I said, "I see 'em."

"Well," Rick said with a chuckle, "you're looking at the new owners of the Whitney Bobcats."

"And you," Joe said, "need a photo for tomorrow's paper."

I was dazed. Rick walked over to Burt's desk where the three of them shuffled through the stack that had captivated Burt and Joe a few minutes before. I sat rigid, frozen in the wingback chair while Rick signed one sheet, then another, and then a third. They all shook hands, and I pulled myself up out of the chair in time to snap off a half roll of film: shots of the three of them huddled over the contracts, of Burt and Joe—looking ridiculous—wearing Bobcats hats with their arms draped over one another. The shock soon faded, and nothing but untainted joy coursed through the veins, arteries, and capillaries of my circulatory system. All I wanted to do was rush home to tell Rose Marie.

Rick was gone as suddenly as he came. The deal was done.

"When did you do this?" I gasped. "And why didn't you tell me?"

Burt gestured toward the chairs where we'd been sitting. "Let's get back to what we're talking about," he said.

"We'll get to that later. I got a story to write and I don't have a lot of time. You gotta fill me in."

"It's all part of the same story," Joe said. "You can't write all of it, but you need to know it. And like it or not, you're a part of all this—and your part's not over."

"What do you mean?"

"Sit down," Burt said, "everything'll come together."

I needed to tell Rose. I had to call Charley. I needed to write. But, dutifully, I returned to the wingback chair. Burt picked up where we'd left off.

"You were asking how we planned to keep the colored folks settled down—"

"And what you just saw," Joe interrupted, "is part of the answer."

"I don't understand," I said. "Why does Phil Edwards—or anybody else down there—care whether or not if you guys own the Bobcats? What's that got to do with them?"

"I don't imagine Phil Edwards could care less," Burt replied. "It's got nothing to do with him—yet. But it will. That's where you come in."

I rolled my eyes, not sure I wanted to hear what was coming. "I'm listening."

Joe perched himself on the edge of Burt's desk; he palmed the top of his head, grimacing. "We need you to set up a meeting for us, that's all for right now."

"A meeting?" I said.

Burt reached over and put his hand on my shoulder. "We want you to set up a meeting with Walter and Percy Jackson. We want to sign Percy right away."

Deep down I was thrilled. But at the same time, and just as profoundly, the idea gnawed at something inside me. This was, as Bud and Cale insisted, not the way things ought to be. But then, when you pondered it further, you came to Walter Jackson. He was a good and decent man, and his presence alone was always enough to lift my spirits. He loved his son as much as I loved mine, and I could practically feel the joy he'd feel when he heard the news.

But blacks and whites mingling together—the mere thought was hard to swallow, like castor oil for the brain. But then, reflecting for a moment more, I came to Percy. He was as harmless as young men come; plainly born to play ball, and now he'd be given the chance. I, along with everybody else in town, would be blessed to watch him.

Still, the whole business felt dirty, like premeditated sin, and the more I thought about it, the more I wanted a hot, soapy shower. And yet … when I thought about it even further, Bea and William and Phil and Walter and Roberta and Chester—and thousands of others just like them would know a new thrill. They'd have a reason to care about baseball, and the Bobcats would survive.

Rose Marie would share none of my ambivalence. I girded myself for what I knew was to come, and headed home to break the news. I told her that the Bobcats had survived; that seven other cities in the Sunshine Circuit would field teams, and that we'd go on living the life we loved. She melted in relief, throwing both arms around me, thrilled at "the wonderful news." But I stood stiffly, resisting the affection.

"There's more," I told her. She backed away, puzzled. And then, as gently as I could, I told her about Percy.

In the fourteen years I've know her, I've never heard a cross word from Rose Marie's lips. I've never seen a tantrum or rage or anything that resembled despair. But that afternoon, at that precise moment, the sweetest woman on earth erupted. Agony and anger flashed through the room, and she collapsed into a kitchen chair. "Life will never be like it was before," she shrieked, "and Joe and Burt are crazy if they think this is going to settle anybody down." She put her hands to her face and began to cry. "You and your colored friends, you're the only ones who're going to sit still for this." She flung her hair away from her eyes. She raised a hand and pointed at me, jabbing her finger through the air. "And you," she screamed, "have you even thought about what this'll do to Chris? Or me?" She pounded the table with her fist. "We've been over this a hundred times," she sobbed.

I struggled to calm her, to find some way to bring her comfort. I hoped to paint the bigger picture, to cover the same territory that Burt had: The world had changed, certain things that had been set in motion—

"Jack," she groaned, "you're the one who can't see the big picture. You put a colored boy on the baseball team, and you think that's going to put an end to it? You think that's going to stop colored kids from wanting to go to Chris's school? You think they'll all of a sudden stop wanting to eat at the diner?" She buried her face in her hands, and the sobs flowed. "Do you think all your friends, all the precious white people in this town, are going to sit back and watch all that happen?"

I slid into the chair beside her, cautious, and despising the world that would make this sweet woman cry. Her eyes were red and tears flooded down her cheeks. "Listen," she sobbed, "you're heading in a direction I can't go. I love you, but I've told you before, I can't watch this, Jack. You gotta hear me on this."

"All I'm doing is setting up a meeting, Rose. I don't know if they'll work anything out or not. After that I write about baseball. That's it."

"You started this," she groaned, "nobody even thought about it until you brought it up."

I reached for her hand. "Rose," I said softly, "colored kids are playing in other towns. I didn't start this. I wish it didn't have to be this way. All I've ever wanted was to keep the team."

She yanked her hand away. "All you want is for us to have a beer in the press box. All you want is to watch Chris play catch … Jack, I can't go to a stadium where coloreds and whites are playing together and sitting together and eating and drinking together."

She gaped at me as if I'd asked her to live in the Kremlin or eat insects. "I can't do it," she sniffed. "And I don't want Chris doing it either."

◆ ◆ ◆ ◆

Three days after the story broke, I drove out to South City High. I had been there three or four times, but never to Walter Jackson's classroom. I peered inside. He was there, sitting behind a desk that had been old when Nathan Bedford Forrest rode through town. He had a red pen in hand and was visibly charmed by the papers he graded. He chuckled softly as he dashed off a check or an X. I noticed the walls were paint-chipped and dirty, and a struggling furnace that wasn't much of a match for Mother Nature heated the room.

I rapped on the door and Walter looked up, surprised. He smiled and cocked his head, plainly happy to see me. He laid his work down and smiled. "You again."

"Yeah." I shrugged defenselessly. "It's me.

"Hey," I asked as I eased into the room, "you see about the Bobcats?"

"Oh yeah," he said, another wide smile staking claim to his face. He said he was glad we'd have Charley around, and that we'd have a place to catch a good game.

"Most of the team is still around," I told him. "Taylor and Little have moved on, but the rest of the guys are back. And Charley's got his eye on a couple of new kids, too."

"Well …" Walter said "… looking forward to seeing 'em, and I know you are too."

He settled back in his chair. "Now tell me what I can do for you, Mr. Hall. I'm pretty sure you didn't ride all the way out here to talk about the Bobcats."

"Yeah," I said, "actually, I came to see if you'd do me a favor."

"Sure," Walter replied, "be happy to."

"I want you to bring Percy over to the *Herald* tomorrow after school. Could you do that?"

"Well," Walter drawled, "I s'pose. How can we help you up there?"

"Just come," I said, "you'll find out when you get there. How's four o'clock?"

"All right," Walter said. "But can't you give some idea what this is about?"

"I wish I could. I just need you to trust me on this one. We'll see you at four, okay?"

◆ ◆ ◆ ◆

My first stop the next morning was Memorial Stadium. Charley was behind his desk, torturing his limping chair and looking like a kid on the first day of Little League. He had checklists and notes scattered everywhere.

Don, the equipment manager, had pulled up a chair so the two veterans could make their plans—uniforms and equipment to buy, a field to get in shape, travel plans to figure.... Players were beginning to gather in the locker room. I saw Jimmy Giles, a promising infielder who was back for his second season. Donny Jones, our starting third baseman, was there, a steady player who was twenty-two, maybe twenty-three years old, and who needed to make a move soon if he had any hope of reaching the big leagues. Denny Douglas walked in just behind me, a power-hitting catcher who was renowned for his tortoise-like speed.

They were all there to let the game seep back into their veins; to smell it and taste it; to be home, and to be with family. They cussed and complained about training. They taunted one another. And did things that only men who have lived in a locker room could ever understand. I swapped insults with Douglas and Giles. And from across the room Jones called out, "Where's that kid of yours, Hall? Haven't seen that boy since September."

"Hey, Donny," I called, happy to see him, "he'll be around. He's been asking about you."

"Gotta teach that boy to hit to the opposite field this year." Donny shook his head soberly. "Kid just didn't get the hang of it last season."

"We got some time," I offered, "he's gonna turn twelve this year."

"He's falling behind, Jack. And you ain't gonna teach him, that's for sure. You get him over here."

I went back across the hall to visit with Charley. "Can you believe it?" I asked.

"I wouldn't have guessed this in a million years, Jack, not in one million dad-gum years. We're gonna give it another go."

"Unreal." I grinned.

Charley sat back and smiled, savoring thoughts of the season to come.

"Hey," I said, turning serious, "you coming over later?"

"Yeah," Charley said, "I'll be there. Me and Percy's old man, I think we got along pretty good. I figure it might help, one baseball man talking to another."

"Think the kid'll sign?" I asked.

"Yeah," Charley said, "he'll sign. This is the chance his old man never got. He's got to give it a try."

"Would you?" I asked. "I mean, let's face it, this ain't gonna be a stroll through the park."

"You're right about that, but, yeah, I think I would. When you're that good, you need to know for sure; you gotta find out for yourself if you're as good as your friends have been telling you."

At about ten 'til four William raced to my desk. Walter and Percy had asked him to let me know that they'd arrived. "Just tell them I'll be there in a minute, would you?"

"Yes, sir," William said. He lingered for a moment, hoping for another morsel of information, but I glanced him away and walked down the hall. I told Joe they had arrived, and that I'd be back down in a minute or two. And then I went to the colored waiting room.

Percy stood with his hands behind his back, staring out the glass door. Walter treaded heavily nearby, rubbing his hands together, a thin coat of sweat beading along his brow.

"Hey," I said, reaching for Walter's hand, "I'm glad you could make it."

Walter forced a smile. He took my hand and said, "Now, Mr. Hall, please, you got to tell us what this is about. What are we doing here?"

"It's okay, Walter, trust me." I turned. "Come on," I said, "we'll go this way."

"I do trust you," Walter said, "but I-I-I'd just like to know what this about."

"It'll be painless. I promise."

We made our way through the easy maze into Joe's office. There, waiting for a Negro schoolteacher and his eighteen-year-old son, were the two most powerful men in Whitney.

After we'd made our introductions, Charley stepped in. Joe took an uneasy glance around the room. "Have a seat," he said. "Everybody just find a seat … don't mean to keep you long." Joe was jumpier than Walter, and Burt was too shaky to help.

"Well," Joe began, "we, uh, appreciate you men coming over. We wanted to, uh, speak to you fellas today—"

This was too much for Charley. "You mind if I jump in here?" he said.

"That's a good idea," Burt offered. "Why don't you go on, Charley?"

"Walter," Charley said, "we finished a half game back last season. If we'd had a little more run production, and maybe a little more speed—why I believe we'd have won another pennant. We've had our eye on two or three kids who can fill in the gaps. Percy here's one of 'em. We'd like him to come play for us." He turned to Percy. "What do you say? Would you like to play for the Bobcats?"

The light from Walter's smile burst into the room. "The thought had crossed my mind," he whispered, "but I just couldn't believe it." He glanced at me. "When you came to the school yesterday, I just couldn't figure it out, and later I thought, maybe it'd be about this. But I didn't dare say it out loud." He turned to his son. "This is a dream come true, boy, a dream come true." Percy sat still, and perfectly silent. "Wouldn't you like to play pro ball?" his dad asked.

"I s'pose," Percy mumbled. Then, with contrition, he added, "We talked about college; about playing football."

"And I want you to go to college," Walter said. "You can do both. But this is baseball, boy—professional baseball." For a moment it was as if they were the only ones in the room. Walter put his hand on Percy's shoulder. "Boys like you don't get this kind of chance," he said. "You hear what I'm saying? We just don't get this kind of chance. And this is your game." He leaned closer, to where he could look Percy in the eyes. "This is the game you were born to play."

Burt smoothed a contract across Joe's desk. And at 4:42, Percy Jackson became a Whitney Bobcat, and the first Negro player to join the Sunshine Circuit.

Chapter 11

The night before the team's first workout I slept about as soundly as a five-year-old on Christmas Eve. I checked the clock at three and again at four. By five I was making coffee, and at half past, when Rose Marie trooped down the stairs, I was in the living room reading, checking my watch, and with all my mental might, urging the day on. She sneered as she passed, slightly amused, but mostly still angry—and still at war with the idea that a colored kid would play on our team.

We learned that two other Sunshine Circuit teams had signed Negroes. And on the fringe of her consciousness, I believe the inevitability of it all had begun to dawn. She, nor I, nor anyone else imagined the world this way. But certain things had been set in motion. They went against the grain of the things that gave us comfort; they defied our notions of what was right and natural. And yet, "these things" would save my favorite team, in the world's best sport, in the town I loved.

I was halfway down the hall on my way to the locker room when I heard the muffled jabs and verbal punches of young men who more than anything else relish the fraternity of the team. I pushed through the swinging doors, pad and pen in hand, eager and perfectly willing to be enthralled by the clichéd thoughts of young ballplayers. Freddy Taylor, our first basemen, lay flat on his back on a wooden bench in front of his locker. He wore a red-sleeved undershirt and jockey shorts; a wad of tobacco stretched his jaw. Billy Henderson, an outfielder, rocked back on the hind legs of a folding chair, feet propped on the same bench, and looking like he shopped at the same store. Jimmy Giles and Denny Douglas were there too. The sweet smell of tape, sweat-soaked jerseys, and analgesic balm filled the air as seductively as salt at the seashore.

I pulled up a chair beside Giles, knowing that this spring was for me, as much as it was for him, a season of rebirth. We were both where we belonged. And we were both silently yet profoundly grateful to have been given six more months in a loud and smelly locker room. We talked about defense. Teddy Little, last season's shortstop, had moved on and we'd be starting Eddie Smith, an untested rookie. We talked about offense and Giles' hopes to add seventy-three points to his .227 average. Pitching, Jimmy thought, looked sturdy enough, but with a couple of guys still in the Phillies' camp, Charley had to look for a fourth starter. "The Phils are loaded," Jimmy told me. "Curt Simmons and Robin Roberts—those guys are young and nobody can touch 'em." And even though Murry Dickson was showing signs of his thirty-seven years, rookies Penson and Mrozinski were waiting right behind him. "Our guys will probably be back," Giles thought, "but you never know."

Johnny Andrews, a good-looking left fielder, dangled his legs over a table as a trainer wrapped both ankles. We bemoaned the injuries that kept him out of last season's final ten games. He was certain, he said dejectedly, that if he'd been healthy down the stretch we would've won. Then he looked up; his eyes were propped wide with hope and he told me how he'd filled the winter months—running, lifting weights, and taking batting practice twice a day. He shook his head earnestly and swore he'd never been in better shape, and I'm not sure who he was trying harder to convince—me or himself. We rambled on about the outfield. It looked like he'd be in left, Murphy in center, and Henderson in right. Johnny thought we had decent speed, good arms, and real good gloves. But nobody was sure if Murphy could hit. And last year Henderson, who hit .277, only batted around .210 with runners in scoring position.

While I was talking with Giles, Donny Jones made his usual entrance. You couldn't help but smile. Jones was full of himself, a clown, and the kind of guy who could make you laugh after you'd gone 0 for 4. I started toward his locker, eager to visit. I was just about to speak when I noticed him gawking; he was staring off in the distance—dumbfounded—like a kid who'd sneaked into his first freak show. The entire room went silent. I followed Donny's gaze—to the locker-room door—to Percy Jackson.

He wore crisp new blue jeans and a white T-shirt. A small duffle bag hung from his right hand, his mitt was looped around his fingers. He stood at the door, black as coal, bewildered, and blocked from coming farther by the startled stares of his new team. An agonizing few moments passed and the whole room remained frozen. Frantically, I searched for Charley, hoping he had a plan. But he was nowhere in sight. Percy showed the first signs of a thaw, taking a hesitant half step inside.

"Hold on there, nigger," Donny sneered, "where you think you're going?" Donny shifted his weight from one foot to the other; he drooled tobacco juice into a cup, a brown trickle loitered on his chin. Percy stopped, the whites of his eyes grew bigger than full moons, and his pupils darted around the room. "You can't come in here," Donny chuckled. Another plop of brown-stained spit splashed into the cup.

Rick Murphy arrived, cheerful as ever and utterly unfazed by the colored kid blocking his path. He squeezed past Percy, smiled, and said, "That boy think he's dressing in here?" He laughed, not waiting for a reply, and headed for his locker—business as usual. Slowly, door hinges began to creak again, tape was stretched and torn, and quiet conversation returned.

Percy remained paralyzed. "Where's he supposed to dress?" I said—to no one in particular.

"At home," Jones said flatly.

"Maybe he can go across the street," Murphy said. "They got a place for coloreds over there."

I walked to Percy. "He's talking about the armory," I explained. "You know where it is?"

Percy nodded yes. "I seen it," he mumbled.

"I'll go over there with you."

We found the equipment manager and gathered up some practice gear. Then Percy and I found a colored dressing room at the National Guard armory.

When Percy and I headed back down the hall toward the dugout, the locker-room doors were propped open and Charley's voice boomed through the stadium. "This kid's on the team," Charley roared, "and you'll treat him that way. He's gonna dress in here, he's gonna sit in the dugout, he's gonna ride the bus. Some of you ain't gonna like it but he's on this team, same as you."

"But he ain't the same," Donny fired back. "There ain't a one of us who'd have him in our house. Why we gotta have him in our shower?"

"He's right," Fred Taylor said, "how we supposed to act like everything's normal when we got a colored boy stripping down naked right here in the same room."

Percy and I stood at the doors, outside and out of sight. He dragged a sleeve across an itchy nose—looking as if he'd just heard the weather report or an update on wheat prices. Inside, silence hung in the air. Then Charley spoke. His voice was calm, sympathetic. "You're gonna do it the same way Duke Snider does. You're gonna get up and go to work just like Carl Erskine. If guys like that can play with colored boys, then I suspect we can find a way too. And if any of you has any hopes of making it to the big leagues, you better get used to it. What're you gonna do, Jones? You get traded to the Dodgers, you gonna tell Walter Alston to send Campanella over to the armory to change his pants?… Find your fanny back here quicker than a Robin Roberts fastball, I guaran-dang-tee you."

I nudged Percy. "Let's go," I whispered, and we tried to creep by the open doors. But Charley turned. "Percy, get in here," he barked. The team was scattered on wooden benches, they sat on the floor, and on chairs strewn around the room. "We're having a team meeting," Charley said, "and you need to be here." Percy inched his way inside. "That's your locker over there," Charley told him, "number forty-two. From now on you get dressed in here just like everybody else."

Donny turned away.

Charley eyed his players. "All right," he said, "be ready in ten minutes."

On the field guys were loosening up. Some ran across the outfield, others sat with their legs extended, stretching toward their toes, loosening up their hamstrings. I walked around the infield, giving my mind its own light workout; getting my thoughts back in baseball shape. I moseyed between first and second, just off the infield. Eddie Smith and Fred Taylor jogged by; Fred slapped me on the butt as he passed. "Looks like you got your nigger, huh, Jack?" he said, grinning.

Percy stood behind third, his glove at his feet. He had his right foot crossed over his left, bending down to touch his toes. I retreated to the dugout, out of the sun, to watch the rest of the day. Percy's swing looked good. He moved around the infield as gracefully as the next guy, and his arm hadn't rusted much in the off-season. He moved from one place to the next by himself, and in silence. He was just eighteen, a colored kid who could hit and throw and catch. And who was surrounded by twenty-five men who couldn't endure the thought.

◆ ◆ ◆ ◆

Bud Parsons was wound up tighter than the core of a Spalding baseball. Every time Percy fielded a ground ball or took a shower, "he made a mockery of the law," Bud grumbled. "And Charley, Burt, and Joe were all accomplices—every bit as guilty."

Bud wasn't the brightest guy in town, but he was the only one who had seen this coming. Like Burt, Bud understood that "things had been set in motion," and he intended to stop them at Whitney's door. He had shrewdly gathered allies and had gotten his ordinance passed. But Burt and Joe had resources of their own. Since the end of the bus boycott the paper printed a series of front-page editorials calling on everyone to show "a new neighborliness." And Burt made a tour of the social and civic clubs, encouraging members to think of new ways to make Whitney a quiet town. Nobody used the words "colored" or "white." We simply laid out a pair of new themes: Whitney would be the world's most peaceful town. A place where everyone would feel at home.

I wrote stories about the Sunshine Circuit's teams, and included photos of the league's three new Negroes—on the field with white players, in the dugout, and drinking from water coolers. I ignored the fact that those cities, like ours, struggled. And that their players, like ours, wrestled with a galling new reality.

◆ ◆ ◆ ◆

Item three on the Tuesday-morning docket was "Amendment to Parks Ordinance." Phil Edwards arrived early and sat beside Chester LaBarr. Walter Jackson was there too. And so were thirty or forty other colored men: business owners, community leaders, and pastors.

Burt presented his case, arguing that three Sunshine Circuit teams now fielded colored players. We faced a whole new set of circumstances, Burt said. This wasn't about a long-shot possibility that a mixed team from New York might wander into town. Percy Jackson would be in the dugout every night. And teams that had been coming to Whitney for years—from right in our own backyard—they'd be bringing colored boys too. "Nobody's trying to overturn this thing," Burt assured the crowd. "The ordinance ought to stay in place for the youth leagues and softball teams." But the stadium was different; Negro players were here, and we had to face the facts.

Bud and Cale pleaded their familiar case. "It was wrong," "not the way things were meant to be," "against God's will…."

Burt pleaded for the greater good of the town. And baseball, he urged, "was an important part of our life together … America's pastime … good for every Whitney family." Cale fired back, arguing for the greater good of society, for the southern way of life, and for living as God intended—at any cost—regardless of what others thought.

"This is exactly why we passed that law," Bud growled. "Now you and Joe, you got to get that nigger off the field. And you need to get him out of our locker room, too."

Burt calmly propped his chin on a fist, hoping a few seconds of silence would cool Bud down. Then he leaned back and faced his adversaries. His voice was easy, like one neighbor talking to another over the backyard fence. "You boys talk about our way of life, about living right, about doing what's best—we all want the same thing." He pushed his seat back from the dais and crossed his legs. "We've known each other a long time, and I know you mean it. Bud, you and Cale, you've both done a lot of good for this town. Nobody knows that better than I do. But here's the thing: We take the hard stand you're laying out and we're gonna put a lot of people out of work, people who look to you to take care of 'em—all those good folks who keep up the field, the high-school groups who sell Cokes and peanuts, the guys who sell tickets, not to mention our players and coaches. Some of those folks are colored, and some are white. And I think we want to do what's right by all of them.

"On top of that, the Bobcats have been a part of Whitney as long as any of us can remember. We all grew up with them. We've all taken our kids out to see 'em." He shook his head, thinking back to easier times. "I'd like my grandkids to see 'em too. And let's just think about it," he pleaded, "forget about Negroes and whites for a minute—what kind of town doesn't have baseball? Now I don't know about you fellas, but I don't especially want to go down in history as the guy who lost our baseball team."

Bud and Cale pronounced their love of the game, but the price, they argued, was too steep. They loved their way of life more.

Phil Edwards bowed his head and Walter Jackson plunged his face into his open hands, praying that he hadn't really heard what had just been said.

Burt pressed his case, talking about fathers and sons, about a wholesome place for Whitney's people, and about what it takes to be a peaceful town. But nobody looked convinced, and from one face to the next all I could see were confused frowns and deep consternation.

Then, from out of nowhere, John Drake slapped the desk in front of him. "You know, I'm sitting here listening and I swear you're both right. Now I know we can't have it both ways—just ain't no way to work that out. But what about this: What if we let the colored boys play on the field—Burt's right, that's coming whether we like it or not … nothing we can do to stop it. But we can make sure they don't use the locker room. We got the armory right across the street. All the colored boys, they can go over there together. And the locker rooms at the stadium—they'll be for the white boys. I know that ain't perfect, but I'd be willing to go for something like that."

Lights clicked on in a dozen eyes. Around the room a few heads wobbled as if they'd heard wisdom from Solomon. Burt didn't like it. And Charley fought every urge within him to leap out of his seat. But I could tell by the look in Burt's eye—he saw an opening that might close fast. He called the question, and the revised amendment passed.

The crowd bottlenecked at the door, everyone hurrying out to spread the news. But Phil Edwards and Walter Jackson kept their seats and waited for the room to clear. I slid into a seat behind them. "Percy doing all right?" I asked.

"Yeah," Walter said, "he's doing petty good."

"He's been dressing in the locker room with the other guys, what's he going to think about this?"

"You know," Walter said, "I think he'll be okay. Might even be better, you know, give him a place to relax a little bit."

"Seems like he's always alone," I replied, "at least it looks that way to me. I'd think that'd be hard."

"Sometimes it is," Edwards answered, "but you've never been the sore thumb, Mr. Hall. You've never stuck out in the crowd, been the one who's different—not because of anything you do—but just because of the way you are."

"When you're by yourself," Walter said, "you don't have to think about it."

My mind wandered back to South City High, to the glances that followed me down the halls, to the wariness that was stirred by nothing more than my presence. At the ball field and in the gym, every moment I was there I was—for a little while—the sore thumb. And I had lived with the uncomfortable weight of self-consciousness.

◆ ◆ ◆ ◆

We opened on April fifth at home. Hours before the game I fluttered around like a hummingbird, slapping guys on the back, wishing them good luck, and asking if they were ready. I hovered around Giles and Jones. They were wide-eyed and yearning to play as they had never yearned before.

Percy wandered in from across the street, dressed in a bright white, brand-new Bobcats uniform. Without a word to anyone he grabbed a seat off to one side. A few guys tossed him a friendly nod or a quick wave; and a couple went so far as to mumble, "Hey, Percy," as they passed. I grabbed a chair and joined him. "Everything okay?" I asked.

"Yessir," he muttered.

"Charley says you're coming along real good."

He nodded slightly. "I s'pose."

"Big night tonight, you nervous?"

He cocked his head. "I'm okay."

I put my hand on the boy's shoulder. I let in linger there for a while, and then said, "Hey, Percy." I waited until he looked up. "Has Charley talked to you about what to expect out there, about what you might hear?"

He twisted his mouth into a grim frown, and nodded yes.

A little more than an hour before the game, I moved through the tunnel that leads from the locker room into the dugout. I ducked my head as I came through the narrow passageway, just as I had a hundred times before, and there—the instant light hit my eye—I saw a sight more astonishing than any sci-fi writer's weirdest dream. I stood in the dugout, gape-mouthed and dumb.

"Something, ain't it?" Charley stood at the other end of the dugout.

The colored bleachers gushed on every side. Negro men and women stood along the foul line—a dark human chain that stretched from the outfield wall to the visitor's dugout. Boys and girls romped in left field and played back behind the bleachers.

"Did you have any idea?" I asked.

"No," Charley laughed. "I thought we'd have plenty of colored folks, but no, I wasn't expecting anything like this."

In the white section, too, people were pouring into the stadium. Blue caps flowed down the aisles, kids scampered everywhere, and like moisture before a storm, a soaring spirit filled the air. I hurried back to find Percy.

"There's a lot of folks out there to see you," I told him, "a lot of folks who're real proud of you."

In the language he liked best, Percy replied with a raised eyebrow and brief nod.

"No matter what," I said, "you just tend to business. Don't worry about anything but baseball, you hear?"

"Yessir."

Charley walked by, heading toward his office. I clapped Percy on the shoulder and wished him luck. Then chased Charley down.

"You gonna get him in?" I asked.

"I don't know." Charley shrugged. "We'll just see how it goes."

"Lot of people out there want to see him, they're going to be awfully disappointed if they don't."

"Yeah, and that's just more pressure on him … everybody'll get to see him soon enough."

A rap at the door cut into the conversation. "Trouble you for a minute, Coach?" It was Doug Russ and Billy Roberts, the umpires.

"Little unusual for you boys to be down here before a game," Charley said. "What's up?"

"Just need to talk for a second," Doug answered.

"Well, come on then."

Billy asked, "You playing the colored kid tonight?"

"Don't think so," Charley said, "but if I need to I will. Why?"

"Mind if we all have a little chat?" Doug asked. "Maybe he could come on in … just take a minute."

Charley turned away, not altogether sure this was a good idea. "All right," he said. He called Percy over, introduced him around.

"There's a good-size crowd out there," Doug began, "and a lot of 'em are here because you're here. Now there's a bunch of 'em who're real glad you're playing. And I s'pect another bunch ain't so glad. And, son, I don't want any trouble from either bunch. We ain't gonna treat you any different than we treat anybody else. But if you come in the game, you can't be arguing with us, you can't so much as look like you don't like a call, you understand?"

"We ain't gonna give anybody any reason to complain," Billy added. "We'll do our best, and you go right on along with it." He looked up at Charley. "We all square on that?"

Percy shifted his eyes up to his manager, and Charley replied, "Sure." He gave Percy a friendly slap on the back. "Percy here gets in the game, he'll be on his best behavior … no matter how many calls you guys miss."

Doug smiled back, and he and Billy got up to go. The head ump put his hand on Percy's shoulder. "Good luck," he said.

"C'mon," his partner snapped, "let's get out of here."

At twelve thirty, still a half hour before the first pitch, players began to trickle out of the locker room to loosen up and work off the jitters. I was standing near the on-deck circle talking to Joe and Burt, who had staked out front-row seats. Out of the corner of my eye I saw Giles and Smith trot out, then Murphy and Jones, and then Johnny Andrews.

Joe took a long, sweeping look around the field, and came as close to looking happy as I'd ever seen him. "Good crowd," he said, "and it's still early."

"Just look out there." Burt gestured toward the colored section. "That's better'n anybody could've guessed, and everyone of 'em's happier than a dad-gum clam." He held up both hands as if to embrace the entire stadium. "Everybody's getting along and having a good time." Then he smiled and took a long swig from a cup of cold Coke.

We started guessing at the crowd size. I thought we'd easily top five thousand five hundred, and Joe said he'd be tickled at anything past four.

"Shoot," Burt said, "I bet we're already past three and we got a half hour to go."

"You might be right," I said. I looked at my watch. "They don't usually get in here until—"

Without warning the colored stands erupted. Fans stood and cheered. They frantically pumped their fists in the air. They began to clap and stomp their feet. Kids and grown-ups alike raced from behind the bleachers. They pointed toward the dugout, and then they stopped and stood still. And stared.

I turned and watched Percy step onto the field. He was still in his long-sleeved undershirt, his cap was pushed back on his head, and his glove was tucked loosely under his arm. At the burst of emotion he stopped, dead still, and gaped at the crowd. The other guys, from wherever they stood, turned too. Taylor shook his head and fired a full load of tobacco-stained spit into the ground. Denny Douglas doubled over laughing, tickled beyond what he could bear that a near-mute rookie could cause this kind of commotion. Giles grinned in harmless surprise, and then he tossed his glove on the ground and joined the applause. And Donny Jones glared at the left-field stands, loathing the thought that his team's new hero was a nigger who'd never played a single pitch of pro ball.

Negroes whooped and whistled, and the left-field bleachers swayed with joy. There were bemused grins scattered among the white faces, and more than a few disgusted frowns. The white crowd generally sat still, absorbing the spectacle, and waiting patiently for the game to begin.

At twelve fifty, Charley headed for home plate to swap lineups with Madison's manager. We'd go with Taylor at first, Giles at second, and Donny Jones at third. Eddie Smith started at short. In the outfield it was Andrews, Murphy, and Henderson. Rob Haddock was on the mound. Charley had done this ten thousand times before, but this afternoon he was jumpier than a congressman on election day.

At five 'til one I bounded up the steps for the press box. Jeff Harrison was already there standing in the back corner, powerless to wipe a little-kid grin off his face. He had a tall Coke in one hand and a hot dog in the other. Dean Duncan, a crabby reporter from Chesterfield, was there too.

"Was starting to wonder if you'd make it," Jeff said.

I grinned back at him. "Oh, I think you knew I'd be along."

"Yeah," Duncan grunted, "from what I hear, this is a big day for you."

I slapped him on the back as I squeezed by. "What are you talking about?"

"Just heard you're the guy put this thing together, that's all; that you're the one who wanted to make sure we got some colored boys in the Sunshine Circuit."

"That's crazy," I said, "you nip that in the bud, will you?" I slid into my usual spot. "Now I will tell you this," I said, pointing out to left field. "I like what I see out there. Must be three thousand colored folks; every one of 'em bought a ticket and most of 'em'll buy a Coke and a hot dog before the day's over. And I don't mind telling you boys: If they weren't here, we wouldn't be either."

"Still makes me queasy as hell," Duncan sputtered.

"It's troublesome," Jeff added, "and it grates on me, too, but by golly we're here and it's opening day."

"It grates hard," Dean mumbled.

Haddock took his warm-up tosses. Charley stood on the dugout steps rubbing his hands together, clapping, shouting to each player and calling him by a favorite nickname. The crowd sang and prayed. And at 1:07, Rob Haddock threw the first pitch of the '54 season.

In the bottom of the seventh the score was tied. Jones was on second, and Murphy was on first. There was one out and Haddock was due up. Charley sent Mike Schaeffer, a reserve outfielder, in to pinch-hit. On a 2-2 count he got a fastball, belt-high on the inside corner—and he got every bit of it. Like a cannon shot, the low line drive took off toward left-center, and Jones instantly broke for third. Instinctively, the shortstop jumped. And as if the ball had eyes, it found his glove. Jones was halfway down the line, and Madison turned the easy double play.

Schaeffer, a good defensive player, stayed in the game and Rick Murphy came out.

In the eighth Denny Douglas led off with a tee shot to right. But Denny is slower than thick ketchup, and somehow managed to shrink an easy triple into a stand-up double. Charley sent Tommy Lewis, another reserve, in to run for him. That meant that Galen West, an eighteen-year-old rookie, would catch the ninth inning.

Eddie Smith hit next—an infield pop to the second baseman for an easy out. Then Andrews stepped to the plate. Our center fielder hit a deep fly to right; Lewis tagged and made it to third, but now there were two outs. Giles, who'd normally swing at anything within smelling distance of the strike zone, drew a rare walk. On the first pitch to Taylor, he stole second, and it looked like we might have something cooking. Fans were on their feet urging Freddie on. But he sent a weak grounder to first, the inning was over, and our eighth-inning hopes were squashed.

In their half of the ninth, with one out, Madison's shortstop—a guy who couldn't have been more than five foot eight and 165 pounds soaking wet—hit a line drive that cleared the fence by eighteen inches.

Marty Davis, a smart reliever, knew it the instant he heard the crack of the bat. Without bothering to look up, he kicked the mound. A fastball had drifted up on him and caught too much of the plate—an early season mistake, and he'd been made to pay.

Jeff Harrison groaned as he watched Henderson leap for the ball. I tossed a pencil across the room, sure the game was over. Dean Duncan rocked on the back legs of his chair and laughed. "Kid won't do that two more times all season," he chuckled.

Davis made short work of the next two batters, but we were down a run with only three outs to go.

Billy Henderson led off the ninth with a sharp ground ball to short: one man up, one down. Jones then blasted a line drive to center—a solid single—and we had the tying run on. Galen West was up next. He dribbled the ball off the end of his bat—the thing couldn't have gone more than twenty feet—but Madison's infield was deep, looking for the double play. The rookie catcher pounded his way toward first. Madison's third baseman charged; he grabbed the ball barehanded, bobbled it once, then twice, then threw hard to first—a step too late. The tying run was in scoring position, and the winning run was aboard.

Now Charley had a chance to show why he makes the big money. Because Lewis had stayed in the game, the pitcher's spot was due up, and there were only two position players left on the bench. Both could run, but one was the better hitter. Charley pored over his lineup card, weighing his limited options—and then he sent Percy to the plate.

Percy shot up from the bench, moving faster than I'd ever seen him move before. He grabbed a couple of bats and swung them in long, looping circles. He took a few practice cuts, tossed one of the bats aside, and strode to the plate.

The colored fans stomped and jumped and screamed. I looked at the crowd below the press box. Helen, my favorite waitress at the diner, stood and waved a poster high in the air screaming toward home plate. I hustled down to the stands for a closer look. Jeff Harrison was on my heels.

Though Percy hadn't stepped foot on the infield, he nervously tapped at his shoes. He adjusted his hat, took a practice cut, and then stepped into the batter's box. He kicked at the dirt with his back cleats and planted his foot. The pitcher took a long look in … then delivered. The first pitch was a fastball—head high and dangerously inside. Percy twisted out of the way. He fell to the ground, and for four or five seconds he stayed there, staring at the sky. The colored crowd was frozen. I looked at Joe. He and Burt were up and out of their seats. Joe had both hands working the top of his head. Percy sat up, and the colored crowd came back to life. He brushed off his hands, eyeing the pitcher angrily. Then he got to his feet, and the Negro fans roared.

In the white section a guy in the third row—no more than fifteen yards from Percy—stood and yelled, "What do you expect, nigger, get back to South City." His two kids and the fans around him giggled.

The next pitch was another fastball, high and inside again, sending Percy to the deck for a second time. This time, like brooding thunder, a chorus of boos rolled in from the left-field stands, and an angry-looking crowd began to gather along the foul line.

Burt hopped down to the field and rushed past the Madison dugout, to where a handful of Whitney's finest had gathered, their hands poised on clubs and holsters. Calmly, and with Burt standing close behind, they spread out along the foul line, showing themselves to the crowd, and to the Madison pitcher.

From the white section's fifth row a young woman—blonde and cheerleader-pretty—stood and screamed, "Niggers don't play ball, they pick cotton." And behind her, a factory worker who could barely control his fury yelled, "Watermelon man!"

In a close game, and in a crucial situation, Madison had used two precious pitches to let Percy know he wasn't welcome. Now they had to throw him strikes. The pitcher went into his stretch for the third time. Another fastball, this time just off the outside corner. Percy swung late and fouled the ball into the third row behind the home-team dugout.

Helen shook her homemade sign, screaming, red-faced and hoarse. She spun to her right and left, proud of the work she'd done. And for twenty rows in every direction, her neighbors read the hand-scrawled words, "Hey nigger, don't you wish you were white."

The count was 2-1, and the fourth pitch to Percy was on the way. He swung for the fence and lined the ball deep to left field … just foul.

The crowd of colored fans swelled along the foul line, restless and eager.

On the next pitch Percy swung and sent a screaming line drive over the shortstop's head. Jones broke from second. He easily scored and the game was tied.

Colored fans screamed, they hugged one another, and rejoiced like those who'd been cured from a long and fatal disease. By instinct rather than choice, white fans threw victorious fists into the air.

Percy stood at second, with his first hit and an RBI.

Schaeffer stepped to the plate. He watched two balls and a strike go by. Then he looped a soft single into right. West beat the throw to the plate, and the Bobcats won.

Jeff and I hustled down to the field. The Bobcats charged from the dugout as if they'd just won the World Series. They swarmed Schaeffer slapping him on the back, and jumping into each other's arms.

Percy trotted in alone. As he neared the dugout, Charley jogged up and threw an arm around his shoulder. They came to the steps where a couple of boys—maybe sixteen—stood and screamed, "Nice hit, dice shooter." Charley pulled Percy close, and the two of them disappeared down the tunnel.

Chapter 12

I pulled into the driveway a little before six. Walking from the car to the kitchen, I glanced to the backyard—to Chris's old swing set, seats swaying; to the sun-bleached picnic table; and the dog toys Slugger had left strewn across the yard. A handful of lanky pines waved in the breeze to welcome me home. The willow, slumped by the weight of a thousand feathery branches, bowed in my direction, while sparrows, robins, and blue jays chirped and darted from limb to wire finishing up their work before dark.

Every once in a while I have moments when I'm overwhelmed by the ordinary—by the commonplace and garden variety—and in this moment, I stood perfectly still on my cracked concrete driveway hoping none of this would ever change. This was a perfect picture. And life here, in this spot, with Rose Marie, Chris, and Slugger was exactly the way it was meant to be.

In the kitchen Rose Marie was bent down, rummaging through the refrigerator. From the living room Buffalo Bob cheered on the Peanut Gallery, "Let's give a rousing cheer, 'cause Howdy Doody's here. It's time to start the show, so kids let's go!"

At the sound of the creaking screen door, Rose Marie glanced over, more anxious than happy. She stood and propped an elbow on the refrigerator door. "Well," she said, "how'd it go?"

"It was perfect. I couldn't have drawn it up better. We were down by one in the ninth; Schaeffer comes off the bench and wins it with a little Texas-league blooper, just like something you'd see in the movies."

She smiled blandly. "And how'd Jackie Robinson Jr. do? Your boy get in the game?"

"Come on, Rose, he's not my boy. But yeah, he came in to pinch-hit, drove in the tying run. Not a bad start."

"And everybody there I s'pose was charmed to see a colored boy on the team?"

"No," I said, "not by a long shot. But there were a bunch of colored people out there, Rose, more than I've ever seen in one place, and every one of 'em paid full price for a ticket."

"Well isn't that nice." She smiled. "A chance for us to get to know our colored neighbors."

"So," I said, desperate to change the subject, "what's for dinner? Anything I can do to help?"

"There's a casserole in the oven," she said. "We'll wait 'til Howdy Doody's over."

Rose Marie lifted the pot's lid and steam rose, ensnaring us with the fragrance of tuna fish, cheese, and noodles. We thanked God for the food and the cook; for swing sets, dogs, and tall, skinny pines—and for all the blessings we'd been given. And then we dove into our dinner.

I commenced a blow-by-blow description of the game, sliding my scorebook over to Chris, and in lifelike color relived every play. He sat mesmerized; his eyes pried wide by a game that came alive in his mind, and he savored the sights he imagined more than the food. In the pauses between plays he asked about Douglas and Giles. He insisted on an up-to-date injury report. It was good, he said soberly, that our relief pitching had held up late in the game.

Then he wanted to know about our plans for Saturday.

His mother shot me a "don't you dare" scowl, and I did what I could to evade the question. "I don't know, pal, we'll talk about it later, okay?"

But Chris, like me, had suffered through a long, drab winter.

"Well," he said, his eyes beseeching, "we're going, aren't we?"

Rose Marie leaned toward him; she looked like an earnest teacher trying to explain algebra to a history major. Things were different this year, she said, and it might not be good for him to be at the ballpark. He looked at me, his eyes pleading for more information. With an expression that begged her to go on, I turned to Rose Marie. She glanced away, contemplating how much her only son loved the game. Then she moved a forkful of noodles to her mouth and sat there, quietly.

"It's been a year," Chris protested. "I haven't been to one practice. I haven't seen Denny or Jimmy. I haven't even seen Uncle Charley since school started."

"I know," Rose Marie said, "we'll have Charley over soon."

"Why can't I go to the game?" he asked. "What's wrong?"

Rose Marie planted both elbows on the table and rested her chin on prayerfully folded hands. "Things are different this year," she began, "and we haven't decided what to do." There was a new player on the team she explained—a colored boy—and it wasn't right for colored people and white people to play with one another.

Chris hiked up an eyebrow, and with unstained innocence said, "Colored men play in the big leagues. It's just like having Jackie Robinson on our team. Or Larry Doby."

Those men played in different leagues, and in another part of the country, his mother explained, where people didn't believe the same way we did.

"What do you mean?" Chris wanted to know.

"It's not right, sweetheart, for colored people and white people to live together and play together. It's important for black people to keep to themselves, to do things they enjoy, to work at the things they're best suited for…." White people needed to do the same, she explained. "And I don't want you getting all mixed up."

Chris angled his head. "I don't know," he replied, "seems like Jackie Robinson is suited for baseball, and Willie Mays … they're as good as anybody."

"Yes," his mother agreed, "they're good players. But it'd be better if they played with other Negroes … you understand?"

He curled his lips, taking this into consideration. Then he said, "But I see 'em playing on TV. What's the difference if I see them in real life? I want to go, Mom. I really want to go."

Rose Marie speared a batch of cold noodles. "We'll think about it," she muttered. "Right now you need to finish your dinner."

◆ ◆ ◆ ◆

For three seasons out of four the early morning creak of Rose Marie's chair is like the voice of a good friend calling for company. Outside, she rocked softly, her hands wrapped around an oversized mug, her head down, and the paper open on her lap.

"Well," I asked, pushing through the screen door, "how'd we do today?"

"Sounds like a great game," she said, doing her best to sound cheerful, "and you captured it perfectly—like always." She looked back and smiled. "Really."

I slid into my chair and reached for the front page. "It *was* a great game, Rose. You would've loved it. And Chris would've had a great time."

"Yeah," she said, the chair creaking cozily, "I know. But all this," she picked up the paper and let it fall to her lap, "the other team throwing at that boy, the colored people looking like they're about to storm the field. We can't take our boy to a riot, Jack. And sooner or later that's what we'll have. We're just asking for it, putting a black boy out there with whites."

"None of that stuff lasted long," I said, "and now that he's been in the game, I don't think it'll happen again."

"Maybe not," she sighed, "but still...." She took a long sip from her mug. "Coloreds and whites on the same field, angry crowds, meanness all over the place.... How do you raise a child with all that mess going on?" She leaned back, the rocker's creak becoming more demanding. "It makes my head hurt just to think about it," she said.

"Yeah, I know." We sat and sipped coffee, and pondered a world gone awry. Then we heard Chris and Slugger tromping down the stairs, scurrying toward the kitchen.

Rose Marie put her hand on top of mind. "Well, you ready to eat?"

◆ ◆ ◆ ◆

I kissed my wife good-bye and stepped outside, eager to conquer a full day, beginning with a stop at the stadium to check in with Charley. From there

I'd drive up to the college; the Raiders' season opened soon, and with everyone hoping for better things, it was time to take a look. Then it was back to the office for some real work before tonight's game.

I opened the Ford's back door and tossed my briefcase inside. Reaching for the front door handle—out of the corner of my eye—I saw the open gas cap. It had been four or five days since I'd stopped for a fill-up. In the same moment I was stabbed by the sight of the long deep gashes, three lesions to the otherwise perfect complexion of my beautiful car stretching across the rear door. I ran my fingers over the wounds, shaking my head, wondering who would do this—and why. I went to close the gas cap, and noticed a trace of white—granules of some kind along the rim of the tank. I touched a finger to them, smelled them, and touched my fingers to the tip of my tongue. Sugar.

I hurried inside and called Ron, my mechanic. "Whatever you do," he warned, "don't start the car. We're going to have to flush that tank real good; probably have to replace it. I'll be out with the wrecker in a while." And then he added, "Somebody don't like you much, Jack. You better be careful."

Every trace of Rose Marie's countenance was wracked with pain. She slumped into a kitchen chair. "First they call our boy a nigger lover, then they pestered us with phone calls, and now this." She buried her face in her hands. "I don't think this is the end of it," she moaned. "There's going to be more."

"Probably just some kids playing a prank," I said feebly.

"No," she groaned, "you know good and well that's not it." She lowered her hands and glared at me. "You put a colored boy's picture in the paper. You talked about how he got some key hit, you ..." she looked away, her lips tight as a clamp. "This was no prank, Jack."

I stood beside her, my hand on her shoulder, and watched her suffer. "Well," I said, "I gotta catch the bus. Ron'll be out soon."

I charged through the *Herald*'s lobby, late and discouraged, but with a list of things I still had to get done. "Hey, Jack," Louise shouted after me, "stop by Joe's office. He wants to see you first thing."

Joe had just arrived and was throwing his suit coat over the back of a chair. I rapped at the door and he turned, scowling like he'd tear the whole day limb from limb as soon as he could get his hands on it.

"Morning," I said.

"Morning's been crap," he snarled.

"Yeah, well, I can't argue with you there."

He rubbed his head, and his lips were screwed into a tight frown. "Same jackass who tore up your car got mine … ran a key up and down the side, dumped a half pound sugar down the tank. I don't know how bad it's tore up. Ron says mine's worse than yours."

So much for my kid-playing-a-prank theory.

"Guess I was lucky," I said, "noticed it before I cranked the engine."

"Hang on a second." Joe reached for the phone. "I meant to check on Burt." He dialed the mayor's number. Burt wasn't in, Margaret said, he'd had car trouble and was running late. "I'll call back," Joe snapped at her. Then he returned to me. "We'll get the cops on this; find the moron who thinks this is funny."

"And that's it …?" I pressed.

Joe peered over his glasses. He shrugged—as if he didn't understand the question. "What do you want?" he asked. "What else is there to do?"

"I'm talking about Percy," I said. "You gonna leave everything the way it is? With him? With the team?"

Joe fell into his chair. "Well, yeah. You think we'd change things because of this?" He leaned across the desk; his eyes narrowed. "Did you see that crowd last night? You ever seen so many happy colored folks in your life? Ain't about to let one idiot change the plan."

"You're not concerned about the screaming? About the signs? About the coloreds bunching up on the foul line?"

"Well, I'd be an idiot if I wasn't concerned, but we ain't gonna give up after nine innings. We had three thousand colored folks out there, Jack. Every one of 'em was proud as punch of their boy. Every one of 'em felt like he owned a piece of the town. That's why we got this kid. For the love of … we got just what we wanted."

"You got a bunch of people who're spittin' mad," I said, "and that's one thing you didn't want."

"Hell, Jack, we had six thousand people out there. Out of six thousand how many screamed at that boy? How many made up a sign? Out of the six thousand, how many really wanted to make trouble?"

"Enough to make trouble," I cracked.

"Yeah, but still," Joe reasoned, "folks like that, they burn out fast." He looked up to see if I bought it. Then, as if to persuade us both, he waved a hand through the air. "This'll die down. You wait and see."

◆ ◆ ◆ ◆

The season got off to a good start. We took two out of three from Madison and were headed to Clayton for a three-game set on the road. Thursday morning the blue and silver Greyhound Scenicruiser idled at the gates of Memorial Stadium, and the air filled with diesel fumes and high expectations.

Duffle bags and coolers sat stacked, waiting to be loaded, and a handful of guys had gathered early, drawn by eagerness they couldn't resist a minute more. One by one, for thirty more minutes, the travel squad arrived. We boarded the bus, and Don went up and down the aisle counting heads, calling names, and tossing out brown-bagged lunches. A few minutes before eleven, the bus lurched away and headed north toward Highway 27.

Pitchers and catchers clumped together toward the back of the bus on the right-hand side. Most of the outfielders bunched up in front of them, and the infielders spread out all along the left. The chatter was loud and breezy.

Percy had drifted up to the top tier, toward the back. He sat by himself with a lapful of comic books and crossword puzzles. As troubled as my life was, I figured his had to be worse. I tossed my briefcase into the overhead rack and slid into the seat behind him. He glanced up, surprised. "Hey, Percy," I said.

"Hey," he said back.

"Mind if I join you?"

"No, sir."

As the bus made its way through town, I talked about the weather, and about his dad. I carried on about how I loved baseball and the newspaper business, but that I hated to be away from home. Then I told him what I knew about Clayton: They had good pitching, the top of the order was tough, but from what we could tell, their six, seven, and eight batters couldn't hit a slow-pitched softball.

Here and there, sprinkled through the monologue, he muttered "yessir," or "uh-huh." He smiled occasionally, even chuckled a time or two, and seemed glad for the company. Thirty minutes into the trip most of the talk had quieted down, and I leaned into the corner of the seat and wandered off into a dream.

After a while we made a sweeping turn into the Clayton City Motel parking lot and pulled around back, out of the way of everyday traffic. The driver jumped down and opened the luggage compartments, then quickly stacked bags and suitcases. Players and coaches lumbered out of the double-decker bus, stretching and yawning. Lazily, they strapped bags over their shoulders and looked for Don to get their room assignments and keys. They paired off, two to a room, and disappeared into the two-story motor inn, where they'd catch one more nap before batting practice.

Percy lingered behind the bus, his bag at his feet, with Charley standing beside him. That seemed odd to me, the two of them just standing there. Prodded by a reporter's meddlesome nature, I asked, "What are you guys doing?"

Charley rolled his eyes. He expelled a chest-full of frustration and said, "Percy's staying with a family that lives on the other side of town. We're just waiting on his ride."

My mind flashed back to Phil Edwards, and I thought: *Guy gets a clutch hit in the bottom of the ninth, and the world reminds him, every chance it gets, that he is something less than everyone around him.* A bright blue Chevy pulled up. We watched a smiling, good-humored colored man bounce out of the car and open the trunk. He took long, purposeful strides around the car and helped Percy with his bag. Charley thanked him, handed over a wad of cash, and said, "He needs to be at the stadium by five."

"He'll be here," the man said with a grin. "Yes, sir, he'll be right on time." Without a word Percy climbed into the car, and the two of them disappeared.

◆ ◆ ◆ ◆

The Clayton crowd was good-sized—somewhere on the north side of five thousand—and fans swamped the colored bleachers, hoping to see a black kid hold his own against the home team.

In the bottom of the fourth with no score, Clayton had a runner on second. Their cleanup man was at the plate, and on a 2-2 count he lifted a high fly ball to right field, just short of the warning track. The runner tagged.

Billy Henderson's got a rocket-powered arm. And he's stunned past belief when anybody who's ever read a scouting report's got the gall to challenge it.

Billy circled under the ball, his body in perfect position; with flawless elegance he caught it and threw. The instant the ball hit Henderson's mitt, the runner broke for third. I, along with the five thousand fans, held my breath, watching the ball and the runner, the ump and the tag.

I believe there is a reason for everything that happens in the world. And from the time I was a boy, when I'd been discouraged or hurt, I'd been taught by parents and preachers the Bible's promise that "... all things work together for good." That assurance, in the midst of lousy times, is a hard one to hold on to. But as we look back at how the events of our lives are seamed together, it is, as I've said before, hard to have faith in chance.

Henderson's throw bounced eighteen inches in front of Donny Jones, who, like any good infielder, was planted firmly in front of the ball and intent on knocking it down. But instead, the short hop struck him flush on the nose and Donny fell as if he'd been shot at close range. Blood spurted everywhere, covering his face, hands, and arms. Charley and Davy

White, our trainer, raced from the dugout. They toweled off Donny's face as best they could, and stuffed cotton up his nose to staunch the flow. Four minutes must have passed before Donny knew his name. Several more dragged by before he could get to his feet. He was wobbly, staggered by the pain. Davy propped him up on one side, and Charley, with Donny's hat and glove tucked under an arm, held him up on the other. With Charley and Davy as crutches, the Bobcats third baseman hobbled away, cheered by an appreciative crowd.

They laid Donny down on the bench and tended to him. Terry Thompson, a utility infielder, and Percy hustled out of the dugout to loosen up. The ump gave them plenty of time, then ambled over to the dugout, a courteous but sure sign that it was time to play. Charley met him at the top step, his lineup card in hand. The two men walked toward the field, talking, pointing, and nodding their heads. Then Charley turned toward his infielders, barked out an order—and Percy broke for third.

In the bleachers beside third base a crowd instantly gathered and set loose a torrent of cold-blooded words that wouldn't be dammed. I had never heard the word nigger repeated so often, or so cruelly.

Percy was at his post, alert and ready to play, numb to the crowd. But the foul-mouthed horde was more than his manager could bear, and before the next pitch flew, Charley popped out of the dugout and ran to the umpire. They talked, both men plainly worried. But the ump raised his hand to the air, as if to say, "What do you want me to do?" He sent Charley back to the dugout, and signaled Haddock to play.

The Bobcats pitcher threw a strike, and the crowd's howls grew louder. On the next pitch the batter sent a routine ground ball to the left side of the diamond. At the crack of the bat Percy broke in front of Eddie Smith, fielded the ball coolly, and threw to first for the easy out.

The mob erupted. The throng retched out every imaginable insult, and Charley charged out again. He put his hands to his hips, and I could practically hear him scream, "Do something!" The ump raised his hands again, palms up, imploring, "What …?"

Finally, the umpire jogged over to the Clayton dugout. A minute later a kid in street clothes rushed up to the press box, and seconds later the PA announcer's voice crackled across the stadium. "Ladies and gentlemen, the Clayton Cowboys would like y'all to refrain from making personal insults. You can cheer and boo just as loud as you like, but please don't insult individual players."

The crowd hissed like a brood of angry vipers. The announcer repeated the message—to no greater avail—then the umpire crouched behind the plate. He signaled Haddock to throw, and the screams reached heights that I'm sure this stadium had never heard.

In our half of the sixth Henderson, Jackson, and Douglas were due up. The Clayton catcher threw down to second, the ball made its way around the horn, and Billy stepped into the batter's box. On an 0-2 count he reached for a lousy pitch and sent a soft grounder to first—out by fifteen feet.

Then Percy stepped to the plate. The colored fans in our opponent's park applauded deliriously. They stood, and more than two thousand souls hoped with all their hearts to see the colored kid do well. Insults continued to rain down from the stands, and white fans with red-flushed faces made no attempt to hide their scorn.

On a 1-1 pitch Percy drilled a fastball back up the middle, a solid single. Black fans jumped and hollered, overjoyed to see their kid handle one of the league's toughest pitchers. At the same time an angry gang swelled near first base, and like a lanced boil they spewed, pouring insults all over the teenager from Whitney. Charley rushed from the dugout for the third time. The ump put his hands on his hips—frustrated. Charley mopped his brow with both shoulders, disgusted with the ump, the crowd, and every inch of Clayton's red clay. He stood chest-to-chest with the shorter man, arms folded, barking out a clipped string of angry complaints. But he had seen and heard enough. Charley said his piece, turned to the dugout, and signaled inside. Thompson jumped out and ran to first to pinch-run. Percy's chin fell to his chest, his shoulders sagged, and he began the painful walk to the dugout.

The victorious crowd screamed in triumph. Charley waited for Percy. He put a hand on the colored kid's shoulder as if to say, "I'm sorry." Then, from out of nowhere, Giles appeared, and in front of five thousand mostly hostile fans, Jimmy gave his teammate a slap on the back. He shook Percy's hand, and he held it for three or four seconds, speaking to him eye-to-eye and man-to-man. Then he patted the colored boy on the butt, and the three of them walked to the dugout together.

The men and women around me—mothers and fathers, office workers, farmers, clerks, and shopkeepers—exploded with undiluted malice. I thought to myself: *In the midst of hard times it is hard to hold on to that promise that all things work together for good.*

Tired and discouraged after the 2-1 loss, the team trudged onto the bus—infielders, outfielders, and pitchers finding their customary spots—Percy drifting away to the back. But Giles wandered off after him and took the seat just in front of Percy. Denny Douglas slid into the one behind, and as the bus pulled into the sparse traffic, Giles and Douglas talked. For the most part the conversation bypassed the quiet colored kid between them, but Percy was a deliberate part of it. And for the first time he looked his teammates in the eye. He smiled at Denny's jokes, and seemed to agree with Jimmy's comments.

It was close to eleven when the bus pulled into Patterson's Diner, a stop we'd been making for years. Patterson's served great food, and it was just the thing to soothe a painful loss. We crowded into the back room and grabbed our seats. And we didn't wait long before three waitresses were clanking down full plates of thick steak, mashed potatoes, and green beans. Moods brightened with the food, and the pain of the season's second loss began to fade.

We'd had a long ride and a tough loss, and most everybody looked forward to a rest that would last well into the next afternoon. While the last few stragglers finished their meal, I strolled out to the front porch, to catch some cool air and to sort through a tense and hard-to-figure night.

As my eyes roved the sky, I caught a glimpse of something—some shadowy motion—inside the team bus. I rushed over figuring somebody was up to no good. I hopped up the three steps and turned into the aisle. There, in the dark, sat Percy and a colored busboy.

"What are you guys doing?" I asked.

"This is Julius," Percy mumbled, his mouth full of meat and potatoes. "He just brought me some dinner."

Back at the hotel we trudged off to our rooms, well fed and eager for rest. And while the rest of us crawled between clean sheets, Percy took off on one more ride—to a colored family's home fifteen miles away.

That night we learned that Jones' nose was broken and he'd be out at least six weeks, probably more. Terry Thompson took over at third. In the next two games he went 1 for 8 at the plate, and Saturday he rushed a throw, sailing the ball three feet over Taylor's head. The runner came around to score the winning run, and we dropped the series two games to one.

I sat with Charley on the ride home. We talked awhile about Clayton, but quickly turned our attention to the upcoming home stand with Leesburg. We were both drowsy, but just before he surrendered to much-needed sleep, Charley said, "We're gonna have to bite the bullet and see if Percy can help."

Chapter 13

Monday night, sometime around seven o'clock, a Negro player would—for the first time in Sunshine Circuit history—start a baseball game.

I hated the bends and folds in my own ambivalence. I was, hard as I fought it, hounded by the notion that this was wrong. I thought about how proximity changes perspective. We had all grown used to Robinson, Doby, Banks, and Mays. We saw them on television, heard about them on the radio, and read their names in the newspaper. But they played far away, in front of huge crowds, in ballparks that bore little resemblance to ours. They were images on a screen or in our imaginations—intangible and somehow something other than real. But I had been face-to-face with Percy Jackson. I'd watched him shuffle around nervously, too jittery to look a white man in the eye. I had talked to him, touched him, heard him speak, stood beside him in a locker room, and smelled his sweat-soaked skin after a two-hour practice beneath a full summer sun. His family worked and played in the town where I lived. They were flesh and blood—as real as people get—and their flesh was darker than mine. There was nothing illusory about it.

At the same time, and I would've never said this out loud, I liked Walter Jackson. Standing behind a backstop bad-mouthing managers' moves, I lost sight of his black skin. And because Percy was Walter's boy, I liked him, too. I just couldn't untangle the knot that was coiled inside: How could I like these people, and not fully hope for their good fortune?

Monday's game was by any measure big news. It was a historic event, and as a journalist I was obliged to give it its due. It was up to me to let the world know that in this town, on this night, a colored kid named

Percy Jackson did a thing that no Negro had ever done before. Posterity would demand the details, and it was up to me to deliver.

As an ordinary guy who wanted baseball to stay in town forever, I longed to see a gigantic crowd—black or white. I prayed that ticket takers would have to ice down their overtired arms. And I hoped to hear turnstiles collapse from utter exhaustion.

As Rose Marie's loving husband there was a tempting urge to let the whole thing pass; to simply record the game like any other. For the sake of my marriage, and for the emotional health of the woman I loved, should I cheat posterity? But then again, how many times does the world turn to a small-town sportswriter? And how often had Providence entrusted Jack Hall with that kind of task?

This story was a burden I'd been given to bear. And late Saturday night, after I'd returned from Clayton and was getting ready for bed, I told Rose Marie that I wanted to go to the early church service—and then go find the Jacksons.

She switched on the light beside her bed, and through tired, squinting eyes looked at me like I'd lost every bit of the good sense God had given. I knew, as surely as I knew it was dark at midnight, that the last thing she wanted was a conversation that included the words "Percy Jackson." "Jack," she groaned, "you don't need to mess up a free Sunday, just stay home."

"I don't want to mess up anything," I replied, "but this has got to be done." I went into the bathroom. "I know how much you hate all this, but don't you wonder what it's like? These people are poor, nobody's ever heard of them, they live within a mile of the chicken plant." I stepped back to the bedroom, my mouth lathered with Colgate. "And now their lives are changed—just because their kid can play ball. Whether we like it or not, Rose, he's going to do something that nobody around here's ever done before." I went to rinse my mouth, and wondered out loud, "What in the world's going on in their heads?"

Rose lay on her side, an elbow on the bed, her head propped on her hand. "You got to start paying attention," she said. "Two or three times some child—prompted by his kindhearted daddy—has called your son a nigger lover. It's been less than a week since somebody nearly ruined your car. Now this colored boy's going to start a baseball game and you mean to turn it into an epic for the ages." She frowned, mystified by her dull-headed husband. "We're about a half inch from getting run out of here, and now you want to go traipsing off to colored town like you're the Jackson family's best friend—this is not a good idea, Hall."

"Rose," I pleaded, "how do I *not* do this? This isn't what we wanted, I know that, but I can't pretend it's not happening. I can't just look the other way." I turned from my dresser to face her. "And you know what, you'd like these people—the same way you like Bea Washington. Same way you like William. Same way you like a dozen colored people in town—the Jacksons aren't any different."

With dramatic flare that I'd only seen on a stage, my wife dropped her head to the pillow. She lifted both arms into the air, wailing, "Not different! Jack, the reason we're talking at quarter past twelve is because they are *entirely* different. The reason you're gallivanting around nigger town on a Sunday afternoon is because these people *are* different. Bea and William and the other colored folks we know—they're not trying to join the Little League. They're not trying to go to Chris's school. And they are certainly not trying to play professional baseball. These people, Jack—these Jacksons—they're the most different people in the whole town."

I slid into bed beside her. "But they don't want trouble, they—"

"Jack, when this kid plays ball, there's a riot, or something that surely resembles one. If that's not trouble, then what exactly is it?"

"A kid playing ball, a father who loves to watch, a mother who wants her boy to do the thing he's good at—"

"Even if it means coloreds and whites mixing together? Jack, this has gone on a long time. You think it's about baseball, and I don't know, maybe the Jacksons do too. But the people who're making all the fuss—they don't give a flip if Percy Jackson plays ninety innings a day." She snapped off her light and turned away. "So long as he does it with his own people in his own part of town."

I switched off my light, struggling to unscramble the mess that was in my mind. "If you just knew these people—"

"Jack," she said flatly, "I'm sure they're very nice. But I assure you, these are people I do not want to know."

Percy Jackson and I had stretched Rose to the breaking point; we had brought this good-natured woman more grief than she could bear. But, throughout our years together, I have been overwhelmed by my wife's boundless capacity to love me. She hated what I was about to do, and she was certain, without question or pause, that I was stupid or wrong or, more likely, some combination of both. She was tired and discouraged and yet, as we moved through our Sunday-morning rituals, she smiled and laughed and sang, never once mentioning the night before or the day ahead. No casual observer could have guessed at the depth of the chill that was in her bones.

In our room, getting dressed, I watched her slip on a yellow dress with red trim. She tugged at it here and there, then shook her hair and fluffed it out over her shoulders. I stared, astonished once more at my good fortune. She was, as she has always been, stunning. And this being Sunday, I thanked God for her.

◆ ◆ ◆ ◆

We normally sit on the right side of our church sanctuary, near the middle where we're a poor target for a pastor who often speaks about life's more tender matters. Alan Spencer's a couple of years older than I am—smart and likeable enough—the kind of guy who doesn't pry too much, but lets you know that he cares, and that he's around if you need him. This morning we followed the familiar pattern: a couple of hymns, the Apostles' Creed, the Lord's Prayer. Then Spencer asked us to turn to Luke, chapter ten. He directed us to the thirtieth verse, and then he began to read: "A certain man went down from Jerusalem to Jericho, and fell among thieves, which stripped him of his raiment, and wounded him, and departed, leaving him half dead. And by chance there came down a certain priest that way…."

At the opening lines of the well-worn passage, my mind begged to wander, and I gave it permission to go. I'd heard the parable of the good Samaritan a thousand times, and I knew to be kind to my neighbor—especially those who were friendless and forsaken. My thoughts glanced off the familiar words and drifted toward Percy and Walter Jackson. These two were, after all, the only people I knew personally who had ever been demeaned and cast down. Percy—a kid still in his teens—had been attacked in two towns, with no one to tend his wounds. My mind had been circling around that thought when I noticed the room had become quiet. A pause in Spencer's rhythm snapped me back to the here and now, to the pastor standing in his pulpit. His eyes traveled the room, and they didn't rest until they came to me.

And then he continued: "We always think about the Samaritan," he said, "about the good guy who stopped to help. And we should; Jesus tells us to 'Go, and do thou likewise.' But there's something else here." He paused to make sure I was listening. "In this story I don't believe we're the Samaritan. I believe we're the man in the ditch; the one who was left to die, the one who, apart from the mercy he was shown, is destitute and doomed. We need to be good neighbors," the pastor said matter-of-factly, "not because it's nice, but because a price has been paid to heal our wounds...."

My mind strayed back to Percy Jackson, and I thought about how—when merciless fans screamed for him to go home, he must surely have ached for the kindness of a merciful God—and to the more ticklish notion that God's comfort is most often dispensed through those who have known it.

◆ ◆ ◆ ◆

After church I dropped my family off at home. Then, against every wish my wife had made, I headed for New Hope Community Church.

It was just past noon when I arrived. The dirt parking lot was three-quarters full, yet perfectly still. I checked my watch again, anxious, wondering how long Edwards would preach. I found some shade where

I parked and waited, and where my mind rambled off, wondering what life was like for the Walter Jackson family. I drifted into my imagination, oblivious to the birds' back-and-forth songs, to the murmur of leaves in the wind, or the whoosh of distant traffic.

Then an organ jolted to life inside. A multitude of voices joined together, loud and brimming with faith, all asking: "What can wash away my sin …?" They paused a beat, and then replied, "Nothing but the blood of Jesus." I sat in the shadow of an ancient oak, humming along. On the chorus my spirit rose with the congregation's, and sitting in the car, alone, I added my off-key voice to theirs: "Oh precious is the flow that makes me white as snow. No other fount I know, nothing but the blood of Jesus."

An instant later the church door burst open, and Phil Edwards appeared. He pumped the hands of his just-fed flock, greeting them as they respectfully passed and complimented his "fine sermon." The men wore their best clothes; mostly work pants and overalls. The women were bedecked in flowing, flowery dresses and wide-brimmed hats. And everyone in that church was clothed in dignity, befitting the occasion.

Before long, Walter emerged, his wife and children close behind. They made their way to the parking lot, stopping friend-by-friend, chatting, and catching up on a week's worth of untold news. Walter, one of the few men in a business suit and black shined shoes, was dressed as finely as any banker. And Percy was eking out the last few miles of a black suit, worn to a gloss and a quarter inch too short at the cuffs and sleeves. Roberta and her daughter wore white gloves and bright dresses, and the family fit right in with the extravagant crowd.

I was sitting on the hood of the car, feet propped on the front bumper, enjoying the parade when Walter caught sight of me. He wandered over, Sunday-slow, his head crooked with curiosity. "Afternoon." He held out his hand. "Now I gotta say you're a sight I did not expect to see here today." He grinned, surprised but pleased to see me. "Is there something I can help you with?"

"Yeah," I said, "and I'm sorry to barge in on your Sunday. I wouldn't normally do something like this. But I wondered if I might talk with you and Roberta, just for a minute or two." A smile swept across my face. "Percy's gonna start tomorrow," I said. "Your boy's going to be the first Negro to do that in the league. I just wanted to know what you two thought about it."

Walter returned the smile. He took off his hat and mopped his brow with a clean white handkerchief. He glanced around the church grounds, looking a little sly—as if he might've clipped a few bucks from the offering plate—then he looked down and kicked at the pine straw. "Well ..." he drawled. "You could come have lunch with us. Roberta's fixed a good meal and there's more than enough, I'm sure about that."

I was dumbstruck.

Walter waited for a reply, still toeing the ground. I just stared away, muzzled by the shock. He and I both knew I could never step foot in his home. I could never—not for any reason—share a meal at a Negro's table, and I sat there, silent as a rock, miffed, but also a little amused. Walter Jackson, I thought to myself, unlike anybody I had ever known, had this amiable way of crossing lines that weren't to be broached.

"Well ..." Walter finally said, now trying to undue the damage. "Maybe we could just sit in the church for a while. It's just about cleared out now."

And then, for reasons my mind still can't fully form, I said, "Lunch at your place would be fine."

Walter's eyes gleamed. "Good," he said. "House isn't far from here."

I was instantly overcome with misgivings, certain that some dreadful thing was in store. I made a manly effort to brush these bothers aside. I was, I told myself, simply doing what had to be done; a reporter following a story. With trepidation that still makes me squirm, I followed Walter to the Jackson family home.

They lived in a modest house, white with garish green shutters, dingy-looking, and faded by the heat of thirty summers. A boxwood hedge was neatly trimmed, level at the sills of three front windows. And the small, weed-speckled lawn looked to have been freshly mowed.

From the front door I stepped directly into the living room where a mangy couch, wilted with age, was flanked by a pair of matching, equally worn chairs. A cramped dining room jutted off to the rear, and a kitchen—broiling hot and too small to hold three people—lay just beyond that.

The windows were wide open, and most of the screens, I saw, had been torn and taped back together. An electric fan patrolled the room, moving left to right, and sending a breeze that made the heat just bearable. I tried to get a feel for what life was like here. The house was tiny and dim, but the presence of a contented family made it seem like home. Their shelves and walls, like mine, were cluttered with pictures and mementos. But it was all so strange—like walking around in an episode of *Amos 'n' Andy*—these dark faces with bright eyes and teeth grinning up from cheap frames. It was, in one way, familiar. But in another, it was unlike anything I'd ever seen.

I stood in the living room trying to catch my full share of the fan's breeze. Roberta hauled a tray of baked pork chops out of her oven. Corn bread, limas-and-spinach, and potato salad, all prepared the night before, suddenly appeared, and Walter took his place at the head of the table. He motioned for me to sit beside him. We joined hands and Walter prayed. He thanked God for the food and for his family. And then, right out loud, he thanked God for me and for the things I had done for them. I was embarrassed at the mention of my name, and surprised that Walter Jackson believed I had done things for which his family owed God thanks. I glanced up bashfully as the bowls and platters began their routes around the table. As I handed off the corn bread, I looked to Justina, Percy's fifteen-year-old sister. "Your brother's going to start tomorrow night for the Bobcats," I told her. "You going to the game?"

Her bright smile lit the room. "We're staying for the whole game," she said, "no matter how late it gets."

"Oh yeah, it's a school night," I said, "I hadn't thought about that."

"It don't matter." Justina sang the words. "We're staying for the whole game."

I had to smile at the pigtailed girl who brimmed with joy, and who, I am certain, would have burst with one more puff of sisterly pride. I took the platter of grease-soaked pork, and turned to her mother. "What about you, Roberta, what do you think about Percy starting tomorrow?"

Roberta Jackson glanced away, and a second or two passed before she said, "We're proud of Percy, real proud."

"But …" I prodded.

By instinct she grabbed hold of her son's arm. She rubbed back and forth, gently. "I'm this boy's mother," she said. Her eyes darted away, and she pressed her lips tight together. "There's some people who've been unkind, who don't want Percy to play—"

"And you're worried?" I asked. "You think somebody might hurt him?"

She nodded. And then, with the slightest tremor, she said, "We've been to the games. Some of those people are very angry, and some …" She looked down again.

"Go on," I nudged her.

She rested her elbows on the table, laced her fingers together, and rested her chin on top of her hands. "I hate the way those people talk," she said, her voice no more than a whisper. She looked down for the third time, too timid to meet my eye. "I know they're angry," she went on, "I understand that. But I never knew anyone could be so mean." She looked up, for just an instant, then quickly turned away. "I don't believe the demons themselves could be that hurtful," she mumbled, "not the demons themselves."

I stopped mid-chew, humiliated and feeling ashamed. I gulped down my food and then twisted around to face Percy Jackson's mother. "I'm sorry about the way they talk," I said, "there's no excuse for it. It's just that this whole thing—having colored boys and white boys playing together—it's different than anything they've ever known. It changes the way we live, the things we think. And for a lot of people, that's scary."

I stared into my plate, embarrassed by the paltry answer.

She still had hold of her son's arm. Her eyes remained cast down. "This boy look scary to you?" she asked.

"No," I said, nodding soberly. "And I don't think anybody's actually afraid of Percy. It's the idea, the fact that things are different." I turned to Walter, grasping for help. "What do you think? You worried about Percy?"

A forkful of pork chop finished its course, and Walter Jackson shook his head. "Not so much," he said, "we've been hearing that talk our whole lives. And that's all it is, just talk." He aimed his fork in Percy's direction. "We're not troublemakers. We don't mean to give anybody one single reason to worry. We don't care where we sit on the bus, or where we wait for it. We don't care what water fountain we drink out of, or what door we use.

"I just wish folks would remember we didn't go looking for this. Mr. Anderson and Mr. Reeves—they came to us. We're mighty grateful, and we mean to make the most out of the chance we've been given. But we never set out to change anything."

"Does it matter to you that Percy's the first Negro to play in the Sunshine Circuit? Does that make you proud?"

"Yessir," Walter said, "but probably not the way you think. I'm proud because he's a good ballplayer … Negro, white …" Walter shrugged. "We're just grateful, that's all. Percy's got a chance that colored boys don't get, and that's a remarkable thing, Mr. Hall … it is a remarkable thing."

Walter scraped his fork over the plate, herding the remnants that remained. "All the things Roberta's talking about, they're hard but they're no surprise. And Percy …" he gestured toward the boy. "He was ready for it."

I turned to Percy. "It's gotten pretty rough out there. Got a lot rougher in Clayton than I ever expected. Hard to imagine anybody could've been ready for that."

Percy, I saw, was more comfortable in his own home than in the other places I'd seen him. He was at ease and willing to speak. "We talked about it," he said, "and I knew it'd happen. I was expectin' it."

"What's it like?" I asked. "How's it feel when people call you names?"

He glanced away. "I just think about Jackie," Percy said. He looked to his father. "We talked about what happened to him."

"That's right," Walter added, "Percy and I talked a lot about Jackie, about the things people did, about the threats they made. He's come through all this—the very same stuff we're seeing and hearing. It hasn't been easy for him, and we knew it wouldn't be easy for us. But Jackie's made it, so we know we can too."

"And you think all this will eventually pass?"

"Oh sure," Walter said, "might take a little longer down here than up north. But sooner or later, if we've got the guts to stick with it—if Mr. Anderson and Mr. Reeves can stick it out—I believe folks'll calm down."

"But you are right, Mr. Hall, it's very hard," Roberta said. "And Percy never meant nobody no harm."

◆ ◆ ◆ ◆

I went back to the office, typed up the story, and then hurried home. Rose Marie and Chris were out front, Chris pitching to his mom, who was crouched down like a catcher and chattering like a zealous Little Leaguer. "You guys're looking pretty serious," I hollered from the car.

"You're just in time," Rose gasped, "I'm just about out of gas."

"It's usually the pitcher who runs out of gas, but I'll be right there."

Chris and I played catch while Rose umped from the front-porch swing. After a while it was time for dinner, and I tossed the gloves and ball to Chris. I followed Rose into the kitchen.

"Well," she said, doing her best to soften the edge on her voice, "you were gone longer than I expected."

"Yeah," I chuckled, "it was weird, they invited me over for lunch; never been to a colored person's house before … was pretty strange."

Rose's mouth fell open. "Come on, Jack, you can't be serious," she said. "Please tell me you didn't go in their house."

"I didn't really mean to," I said, "it just sort of happened. Walter asked, and, well, I guess without really thinking about it, I thought it was the best way to get the story; to get a feel for how they lived, for what this really meant to them."

She pushed the oven door shut. With one hand lingering on the handle, she turned, her eyes restless. "Do you have any idea what this will mean if someone finds out? Do you know what people will think? What they'd do to us?"

"Who'd see me down there, Rose? And who could they possibly tell?"

She rolled her eyes. "You got no business going in there whether anybody knows it or not."

I saw a chill run the length of her spine. "Yeah, I know," I said, "and the whole thing felt weird, but it wasn't that bad."

She stared at me, eyes wide with disbelief, and then turned away. "Well," she said, "I hope you got what you were looking for."

"I think I did. And it was different than what I expected."

"Different?"

"I thought I'd hear about how proud they were; about how happy they'd be to see their boy step out on the field … and I got a little of that. But his mother's scared more than anything else; afraid somebody's going to hurt her kid. And Walter … he doesn't want to let on, but I think he's worried about whether or not Percy can take it, if the kid's got the guts to stick it out."

"Well, from the things you've written, if I was that boy's mother, I'd be scared too." Rose Marie cut a glance my way. "I don't know how the woman sleeps."

"Well," I said, "we're lucky. We'll never know what it's like."

◆ ◆ ◆ ◆

On page three of Monday's paper the story appeared. Beneath a small action shot the modest headline proclaimed: "First Negro to Start Sunshine Circuit Game."

I opened with the facts, telling readers that Percy Jackson had appeared in a couple of games this season: one at home and one in Clayton. That he was 2 for 2 at the plate, and had nicely handled his only fielding chance. That he had been greeted roughly on opening day at Memorial Stadium. And that last Thursday night, in Clayton, a hostile crowd had run him right off the field.

And then, with my pastor's words rambling round in the distance, and with Sunday's lunch conversation still fresh in my mind, I recorded a few thoughts about Percy Jackson and Jackie Robinson.

Jackson, I suggested, heard the same taunts that Robinson had a few years before. But the *New York Times* would never tell Percy's story. WNBC radio would never mention his name. And it wasn't likely that a TV network would ever beam his image from New York to Los Angeles. Percy Jackson, I mused, wasn't part of a flamboyant scheme to change the game. He was a local kid, putting up with the worst kind of slurs for nothing more than a chance to play the game he loved. He was an eighteen-year-old boy who, for a few measly bucks and the thrill of wearing a Bobcats uniform, suffered abuse the likes of which most men could never bear. It was one thing, I wrote, to endure threats for fame, and insults for fortune. But it was something else to endure them for the joy of playing at Memorial Stadium.

There were, I confessed, things about seeing a Negro play that were troubling, especially in a small town like ours. But whether or not one liked the idea of a colored boy on the team, Percy Jackson reminded us of why we loved the game. And why it was important to keep baseball in Whitney.

It was a few minutes shy of seven o'clock when I took my coffee out to the front porch. The screen door rattled shut. My wife glanced up and said, "Fuel on the fire, huh, Hall."

"I hope not. It's just … if you'd seen what this kid's put up with, if you'd heard the crowd over in Clayton …" My voice faded as I wrestled with my own thoughts. I sipped a few times from my cup. "Honest to goodness, Rose, you'd like these people."

She kept her eyes on the paper. "I'm sure they're sweeter than your mother's tea," she said, "really." She reached over and put her hand on top of mine. "It's okay with me if you like these people," she said, "and maybe you're right, maybe I'd like them too." Then she lifted the paper from her lap. "But you're making life tough on us, Hall. On me and Chris. On the whole town. This kind of stuff … it makes people squirm."

◆ ◆ ◆ ◆

The crowd gathered early, and colored fans for fifty miles around staked out places in the stands and along the left-field foul line. Some brought chairs and picnics; they filled the air with exhilaration.

White fans gathered too, a number carrying homemade signs intended to let Burt and Joe—and maybe me—know what they thought about coloreds and whites playing baseball together. It seemed every cop in the state was there too. They arrived early and walked the grounds, sending a signal that only a blind man could miss: There would be trouble.

At six thirty Percy trotted onto the field, and the colored crowd erupted in pure delight. In reply, for the first time that night, a sign appeared: "Cotton picker go home." And then a second one: "Niggers don't belong." More than six thousand people were there, the biggest crowd I'd ever seen at Memorial Stadium. Section 104 of the grandstand, the cheap seats on the third-base side, had, at the last minute, been converted to a colored section to handle the overflow crowd.

In the first inning Percy fielded a sharply hit grounder and gunned the ball to first for an easy out. In the bottom of the second he grounded out to short. And in the top of the fourth he turned a textbook-smooth double play, as beautiful as any I'd ever seen.

Black and white fans sat close together; they took turns cheering and jeering, but the white crowd was easily overmatched. At the end of each half inning cops marched out to the foul lines, their hands resting on billy-club handles. The umps called the game tight, and kept play under control. But, plain as the moon and stars, tension hung in the nighttime air. The crowd—black and white—was strung tighter than Tony Trabert's racquet.

In the bottom of the fourth Percy dropped a nice single in front of the Leesburg right fielder, but didn't advance. In the fifth he had two fielding opportunities and handled them both perfectly. In the sixth, with one out and a man on first, he hit a sharp ground ball to short, and Leesburg turned a double play to end the inning.

He was, at this point, 1 for 3 on the night.

In the eighth we were up a run. Taylor was on second and we had two outs. Percy lined a fastball straight up the middle and Fred scored easily, adding a little insurance.

In the top of the ninth, with one out, the Leesburg right fielder hit a solo shot to right-center field, bringing the Generals to within one. Then, with two outs and a man on first, a two-hopper bounced Percy's way. He fielded the ball cleanly, glided toward first, and rifled the ball to Freddy for the game's final out. His RBI single was, as things turned out, the difference in the game.

Up in the press box I grinned, pleased not only with the win, but with Percy's performance. But I was torn, too. On one hand Sam Fowler pitched great; he held Leesburg to five hits and one run. And this was a story worth telling. On the other hand Percy's steady play, the RBI, and the historical significance of his starting role made him the night's big news.

But my wife's lament wouldn't yield. I told myself that Walter Jackson was right, that this was going to take time. The idea of a colored kid on the field—that was going to take Whitney some getting used to. And maybe the best thing I could do was to dish out Percy Jackson in small doses. I nodded my head, confirming the quick and wobbly decision. I'd make sure the headline read something like: "Fowler Throws Gem." And in a two-hundred-word sidebar with no photo, I'd add something along the lines of, "Jackson Makes Sunshine Circuit History." And there, to meet posterity's demands, I'd give a sketch of Percy's first game.

◆ ◆ ◆ ◆

Tuesday morning I wandered out to the front porch as usual. But Rose Marie wasn't there. She was standing in the driveway, face buried in her hands, staring straight down. As I hurried to her, four words that had been spray-painted on the driveway came into focus: "Nigger Lovers Get Out."

My heart fell. We had lived in this town for thirteen years. We were friendly with just about everybody; I couldn't cross the street without four people calling me by name. This defied the most depraved imagination. It was a thought that wouldn't form, an idea that couldn't be conceived. And if, at the precise moment, the culprit had been within my grasp, I swear, with God as my witness, I would have joyfully hacked and shredded him into unrecognizable pieces.

This was more than my wife could endure. And with all we'd been through: the conversations, the disagreements, the tense times....

Tears streamed down her face and she swayed back and forth, mumbling, "I can't believe this. I cannot believe this."

"I'm sorry, Rose. I'm sorry."

She stared down and mumbled again, "I can't believe this."

"Let's go inside," I said, putting my arm around her. "I'll get this taken care of. Come on."

I called Burt. He had gotten the same treatment, and that meant that Joe and maybe Charley had too. Burt said he'd have a city crew come out to the house and clean it up right away. "We don't want people thinking this is more than it is," he said. "Gotta be one or two guys with too much time on their hands, that's all. We'll have somebody out there inside the hour." And the police, he added, would be watching our houses round the clock.

I told Rose that it'd soon be gone, but the tears still trickled. She looked up at me, her eyes wet and frightened. And then, without a word, she disappeared up the stairs.

Chapter 14

From the moment he stepped on the field, Percy was a picture of near perfection, devouring grounders that came anywhere near, and punishing the ball as if it embodied every cruel name he'd ever been called.

As April gave way to May, his average bounced around in the .330 to .340 range. In Sunshine Circuit towns the talk of Whitney's third baseman spread like mist from a fleet of crop dusters. We marched through Leesburg, Madison, and Jeffersonville. At each stop the white crowds came ready to out-slur the town that had come before. And night after night Negroes jammed into the stands, past capacity, to cheer for Percy Jackson.

In Jeffersonville they had to stretch rope from the grandstand to the outfield wall to keep the colored crowd from seeping onto the field. In Leesburg, where they'd averaged about fifty colored fans a game in 1953, they drew six thousand over the three nights of our first visit. And in Madison you could see thousands of colored folks, all swelled up with pride, standing tall, and feeling, as Joe liked to say, as if they owned a tiny piece of the town. We weren't but a few weeks into the season, and no one could say for sure that any of this would last. But these signs held great promise.

Through the protests and past the heckling, Joe and Burt saw their plan coming together. They believed, as Walter Jackson did, that the taunting would soon pass. We reminded ourselves, in the midst of the worst rages, that Robinson, Doby, and Mays had come through a gauntlet that looked a lot like ours. We assured ourselves with perfect hindsight that cities like New York and Cleveland were at peace with their Negro players—and that eventually we would be too. If we hoped to survive, we had no choice.

But I wondered sometimes about the thoughts that passed through Percy's mind. I never saw him flustered, never saw him look like he wanted to lash back. I know he would've made Jackie Robinson proud. But he lived a life that could only consume the spirit.

In Jeffersonville the visiting team has to walk alongside the stands to get to the dugout. Percy dressed by six for the eight o'clock game, hoping to dodge at least one round of humiliation, but fifty or sixty devoted fans arrived early, making the special effort to remind him that he was black and that his great-grandfather had been dragged to town to pick a white man's cotton. At home one night he struck out twice—once late in the game with two men on—and Burt had to have four cops walk him to his father's car, shielding both men from bottle-wielding fans who screamed familiar, angry taunts.

Plenty of trouble was still brewing in the dugout, too. Every time Percy got a hit, earned a walk, or made a nice play in the field, Donny Jones—his face plastered with bandages and tape—smoldered on the bench. Against Kingstown, Percy lunged at a scalded line drive, snagging it out of the air so fast the crowd lost sight of the ball. Slowly, he picked himself up, pulled the ball out of his glove, and calmly started it around the horn. A stunned crowed—white and black—instinctively rose and cheered the indescribable play. I watched Jones from the press box. He eyed Fred Taylor and neither man could bring himself to concede Percy's feat. Later in the same game Kingstown pinch-hit Nat Quaid, a nineteen-year-old Negro they'd signed a week after we'd enlisted Percy. He worked our pitcher over good, fouling off four or five fastballs before finally drawing the walk. Jones threw a towel in disgust, he kicked a water bucket, and from a hundred yards away I could read his lips as he screamed, "Damn niggers!" Percy sat on the bench, just three players down, and no more than ten feet away.

Jones was five years older than the rookie sub, and he knew—we all knew—that his hourglass had just about emptied. Day after day he and Taylor watched every move Percy made, hoping to find a flaw in the rookie's game. But the pickings were slim.

When we were on the road, Percy's spirit could've only journeyed south. In Class C ball nobody lives in anything that resembles luxury, but we stayed in respectable hotels and slept between clean sheets in air-conditioned rooms—except for Percy—who was dispatched to run-down boardinghouses I wouldn't have found fit for Slugger, or taxied to some stranger's rickety home fifteen miles from the rest of the team.

I remember our first trip to Leesburg. After the game we'd pulled into the Travel Right Hotel parking lot—around midnight—and a couple of cabs were waiting for a fare. Percy waited beside them, past one, for the colored cab company to send a car. I'll never forget, late one night on the bus ride home from Jeffersonville, Percy was more talkative than I'd ever seen. He told me and Giles that Don had put him up with an old woman on the outskirts of town. She was, Don had promised, a great cook, "and that was the truth," Percy said. Then he looked at us both with bright but dubious eyes. "It must've been a hundred degrees in that house, and all she had to cool the place down was some old tiny fan." She had been real polite, Percy explained, and promised that he could use it, 'cause he was a ballplayer who needed his rest. "I drifted off," Percy went on, "and was feeling pretty good. Next thing I know, it must be 'bout four in the morning … whole bed ain't nothing but a pool of sweat." He shook his head and peered up. "That old lady, she must've come in 'bout midnight and took that fan for herself. I could hear it down the hall, just blowing away."

Giles and I cracked up. We laughed 'til we had to wipe away the tears, picturing the run-down house, and the shriveled-up woman sneaking down the hall in the middle of the night, pulling a fast one on her young boarder. Percy grinned, looking as if it had been worth the pain to share a few laughs.

The heat, I am certain, was the lightest load he had to bear. After every game he was cast away from the team. He never lay awake at night making jokes with his friends. He never traded lies in the locker room about the girls he'd kissed or the home runs he'd hit in high school. While his teammates showered and dressed, and talked about parties and good times, Percy had been banished to the armory, to a public restroom down the street, or he simply had to wait outside—dirty and smelling to high heaven—'til his teammates were ready to move on.

Night after night, at home and away, fans called him a hundred different names, but never Percy or Jackson. In a hundred different ways they made one thing known: We don't want you here. The "sore thumb" was hammered without mercy. And as I watched him—day after day, and town by town—I was dogged by uninvited thoughts, forced against my will to wonder how much pain one kid could bear—and whether or not his plan was coming together as neatly as Joe's.

◆ ◆ ◆ ◆

In the middle of May a fateful new twist that none of us could have imagined swept into our lives. On Monday the seventeenth, nine black-robed men a thousand miles away—men who'd never once stepped foot in our town—declared that our lives must take a new turn. Time was split in two. From that day forward we would remember life before the seventeenth—and after.

When I think back to that day, the first thing I see in my mind's eye is Joe racing across the town square. I had gone to the window, wondering whether or not I'd need an umbrella, and I spotted him barreling for the office, his short, middle-aged legs churning as fast as they'd go. He burst through the front doors, past Louise, rushing for the newsroom. Puffing hard and sounding dangerously out of breath, he sped to the Teletype as it pounded out the news, paper lurching upward in urgent spasms. Joe's eyes kept pace, moving back and forth across the page, a frown furrowing deep into his brow. Others circled round, looking glum. Then the machine came still, and the room fell silent. They all turned, staggered and speechless. Joe rubbed his head, confused—as if he'd been looking at a language he couldn't read. He ripped the paper out of the machine and started from the top, rereading the words that had just raced across the wire.

"What is it?" I whispered, expecting to hear something about Ike having a heart attack or stroke.

Joe peered up over his glasses. "The Supreme Court," he said, "they're gonna make us put colored kids in the schools." He shook his head, perplexed by the news he couldn't comprehend. He reread the words a third time and a fourth, and then handed me the AP report.

Within minutes radio reports flew through the air. And that evening, just before the Bobcats' game with Kingstown, Douglas Edwards and John Cameron Swayze devoted all fifteen minutes of the network newscast to Oliver Brown's legal victory over the Topeka, Kansas, school board. By game time everybody in Whitney had heard the news, and no one was unaffected by it.

From the press box that night, an hour before the game, I looked at the parking lot, down the entrance road, and watched a long string of green, blue, and white cars snake up the red-clay road to the stadium. The Negro crowd was pouring in early. They lined up at the colored ticket window and marched through the side entrance to the grandstand. And it seemed to me, though who can say what my own imagination fashioned, that they had been filled with a new spirit. Possibilities dawned late that afternoon that no Negro had ever imagined, and a buoyant crowd of black men swelled within the walls of Memorial Stadium.

The white crowd was small and quiet; a brooding bunch who had been muzzled by the day's news and who, in grim contrast to their colored neighbors, were tenuous and restrained.

This was the eye of a gathering storm. Nine men who knew nothing about us had forever altered the foundation of our lives. No one could imagine where their decision would lead, but the imagining alone sent shudders through the neighbors I'd known for years. And as I sat in the press box that night, watching and listening, I knew this calm couldn't last.

The next morning, in 125-point type, the headline roared, "School Segregation Banned." A subhead added, "Supreme Court refutes separate but equal."

If you were on earth at the time, you know all about the case of Oliver Brown, a Negro in Topeka, Kansas, who demanded the right to enroll his little girl in the white school near his home. Only a few words from the Court's opinion matter: *We conclude that, in the field of public education, the doctrine of "separate but equal" has no place. Separate educational facilities are inherently unequal.* With those twenty-four words Earl Warren had pulled the rug out from under our world.

Ten seconds after Helen unlocked the diner's doors, speculation coursed through the place like blood, giving it life like I had never seen before. Newspapers littered the countertop, splayed across every table, and troubled neighbors leaned toward one another asking what kind of grief these words would bring. For the second time in all the years I'd know her, Helen had come unglued.

She and I had gone around a time or two on the subject of Percy Jackson. The day after he signed, she had, in front of my friends and loyal readers, thrown me out of her restaurant—hungry and humiliated. A few hours later, when business was slow, I slithered back, and while we had the place to ourselves, we pulled out our full quiver of verbal weapons and had at it, knocking one another down and dragging one another out for as good a thrashing as each was able to give. In the end we made peace, but she had not come to terms with the notion of mixing races.

I sat at the counter and she banged a cup down in front of me. She poured and the coffee sloshed into the saucer. Her eyes were dim, and without looking up she said, "Do you see? Do you see what happens when we let 'em play ball? This is what we get!"

"Helen," I said calmly, "I don't think this has anything to do with baseball."

She looked down and away, and off to one side—everywhere but in my eyes. "I wouldn't be too sure about that, Jack. We let 'em on a baseball field one minute, and the next thing you know they're in our kids' schools … heaven only knows what's next." She brushed a tear aside, scribbled down my order, and wandered away, coffeepot in hand, searching for consolation.

"This is just horrible," the woman sitting beside me said to herself. "People was saying they'd do it, but I didn't imagine it'd ever happen." She dragged a fork through her grits, mumbling, "Colored kids at Jefferson Davis High … can no more imagine that than a man on the moon."

Helen was back a few minutes later, sliding a plate across the counter.

She was angry and hurt, and still half-blaming me for most of the town's woes. But there was despair in her eyes and she knew, regardless of what had passed between us, that I was a friend. "What do you s'pose is gonna happen, Jack? They gonna do this for real?"

"I don't see how," I answered. "It's just too much, I don't think anybody's going to go along with it."

"So what'll they do?" Helen asked. "They can't toss us all in jail."

"They'll come to some kind of compromise," I said, "they don't really have a choice. There's not a senator or congressman for ten states around who's going to stand for this—not if he wants to get reelected."

She stared out the big glass widows. "We never should've put a colored boy on that baseball team, Jack … should've never done that."

"Helen, I don't think Earl Warren's keeping up with Percy Jackson's batting average. And I'd bet you dollars to dimes, he doesn't know Roy Campanella from Roy Rogers."

"Maybe not. But how we gonna fight this? If we put colored boys on the baseball team, why wouldn't we put 'em in the schools? How's anybody gonna argue that?"

"It's not the same thing. A baseball team's a private business, and nobody's forcing anybody to go to the games." I swirled the coffee, searching for words. "Look, Helen, we don't get to choose team owners; we got no say in what they do. But we dang sure elect governors and congressmen. They can't lie down on this, not if they want to keep their jobs." I took a sip of coffee, and then, in my most consoling voice, I said, "We've got some time here. Nobody's saying this is going to happen next year, or even the year after that. We got time to figure something out."

She refilled my cup, brushing one more tear aside as she strolled away.

"You're right," a voice behind me said, "we got time, but it's hard to say how much." Dick Reeves, Burt's brother and the proprietor of Reeves Department Store, slid onto the stool beside me.

"Hey," I said, "haven't seen you in a while. How's business?"

"Can't complain," he answered, "least not about business."

"You're not too pleased with this morning's news …?"

"This ain't good. People who do stuff like this," he jabbed a finger at the paper, poking at the group shot of the nine justices, "they got no idea what kind of trouble they're causing." He spread a menu open. "This is so stupid," he said, "and there ain't no way we're gonna do it."

"Well, I've got a hunch the governor's on it," I said.

"Yeah, I'm sure he is," Dick replied. "But I'm not sure we can leave it there."

"What do you mean?"

"I don't know," he answered, "I really don't. Just seems like something we ought to put some thought to, that's all."

The diner teemed with rumors all day long, and the day after that, and every day for the rest of the week—the men and women of Whitney wondering aloud what we'd do, and hoping for an answer.

At the stadium Tuesday night the white crowd began inching out of its shell. But they were, compared to what we'd seen in weeks past, subdued … still simmering and mulling over the news.

We won the game, 6–2. And it was Fred Taylor who blew things wide open, blasting a three-run homer in the fourth. After the game I went down to the locker room to find Freddie, to get a quote from him and maybe a couple of the others. The mood was good, and Joe and Burt were there, patting backs and soaking up some locker-room revelry. I finished my interviews and checked the time; the story had to be typeset and on the press soon. As I hustled out the door, Burt called, "Hey, Jack." I turned. "You got some time in the morning?"

"Sure," I answered. "What's up?"

"Stop by around eight, will ya?"

◆ ◆ ◆ ◆

Just past midnight, turning onto Pine Cove Lane, our porch light alone cast a friendly greeting, beckoning me home. Inside the house, guided by the night-light upstairs, I climbed to Chris's room and peeked inside. At once I wanted to laugh and cry. In his narrow twin bed—tucked under a bedspread dotted with pictures of bats and balls, sliding base runners and diving outfielders—my wife and son lay cuddled together in a cozy ball. There's nothing that warms me more than the fondness they have for one another, and to see the inexhaustible love she pours out on him. But I knew why she was there. Monday's news was like a ransom notice, and she was overcome with fear. She was here shielding our son from the corruption outside, guarding our family against all the invisible forces, holding on to her son—giving and getting comfort the world couldn't offer.

I stood over the two of them, watching and smiling, and at the same time hating my own helplessness—hating that I couldn't defend her, that I couldn't chase this trouble away. I ran my hand over Chris's face and hair, then gently shook Rose's arm and whispered to her. She squinted, rubbing her eyes. Groggily, she murmured, "Oh, hi. We were just saying prayers ... guess I fell asleep."

"Yeah," I whispered, "why don't you come on with me." We walked down the hall; she headed straight for bed and slipped under the covers, pulling them up to her chin while I got ready. I crawled in beside her and took her hand. She was alert now. I had, by waking her, made her vulnerable to the dark thoughts that were crouched and waiting—and that wasted no time mugging her imagination. She squeezed my hand, and said, "I'll never let anything happen to him, Jack. I don't care if Dwight Eisenhower comes to our front door, I'll never send him where he ought not go."

"Yeah," I said, "I know."

"We'll need to think about this, come up with a plan, think about what we'll do if they try to mix his school."

"Nothing's going to happen for a while," I said.

"I don't want to wait 'til it's too late. I want this figured out. Chris will not spend one minute in a mixed school." She drew up her knees, and I could practically feel her eyes flashing back and forth across the ceiling, her mind roiling.

"Well," I said, "I'll be with Burt first thing in the morning. I'll hear what he's thinking. That might help us know what to do."

She kicked off the bedspread, nervous and trying to cool down. "That's fine," she said. "But I'm not trusting this to anybody else. We're that boy's parents, and we have got to be sure."

"We'll be sure," I said. "And we'll get through this."

Rose Marie lay wide-awake, staring at the ceiling, and sorting through the dark thoughts.

◆ ◆ ◆ ◆

I got to Burt's office early, feeling more hopeful than I had any reason or right to be. The coffeepot gurgled, adding the sounds and smells of good things to come. Margaret, fresh and pretty and in a playful mood, made it hard for a man to think grim thoughts. Joe was at the window, his suit coat still on. Burt was behind his desk glancing over the papers that were stacked up and ready to fill his day. Charley strolled in a few seconds behind me.

"So what's up?" I asked.

Joe took a seat and motioned for Charley and me to do the same. Burt tossed his reading glasses aside and began. "Nobody's had much time to think about Monday's news," he said. "You've seen what the governor's had to say. He's been calling around letting mayors know that he's got no intention of putting colored kids in our schools." Burt sat back, massaging his forehead and rubbing his eyes. "I don't know what we're going to do around here, but I'm not in the mood to let some bunch a thousand miles away mess everything up, I can tell you that." He glanced away, fuming, and looking like he'd strangle Earl Warren if the justice had been within reach. But he was also in pain. His town—the people who made Whitney their home—we were all coming to a rough spot in the road, and I could see in Burt's eyes, he wasn't sure he could fix it.

"Nobody knows what the colored folks'll do about all of this," Joe added. "To tell you the truth, I don't s'pect most of 'em care one way or the other. Far as I can see, everybody's pretty happy. But some might want to make something out of it, and we got to be ready."

"This ain't a good thing for us," Burt mumbled, mostly to himself. "Ain't gonna make things better for one single person."

Charley leaned forward, looking at Joe. "I know you guys are wrestling with this, but what's it got to do with me and Jack?"

"Yeah," Joe said, "we're coming to that. How's Jones' nose?"

Charley flinched at the change in subject. "He's coming along. Still swollen up pretty bad; gonna take longer than we thought, but he'll be ready soon."

"Jackson kid's playing good ball," Burt offered, forcing a weak smile.

"Yeah," Charley said, "he looks real good."

"Charley," Joe bent forward clasping his hands together, "we want you to play Percy. For right now we want him on the field every second there's an excuse to put him there."

Charley blew out a long breath. "Look," he said, "Percy's doing great. And I'm tickled as I can be about that. But Jones has more experience. He's been around the block." Charley mimicked Joe, folding his hands. He steepled his forefingers together, aiming them in Joe's direction. "And if we bench him, it's the last nail in his coffin. He'll be back at the chicken plant by October making a buck an hour for the rest of his life."

"More'n he's making now," Joe said with a shrug.

"Look," Charley continued, "I don't know if Jones can make it in the big leagues. Nobody's given him a shot so far. But this is it for him. We all know Jackson's a better player. But he's still a pup; he's got all the time in the world." Charley got up and began drifting around the room: hands on hips, then arms folded over the chest. "We try to win games," Charley said. "We take the talent we got and do what we can with it. But that's only half the job." He turned and looked at us. "We're here to get these kids ready for the next level, to get 'em ready for big-league ball. We bench Jones and we screw that up. We screw up the thing we're here to do."

Burt rocked behind his desk, looking at the ceiling. "You said yourself, it ain't likely he's going to make it. And, I don't want to mess up a guy's career, but we gotta think about the big picture here."

Charley leaned into the window frame, looking outside. Then he glanced at Burt. "I don't know anything about politics, and—no offense—never really cared." His eyes steadied on the mayor. "But you gotta leave ballplayers out of this. We got nothing to do with it."

Burt spun around in his chair. "Sure you do," he fired back. "One way or another, everything's about politics. And if it isn't now …" he picked up a copy of Tuesday's paper making sure we saw the headline "… it will be real soon."

"And you." Joe's eyes shifted to me. "I want you to get serious about letting people know how good this kid is. Turn him into Whitney's own Willie Mays. Or that other guy for the Giants, the colored boy they got playing third, what's his name … Hank Thompson. You make him our own Hank Thompson."

It was my turn to heave a long sigh. "You know what happens to me when I write his name? When I show his picture? When I so much as suggest he might be any good?"

"I believe I could ballpark it," Joe said. "The same thing happens to me. Same thing happens to Burt."

"And you want more of it? You want to see me divorced? You want to see my kid scarred from all the garbage he gets at school?"

Burt said, "No, we don't want to see any of that. But what's going to scar your boy more, Jack: some white kids teasing him, or colored kids sitting beside him in the school cafeteria? People are messing up my car just like they're doing to yours, and I don't like it any more than you do. But if I gotta pick, I'll tell you what: I'll take a messed-up car over having some colored boy come calling for my daughter when she's sixteen.

"Right now we're picking the lesser of evils." He tossed a pen onto the desk. "And I'm afraid that's the only choice we got."

"We don't know what Phil Edwards is thinking," Joe added. "But we got to be able to point to something and say, 'See here, this is what we're doing for the Negro.'"

From the window Charley said, "You think baseball's gonna do it? You got the Supreme Court of the United States saying to mix the schools and you guys are tinkering with a Class C baseball team?"

Joe looked at his manager and said, "Yeah. If you gotta a better idea, this ain't the time to hold back. That man over there," he gestured toward Burt, "right now he's got the biggest ears in town … you got a solution, he's listening." A pause hung in the air, the four of us trying to soak it all in.

"There's one more thing," Joe said.

Charley and I glanced over.

"We want you guys to be looking for another one." He looked at me. "Maybe write up a story about some prospects, and include a colored kid or two. When somebody comes asking about the black man and equality, we gotta show 'em we're serious."

"That's right," Burt said, "and we ain't gonna show 'em our schools."

I walked back to the office through the town square, passing the barbershop, Reeves Department Store, the diner, the hardware store, and I thought, *Why not?* Why wouldn't baseball be the thing that wrapped around our town and held it together? I understood Charley's point. He lived for the game, for wins and losses, for outsmarting the guy in the other dugout, for transforming raw kids into graceful athletes who would, one day, take all that he'd preached and practice it in the game's great cathedrals: Connie Mack Stadium, Sportsman's Park, and Wrigley Field.

But I had the advantage of distance. I could see the game from a different perspective. And I understood, in a way Charley couldn't, that baseball's about more than wins and losses, or strategy, or the players' performance. For six months a year baseball is the glue that binds fathers to sons; a topic that makes supper a time to look forward to; a season when moms, dads, kids, and neighbors all share the same hope. When I was sixteen and knew the answers to most of the world's questions—when I couldn't find a thing in common with a father who'd suddenly gone stupid—we had baseball and box scores. While guys like Charley schemed to win games—when they plotted hit-and-run attempts, sac flies, and pickoff plays—baseball sustained a bond that had, in every other place, come unglued.

Far away in the back of my mind, I thought, though never dared to whisper, that baseball had cast its spell on me and Walter Jackson—a colored man and white man, who, if nothing else, shared a love for the game. So why couldn't baseball be a bridge from Burt to Phil Edwards? From Joe to Chester LaBarr? From Helen to a waitress in Walter's part of town?

Baseball was woven into our lives as seamlessly as our churches and schools. And because of Burt and Joe and Percy, it was a cloth that now covered the whole town.

Baseball's purpose, I thought, was surely nobler than Donny Jones' long and last shot at a big-league career.

Chapter 15

From one end of Dixie to the other, reaction to the Court's decision was fast and defiant. Governors and congressmen, city councilmen and school-board members—all assailed the logic they couldn't conceive. From the capitol steps one governor swore that the good citizens of his state would never stand for mixing races. One border away a candidate for high office issued the ominous warning that the decision "pointed directly at the bedroom door and it'll get there soon 'less we make a determined stand." A congressman to our east proclaimed that southerners would never swallow so bitter a pill. A senator to the south decreed that this was "the most serious blow ever struck against states' rights." There was even talk about the need for soldiers to quell the coming violence.

You could see the same thing all around town—among store clerks and salesmen, and doctors and lawyers: Stubbornness was firming up like four-hour-old cement. You could hear it too—in the bars and diners, in churches and clubs, and down at the Piggly Wiggly—aggravation was taking hold, and the thought was festering in the minds of ordinary men: Those who knew nothing about us had meddled where they didn't belong. Earl Warren, Hugo Black, William Douglas, Felix Frankfurter—they and the other five—for reasons my friends could never fathom, had taken a thing that worked perfectly well and destroyed it. My neighbors did not take it kindly, or lightly. Everyday hardness tightened its grip on their hearts, and I thought to myself: *There is only one Negro in Whitney who has ever integrated anything, and this doesn't bode well for him.*

The final game of the Kingstown series took place Wednesday night. In the stands behind home plate, bitterness had replaced shock. The crowd came ready to spew two full days of bottled-up gall. The hand-scrawled signs were back, and one look at their language revealed that vengeance was in the hearts of their authors. The taunting returned to full volume and was as ferocious as ever.

Nine men a thousand miles away had trespassed into our lives. And Percy Jackson was paying the price, taking the full measure of the crowd's scorn … the object of wrath he didn't deserve. I thought about Roberta Jackson sitting in the colored section, hearing every angry word fired like a bullet at her only son. I sat in the press box trying to get my mind on the game, and I was, without warning, struck with an unsettling thought: I was the only one who had the means to absolve him. Every one of these people read the words I wrote. They knew me and trusted me. I had, literally at my fingertips, the means to remind them that this young boy wasn't to blame.

◆ ◆ ◆ ◆

With the late start the season was shortened to ninety-four games: forty-seven at home, forty-seven away. And it was, impossible as it seemed, time to head back to Clayton. After a day off on Thursday we boarded the bus and trekked back to the toughest town on the Circuit.

Charley planned to start Thompson at third. Despite the conversation we'd had with Joe and Burt, and in spite of Percy's .336 batting average, he'd thought it over. "We couldn't play him a month ago," Charley said. "With all that's happened since, it ain't likely anybody's calmed down." Burt and Joe didn't argue. And I didn't sense much disappointment from Percy after he'd heard the news. But Charley's plan hadn't reached the Clayton crowd, and Friday night they'd gathered early—black and white, both—eager to welcome Percy back to town.

The sounds were vivid that night. The smells were pure. The colors were bright. And the air was fresh and warm and perfect for baseball. Negro fans swarmed into the stadium. This was, by far, the biggest colored crowd we'd seen. Five minutes before game time the ushers and grounds crew frantically roped off the field, corraling them all into foul territory. But failing, utterly, to corral their enthusiasm. The colored fans stood tall and eager to cheer for one of their own. The white fans were restless too. And when the PA announcer came to Thompson's name, both crowds booed with bitter disappointment.

In the top of the eighth we were down by a run. Billy Henderson led off with a single. Then Thompson flied out to short right field. Douglas singled to left, moving Henderson into scoring position. Rick Murphy was up. On a 1-1 pitch he drove the ball straight into the rock-hard dirt in front of home plate. The ball bounced fifty feet into the air. The Clayton third baseman charged. The catcher threw off his mask, and both players stood, mitts poised, waiting and waiting and waiting for the inevitable effect of gravity. When the ball finally fell, Rick was standing safely at first. The ball hadn't traveled fifteen feet from home, but now the bases were loaded and there was only one out.

It was late in the game, bases filled, one out, and the pitcher's spot was due. We were in the league's toughest town, and on the bench we had a handful of guys who could pinch-hit. One was batting .213, another .186, a third .210. The fourth guy, a rookie, was hitting .333, but he'd only had six at bats, none of them in a situation like this.

And there was Percy.

I stared into the dugout, my heart pounding as hard as his. Charley sat beside him, his arm around his shoulder, their noses no more than an inch apart. Percy's head moved up and down, answering yes to whatever Charley was asking. Charley looked sober as a nun, and I could almost hear him saying, "Are you sure? Are you really sure?" Percy's nods grew more insistent. Charley looked to the field and to the crowd—worry covering him like a pair of long johns. The ump stared into our dugout, hands on his hips, silently demanding, "What are you gonna do?" Charley looked at Percy again while our pitcher loitered in the on-deck circle, waiting for the call.

Percy jumped up and grabbed a couple of bats. He hopped out of the dugout, swinging them and stretching, trying to get loose in a hurry.

The fans exploded, colored and white at the same time—one, a force for jubilation—the other, for sheer contempt. I glanced at the PA announcer, waiting for him to call Percy's name, but he sat perfectly still. I looked to the field. Percy limbered up while a pack of rejuvenated fans pelted him with peanuts and ice. He waited, inching toward the plate to avoid the barrage. The PA announcer didn't move. A full minute passed.

And then, when everybody in the place was wondering what was going on, the Clayton County sheriff charged onto the field. He blew his whistle—three shrill blasts—and waved his hands over his head, extravagant gestures that quickly arrested the crowd's attention. A handful of deputies waddled behind him; they all circled around home. Charley blasted out of the dugout, a practice he'd perfected here, while the Cowboys manager ambled out to meet him.

Umpires, managers, and sheriff huddled at the plate. Percy stood to one side, his bat on his shoulder. The Clayton pitcher waited, arms dangling impatiently at his sides. The catcher strolled away to the backstop, his mask hanging loosely from his right hand as he, like six thousand others, waited to see what this was all about.

Charley's contempt for the city of Clayton had risen to a level it had not known before. But he stayed calm: no wild gestures, no ranting, no debate—just a seething revulsion he couldn't conceal.

A man in a shirt and tie stood in the first row behind the Clayton dugout. His hair was thick and brushed straight back; glasses were black and horn-rimmed. His arms were folded, and his eyes never wavered from the meeting that had taken the whole crowd by surprise. I nudged the Clayton sportswriter beside me. "Who's that?" I asked.

"Mayor," he said blandly.

"You know what's going on?"

"Yeah," the reporter said, a trace of hesitation in his voice.

I opened my hands, silently prodding him on. He shifted in his seat uneasily. "Last night he called an emergency meeting. The city banned all Negroes from the public parks, especially this one. I believe your boy's being asked to leave the field."

I looked down at my scorebook and doodled for a second or two. Without looking up, I said, "They did this last night?"

"Yeah."

"Might've been nice if somebody had mentioned it a bit sooner," I said, lacing the remark with disgust.

"Yeah, well, you might've guessed by now that he wanted to make a show of it; wanted to let folks know this ain't Washington, D.C." He glanced over again, embarrassed. "Sorry, Jack."

The meeting broke up. Charley and Percy walked back to the dugout side by side. A moment later Galen West hit into a double play to end the inning.

Saturday morning Percy's name would be erased from the Bobcats roster. And Saturday night he'd sit in the colored bleachers—alone and anonymous—in the midst of a very small crowd.

◆ ◆ ◆ ◆

That night I stared at the walls, the ceiling, and at the window where a thin sheet of annoying light crept in under the curtains. The air conditioner droned, and I hoped the steady sound would lull me to sleep, but it failed. I could not, no matter how hard I strained, expel the images from my mind: the sheriff waving his arms; the mayor standing placidly, eyes fixed on the meeting he'd orchestrated the night before; Percy and Charley trudging back to the dugout, humiliated and jeered by the strident mob.

My spirit churned, and I couldn't get rid of this inkling—compulsion might be the better word—that I ought to do something. For a moment my thoughts drifted to Walter and Roberta, and to how they'd feel when they got the news. Then I could see the Clayton fans—overtaken by the frenzy—hurling ice and insults. I could read the taunting signs. And it was at that moment, lying there in the Clayton Motor Lodge struggling to find more peaceful thoughts, that it came to me for the first time—this burst of insight into the obvious—that Percy Jackson didn't matter. He was a pawn in a game that he wasn't even aware of. He and the other Negro players were nothing more than tokens, moved from one square to the next, with no reason to weigh their ambitions, to consider their hopes, or to care for their families. They were, to the politicians and businessmen, a kind of currency—to buy peace, favor, votes, or acclaim. The Clayton sheriff and mayor were, without question, the most loathsome offenders, but there was ample guilt to go around. Some of it belonged to Burt and Joe.

And some of it was mine.

I hopped out of bed and went to the small desk that was angled into a corner of my room. I switched on the lamp and began rapping out the random thoughts that streamed through my mind. In the smallest hours of Saturday morning, on the paper before me, cranking up a line at a time, a new angle on Percy Jackson began to emerge. I typed without thinking. As my fingers punched keys, I felt scales falling from my eyes, and there—in a hostile town, in the middle of the night, all alone—I saw things in a new light.

The headline, I quickly imagined, would say it straight: "Jackson Tossed Out of Clayton." I pulled no punches, describing the mayor and sheriff as bush leaguers, who had, for nothing more than selfish gain, gone to extraordinary lengths to humiliate a Bobcats player.

At the same time I wanted to sympathize with my readers, knowing that we were all confused and frustrated; understanding that life had suddenly become uncertain. "People across the South," I conceded, "are rightly concerned about the recent Supreme Court ruling. But how could that prompt a man to call secret meetings in the middle of the night for the sole purpose of disrupting a baseball game?" What right did it give the city of Clayton to intentionally shame members of an opposing team? And how could they justify luring Charley Baxter into a trap that was not only embarrassing, but that might affect the outcome of the game—and perhaps, a few months from now, of the season?

Fans, too, I said, even those in Whitney, had been unfair. "There's good reason for us all to be concerned," I granted, "and even angry. But wrath, if it is to be rightly expressed, must be properly placed." Baseball, I reminded everyone, had been integrated for more than five years. The Court's decision had nothing to do with Jackie Robinson or Larry Doby. And for Sunshine

Circuit fans to pour out their rage on Percy Jackson, Nat Quaid, and Wendell Hoskins simply made no sense. "Let's be honest," I said, "these men saved our league. They, more than other players, managers, or owners were responsible for attendance records, increased revenues, and, at least for now, the financial viability of the Sunshine Circuit.

"In Whitney," I went on, "we had one man to thank for a 43 percent increase at the gate: Percy Jackson. And yet, instead of gratitude, he receives our scorn." I made an appeal to died-in-the-wool fans: "If you like baseball, if you like having professional teams in our part of the country, then you have three Negroes to thank, and none more than Percy Jackson.

"This kid just might be," I rattled on, "one of the best players in the league. Since Donny Jones went down, Jackson's been hitting near .340—sixty points better than Jones. He's third in RBIs, and he has yet to make an error. The young Negro," I explained, "is contributing on the field, he's bringing new fans to the stadium; moreover, while the wounds from the bus boycott were still tender, his presence had been a salve to our Negro population. It wouldn't cost much—if we couldn't express gratitude—to at least show good manners.

"Percy Jackson, like Jackie Robinson, has quietly endured. He's never returned evil for evil, and he's demonstrated more patience than a kindergarten teacher. But at the end of the day, Whitney's third baseman is a flesh-and-blood human being, as easily wounded by insults as the rest of us. We are a Christian and God-fearing people who believe in treating others as we want to be treated. We hold fast to our way of life and to the notion of 'separate but equal.' But do we not also believe, with equal fervor, in loving our neighbor as ourselves? For us, for Clayton, and for the other towns in the Sunshine Circuit, it makes no sense to punish a ballplayer for problems he has not caused."

The words spilled out in a torrent I didn't control. For two hours I typed, and it was as if my fingers moved on their own accord. After the revelation had ceased, I slept like a just-fed baby. Later I freshened up what I'd written, and without thinking about it nearly long enough, phoned it in for Sunday's paper.

◆ ◆ ◆ ◆

Sunday afternoon you would've had a hard time telling that we'd lost the series two games to one, and that we'd never really been in Sunday's 8-1 loss. Don't get me wrong, nobody at this level likes to lose, but as the players mingled outside, their spirits were high. They laughed and joked with one another. And even Charley, who takes the game as seriously as generals take war, seemed unbothered by two losses in the past three days.

I've never pondered for very long on the emotional lives of twenty-year-old ballplayers, but I had a hunch about this. I've seen it—in every sport, in every town, from little leagues to big leagues: There is a force—a bond of some kind—that draws men together when they give a game all they've got, when they sweat and strain side by side, and when each one pulls his weight in the joint effort to win.

When Percy joined the team, that bond began to dissolve. When Jones went down, it weakened more. And then, when a lone player was heckled by the crowd and exiled from the team, it was nearly impossible for nine men to play together. But Friday night something changed. Clayton's deception, their undisguised malice, and the production of a bizarre spectacle—these were blows that had been dealt to them all; humiliations they were forced to share, and insults that stung every man in a Bobcats uniform. Something was different now—something faint and just emerging. As the afternoon faded to dusk, we passed the Clayton city limit sign for the last time that season, glad to have it behind us. But I wondered if some good had come from a terrible night.

An hour farther along the road, the Greyhound swung into the parking lot of the Big Chicken, one of our favorite places along the two-lane stretch that connects Whitney to Clayton. The place was an enormous barnlike building, bright yellow, with a giant chicken head on the west end that bobbed up and down pecking in the air. Inside, the dining room was cavernous—wide and high, and filled with the sounds of a feasting crowd. Long picnic tables stretched from one end of the room to the other, and a flock of yellow-clad waitresses hurried in and out of a bustling kitchen, all of them rushing to deliver platters full of the best fried chicken any mortal has ever known.

In a long single file we marched toward the back. Along the way we eyed Texas-sized bowls of mashed potatoes, green beans, and coleslaw; we passed trays of corn bread and biscuits; plates covered with black-eyed peas and corn on the cob that soaked in deep pools of melted butter.

By the time we reached our seats, our mouths were well watered, and the second our fannies hit the benches, platters suddenly appeared. Nobody wasted time digging in. Plates were quickly piled high with food that tasted so good you couldn't imagine you'd ever want to stop eating. I took a swig of sweet tea from a glass bigger than a kid's sand pail. Giles and Douglas sat at the other end of the table, heaping mountains of potatoes and peas onto their plates. Eddie Smith, Johnny Andrews, and Billy Henderson sat side by side, taking platters from the left and passing them to the right. Charley and Don and the coaches sat together two tables down, and everyone's mood began to brighten, roused by the good food and friendly conversation.

Harried again by uninvited thoughts—I wondered about Percy. I slipped outside to check the bus—there was no sign of him, so I asked Charley if he'd seen Percy. He motioned to his right. "Check the kitchen," he said, "they got a place all set up for him."

"No need," I answered, "I was just wondering where he was."

I wedged my way between Murphy and Haddock, trying to picture what it must be like for him. I took a bite of black-eyed peas, but didn't notice if they were spicy or bland. I chomped into a chicken breast that could've come from a small ostrich, but I couldn't tell you if it was moist or dry. I sipped at the tea and then pushed coleslaw around my plate for a while, oblivious to the chatter that buzzed around me.

And then, without saying anything to anybody, I picked up my plate and glass. I brushed by a few waitresses and backed my way through the swinging doors into the kitchen. I wandered around, drawing odd stares from cooks and busboys. I peeked past the shiny sinks and stoves, and I spotted him, sitting alone at a table that had been crammed into an out-of-the-way corner.

Plate in hand, I walked up to Percy. "Mind if I join you?"

He glanced up. Then he looked around the room, his eyes darting right then left.

"Would it be okay?" I asked. "Or would you rather be by yourself?"

"I s'pose it's fine," Percy said, but he wasn't sure.

I sat down and spread a napkin over my lap.

Percy leaned toward me, a fork in his left hand, a knife in the right. "You sure this is all right?" he asked, eyes still shifting back and forth like a kid who's worried about getting caught.

"You let me worry about that." Then, changing the subject, I said, "Bet you're glad to be heading home?"

"Yessir," Percy mumbled, "glad we done with that town for good."

"Yeah," I said, "I think we're all glad."

I threw back a gulp of iced tea and noticed Percy gawking at something behind me. I turned. Giles and Douglas marched toward us. Andrews was right behind, the three of them loaded down with plates, glasses, and silverware. Giles went to one side of the table, Andrews and Douglas split off to the other. As he slid onto the bench, Douglas slapped Percy on the back. He laughed and said, "You had a heck of a series, man. You showed 'em a thing or two out there, didn't ya?"

The five of us sat together, tucked away where the sight of a colored kid eating with white men wouldn't spoil others' appetites. There, amidst the heat and noise of a hectic kitchen, we talked and teased, and savored a meal that satisfied a multitude of the things we were hungry for.

Giles tipped his glass Percy's way. "Don't you worry about Clayton," he said, "the place is a toilet, and we'll be home real soon." Percy nodded as if to say "yeah," and shoveled in a mouthful of black-eyed peas.

Andrews, who as far as I know had resented Percy as much as anyone, sat beside him, inches away. Johnny looked at his Negro teammate—looked him straight on—and said, "I can't believe what they did to you the other night. That was wrong, man. It was just wrong."

Percy pressed his lips together and dipped his chin in reply. Then reached for a fresh bowl of mashed potatoes.

We polished off another plate of chicken and two more dishes of black-eyed peas. We made short work of too much bread pudding. And then, stuffed full of food and good companionship, we headed for the bus.

It was dark outside, and we were all ready to sleep our way back to Whitney. I trailed Douglas into the bus and started down the aisle. Donny Jones was five seats back, his face streaked by three rows of white tape. He leaned back and stared at me, daring me to return his gaze. All the warmth that I'd gathered up over the past hour went cold. I glanced at him, and then looked away, thinking about what I'd written and wondering if he'd somehow seen it or heard about it. I walked on, almost certain I'd done the wrong thing.

I found my spot and put one hand on the back of the seat as I slid in. With the other hand I reached into my shirt pocket for my notepad. I patted there two or three times, I checked my pants pockets, then searched the floor and under my seat. My mind raced, trying to recall where I'd seen it last. I scrambled out the back of the bus and hustled into the restaurant. I rushed through the kitchen doors, past the sinks and stoves, to our table. As I neared the last turn, I stopped. There was a gruff voice, one tinged with revulsion. "What are we gonna do with the nigger's stuff?" someone wondered.

"I don't wanna touch it," a kid replied.

"That makes two of us," a third voice agreed.

Then a fourth kid spoke up, his voice full of defiance. "I'll touch it," he sneered. An instant later glass shattered. I spun around the corner. A pimply-faced kid—a busboy, maybe seventeen, wearing a filthy wrap around apron, stood at Percy's seat. Crushed ice and slivers of a broken tea glass were scattered at his feet. The others, two boys and a girl, surrounded the table.

I watched in silence.

The girl, cute, with short blonde hair and braces, grabbed Douglas's napkin. She covered her hand and gingerly reached down. "Disgusting," she sneered, as she flung Percy's fork into a trash can.

From the corner of my eye, and for the first time that night, I noticed a colored man standing fifteen feet from our table. He was bent over a sink, steam rising around him, as he scoured a dish that he'd just plucked from a stack that stood thirty plates high. His hair was gray-flecked, and he was thin and muscular and still strong for a man who had to have passed sixty.

"I wouldn't let my dog eat off that plate," one of the boys cracked.

The girl shivered from a chill. "I can't believe a nigger had one of our forks in his mouth."

The dishwasher glanced over, said nothing, and then reached for the next plate.

The busboy noticed. "So what do you think, Nathaniel," he hollered across the room, "that plate fit for Will's old mutt?"

Nathaniel mutely stacked the dish in the drip rack beside him.

"What are we going to do with it?" the girl asked. "I sure don't want to eat off it."

"We ain't gonna take that chance," the busboy promised. He grabbed the china plate, then he turned slightly, making sure Nathaniel had a clear view. With both hands he lifted it high over his head. "Here goes," he exclaimed. With violence and glee, he slammed the plate to the floor, smashing it into a hundred tiny pieces. The teenagers clapped and roared with laughter.

"What the … what in the world are you doing?" I gasped.

The busboy looked up, a smug grin plastered wide across his face. "Nigger's plate," he sneered, "wouldn't give it to nobody else now." He turned, still looking proud, and began loading the other plates into a silver tub. The young girl squeamishly deposited Percy's spoon into the trash.

I looked at Nathaniel—his eyes cast down, suds up to his elbows slaving away at the next dirty dish—and I stopped worrying about what I had written.

Chapter 16

During the week of May seventeenth I learned more surely than I had ever known it before that man was not meant to live with fretfulness. It deprives you of sleep. It plagues the mind with poisonous thoughts. And like a well-bred hound, it keeps contentment at bay.

When I got home, I saw no sign of hospitality, no glimmer of warmth, not a clue that anyone—known or unknown—would find a friendly reception there.

And so, with a twinge of doubt, I ventured into my own home. The screen door slammed shut behind me, I fumbled for the light switch on the kitchen wall, and followed the sounds of the TV into the living room where Rose Marie rested on the couch reading the newspaper, keeping company with Jack Benny. She didn't get up, or look over, or so much as speak when I came into the room. Warily, and bluffing cheerfulness, I said, "Hey, babe," and dropped my suitcase at the foot of the stairs.

A couple of uneasy seconds passed. "You outdid yourself," she declared, still not looking up. "This was a … oh, I don't know, let's call it … spirited; we were treated to a spirited piece by the Whitney sports editor today."

"Yeah." I chuckled clumsily. "I suppose so. I'm sorry. I probably should've called to tell you."

She lowered the paper, and we looked at one another. Neither of us spoke. She didn't seem angry. I couldn't find a hint of hostility—not in her eyes, or in the cast of her jaw, or the posture of her lips. She looked worn out and beaten down. My wariness turned to regret.

"Yeah," she whispered flatly, "that would've been nice." She returned to the paper, adding, "It would've been nicer if you'd thought a little more about us—about me and Chris—about what this would do to your own family."

I lowered myself into the chair beside her and told her about the sheriff and mayor, and about how I couldn't sleep. I described the images that had hounded me. I recounted how the words flowed from out of nowhere.

And then I stopped. I watched her staring at the newspaper, wanting her to understand what had happened, needing to make that night as raw to her as it had been for me. "I didn't plan it," I said, "and I know it sounds weird, but I couldn't just lie there. I had to do something." I reached over and picked up the sports page. "And this is all I know how to do."

Rose Marie studied me, weighing the words. "And while you were in the midst of all this," she asked, "did you give your wife and son a passing thought? Did it occur to you—for even a second—that this would affect *us*?"

After three or four seconds of punishing silence, she looked away, knifed by the tacit admission that for three hours she had not crossed my mind. She stared at the television, then she said, "It's all real noble, Hall. Honest, it is. Just seems like you'd think about us, that's all, that you'd worry about me and Chris, that you'd care about the way people treat us…."

The light flickered on her cheeks and nose, revealing the toll this had taken. Staring straight ahead, in a voice tinged with regret, she said, "Now we sit here and wait." She leaned back and pondered the ceiling, her imagination filling with images of things to come. "Haven't gotten any crank calls," she mused. "Who knows, maybe we got a break because it's Sunday. Or maybe everybody who's of a mind to call has already done it." She cut her eyes to me. "What do you suppose they do after they've poured sugar in the gas tank, Hall? Once they've painted the driveway, what do you suppose they do after that?"

We sat quietly, Jack Benny and Rochester adding laughter to a scene that wasn't funny. Rose Marie sat up and gave the paper a hard shake. She turned the page and said, "I ran into Kitty Patterson at church this morning. She didn't mention the article, probably hadn't even had a chance to look at the paper, but I thought it was peculiar: A bunch of us had gotten together a group to play bridge at her house on Tuesdays." She peered over the top of the paper. "I might've mentioned that to you. Well, as it turns out they're not going to be able to play after all, had to cancel the whole thing for some reason. I never could figure out exactly why."

She turned another page and stabbed at it to straighten an errant fold. "And after Sunday school I saw Jean Simpson. Chris was going to go over to their house on Saturday for a party, but it's the oddest thing: They're going to have to reschedule." Brusquely, she turned the page again. "Yeah, she apologized, said she felt real bad about it; some kind of family problem that needs tending to." She glanced up for a third time. "Can you imagine that, two things cancelled on the same day?"

I leaned back in the chair, and I told her I was sorry. I told her that I loved her more than any combination of words could ever express. And I promised her that nothing was more important to me than she and Chris were.

"I want to believe that," she said, "and there was a time when I wouldn't have doubted it; not for a single second. But you write these things, Hall, and you know what's going to happen, you know that me and Chris are going to pay the price. But you go right on ahead…." She picked up the sports page, brandishing it wearily. "You did it on purpose, Jack. You wrote it and you put it in the paper. And now we're losing our friends."

She let the paper fall. And then, as if trying to ease the blow she'd just landed, she said, "Look, I know you love me. And I know you love Chris. But right now, Jack—right this very minute—this thing with Percy Jackson looks to be giving us a run for our money."

I had told her the absolute and unvarnished truth: I did love her more than words could convey. She is an inseparable part of me, and there is no one—not alive or dead or who will ever live—who loves his wife more than I love mine. But—and this is something that pains me now, a part of my own character I don't understand—she was right. If I had known that her friends would forsake her, I would have written the article anyway. And if I could have foreseen that Sammy Simpson's family would renounce my own son, I still would have sent the story to press.

My eyes lingered on her. Weakly, I said, "I can't explain it, Rose, there's just something about this…." My voice trailed away. A Pepsi-Cola jingle bounced around the room as I struggled to find a few words that might make sense. "You know," I began again, "there are mornings when we sit out on the porch talking about whatever's in the paper, and I don't want to leave. I look at you and I want to stay here, I just want to stay close to you. But I get up and go to work because that's what I'm supposed to do."

Rose stared at the television.

"And at the end of the month," I trudged on, "when I pay for the electricity and phone, I look at all the money we're spending, and I want to take every nickel of it and buy you jewelry or nice clothes, or something a lot sexier than electricity. But I pay the bills. I don't buy you the nice things because—" I stopped, frustrated and feeling stupid, and knowing that this wasn't getting me where I wanted to go.

"Look," I stumbled on, "I know this doesn't make any sense, but as much as I love you, I had to write the article. They were killing this kid, Rose, and I was lying there with a typewriter ten feet away. And I don't know, for some reason I thought I could do something about it." I stopped again, my thoughts too tangled to go on.

"I get it," Rose said, still intent on the television. "I know what you're trying to say. And ninety-nine out of a hundred times I'd go along with you. But why now, Jack?" She turned to face me. "The people in this town—we've all got boys and girls who are this close to being in school with colored kids. Everybody's trying to get this figured out, we're trying to keep life sane, and you go filling up fifty column inches telling us to be nice to the colored boys. It might be real decent, Hall, but why now?"

I was spent—emotionally, physically, mentally—and there wasn't a lot of fight left in me. "I didn't choose the time," I murmured. "The Clayton mayor, the sheriff, the city council—even the PA announcer for crying out loud—grown men got together in the middle of the night; they made a plan to ruin a boy's life—a boy who's only six years older than Chris. How do I say, 'It's not a good time'?" I frowned and threw up my hands, not the least bit sure of the answer to my own question.

"There's no law that says you got to write an article, Jack. You just wait, that's all. You wait until people are ready to hear. You wait until this mess gets sorted out."

"If you'd been there, Rose, if you had seen it; if you had heard what—"

Rose's eyes circled in disbelief. "I've been to worse places," she said, "and I've seen things you pray to God you never see." She tossed the paper onto the floor. "I've told you, Jack, I've told you umpteen times: Mixing coloreds and whites makes us do ugly things, things we'd never do, never even think in any other situation." Her gaze sharpened. "I'm sure this poor colored boy's getting all kinds of grief he doesn't deserve, Jack, but what'd you expect?" She paused, as if waiting for an answer. Then she said, "Anybody who's anywhere close to this is going to see something he wished he hadn't, Jack—including me and Chris. And we don't deserve it either."

I was at the kitchen table when Chris and Slugger romped down the stairs, bright-eyed and ready to tackle whatever the world might throw their way. Chris patted me on the back as he passed; he grabbed the Frosted Flakes and asked about yesterday's games. I gave him a few highlights, and we both checked the box score to see how Musial and Moon had done against the Pirates. He plopped into his chair and we skimmed over our plans for the day. And then, at the conversation's first pause, I said, "Mom told me about Sammy's party."

Chris shrugged; he poured milk into his bowl and then turned the box to see what sort of treasure a box top might bring from Battle Creek, Michigan. "You know," I said, "they probably didn't really cancel the party. They probably didn't want you to come because they're mad at me."

He peeked up. "'Cause you're a nigger lover?" he asked. He wore the purity of an innocent child, simply repeating words that had been whispered behind his back.

"Well," I said, "probably not the way you mean."

He slurped up a spoonful of cereal. "Like what, then?" he asked.

I began with the sermon about the Good Samaritan. "I was just trying to take care of my neighbor," I explained. Chris read about Tony the Tiger's secret decoder ring, while I explained that people were nervous and that some thought I was helping the wrong way. “Anyway,” I said, “they’re mad at me. And they might get mad at you and Mom, too.”

“That’s dumb,” Chris mumbled, now studying the fine print of Kellogg’s latest offer.

“Well, people are saying a lot of things they don’t really mean. But it’ll all get back to normal soon. And Chris …”

“Yes, sir?”

“I didn’t mean for people to get mad at you. I’m just trying to do the right thing, you understand?”

He looked up from the cereal box. “I guess so,” he said. But his eyes lingered, as if he wanted to say more.

“What is it?” I asked him. “What’s on your mind?”

“There are kids who won’t eat lunch with me anymore,” he said. “And at recess, a lot of times I end up doing something by myself, or just watching.”

I put my hand on his shoulder and said, “I’m sorry, pal. I never meant for anything like that to happen.”

“Even Sammy,” he said, “he’s not allowed to walk with me to school anymore.” Chris peered up. “I don’t really have any friends right now.”

“I’ll talk to Sammy’s parents, okay? And I think things’ll get back to normal soon.”

Chris nodded silently, and turned back to his cereal.

Rose Marie swept in from the porch. “Everybody got what they need?” she asked.

Chris looked up and grunted, “Yes, ma’am.” Then, pushing the cereal box aside, he eyed his mother cautiously. He turned to me and said, “I want to see Percy Jackson play. Can we go to the game Saturday?”

◆ ◆ ◆ ◆

I had one more reaction to face, and Monday morning—bellowing from clear down the corridor—came the expected roar: “Hall, I need to see you. Now.”

Joe sat behind a dozen foot-high stacks of paper, reading glasses perched in their proper position, scanning Sunday's *Atlanta Constitution*. I rapped on the door; he tossed the paper aside and motioned me to a chair. Yesterday's sports section was folded into a tight square, to the piece I'd done on Percy. He flipped it to the edge of the desk, and I don't remember exactly what he said, but it was something to the effect of, "Son, I didn't tell you to scold white people, I just wanted you to let 'em know that Percy's playing some good ball."

I hadn't sorted all this out in my own mind, and I wasn't ready for a debate, so I just nodded amiably and said "sure" or "no problem" or "fine"—something that I hoped would end the conversation quickly. But the off-the-cuff answer had the opposite effect; it summoned an even deeper suspicion. Joe leaned forward. He peered over the glasses and said, "Now you aren't thinking about turning this into some kind of crusade, are you? I mean, you aren't gonna start using my sports section as your personal pulpit? Please tell me this isn't gonna turn into something like that."

"No," I assured him, "I don't have anything like that even remotely in mind."

"That's good to hear," he replied, "'cause I tell you what, we've been getting the calls again; people saying if they see any more of this, they're gonna cancel their subscriptions. And I'll bet you a week's salary you'll be getting a sack of mail saying the same thing."

He ran a hand over his head. Then he reached over for the paper; he looked at it, scowling. "I don't like unhappy subscribers," he declared, "but that ain't the worst of it." He peered over his glasses again. "I just got off the phone with Good Buy Bob Bouchard." Joe shook his head, disdaining the folksy nickname. "He carried on for a half hour about how the radio station's got their head on straight, 'bout how they're trying to keep folks where they belong. Then he went on and on about how a merchant's got to make sure his advertising's in a place the people respect." Joe glanced up to catch my eye. "Now I don't think he can afford to drop us any more than we can afford to lose him. But there's been others making the same kind of noise." Joe leaned forward across his desk again, and said, "Look, write all day long about how good this boy is. Put his picture in the paper. Call him the best player to come through here since Grady Wolf. That's all fine. But don't insult folks. That's just not good business."

Despite all my own doubts this conversation rubbed me wrong, and my irritation seeped out into the open. "Yeah," I groused, "that's fine."

Joe pinched up his face. "What's your problem?" he grumbled. "I'm the one who's got to talk to these people."

I mustered boldness I didn't really feel and said, "I don't think you'd ever ask a guy in news to change what he was doing because a car dealer didn't like it."

"Well," Joe said, a thin smile inching across his lips, "maybe not. And the truth is we're in a prickly spot here—editorially, I mean. Over in news everybody knows we're not for race mixing, or integrating schools, or for the Supreme Court messing with states' rights. And you know what the deal is with Percy: We put him on that team to keep the colored folks calmed down. We're trying to thread a tiny dad-gum needle here, Jack. And we got to be careful—news or sports, don't really matter right now—we can't be giving people the wrong idea."

"I understand all that," I told Joe. "But we give people the wrong idea by what we don't print too." I stood and paced along the bookcases on the back wall. For as long as I had been around, I said, the paper had stood for decency. It had been for doing the right thing—no matter what the car dealers thought. I turned back to Joe. "Silence sends a message too."

"Yeah." Joe nodded, his smile now widening. "You're right about that."

He took his glasses off and let them drop to his chest. Then he leaned back; he laced his fingers on top of his head and said, "So what's got into you? Wasn't but a couple of days ago you were whining like a baby, crying about what happens when you write something good about this boy. Now you're telling everybody in town they better be nice."

I frowned. Or it might have been an embarrassed smile. "I don't know," I sighed. "You weren't there the other night. I wished you had seen it. Burt, too. It got ugly and …" I broke off and glanced around the office—at all the photos of Joe and Burt posing with governors and congressmen, at Joe cutting ribbons from every landmark in town, and waving from convertibles at the Fourth of July parades. I walked along the wall of photos. "I love this place," I said, "and I don't want it to ever look or sound like Clayton." I turned to face him again. "You don't either. And we don't want people getting the wrong idea about that."

◆ ◆ ◆ ◆

At five o'clock that afternoon I was puzzled. And by five thirty I was in pain.

Puzzled because there had only been a handful of troublesome phone calls at the paper, maybe three cancelled subscriptions, and no more than a pair of contemptuous glares from my coworkers.

And wounded because at home the news was not what I had expected.

To our great relief Rose Marie had been spared the flood of angry calls that she'd braced for. But a pair of replies from the Whitney Elementary School stunned us, and they would, I knew the moment I'd heard about them, cast a pall over my family for as far into the future as I could see.

Rose had run into the principal, Jed Hampton, that afternoon after school. "Yeah," she reported, "he was real glad to catch up with me; said he had something he needed to go over with us." The school, Hampton said, had decided that they'd choose new patrol boys at the end of the semester. "Now we've never done that before," he quipped, "always been a yearlong thing. But the faculty thought it'd be nice to give some other boys a chance—you know, the ones who've been bringing up their grades, who're starting to measure up to their potential.... Got nothing to do with Chris," he assured her.

And then, just a few minutes before I got home, his teacher had called. Outside our own family there is not a soul on the planet who loves Chris more than Jane Lizenbee. "Her voice was sad," Rose Marie said, "but she could not have been clearer." It wouldn't be a good idea, the teacher had insisted, for Chris to go to the county spelling bee next week. "With all that's been going on, I believe it'd just cause a stir," she told Rose Marie. "At least for right now." She was afraid that the other children might be rough on him, and that Rose Marie and I might not feel welcomed. And the school, she said, would have to deal with all sorts of issues at a time "when we're trying so hard to keep everybody settled down.

"Chris is such a smart boy," Miss Lizenbee had assured Rose, "he'll have lots of chances in the future."

"This'll kill that poor child," my wife moaned. "He's taken it all in stride up 'til now; taken it much better than I ever imagined a boy his age could, but this…."

I sat beside her at the kitchen table. "I'll see what we can do," I said. "Maybe we can work something out."

She grabbed my hand, and I felt every ounce of her apprehension. "Things seemed so quiet," she said. She reached up to dab at her eyes. "We're not getting calls from a bunch of crazy people, Jack. We're not seeing pranks from strangers in the middle of the night." She squeezed my hand harder. "Now it's coming from our friends."

"He's upstairs?" I asked.

"Yeah," Rose sniffed, "he just got home."

I tramped up to his room, rapped on the door, and pushed my way inside. "Can we talk for a second, pal?"

He looked up from his schoolbook and said, "Sure."

I delivered the news. I explained that it was all my fault, that he hadn't done anything wrong. And I told him, again, that I was sorry.

He did his best to stay tough and to hold back the tears, but this surge of events, poured onto what he'd already endured, breached every façade, and he crumpled under the weight.

I put an arm around his shoulder. "You know," I told him, "we've always been pretty lucky, we've hardly ever had anything bad happen to us. And I'm really sorry about this time. But I want you to know a couple of things, pal. One, this'll all be over one day. You're going to have plenty of friends and your teachers are going to include you in the spelling bees and science fairs and all that stuff. I don't know when, Chris, and it may be a long time, but things are going to be okay for you. I promise."

He glowered up at me, his eyes silently scoffing back: *Sure, that's what parents always say.*

Then I leaned forward, elbows on my knees, hands dangling between them, and said, "Here's the other thing: I could make a lot of this stuff go away, Chris. I could write things that would make everybody happy; that'd make them love you and me and Mom just the way they always have … be the easiest thing in the world. But sometimes we've got to do what's right, and not what's safe, especially in the newspaper business. You know what I mean?"

He dragged a hand over his eyes and nose. "Sort of," he sniffed. "But you don't know what it's like, Dad. Kids call us nigger lovers almost every day. Mike and Jimmy, they're not allowed to play with me anymore. And at baseball practice, there are three guys who won't even sit next to me on the bench." He flopped down on his bed and turned away. "I hate this," he said.

"Look, I know what it's like, really. And I'm sorry. I don't want you to have to go through any of this, pal. I'll try to make it easier, okay?"

"When?" his voice heaved.

"As soon as I can," I promised. "I'll start right now, today. I don't want to hurt you, Chris." I rubbed up and down his back. "I've got to tell the truth; I've still got to do what's right, even if it's risky. But I'll try to take it easy, okay?"

"Yeah," he said. "But Dad." He rolled over to face me. "I want to see him play. I think I deserve to see him."

◆ ◆ ◆ ◆

I felt bad leaving Rose Marie, as though I had abandoned her and left her to stew in a terrible mess I had made. But I was glad for tonight's game, relieved to have a diversion, and looking forward to some time with the team.

I stopped by Charley's office, but no one was there. So I wandered across the hall, into the locker room, hoping to spot Giles, Andrews, or Douglas. My foot had barely touched the concrete floor when something flashed. I ducked, and in an instant panic, threw up both hands. There was a crash inches away from my right ear—then a baseball dribbling away from the lockers beside me. My heart tried to pound its way out of my chest. My breath came hard. And my eyes found the fresh inch-deep dent in the nearest locker.

Donny Jones sat fifteen feet in front of me wearing boxer shorts and a menacing grin. "Sorry, Jack, didn't see you come in," he cracked.

"What the … what are you doing?" I snapped.

"Hey, I was just playing around with you."

My panic turned to rage. "Well knock it off. You scared the daylights out of me."

There were only a few players inside: Johnny Andrews and Billy Henderson; Fred Taylor sat at his locker, a snarl smeared across his face too. "Come on, Donny," Fred ragged, "you almost hit Jack. And if we didn't have him around, who'd tell everybody the nigger's better'n you are?"

Andrews and Henderson turned away, hoping to steer clear of this conversation. "Yeah," Donny sneered, "that'd be a real serious shame, now wouldn't it?"

I looked at Donny. "Are you threatening me?" I laughed. "Is that what this is about?"

Jones stood up, folding his arms across his forty-eight-inch chest. "No," he said, "if I wanted to hurt you, I'd just come over there and do it." His looked down, and I could see that he wasn't comfortable with this, that he might even be embarrassed. And then, more contritely, he said, "I just want to know what you're doing. Since when is it your job to help the nigger take mine? That's what I want to know."

Taylor had Sunday's sports section on the bench beside him. He gestured toward it and said, "This is what happens; you start mixing up coloreds and whites and pretty soon white guys lose their jobs. The coloreds start thinking they're as good as anybody else." He flung the paper at me. "You need to mind your own business, Jack. Let Charley run the team."

"Knock it off," Andrews snapped from across the room. "Jack didn't mean no harm."

Donny didn't turn. He just stood there staring at me and said, "Jack reminded the whole town that this little nigger's hitting sixty points better'n I am. That your idea of no harm?"

"He's hitting sixty points better'n most of us," Johnny replied.

"He don't play the same position you do," Donny shot back, "don't exactly have the same effect on you, does it?"

"Maybe not," Andrews admitted, "but what happened the other night was wrong. And all the stuff he puts up with … that ain't right. You can't argue 'bout that."

"Sure I can." Donny hissed. "What happened over there—those folks stood up for what's right. They ain't caving in, letting a bunch of outsiders tell 'em what to do. They're seeing to it that everybody stays with their own kind. You telling me you got a problem with that?"

Denny Douglas strolled into the room. "Well, right now that boy's hitting somewhere in the neighborhood of .330," he said. "He's catching anything that's hit to the left side of second base. I got to tell you the truth, at least for right now, I got a serious problem with it."

"It ain't right," Freddie stormed, "and we ain't gonna have it."

"Look," I said to Donny, "we've known each other for a while, and I've been a big fan of yours. But Percy's here, and right now he's a human bull's-eye. People are blaming him for all kinds of stuff that's not his fault, and it's not fair. That's all I'm saying."

"And you think the way they're treating me is fair—giving my job to this colored boy."

"I don't want you to lose your job," I said, "not to anybody. But we all gotta face the facts. The big-league teams are signing colored players. And if they sign 'em, they gotta put 'em someplace, they gotta play 'em. That cow's not going back in the barn."

"Well," Freddie countered, "there's a few of us think it's worth a try."

"Now you boys listen up," Denny said, "I'm not exactly sure what you mean by that, but you leave Percy alone. You ain't gotta be best friends with him, I ain't saying that. But this boy's on the team. You just let him be."

Donny spit a wad a tobacco juice into a mangled coffee can. "Yeah," he sneered, "we'll see. We'll get us a colored catcher down here—some ol' boy who don't need a week and a half to run to first base—see what you think about it then."

Denny howled. "Now come on, Donny," he laughed, "you get Roy Campanella down here right this minute. I'll run circles 'round that boy."

In the first inning Smith, Andrews, and Giles went down in order. Then, in the second, Taylor led off with a single. Henderson followed with a soft grounder to short; Taylor slid into second hard, breaking up the double play, and leaving Billy on first with Percy coming to the plate.

Percy lifted the bat over his head and stretched right and left to get loose, then stepped in the batter's box. I can't say for sure but I like to think that the crowd was tamer than they'd been before; that they'd responded to Sunday's rebuke, and some—a few, at least—believed kindness was in order. But there were plenty who felt obliged to make their displeasure known. They had, within the past few days, come up with a new slogan, "Back to nigger school." And the chant—though bridled—began to make a run around the stadium.

Denny Douglas moved into the on-deck circle. He gawked at the crowd, shaking his head dolefully. Percy watched the first pitch go by, high and outside for ball one. The second pitch was a called strike, a fastball just off the corner.

"Back to nigger school," gathered speed, and here and there it was garnished with other taunts.

On the next pitch Percy swung hard, and whiffed at a high fastball—strike two.

Spurred by the crowd's fervor, a man had drifted down to the aisle near the on-deck circle. He was paunchy and wore blue jeans and a green T-shirt. He was the kind of guy you'd never give a second look. But without warning he began screaming, "You'll never be a white man! You were born a nigger, you'll die a nigger!"

Percy stepped out of the box. He took off his hat and shouldered the sweat from his brow, gaping at the man and wondering what had gotten him so suddenly riled. He stepped back to the plate and the man shrieked again. Before the pitcher could begin his windup, Percy raised a hand, asking the ump for time.

And at that moment Denny charged the belligerent fan. He swelled up to his full six feet two inches, squared around, and stood before him—nose-to-nose. Muscles bulged at his sleeves, and he gripped his thirty-eight-ounce bat as if he meant to do it harm. His head rocked. His forearms flexed. The bat twitched in his hands. The paunchy man recoiled faster than a just-fired Winchester. Denny stabbed a finger in his face, and pointed away, somewhere off in the distance. The man—shocked and suddenly afraid—backed away and disappeared, I suspect right out of the stadium.

Denny turned, still strangling the bat and wordlessly asking the crowd, "Is there anybody else?"

The next pitch was a called strike—a questionable call from a nervous ump who was eager to move on. Percy shot him a you-gotta-be-kidding-me glare, then, amidst the scattered boos, trudged away. As their paths crossed, Denny slapped Percy on the backside, and if I read his lips right he said, "You'll get 'em next time."

Percy tramped down the steps to the water buckets at the home-plate end of the dugout. Donny Jones was there, perched on the bench's backrest. Percy, gazing out toward the field, put the ladle to his lips. Quicker than a cobra strikes, Donny slapped it out of his hands, slamming the ladle into the back wall. I grabbed my binoculars and watched Jones glower at his Negro teammate. He snarled and pointed to another bucket. It had a single dipper in it, and on the outside, on a wide strip of tape, someone had scrawled, "Colored."

Percy froze. Others quickly began to gather, and Charley hurried down too. He stood before Jones, hands on his hips. Donny spat out his side of the story, gesturing with his hands and head, making his disgust evident—even to me—thirty rows above him. Charley tore off his cap and stabbed his fingers through his sweaty hair—mystified by whatever he'd heard. Then he walked over and picked up the ladle that had been slapped from Percy's hand. He rubbed it against his pant leg, dipped it into the "Colored" bucket, and took a long sip of the lukewarm water. He gave Jones a pained and pitiful look, and hobbled away. Andrews grabbed a second ladle and dipped it into the same bucket, drank, and left it there. Then Galen West, the reserve catcher, walked over. He stretched a new piece of tape over the one that read "Colored." On it he had scribbled, "Bobcats."

◆ ◆ ◆ ◆

Tuesday morning I ventured into the diner, a courageous act under the circumstances—or perhaps just a stupid one. But curiosity won the tug-of-war with common sense, and I went to see what my neighbors had to say.

Helen was quiet, still sulking, and not in much of a mood to talk. The little I could pry out of her had to do with the "bigger picture."

"You just don't understand," she huffed at me, "once we start, once we head down this road, there's no turning back." She gave me a hard, pleading look. "I'm telling you, Jack, you got to help put a stop to this." She tramped away, armed with a pair of coffeepots, and filled with fear of what lay ahead.

Mike Warren, my banker friend, was in his spot at the end of the counter, strolling through the morning paper. "You still talking to me?" I asked.

He cracked a slight, almost kindly smile. "You've done worse," he said. The smile widened. "But I got to tell you something: I used to think you were a pretty bright guy. I'm not all that sure anymore."

"Yeah," I granted, sliding onto the stool beside him, "you, my wife, my boss … that list is getting pretty long." I frowned. "So what did you think … go too far this time?"

Mike wrapped his toast around a few strips of leftover bacon and stared at his plate. "You gotta understand something," he said, "I'm not about to send my kids to school with 'em, ain't gonna sit beside 'em at the movie theater, either—but professional baseball … I can't get too worked up about that. These colored boys have proved they can play, and I don't know … a bunch of guys hanging out in the dugout, that just don't bother me."

I gestured toward Helen. "She thinks we're halfway down the road to ruin, that we'll regret the day I ever mentioned Percy Jackson's name."

"Naw," Mike said, "I wouldn't go that far." Between bites of his bacon sandwich he said he wouldn't care if his own son played ball with colored boys. Then the easiness vanished. He swiveled toward me and said, "But I'd make dang sure they didn't get within a mile of my daughter." He gulped his food down. "This kid, Jackson, he's just a ballplayer," Mike said. "I don't see the sense in shaming him like they did. And calling him a bunch of names." He glanced up at me. "How's that solve any of the problems we're facing?"

Luther, the foreman from the plant, and the only man I've ever known who could chew with a toothpick dangling from his lips, was scraping up the last bit of his breakfast. I asked him what he thought, and in a voice that bordered on being forlorn, he said, "I don't really know, to tell you the truth.… I wish we didn't have to talk about it all; wish we could just turn the clock back. I wish that real hard." He peeked up, a neighborly look on his face, and with a trace of sympathy he said, "I ain't mad at you, if that's what you're getting at. And you know what, I might could bring myself to feel sorry for that Jackson boy. I work with colored fellas every day; we don't have problems like the ones you're talking about. Everybody just does what he's supposed to do, and then they go home—we never have any trouble.

"I don't know," Luther continued, "just seems like this hit us from out of the blue … don't know why we couldn't have left things alone."

"It bother you that Percy's on our team?"

Luther held his cup out for Helen to fill as she passed. "Well," he drawled, "when you get right down to it, I s'pose it does. If the boy could play ball and that'd be the end of it—well, I'd probably be fine with that. But somebody's always got to make something more of it, you know what I mean?" He pushed his plate away and cupped the warm coffee in both hands. A moment or two floated by, and then he said, "You know, I like this new kid the Braves got out of Jacksonville, this Aaron fella. I betcha he's gonna be real good and I like to watch him play. But that don't mean I want him in here eating with us—you know what I'm saying? I mean, as long as he's up in Milwaukee, I don't care one way or the other 'bout where he goes or what he does." His eyes dropped, perhaps picturing Henry Aaron at the table beside him. "But when it gets closer to home … I don't know, it just don't sit right."

Chapter 17

Saturday morning dawned, and in her eyes and along her forehead you could see the strain. In an occasional fluttery breath you could hear the burden of pestering doubts, but one thing was plain: Rose Marie was ready for baseball.

I don't think she would have admitted it for every dime in the Whitney National Bank, but she had missed it nearly as much as Chris—the sunshine and fresh air, the gasps of the crowd at a diving catch, the cry of concessionaires hawking peanuts and popcorn. And she longed to be in the ballpark, sitting beside Chris as he watched—enchanted—for the better part of an afternoon.

We made our way into the stadium ninety minutes before most of the crowd and hurried to Rose Marie's favorite spot along the third-base line. She stretched both arms to the sky looking to right field, slowly twisting toward left, soaking it all in—the grass and clay, the just-painted scoreboard, the familiar ads painted on the outfield wall—making sure everything was just the way she had left it. Wrapped in the warm surroundings, she folded herself into the seat and rubbed suntan lotion into her arms, legs, and shoulders. She roped her hair into a ponytail, pulled out her book, and then, stretching her legs across the seat in front of her, waved us away saying she'd see us in an hour.

Chris and I bolted for the locker room. We marched down the hall, side by side, then crashed through the doors. Chris was, in an instant, dazzled. Giles, Andrews, and Douglas all saw him at the same time and the room erupted into shouts of "kid," "runt," and "slugger." He got his back slapped and his head rubbed, and he warmed up the musty room like a puppy at a church picnic. Chris darted from locker to locker, catching up with guys he hadn't seen since last September. And as they began drifting out to the field, Chris tagged along right behind, his glove and cap on—ready to play. I walked with him through the tunnel and out toward the field. Before he crossed the foul line, Giles called him over to play catch, and I watched as he stood beside the players, shoulder high to them, tossing the ball like a pro. Douglas clambered through the passageway, then Eddie Smith and Rick Murphy. Billy Henderson followed a minute or two behind. And then, dressed-out as if he meant to play—with bandages still splayed across his face—came Donny Jones. He hurried toward Chris and playfully knocked the cap off his head, grinning as he passed. Chris bent down to pick it up and—I suspect threatening an act of unspeakable revenge—beamed back at Donny.

For a few seconds the world was the way it had always been.

Half an hour still remained before the game against Dittmer, and four of us were in the press box finishing up our last-minute chores. Jeff Harrison roamed around in the tight space behind Jim Holby mumbling about the weather, Giles' five-game hitting streak, and Dittmer's four consecutive losses. Nobody paid him much attention. He was, at least for the time being, background noise to the work at hand. But then, in the middle of a sentence, his rhythm broke. After a two- or three-beat pause, Jeff gasped, "Would you look at—now, I don't believe I've seen anything quite like that."

"What?" I mumbled back.

"Line of colored folks must stretch halfway back to town," he marveled.

"Well," I answered, still not impressed enough to look up, "Percy's playing good, it's a nice day—"

"Yeah, yeah, yeah," Jeff cut in, "that's all fine, but it don't explain what I'm seeing. There's something else going on here."

I glimpsed out at the colored grandstand; it was packed tighter than a church on Easter morning. Then I checked the Negro entrance where fans gushed through the gate, still a good twenty-five minutes before game time. "Now that is odd," I whispered. I watched for a while, drumming a pencil against the desk, wondering. Then I looked at Jeff. "We got a little time," I said, "let's check this out." The two of us hustled down to the colored section, and I started sorting through the crowd, searching for familiar faces. We walked along the foul line and behind the stands. I scanned the first few rows of the bleachers, and there, sitting three or four rows up, I spotted Horace, the old sharecropper who'd loaned me a lawn chair the first time I'd ever seen Percy play. I reached out my hand to him and he clambered down to meet me, overjoyed to remake the acquaintance. "Horace," I said, "what in the world is going on here?" His friendly face became earnest; he jammed both hands into his overall pockets and, rocking heel to toe, he said, "We been having a ticket drive down our way. Pastor Edwards—he's the one been putting it on—been telling everybody we got to support the team."

"How's that work?" I asked. "What kind of ticket drive you talking about?"

Horace's eyes sparkled. "All kinds of things," he said, "the churches all been taking up collections to buy tickets, then holding raffles for 'em. Just about all the colored businesses been buying 'em up and giving 'em away. And Mr. LaBarr—he's passing out a whole mess of 'em down at the radio station."

"That's real nice," Jeff said with a nod, "it's real nice." He pondered the crowd for a second or two, and then, with a slight tilt of his head he said, "I wonder why that it is. You got any idea?"

"Oh yeah." Horace beamed. "Pastor says we got to support anything that gives the Negro a fair shake; says if there's something that lets the colored man show what he can do, well then, we got to get behind it."

"Uh-huh," Jeff muttered. "He say anything else?"

"Naw," Horace said, brushing the question aside, "least not for anybody 'round here."

"What do you mean?" Jeff asked.

Horace paused. He cut his eyes toward me.

"It's okay," I told him.

"Well," he said, "he goes over to Clayton nowadays telling the colored folks over there to stay away from the ball games."

"Is that right?" I asked, wondering how I hadn't heard about this before.

"Yessir," he answered, "he's got a little saying going on now; got everybody repeatin' it: 'If we can't play, we won't pay.'"

For the second time this season, to absorb the overflow crowd, ushers rushed to convert a portion of the main grandstand to "colored." I had seen Rose Marie talking with a few of them, at first looking confused, and then cautious as Negro fans advanced into the stadium. She glanced at the oncoming crowd suspiciously. White people all around her squirmed, looking clumsy and unsure until the National Anthem reclaimed their attention. The Bobcats trotted onto the field as Jim Holby called out their names and positions. The near sellout crowd, white and colored alike, settled back into their seats calmly. And the first couple of innings moved right along with neither team able to get a man on base.

Then Percy led off our half of the third.

Since my rant in last Sunday's paper, a discernable change had taken place in the character of the crowd. And I had even seen, on at least three occasions, pleas from a few of the gentler fans to "leave the boy alone." But as the week wore on, an undeniable truth was revealed: There were, among my neighbors, some who had an unquenchable thirst to belittle Percy Jackson. And my editorial, coupled with all the national news, had probably hardened their hearts as well as their determination.

As Percy stepped to the plate, a lone voice from behind the dugout hollered, "Back to nigger school." It was instantly echoed from the third-base side of the stands, and then answered again by a gaggle of voices from up higher and behind home plate. From the press box I watched my wife inch toward our son, leaning over the armrest to pull him closer. A man sitting behind them began to inspire the chorus, standing and turning to face the crowd, merrily swinging his arms back and forth like a choir conductor. Below them, closer to home plate, I spotted Helen holding the sign she'd brought on opening day. It bobbed with the swelling tempo, and she spun right and left so everyone could read, "Hey nigger, don't you wish you were white?"

Rose Marie gently rubbed Chris's head; she patted him on the back, and then hugged him again. As the man behind them swayed with the chorus, she peeked at the Negro fans to her left, who sat peaceably, seeming deaf to the uproar around them.

With the count full Percy crowded the plate and crouched low to shrink the strike zone. On an inside fastball he spun away, looking as if he'd been nearly hit. The ump called ball four, and the day's first round of barbs faded beneath light applause for his smart play.

In the sixth inning, with no score, Billy Henderson blasted a solo home run. He knew it at the crack of the bat. He stood and watched it sail, then flipped his bat aside and began a slow trot around the bases, savoring his first home run of the season. The Dittmer players, already sour from a four-game losing streak, were in no mood for further humiliation. As Billy made his way from third to home, the pitcher glared, and I don't believe there could have been a purer declaration of his team's disdain. Billy crossed the plate grinning, shaking hands with Percy, Jones, and the bat boy as he made his way back to the dugout.

Then Percy stepped into the box. And the Dittmer pitcher, with barely enough time to have gotten a sign, fired a fastball directly at his head. Percy dove. The bat flew out of his hands. And the colored crowd flashed to its feet, their boos storming across the field. Rose Marie glanced around nervously. Chris was on his feet, jeering and turning purple from the strain. Others around the grandstand did the same.

Percy raged back into the box, digging his back foot deep into the dirt—steaming for revenge. He drilled the next pitch down the left-field line to the wall—a stand-up double—and the home crowd, white and colored, surged to its feet, reveling in the just reprisal.

The Dittmer pitcher, now thoroughly rattled, threw a wild pitch to Douglas, outside and in the dirt. It bounced to the backstop and Percy strolled to third. The next pitch was a fastball, letter high. It caught the fat part of the plate, right where Denny likes it, and he lifted the ball deep to right field. Percy tagged and slowly jogged home, eyeing the Dittmer pitcher every step of the way with a glare that screamed, "Don't ever do that again." The colored crowd was on its feet, clapping and hollering, and making sure the world knew they were watching.

The Bobcats took the first game of the series, 2-0.

On my way to locker room I stopped to pick up Chris. Rose Marie grabbed her book and said she'd wait. I glanced up at the colored crowd still mingling beside her and asked, "Are you sure?"

"I'll be fine." Then she wiggled her four fingers and shooed us out of the stands.

Chris and I climbed down to the field and into the dugout on our way to the locker room. Percy was there on the bench, alone, shoving his cleats into a bag and changing into a pair of sneakers for his walk to the armory.

"Great game," I said.

Percy looked at Chris, then to me. "Thanks," he replied.

I introduced the two boys. They shook hands, both reluctant. "Hey," Percy said.

Chris returned a nod. "Can't believe you got a double off that guy after he knocked you down."

A grin crept across Percy's lips. "Made me mad," he said softly.

"Made everybody mad," I shot back.

The colored boy shrugged and smiled. "Felt good," he said.

Chris took a seat beside Percy. "Turned a real nice double play, too," he added.

Percy had leaned down to lace up his shoes. He turned his head up and said, "Thanks, 'preciate it." Then the three of us started down the tunnel—Chris and I to visit with the team—Percy on his way to the armory. We were in the locker room, Percy hurrying through and nearly to the doors when Chris called, "Hey, Percy." He and a handful of others stopped and turned. "That double …" he gave his head a little crook to the side. "That was swift."

Forty-five minutes later we strolled through the parking lot; just a smattering of cars and a handful of people lingered there, including Joe and Burt, who were huddled at the hood of the mayor's car. I opened the door for Rose Marie and saw that Dick Reeves was with them. Joe gestured toward us and Dick turned. He waved and jogged over to the car.

"I need to get with you," he said, "how about breakfast Monday morning?"

The expression on Joe's face looked like an order to say yes. "Seven thirty," I suggested.

With a firm nod Dick confirmed the time.

We hadn't been home for ten minutes before Chris plunged into the scorebook, and the three of us spent our supper time reliving the game and relishing a conversation in which every sentence began with, "Did you see …?" Could you believe …?" or, "Remember when …?"

Chris was red-cheeked from a day in the sun, and his mother's tan had deepened by at least one shade. He put the scorebook in his lap, scanning the action for the third or fourth time; then he glanced up, oblivious for the moment to spelling bees, teachers, and school principals. His eyes shifted from his mother to me, and he asked, "Can we go again tomorrow?" I looked at Rose Marie hoping to see an encouraging sign. And seeing no sign at all, I said, "You bet. Maybe Charley'll let you take a few swings in the batting cage."

I put Chris to bed that night. And after his prayers, as I reached for the light, he softly called, "Dad?"

I turned. "What is it, pal?"

"Percy Jackson," he said. "He was nice. There was nothing scary about him."

"No," I chuckled, "there's nothing scary about Percy."

"It's just because he's colored, then. That's the only reason people get mad at him?"

"Well, there's a little more to it than that," I explained. "They're afraid that if Percy can play for the Bobcats, then other Negroes will want to work and play with white people too. And that's what scares them."

He propped his head on a hand. "But you think it's okay? You want him on the team?"

I sighed and leaned into the doorjamb. "It's not ideal, Chris. It's not how we'd want things to be. But he's a nice guy and he's helped the team; I'm happy about that."

In light that had crept in from the hall, I could see confusion plowed across his forehead. Then, phrase by phrase, he tried to parse the logic:

"So you like Percy.

"And you're glad he's helping the team.

"But you're not really glad that he's on the team?"

I walked back to his bed and sat beside him. "Which means I'm still confused," I confessed. "I think we're all a little mixed up right now; everybody's trying to figure out some new things. But we'll work through it," I said. "And you and me, we'll work through this together, okay?"

I rubbed his back and got up to go, was to the doorway, one foot into the hall.

"Dad?" Chris called again.

"Yeah, pal?"

"I'm thinking you should write the truth about him."

Rose Marie was in bed with her book open; I climbed in beside her. "So all in all," I said, "things went okay today?"

"It was nice to be outside," she replied. "And even with the crowd carrying on, I liked being there, being in the sun. But I don't know, Hall…." She leaned against the headboard. "It got a little frightening out there."

"Yeah, it did get a little rough," I conceded. "Honest to goodness, Rose, I don't know how that kid puts up with it."

"And it's all so sad," she replied, "for him, and for all those people who get so worked up."

"I think it just eggs him on," I said. "That double he hit today, I believe that fastball took a beating that was meant for a few of the loudmouths in the crowd."

"It can't be worth it," Rose mused. "When you see all that, when you hear it …" her eyes wandered, finally coming to rest on the book. "If I were that boy, I simply couldn't do it. And if I were his mother—well, I don't believe I could bear to hear those things."

"If you were his mother, there's not much you could do except bear it," I replied.

Rose glanced over. "Like I said," she whispered, "I don't believe it's worth it."

I moved on to the lighter side of the afternoon. "Chris had a good time," I said.

She smiled. "That's an understatement. And he was so wrapped up in the game, he hardly noticed the crowd."

"One thing to be thankful for."

"Yeah," Rose said, "I suppose." She closed the book, tucking a finger to mark her spot. "But I don't know…."

"What do you mean?" I asked.

"It's what's been bothering me about this the whole time," she said. "I don't want him caught up in all the meanness. I don't want our boy off doing some awful thing. But he's got to see what's going on. I mean … he starts cheering for Percy Jackson the same way he cheers for Jimmy or Johnny and he won't even think about one being white and the other one being colored." She flopped the book open but didn't look down. "A boy his age thinking everybody's just the same … an idea like that's going to land him in trouble."

◆ ◆ ◆ ◆

After church we changed clothes and sped to the stadium. A long column of colored fans had already formed at the side entrance. White fans were there too—picnicking in the parking lot, fathers playing catch with sons, friends leaning into their cars and talking with neighbors about baseball. A bounce is in the air on Sundays that's absent the other six days. The crowds are more expectant; they're keener and more perceptive of all the things around them.

And if you're the first Negro to play for a Sunshine Circuit team, Sunday is a bad time to have a lousy day.

In the second inning Dittmer's leadoff batter scorched a ground ball through the hole between short and third. Percy dove, lunging to the full limit of his thirty-five-inch arm, but the ball glanced off the tip of his glove, and as it trickled into the outfield, the scorer charged him with his first error of the season. He picked himself up, dusting the red clay from his uniform while a dozen fans screamed tired, but pointed insults.

In the bottom of the same inning, with Taylor on second, Percy was fooled by a curve ball and caught looking at strike three. The name-calling went one level louder. In the fifth Percy struck out again, and like a gathering storm, the name-calling grew stronger. Then, in the eighth, with two men on and with the Bobcats down by a run, he popped up to the second baseman and "Back to nigger school" poured from every part of the stadium.

But it was different this time. There was not, in the tenor of this crowd, the undiluted malice that had inspired the crowds before them. This seemed more like Sunday afternoon fun; like an amusement they all shared. With all that had been in the news, with my editorial from a week ago, and with worry swirling at the surface of their everyday lives—these fans just needed a place to vent. Percy was black, he had gone 0 for 3 and committed an error, and it never occurred to most of the white fans that he might have feelings. Today, it was as if someone opened a valve, as if gas, seconds before an explosion, spewed free. There was a whoosh, a purge, a sudden rush … and then it was over.

After my work was done for the day, the three of us trooped down the tire-worn aisle of the stadium lot. I was roughing up Chris's hair, and we tossed a ball back and forth, making our way to the car. In the distance a familiar voice called, "Mr. Hall, Mr. Hall." I turned and found Walter Jackson. He and Roberta were across the street at the armory waiting for Percy, who, just then, appeared at the side door with his bag slung across his shoulder. The three of them started in our direction. Walter's grin was a magnet coaxing me in theirs. As they came nearer, I could sense Rose Marie squirm. She took hold of my hand. "We really ought to be getting home," she said.

In another moment we stood in the Memorial Stadium parking lot, family to family: Walter in front of me, Roberta face-to-face with Rose Marie, and Percy across from Chris.

"Tough day," I said to Percy.

Walter shoved both hands into his back pockets. "Whew," he said, "we are glad this day's done. Hope to never see the likes of it again."

Roberta rubbed Percy's arm. Slowly but steadily, she shifted her weight from left foot to right, and then back again, her eyes damp.

Rose Marie stood quietly, looking down, or away, or up to the sky. I introduced her to the Jacksons, and you would've thought, by the way she labored to shake their hands, that we had greeted a family infected with the mumps, measles, *and* polio.

"Everybody has a bad day," I offered. "You'll be back."

Roberta took a deep breath, shuddering slightly, and hid her face behind Percy.

Walter clapped his son on the back and flashed a grin. "That's right," he said. "Ain't a ballplayer alive who hadn't had a day like that. That's why the good Lord makes tomorrows."

Roberta leaned her head into Percy, gripping his arm, sniffing. Lightly, Walter touched her shoulder and said, "It'll be okay. Yeah," he soothed her, "everything's going to be just fine."

She raised her head nodding yes and reached into her purse for a tissue. She dabbed at the tears and touched it gently to her nose. Then she slowly rubbed her son's back and shoulder.

"A hard day for you is much harder than it is for us," Rose Marie said, speaking to Roberta Jackson.

Roberta pressed her lips together and bowed her head again, appreciatively.

"I'm real sorry for the way people treat your boy," Rose went on. She glanced at Percy, and then put her arm around Chris. "I know that must be very hard."

Roberta dabbed at her eyes again and said, "Thank you, ma'am."

Chapter 18

Through the long glass panes of the diner, I spotted Dick Reeves in the third booth from the door, head down and jotting notes on a white paper napkin. I slid into the opposite seat and Helen appeared, as if from thin air, armed with dual pots of Whitney's most revered coffee. Dick laid his pen aside and we began with small talk about weather that was getting too hot, and kids who were growing too fast. And then, about the time our coffee had cooled, Helen reappeared, this time with plates full of eggs, and grits, and biscuits, and thick strips of crisp bacon. Dick scraped three pats of butter onto the grits, and then, reaching for the salt, he eased into the morning's main topic.

"So," he said, "it's been a few days, you got any new thoughts on our Negro situation?"

I shook my head no and rehashed what I'd said before; that I thought it'd all work out, and that everybody ought to just stay calm. Dick grinned, and with his fork poised in the air halfway between us, he said, "That's why everybody likes you, you're always looking on the bright side." He held his cup out to Helen for a refill and repeated what he'd said—about not leaving things up to governors and mayors.

I took the bait. "So what do you have in mind?" I asked.

Dick said that he'd been kicking it around with Burt and Joe. "We talked for a good eight innings the other day—you know—about what it'd take to keep everybody calm." He blew on the hot coffee and slurped it cautiously. "And the more we talked," he said, "the more one thing became clear." His eyes turned up to meet mine. "The best thing for everybody is to keep things the way they are." He brought his cup down to the table. "So before a bunch of people get all worked up, we got to let the colored folks know there ain't a whole lot for them to gain by pressing this thing—but there's sure enough plenty to lose."

I mopped at my plate with a scrap of biscuit. "How you figure," I asked, "that there's not much for them to gain?"

Dick leaned toward me. "Just think about it," he said. "For one thing, everybody who works in the colored schools'll be out of a job. Your buddy down there—Jackson's old man—you really think he's gonna teach white kids in our school?" Dick rolled his eyes. "All the teachers and principals, they're the ones who run that neighborhood, the ones everybody looks up to. Even if they could keep a job they'll go from top of the heap to bottom of the barrel—just like that." Dick snapped his fingers.

"Hadn't really thought about it," I said, "but I s'pose that's likely."

"And the colored kids," Dick went on, "they ain't gonna be able to keep up. The classes'll get bigger, and that ain't good for nobody, but it's gonna be a whole lot harder on them." He paused for a bite of eggs and grits.

"So what do you want to do?" I asked.

He poked at his food, and looking down at his plate he said, "Here's what I'm thinking: First, we need to let folks down there know we care about 'em. I mean we got to make 'em understand that we honest to goodness want to do what's best."

"Uh-huh," I muttered, "and exactly how are they supposed to come to this conclusion?"

"These folks got common sense," Dick said, "and mixing the schools—nobody 'round here thinks that's a good idea, not really. They got to hear the truth." Dick raised his fork again. "But I believe they got to hear it from their own kind, from the folks down there who've been looking out for 'em all along."

I tore off a piece of biscuit and popped into my mouth. "Well, that'd be nice," I said, "if you could get any of them to do it."

Dick set his fork down. Then, sounding like a coach who'd just come up with a surefire play, he said, "Here's how we go about that. Right now I'm trying to get everybody together—all the businessmen, I mean—and I'm gonna tell 'em that it's up to us to put an end to this."

"Uh-huh. And you're going to do this … how?"

"For openers," he continued, "we get to the right people down there, and we make 'em listen. We help them see this thing right." He leaned forward again. "And we ought to do it," he said, "not because we don't like the colored folks, but because we do."

"All right," I muttered, trying to follow. "And exactly who are the right people?"

Dick backed up against the wall and propped his feet on the bench. "We start with Chester," he said. "We get every storeowner in town to advertise on that old boy's radio station. We all buy ads," he said gleaming, "more than he's ever seen in his life, and we keep at it for as long as he keeps folks thinking right. Then we do the same thing for that fella who puts out the little weekly newspaper. We treat these boys right. We make them a part of what's going on around town—and they make sure all their neighbors understand just how good they really got it."

"Interesting idea," I granted, "but even if you can buy these guys off, you still got Phil Edwards to deal with."

Dick cringed. "You gotta understand something," he complained, "this ain't about buying anybody off. We're just helping 'em to see the facts."

Then he squirmed and frowned. "But you're right about Edwards. And that's exactly why we got to get to these other boys. We can't leave this up to Phil. We go to—"

"But you got to get to the churches," I cut in, "they pull more weight than the radio station or that little paper. And Edwards—whether you like it or not—he pretty much is the church down there."

"Yeah, I know," Dick said, "and we'll talk to him; we'll see what happens. But if he's blind to the facts … well then, we'll have to get behind some of the others down there." Dick sat back and rubbed his face wearily. "I like Phil," he muttered, "always thought he was one of the good ones. But if this mixing bug's bit him … well then, I reckon we'll just have to rearrange the power."

"Rearrange the power?" This time I leaned across the table. "He *is* the power down there," I said. "How you gonna rearrange something you don't have?"

Dick glanced up at me, amused. "We got plenty of power." He winked.

"And let me tell you something: There ain't a thing in this world we'd rather do than share it with the good Negroes down there—you know—with the ones who'll use it to do what's best."

I offered a puzzled frown, and Dick, looking like a kind teacher with a slow child, said, "Listen, we're gonna grab some attention down there and we're gonna help those folks see a few simple facts. We might make a donation here and there—you know—get a building project going at a church or something. We get a couple of pastors to some planning meetings; give 'em a real good spot on a committee. And you know what?" He slapped the table. "I betcha we can get their picture in the paper standing alongside the mayor."

Dick smiled. And I sat there dumbly, trying to get a grasp on the scope of his plan.

That wasn't all. Dick's plan also included putting a bunch of money in the colored school. He had talked to Burt, the city council, and the school board. "Everybody's willing to do whatever they can." And Joe was sure that it'd be easy to raise all kinds of private money. "It's a good cause." Dick grinned. "And folks are generous when the cause is right. We get the colored schools up to par and everybody's gonna be just fine."

He took a long gulp from his bright yellow mug, and then looked away—at the waitresses flitting from table to table, and at our friends fueling up for the new day. "But we gotta get with the folks who work down there," he said, "the teachers, the principals." He turned back to me. "Somebody they trust has got to tell 'em that if the Supreme Court gets its way, they're all gonna lose their jobs."

I swirled the coffee in my half-empty cup. "And you're thinking this is where I fit in?"

He nodded. "From what I hear, you and Mr. Jackson get along real good. And to tell you the truth, Jack, I think that's just fine. Who knows, maybe there's been a reason for it all along. Maybe it's been a part of the bigger plan, you know, for such a time as this."

I frowned. Dick pushed his plate aside, and looking more earnest than a graveside preacher, he said, "Listen, if I had a friend down there, I mean, if there was somebody I honest to goodness cared about, I'd do what I'm asking you to do. I really would. Right now I believe I'm asking you to be this man's friend."

Everything Dick said made sense, and he was a good man who, as far as I'd ever known, had always done the right thing, and done it for the right reasons. But this was new ground. This was a thing we'd never faced before, and the line between right and wrong had become faint and hard to find. Something about this conversation pinched like an old suit that didn't fit anymore. And as I walked to the office I couldn't shake the nagging sense that I'd never quite fit into my own life again. Nevertheless, late that afternoon, I asked William to give Walter a message. "No rush," I said to the janitor, "just tell him the next time he's at the stadium to meet me behind the visitor's dugout after the game. I'll find him."

◆ ◆ ◆ ◆

That night we played Kingstown, and Nat Quaid, one of the other Negroes in the league, was in the lineup. In the past five games, Quaid had collected eight hits in twenty chances. On a club whose team average had yet to crack .250, that had earned him a spot as an everyday player. I watched him take a few cuts in the batting cage, and after seeing him drill five straight pitches to the left-field wall, I pitied Sam Fowler, tonight's starter, who'd have to figure this kid out in a hurry.

When Nat relinquished the cage, I wandered out toward right field where Percy was warming up with Giles and Taylor. I did my best to manufacture an innocent smile, and then, with all the sincerity I could feign, I reminded Freddie that the last time he'd faced Rick Hardy, Kingstown's starter, he'd gone 0 for 4. Taylor's eyes promptly flooded with the hope that lightning would fry the spot where I stood, and he was quick with a comeback, instantly reminding me that the last time he faced Hardy had also been the first time. "I got this guy figured now," he growled, "and there ain't gonna be any oh-fors tonight."

"You ain't in the lineup?" Giles teased.

Freddie sneered. “You’ll see,” he said as he tossed the ball to Percy. “Both you losers, you’ll see.”

I turned to Giles, who couldn’t contain a sly grin, and mentioned that Kingstown’s offense had come alive; that they’d averaged more than five and a half runs in their last five games. Jimmy lobbed the ball to Percy. “Yeah,” he said, the smirk lingering, “key to these guys right now is that new boy, Quaid. If we can keep their nigger off the bases, well then,” Jimmy figured, “we’ll be all right.”

Percy’s arms collapsed at his sides and he flung daggers at Giles. “I ain’t believing that,” he flared.

Jimmy spun around, rattled. “What?” he blurted, the smile suddenly gone. “What are you talking about?”

Percy turned away, shaking his head, and tossed the ball to Taylor. Giles appealed to the first baseman. “What’s with him?” he asked. Freddie turned aside and spit, shrugging.

With his eyes still blazing, Percy answered for him. “You call Nat a nigger and you ain’t standing fifty feet away.” He zipped the ball to Taylor and you could hear his irritation in the unexpected pop of Freddie’s glove. “You call him nigger, that ain’t no different than calling me nigger.”

The ball floated back to Jimmy. “Well …” he stammered “… I-I-I guess you’re right. Sorry, Perce, just didn’t think about it.”

Taylor launched a second wad of brown spit to the ground. “Ain’t nothing to worry about,” he consoled Giles, “let’s just throw.”

This was the first time in Sunshine Circuit history that Negro players would start for both teams. The bleachers were packed tighter than a buffet line on all-you-can-eat Tuesday. Hundreds of black fans had again streamed onto the field. From the press box, as the ushers herded them back into foul territory, I thought about how everything looked and felt different. The spring air was as appealing as it had ever been. The sounds and smells were just as inviting. The promise of a thrill was still keen. But as I watched the ushers corral unruly strays, I longed for the game I'd always known; for easygoing fans, and for nights when the heaviest thought on anybody's mind was whether we'd pull through in the ninth.

Percy and Nat had both fulfilled their promise. They'd brought this new throng, and the throng had brought salvation to the league. But baseball in the Deep South had become messy and surreal, and on nights like this I felt trapped in a restless dream.

For the better part of the next three hours both boys felt the wrath of white fans. Percy was batting sixth in our order, Nat hit third in theirs, which meant that one of them was up almost every inning. Percy went 2 for 4 and was impeccable in the field. Quaid was good too, going 1 for 3 and drawing a walk in the sixth. He caught three fly balls, and in our half of the third he nailed Andrews at second when Johnny dared his untested arm.

Throughout the night, every time the colored fans cheered, my thoughts veered to the left-field bleachers. I wondered again why they had all come. An assortment of thoughts straggled through my mind, but by the fourth inning I suspected this: They came to see with their own eyes that a colored man was a white man's equal. These people had spent their whole lives tucked away in a tiny corner of a no-account town where Jackie Robinson and Willie Mays were never more than faint images on the tiny TV at Rodney's Barbershop. They were names on the radio, or grainy figures in the *Whitney Herald*, but nobody in the colored bleachers had ever seen them. Nobody had ever spoken to them, or touched them, or knew their kid sisters by name. Black fans thronged to Memorial Stadium to see if a boy from their own town could play even up with the white kids.

By the seventh inning it dawned on me that these two boys—one eighteen, the other nineteen—carried a burden no white player had ever lifted. Percy and Nat, and the recent news, teased the colored crowd with notions of new things the world might one day offer. And like kids at Christmas, they rushed to the ballpark, longing to unwrap the gift that would make life grand. That night a pair of colored kids ran faster, hit harder, and threw better than most of the other men around them. They showed the hometown crowd what Robinson, Mays, and Doby had already shown the world. For half the crowd they were a prophecy of the new life to come. The other half watched too, but they were certain that neither boy belonged, confident that Negroes and whites were as different as cats from lions, utterly convinced that segregation was the way of the world—and not a thing with which man should trifle.

I was the last one to leave the press box that night, and was on my way to the locker room when I caught sight of Walter Jackson. I hadn't expected to see him so soon, hadn't rehearsed what I wanted to say. A pang of dread stabbed me. I glanced around, hoping to find some way of escape. But then second thoughts came to the rescue, and I started down the stadium steps calling his name. He turned, and when he grinned, it was as if someone had flipped the switch on a beacon to light the path between us. We grabbed a pair of handy seats and eased in to a conversation about the history we'd just seen. The talk flowed as freely as the river beside us, the way it always does with a well-worn friend, and I hated to change the subject. But it was late, and I knew that Walter was anxious. And so, without giving much thought to a smooth transition, I asked what his friends thought about the Supreme Court.

He shifted in his seat, looking like somebody had stuck a pebble into his back pocket. He said that some people thought it was the best news they'd ever heard, but most weren't so sure. They were nervous, Walter said; they knew that white folks weren't happy, and, "'round here," he said, "when white people get nervous, colored people got reason to get nervous too."

"What about the ones who think it's good news?" I asked.

For them, Walter said, this was the chance of a lifetime, an opportunity not to be missed no matter what the costs.

"What do you suppose that means?" I asked.

Walter couldn't say for sure, but he'd watched Phil Edwards work. The pastor was likely to gather up some key people, Walter guessed, and they'd organize the neighborhood street by street. He'd put the pressure on where he could. And one event at a time, one meeting at a time, one confrontation at a time—all orchestrated with battle-plan precision—"he'll start bangin' on schoolhouse doors."

I stared out to right field and thought about Dick Reeves. I could see him sitting at the diner saying, "I like Phil ... but if the mixin' bug's bit him…." Here were a pair of good men, I thought, both trying to do what's best, both organizing, making plans, arraying forces—and one was utterly opposed to the other.

Without glancing back, I said to Walter, "And what do you think?"

He sat up straight and folded his arms. "I don't like trouble," he replied, "you know that. I like to do what I can and not worry so much about what I can't. Got a wife and two kids. I got a job. And I'll be honest with you, I'm pretty happy with things just the way they are."

"You thought about what this would mean for you, if the colored kids went to white schools?"

There was a long pause. "Yes, sir, it's crossed my mind." Then he chuckled softly. "But I ain't losing sleep over it just yet." He lingered on the thought, and then the chuckle trailed away. "But yes, sir," he said, "I have thought about it."

We talked about what it would be like if South City High faded away. It'd no longer be a place where friends and families gathered, where moms and dads watched their kids learn and play. Teachers would no longer be neighbors, and the current of life would begin to flow north. "It'd change the way we live," Walter reflected, trying to picture his part of town without its schools. "I'm not sure everybody's really thought about it: The ball games, PTA, kids hanging out at the dime store, running after-school errands to the butcher shop—I think we'd miss that."

I let the silence lay there for a while. Then I asked, "Is it worth it? For you, I mean. Is this a thing you want to see happen?"

Walter propped his feet on the seat in front of him. "Tell you the truth, Mr. Hall, I'm not sure what I think really matters. If it were up to me, I'd leave well enough alone. The way I see it, if a man don't want me in his school, I'll go to my own school. He don't want me in his movie theater, I'll go to my own theater." He looked down, resting his chin on his chest. "But some of the young folks coming up, I'm not sure they see things the same way. And sooner or later, it's them we got to be concerned about."

"So you'd like to see things stay the way they are? Is that what you're telling me?"

Walter scanned the field, peered into the dugout, and then looked back toward third base. Finally, and just above a whisper, he said, "Yes, sir, most of the time." He sat quietly for a second or two. "But every now and again …" He made a quarter turn in my direction. "Mixing the schools is a terrible idea," he said, "for all the reasons we just talked about. But …" His voice faded and he looked away.

"But …?" I prodded.

"Let me ask you something," he said. Then, sweeping his hand across the diamond, he posed a question: "You think the Bobcats are better with Percy, or without him?"

"That's more complicated than it sounds," I replied. "On the field they're better, there's no doubt about that. But in the locker room, in the stands … it's harder to say."

Walter stroked his chin. "I understand," he said, "but on the field, they're better. You'd say that a colored boy caused the baseball team to play better baseball, am I right?"

I nodded. "Yeah, that's right."

"That's the problem," he said, "that's the one thing…." He bent forward, folding his hands between his knees. "You ask me if I want to mix the schools, and the answer is no. That ain't gonna mean nothing but trouble, especially for Negroes. But then I think about this team and about what we saw here tonight. I mean, right here we watched a pair of integrated baseball teams, and you and I both know they're better for it. And no matter how hard I try, I can't get that out of my mind."

The grounds crew began raking the field and gathering up the bases. In a quiet, distant tone, Walter said, "You ever think that maybe other things would get better too?"

I didn't reply.

Walter continued, "Mixing kids in the schools—there ain't a dozen people 'round here who honest to goodness want that. But way in the back of my mind, I keep thinking that maybe—I don't know—maybe it could make things better." I saw no smile or any trace of the Walter Jackson glimmer. "I don't know. I try not to dwell on it."

We talked about what was likely to happen in the next days, weeks, and months. We'd read the same news, heard the same talk from governors and congressmen, and we both believed we'd flip two-dozen pages on the calendar before a colored kid got close to Jefferson Davis High. Then I told him about Dick Reeves. I explained that the mayor's brother wanted to raise money for South City; that he wanted to buy books, start a library, and give the teachers a raise. Struck by the shameless irony, Walter grinned. "Well," he chuckled, "nice to see folks so concerned about Negro education."

"Look," I told him, "if you go along with him, you keep your job, the school gets a lot of stuff it needs, and who knows, in the end maybe everybody's better off."

"Yes, sir," Walter murmured, "I suppose that could be." We sat quietly for a moment, and then he asked, "So why exactly are we here, Mr. Hall? I'm guessing there's something you'd like me to do?"

"Yeah," I said, "and it's real simple. Just let the other teachers know that this can work out for the best—for them, for the kids, for the schools."

"So long as we all go along with Mr. Reeves."

I put a hand on the back of my friend's seat and leaned close. "Listen," I said, "and this is just between you and me, but if I were in your shoes, I'd play this for all it's worth. If they offer you five hundred books, tell 'em you've got to have six hundred. If they offer you a 5 percent raise, ask for ten. You don't have to go along with everything he says. You just gotta keep the white schools white. And like we just said, that ain't likely to change anytime soon."

Walter pressed a finger to his lips. He, too, had to ponder the changes to our once steady lives, but before he could think for too long a voice called out, "We're ready." Percy and Nat Quaid ambled toward us, back from the armory where they'd showered and changed. At the sight of them Walter swelled up and glowed. "Now that was some fine baseball out there tonight," he boomed, "'bout as fine as I've ever seen." The boys grinned and looked away, embarrassed.

I reached over the brick wall to introduce myself to Nat. "Mr. Jackson's right," I said, "you guys looked real good."

"Well …" Walter slapped his hands on his knees "… there's some dinner waiting for you boys at home. I s'pect we best be heading on."

"You staying with the Jacksons?" I asked Nat.

He nodded yes and Walter added, "We're mighty glad to have him. His folks were real good to Percy last time we were in Kingstown."

"Well, that's real nice," I said, happy to know that both boys had a place to stay where they felt at home, and where weird old women wouldn't steal the fan.

I drove home with Walter's words rattling around my mind, and I pondered the absurdity of the thought that schools, or businesses, or anything else might be better by mixing races. And then I laughed out loud, thinking that only Walter Jackson, with his kindly smile and benign manner, could have gotten away with suggesting that sharecroppers, janitors, and maids might improve man's more serious work in the world. But then again, there was only one place where it had ever been tried in plain view. Baseball. In grandstands and locker rooms the formula had proved to be temperamental, and at times explosive. But Percy and Nat, and a hundred others in every part of the country had proved that colored kids could play. And almost every team who had signed Negro players—in the big leagues and the minors—was better than they'd been before.

The thought still seemed preposterous, but for an instant, for whatever fragment of time is less than a split second, I thought that maybe I was blind to a truth that was plainly visible.

◆ ◆ ◆ ◆

The next night Walter and I visited again. He had decided he'd let the other teachers know what Dick Reeves had in mind. "But I want to be very clear," he insisted, "I'm doing this for the school and the kids. I don't mean no disrespect, but please let Mr. Reeves know that I'll do what's best for our kids. But what's best today," he said solemnly, "may not be best tomorrow."

On my way to work the next morning I swung by Reeves Department Store and repeated to Dick what Walter Jackson had told me. Dick clinched a fist. "Perfect," he proclaimed, "this is perfect. And you let him know, you give that old boy every assurance in the whole wide world that we're on the same page, everybody's wantin' to do what's best."

Three days later Dick Reeves gathered a host of influential men together, and in the Stonewall Jackson auditorium they pledged to keep Whitney peaceful and prosperous. They vowed to look out for their neighbors, to do what was right, and, by every peaceful means possible, to preserve the only way of life that any of us had ever known.

◆ ◆ ◆ ◆

Within two weeks Chester LaBarr's radio station had sold every minute of airtime it owned, and Reeves Department Store had become its biggest client. The South Town Weekly, with a circulation around two thousand five hundred, expanded from twelve pages to sixteen, and ran full-page ads from Whitney Western Auto, Woolworth's, and Reeves Department Store. And the colored-owned media never whispered a word about the Supreme Court of the United States.

In early June the governor called an emergency session of the state legislature, and by a unanimous vote they vowed to abolish the public schools if the federal government showed the first sign of enforcing the Court's edict. They'd free citizens to divert tax money to private schools, leaving the poor with no options. By nine o'clock the next morning our county school board, at Burt's prompting, offered Negro teachers a 3 percent raise. And by ten thirty the teachers had eagerly accepted. The *Herald* ran a front-page story announcing the deal, and any thought of mixing races in the Whitney public schools was put to rest for the coming year.

Dick and Burt Reeves walked tall, like new men, relieved, and in control of their town. The weight of unbearable responsibility appeared to have been lifted from Joe Anderson's shoulders. And the whole town seemed to heave a collective sigh.

In the weeks that followed, the school board and the Whitney Chamber of Commerce invaded the south side of town with a benevolent form of the same determination that Sherman took to Atlanta. The Monday after the school year ended, painters, carpenters, and plumbers headed out to the Negro schools, a citywide book drive quickly amassed old volumes for their libraries, and every kind of ball, bat, and athletic shoe appeared in the South City locker room.

Chester LaBarr and the publisher of the *South Town News* both took notice, and both lavished high praise on the sudden improvements.

Chapter 19

The Bobcats now led the league by three games, and it looked as though a handful of our guys were on their way to career seasons: Sam Fowler led the league in wins, Haddock sported the circuit's best ERA—a flashy 2.40. Our outfield looked as good as any I'd ever seen, covering ground like the seven seas cover the earth. They were smart, too, and they all had bazookas for arms.

Denny Douglas had discovered his game and was quickly becoming the player Charley envisioned when he saw him for the first time two seasons before. His batting average had climbed to .270. He could throw lightning bolts while still in his crouch, and even the fastest men on the other seven teams lived in fear of our jovial catcher. Only the brave or stupid even dreamed of stealing bases.

But Percy Jackson had been the biggest shock to the Sunshine Circuit's system. Against all odds, and to the dismay of almost everyone, he now paraded a .347 batting average, leading the league by a spacious twenty-three points. A league full of pitchers helped him, all who suffered a collective form of incurable denial—who refused to believe statistics and scouting reports—and who, in acts of inconceivably poor judgment, continued to throw him strikes. But even those with better sense hadn't figured him out. And for reasons that went far deeper than his dark complexion, he'd become a troublesome guest in the other seven stadiums where he wore out the league's best arms.

Things were going our way, and the Bobcats swaggered into Madison for a four-game series—the esprit de corps that had taken root in Clayton continued to blossom, and it was wrapping itself around Percy Jackson like kudzu on a sapling pine. The other players, with only a few exceptions, now shared water buckets with him, sat beside him, and welcomed him into their everyday conversation. In mid-May, Giles had called a team meeting and asked the players to ban the word "nigger" from the locker room, dugout, bus, and field. His motion passed with only five objections. In every town where the Bobcats played, Percy was barred by ordinance from locker rooms, motels, and restaurants. But one play at a time, one at bat at a time, one game at a time, he had become a full-fledged member of the Sunshine Circuit's best team.

◆ ◆ ◆ ◆

One thing I knew we could all use was a change of scenery, and Madison is one of the world's most beautiful towns. It enchants its guests, captivating them with the South's winsome charm from the moment they ease past the city-limits sign. Century-old mansions grace the outskirts. Magnolias and live oaks laced with Spanish moss border the streets, creating a landscape that's more delightful than any artist could ever imagine. Two of the best restaurants I've ever known are there. They specialize in delicacies that no Frenchman or Italian has ever savored: green tomatoes, catfish, hush puppies, and jambalaya that the chefs of New Orleans envy. And best of all, twelve miles from the center of town, standing guard at a pivotal bend in the river, is a Confederate fort where my son's imagination has yet to find its limit.

Within this town's embrace the three of us had enjoyed a full day by the time we arrived at the ballpark, and the game was a respite we all needed. Chris had come alive at Fort Polk, traveling back to another time where he was surrounded by gallantry, defending the homeland's noble cause—unthreatened by neighborhood kids who, goaded by nervous parents, had labeled him a "nigger lover." And Rose Marie had escaped too, distracted by the charm of Madison's town square, by quaint shops, and by the freedom to stroll where nobody lurked around the next corner waiting to give a lecture on Percy Jackson. By the seventh inning we'd be exhausted, but the day had been worth the wear. Our troubles had faded, taken leave in Madison's charms.

Hank Wheeler was in the press box when I got there. Neal Bates, the PA announcer, was there too. And Jerry Atkins, the scorer, was perched beside him, both men nursing a cup of the beer that made Milwaukee famous. With the Mocs quickly fading from contention, the mood was light. There was beer and bourbon to go around, lavishly garnished with wisecracks and well-seasoned wit. I was surrounded by guys I liked, by men who all loved the same rituals, who were drawn to baseball by the same instinct that propels birds south in winter. We were kindred souls, gathered in the place where we felt most comfortable.

Percy came up in the second inning. With no score and with nobody on, he drilled the first pitch four hundred feet to left field, but foul. He fouled off the second pitch, too, back toward the press box a few rows below us. Neither pitch had fooled him, but he was behind in the count, and not likely to see another strike anytime soon. The Madison catcher set up outside and a third fastball swooped away, well off the plate. I glanced down to mark my scorebook and heard a surprised "ooh" rise from the crowd. There was a mysterious round of applause, and I glanced up and saw Percy frozen in the box. Charley suddenly rushed up the steps of the dugout and stood there with both arms clamped around his chest, glaring toward home. I realized that Percy had been called out; the ump had rung him up on a pitch that was nowhere near the strike zone.

I looked down at Chris and Rose Marie. Chris was on his feet, both hands on his head, staring at the ump in disbelief.

"Might've got a break there, huh, Jack," Hank Wheeler said with a grin.

"Yeah," I said, "close one there."

Percy came up again in the fourth, still no score, but this time Billy Henderson was on first. Percy sent a slow two-hopper to the left side of the diamond. The third baseman broke quickly and threw to second for the force. The second baseman wheeled and threw to first. Percy lunged for the bag and beat a good throw by a split second, barely avoiding the double play. The ump, standing where the second baseman normally plays, paused and stared. Then he pointed at the base; he theatrically threw up his right hand and declared Percy out. I slammed a pencil to the desk. Hank Wheeler rocked back in his seat and cried, "Good grief."

Chris had covered his face with his hands and was shaking his head back and forth in misery. He turned to his mom, incredulous, finding it impossible to believe that two umps could be that bad.

In the home team's half of the same inning Madison's cleanup man blasted a line drive directly at Percy's nose. Fueled by instinct and adrenaline, Percy threw up his hands, and the crowd gasped as the ball grazed his glove on its way to the left-field warning track. The ump called time, and Fowler and Eddie Smith rushed over, hoping he wasn't hurt. Percy got to his knees, then slowly to his feet, taking inventory of his body parts and making sure they were all in working order. As he regathered his wits, Jerry Atkins shook his head and mumbled, "Boy shoulda had it," and assigned an error to the Bobcats third baseman.

I looked at Jerry as if he'd just bestowed sainthood on Joseph Stalin. He glanced at me out of the corner of his eye, tossed me a stiff smirk, and said, "What can I do, Jack, the ball hit him right in the glove."

"He's lucky he's got his teeth," I gasped. "For crying out loud, Jerry, the ball about took his head off!" I looked at Wheeler, who was staring out to the field, about to chew off a good-sized chunk of his lower lip.

◆ ◆ ◆ ◆

In the motel room that night Chris was wide-awake and storming back and forth from door to balcony, jabbering ceaselessly about the assault on Percy Jackson. "They got it in for him, everybody—they're all out to get him. It's just not fair."

His mother tried to console him. "Umpires can have a bad night too."

Chris plunged his face into both hands, shaking his head miserably. "Nobody's that bad, Mom. They just don't want him around, that's all." He flopped onto his rollaway bed, reimagining the shady calls and magnifying each one in memories that would last his lifetime. "The fans are always screaming at him; now the umps are cheating him." Chris stared at the motel-room ceiling. "It's not right. He's never hurt anybody."

Rose Marie sat on the bed beside him, sad-eyed and dispirited. "We've talked about this, honey, about Negroes and white people playing together. It's not the way we do things, Chris. It's not the way things are supposed to be, and people are having a hard time. We've been over this, remember?"

"Yes, ma'am," Chris answered. "But still, he didn't deserve all that."

"You're right, pal. But your mom's right too," I said. "It's going to take a long time for people to get used to seeing Percy out there. And a lot of them never will, that's just the way it is." I sat beside him. "We're going to have to be patient."

Chris looked up, trying to understand something that made no sense to a boy who hadn't yet been schooled in the world's ways. "I wish we could have left things the way they were," I told him. "And I wish Percy didn't have to go through any of this. But I think he's going to be fine."

Fatigue finally overcame him. His face softened and his eyes began to droop. "Baseball matters, pal. It's a beautiful and glorious game. It's fun to watch, it's good for moms and dads and kids to go to games together. Percy's playing great," I said softly, "he's keeping the team alive, and he's not hurting a soul. People just need time to see it, even the umps."

◆ ◆ ◆ ◆

The next night Percy came to the plate in the top of the first. The Bobcats had already scored twice and were poised for a big inning with runners at second and third. The first pitch was good, a fastball no more than an inch off the outside corner—a called strike. The next pitch was good too, a little farther outside—called strike two. Percy backed away. He knocked dirt from his cleats and looked down, mumbling—probably to himself, but loud enough for the ump to hear—that he couldn't catch a break on a close call. He shed his cap and wiped away the sweat, then stepped to the plate. The third pitch was way outside, and Percy backed away again. He lifted the bat over his head and twisted right and left to get limber. The ump, in a climactic gesture, punched the air with his right hand, emphatically proclaiming strike three. The inning was over.

Whitney's hopes for more early runs had been dashed by a terrible call. And the league's best hitter stood there, as still as James Madison's statue in the town square, baffled by what had just happened.

As the Bobcats trotted onto the field, Charley streaked for the plate. His face throbbed like overheated coals, and he launched a blistering attack on the home-plate ump. The ump stood calmly, a willing sponge for Charley's wrath, barely offering any resistance. Charley screamed; he flailed at the air, bullying the ump and doing his best to force a fight, or at least an explanation. But the umpire took the beating—meekly—without protest or retribution.

In the fourth inning Madison had men on first and second with one out. The batter sent a crisp ground ball between short and third, and Percy was all over it. At the crack of the bat the runner on second broke. Percy flung his glove to the left and brushed his jersey for one out; then he threw to first for the slickest double play I'd seen all season. But as the Bobcats loped toward the dugout, the infield umpire motioned frantically that Percy had missed the tag. In the same instant the home-plate ump signaled that the throw to first was late. Both runners were safe. The bases were now loaded. And Jerry Atkins charged Percy with a throwing error.

Charley skidded to the top step again and rage poured off him like heat from a blacktop on an August afternoon.

◆ ◆ ◆ ◆

The next night, early in the game, Percy sent a line drive deep to the left-field gap. He raced for first, and then made a wide turn, barreling for second, sliding hard to the inside of the bag, beating the throw by a step and a half. The umpire was in perfect position. He saw Percy's foot hit the bag. He could not have missed the late tag. Yet, with Shakespearian flair, he threw his thumb high into the air and screamed, "Got him!"

I creased my lips so tight they hurt. Hank was as mystified as I was by what he'd seen. He shot a puzzled frown toward Jerry, who sat calmly and offered no reaction.

◆ ◆ ◆ ◆

On our way back to Whitney, Chris complained that the umps had gone crazy. His mother turned to him in the backseat and said, "They had an awful series, there's no getting around that."

"Only when it came to Percy," Chris charged. "The rest of the time they were fair."

Rose Marie glanced toward me. "What do you suppose is going on, Hall? What are they up to?"

Before I had time to reply, Chris scoffed loudly, "They're trying to run him off. That's what the two guys behind us were saying."

Rose put her hand out her window and watched it glide in the wind. "Why doesn't he just go, Jack? This can't be fun for him; it can't be a bit of fun for his poor family." She watched the scenery pass for a while. Then she said, "I feel so sorry for that boy's mother—she must get her heart broken every night."

◆ ◆ ◆ ◆

From Madison the Bobcats traveled to Fulton, and in the third inning of the first game, Percy chased a pop fly deep into foul territory. He sprinted after the ball as fast as he could. At the last second he dove, plowing a five-foot row of dirt and overgrown grass with his chest, knees, and elbows—but the ball bounced two feet in front of his glove. The scorer, sitting just two seats away from me, groaned, "Ohhh, that was close." He made this melodramatic tisking sound and shook his head. "Kid should've had it," he said, and charged Percy with his third error of the week.

In the next inning, with a full count, Percy leaned toward a pitch that was chin high and outside—and was called out on strikes.

The next night he fell victim to three more impossibly bad calls.

After the game I pulled into the ESSO station across from the stadium and waited for Doug Russ, the home-plate umpire. Ten minutes later he and his partner strolled out to the parking lot. Doug climbed into a baby blue Dodge and pulled away. Doing a bad imitation of

Dick Tracy, I tailed him to a steak house on the outskirts of town. From the fringe of the unpaved lot, I watched him go inside and wondered what I was going to do. I sat in the car long enough for Dean Martin to finish "That's Amore," then straggled into the bar and ordered a beer. I sat there, staring straight ahead, trying to imagine what I'd say to a good ump who was barely hiding the fact that he'd gone bad. Three-fourths of the way through the beer, I swiveled around on the bar stool and spotted both umps in a booth across the room. I downed one last gulp, banged the bottle down on the bar, and headed their way.

Umpires make a modest effort to keep their distance from coaches, players, and reporters, and we make a slender try to respect it, so both men were surprised to see me. A prophetic waitress plunked down three bottles of ice-cold Schlitz, and I grabbed a nearby chair, straddling it backward, staking claim to the head of the table.

For ninety minutes we ate and drank and talked easily about good teams and bad ones, about players who were having great years, and those who'd been disappointing. We rattled on effortlessly about guys who were on hot streaks, and those who were slumping. And despite the fact that the league's best hitter had just had the worst week of his rookie season, no one mentioned Percy's name.

◆ ◆ ◆ ◆

The next morning, spurred by a reporter's mistrustful nature, I called Brent Moore at the Leesburg Guardian and asked how Nat was playing. After a long pause on the Leesburg end of the line, Brent answered. "Last four or five games—they been a nightmare for that boy; things have been awful." The league's only other Negro starter, I learned, had made two throwing errors, he'd been called out on strikes four times, and couldn't seem to buy a call on the bases. "I don't like that boy being out there," Moore bristled, "but it's been ugly 'round here. They might as well've put an ad in the paper telling everybody they ain't gonna let him be any good."

The stench had become too strong to ignore, and I took a ride out to see Doug Russ. I got his room number from the desk clerk and rapped on the door. From the back of the room he hollered, "Hang on, be right there." Then, with a toothbrush dangling from his mouth, and wearing blue jeans and a St. Louis Cardinals T-shirt, Doug opened the door.

"Jack," he said hesitantly, "what're you doing here?"

"Got a second?" I asked.

Doug poked his head out the door and looked up and down the hallway. "I don't know, Jack, what are you up to?"

"Just want to talk, that's all."

"We don't do interviews," he said, "you know that."

"Oh, come on," I sneered, "you and I have talked hundreds of times."

"Yeah, but not in my motel room. And not the day after we had dinner together." He sneaked another peek down the hallway. "This doesn't look good, Jack."

"Well ..." I drawled "... there's a lot that doesn't look good these days."

For the third time in thirty seconds, Doug checked to see if anyone might be looking, then he stepped aside. "All right," he said, "what's on your mind?"

"Take a wild guess," I answered.

Doug didn't bother to bluff ignorance or innocence. He sat on the bed and motioned me to a chair. "Look," he said, "I'm not the guy you need to be talking to about this."

"Sure you are. You've been around the league for a while, and you might've missed a call here and there, but you've never done it on purpose—least not 'til now."

Doug ran a few fingers through his still-snarled hair. "You shouldn't be here," he grumbled. "You're a reporter; if you think I'm making bad calls, you're free to tell the whole dad-gum world. If you think I'm throwing games, well, you can say that, too. But we got no business having this conversation."

"If I knew an ump had gone bad, I'd blow the whistle in a heartbeat. But there's something else going on here, and it's all aimed at two guys." I stood up and paced the tiny room. "I don't know you that well, but I don't think you'd throw games; I can't believe you're on the take. So you gotta tell me, what's going on?"

Doug scooted up to the edge of the bed. "Listen," he said, and his eyes telegraphed meaning that went beyond the words, "if you got a problem with the umpiring, or if you don't like the scoring, you need to take it up with the league office." He inched farther forward. "You might even want to go to the president of the league."

"I never said anything about scoring," I replied. "Are you telling me Pete Fry is forcing umps to throw games?"

"No," Doug fired back. "As far as I know, nobody has ever deliberately changed the outcome of a game." He stood up and reached for the door, and with his hand wrapped around the handle, he said, "All I'm saying is, if you got questions about the umpiring, you ought to take it up with Pete."

I hurried back to my room and phoned Hank Wheeler. I told him that the league president might be pressuring umps and scorers to make Percy and Nat look bad.

"Yep," Wheeler agreed, "from what I got, it looks that way."

"What do you know?" I asked.

Hank laughed, but his tone was a blend of sarcasm and dejection. "You get anything from Fry's office in the mail lately?" he asked.

I thought for a minute. "My all-star ballot," I said, "that's the only thing I can think of."

"Bingo," Wheeler called. "Mystery solved."

On the Fourth of July the Sunshine Circuit all-stars play the best players from the Piedmont League. Managers and writers select the teams, and according to Wheeler's source, Pete Fry thought the voters needed help. He'd met with the umps and scorers, Wheeler said, and he told them all to do whatever they had to, to keep Jackson and Quaid out of the game.

"You gotta be kidding me," I cried, "that's the dumbest thing I've ever heard."

"Well, whether it is or not, that's what's going on."

"Who else knows about this?" I asked.

"Still checking," Wheeler replied.

"And you haven't talked to Fry?"

"Left messages, but haven't heard back."

"What are you going to do with this?" I asked.

"I don't know," Hank said. "I'm half expecting my editor to tell me to drop it. And with everything that's going on in the world right now, who knows, it might be best to look the other way."

The sheer wrongness of Fry's plan infuriated me, and I tramped back and forth—stewing in indignation—until my own small room couldn't contain the anger. I sped back to see Doug Russ. I pounded on the door, and the instant it opened, I told him that I had phoned Pete Fry. "He won't take the call," I raged, "but I know what's going on. I know he told you to keep Percy off the all-star team."

Doug stood in the doorway defending passage to his room. "I've already told you too much," he said. "You're gonna have to talk to somebody else."

"How'd all this happen?" I pressed him. "How'd a guy like you get roped into something this stupid?"

Russ stepped aside. He flopped down on the bed, kneading his forehead, trying to rub away his pain. "There's no good choice here. No matter what I do, something bad happens." He looked at me, hoping to find some sympathy. "You know what I mean, Jack?"

"No, I don't," I said. "As far as I can see, you got one choice: You either call the game the way you see it, or you don't. The other choices all belong to somebody else."

"It ain't anywhere near that easy," Doug argued.

I slumped into the plastic upholstered chair. "Why not?"

He leaned against the wall at the head of the bed and chuckled wryly. "You know I took this job the week before Jackie Robinson signed with the Dodgers. I knew those people were crazy," he said, "knew it'd be a disaster...." Doug stuffed a pillow behind his head, and then every reporter's dream came true: Without another word from me, his story began to flow like water through a burst dam.

Doug Russ, like everybody else I knew, never dreamed he'd see the day when Negroes played in the Sunshine Circuit. But when Percy and Nat came along, he did his best to be fair. "I warned them to stay calm," he said, "I told them they had to ignore all the guff they got from the crowd and the other players. But that's the only thing I ever did different." He paused for a second, collecting more thoughts. "I hate those boys being out there, Jack. Coloreds on the same field with white boys …" he tilted his head to the ceiling "… but I never treated them any different."

They seemed like nice enough boys, Doug thought, but when they stepped foot on the field, a sad, sinking feeling welled up inside. "Every time I see one of those boys trot out there," he said, "I get a twinge in the gut … like somebody just died. But I did my job."

Then Percy started knocking the cover off the ball. He attacked grounders like a boll weevil pounces on cotton. "Whenever I call one of your games," Doug marveled, "I can't believe that kid; can't believe he's that good."

Then he told me Pete Fry had started going town to town, gathering umpires and scorers together in closed meetings. "He thinks we've got to give the voters some help," Doug said, "and he knows it sounds wrong, knows it's got to rub us the wrong way, but we got to think about what's important here." He paused again, turning his palms toward the ceiling.

"And exactly what is important?" I prodded.

"Come on, Jack … a nigger on the all-star team?"

"He's the best third baseman we got," I said, "and probably the best player in the league."

We looked at one another, each waiting for the other to speak.

"Look, Jack," he finally said, "it just can't happen. You know that."

"So we're all gonna lie?" I said. "You're gonna make ridiculous calls; I'm going to report that he's making errors and striking out. And then we're all going to tell ourselves that the colored kids aren't any good? Maybe you can keep him off the all-star team. But you can't keep people from seeing the truth. We're not blind. We know he's good, and we all know this is a lie."

"Can you imagine what would happen?" Doug stammered. "Are we really gonna say that Jackson's better than the white kids? You gonna admit that?"

"A little hard-pressed to deny it," I said.

Doug looked away. "What's that gonna mean?" he asked. "What's that say to our kids? How do we explain that?"

"How do we explain that umpires cheat? You guys should've protected the game," I said. "You should've kept it clean."

"It ain't like we're on the take, Jack. Nobody's getting paid, nobody's in this for themselves."

"You're not taking money," I argued, "but you're cheating to get what you want, and you've tarnished the game. We'll never be able to look at it the same way again. Every time we see a bad call, we'll be wondering what you're up to."

"So what are you saying?" Doug flared. "You want your kid believing that a nigger's the best infielder we got; that he's better than the six white kids who play the same position?"

"I'm saying I want you to call the game right. It's up to you to protect the game, that's your job. And you know what? My kid already knows Percy's the best player in the league. And if you got a kid, he does too."

"You and those other teams, you signed these boys to bring in more money," he argued. "And you guys," he stabbed a finger at me, "you signed Jackson to keep that bigmouthed preacher off the mayor's back. You're the ones who used the game to get what you wanted. You weren't protecting baseball. You were trying to keep the niggers quiet. Well, Pete's trying to keep some white folks quiet. I'm not seeing a real big difference here."

"Then you need to look harder," I said. "The money Percy brings in keeps the team alive. Every white kid on the field is there because Percy Jackson brings fans. And yeah, Joe and Burt wanted to keep Phil Edwards from going crazy. But they didn't cheat anybody to do it."

"They cheated everybody," Russ sneered. "They brought this whole mess on. They did it to make their own lives easier, but instead they made things hard—they made 'em harder for every human being on the planet."

◆ ◆ ◆ ◆

The day after we got home, I went looking for Walter Jackson. School was out for the summer but teachers had a few more days to finish up, and I was sure that Walter would stick around for as long as it took to organize South City's new library. By the time I arrived, painters were already at work; green- and orange-splattered drop cloths covered the sidewalk, and long wooden ladders were propped against walls. Carpenters hammered and sawed somewhere in the distance. And a plumber's truck was backed up to the school's main entrance, its back doors swung wide for easy access to pipes, tools, and new fixtures.

I found Walter directing traffic in the gym, where book cartons were stacked two and three high in no evident order. Busy people swarmed the place, and each time they pried a box open, their eyes gaped wide with the discovery of new pearls. Intent teachers sat beside eager students in brown folding chairs organizing their new treasure by author's last name or Dewey decimal numbers. I caught Walter's eye, and he set his work aside. We met under the south goal and Walter placed a hand on my shoulder, the way a close friend silently conveys his thanks. As we made our way to the stands, a woman greeted me by name. Another grinned shyly, then quickly glanced away. Teachers discreetly caught my eye, and some dipped their heads vaguely in my direction. Even students ventured uncertain smiles—all believing, I guessed, that I bore some responsibility for their school's good fortune. This was the first time I'd ever been warmly received here. The smiles and frail gestures made the place feel more familiar, and the burden of being different was lighter than it had ever been before.

As Walter and I slid into the front row, I asked how Percy was holding up. Walter ran an open hand over the top of his head; he looked a little like Joe, frustrated beyond what words can describe.

"What's he saying about the umpires?" I asked.

"It's just one more thing," Walter huffed. He explained that Charley knew something was up, he knew that Percy was as good as he'd ever been.

"I'm sorry about all this," I said weakly.

"Yes sir," Walter replied, "and it's too bad, life was getting to be tolerable, you know, with the team." He scratched at his head again. "A boy gets a bunch of static from the crowd … well, he can play through that. But when the game itself turns on you—when the people making the rules turn against you—well, that's a different ball game." He leaned back, resting his elbows on the bench behind us. "This keeps up and our only hope is that Mr. Baxter can move him up north where he might get a fair shot."

"I hope this'll pass," I said. "And I'm guessing Charley wants to keep Percy here until he's sure it's time to move on."

"For a colored boy," Walter said, "I believe the time to move on's coming pretty quick." Walter puckered his lips. "Just don't make sense. Boy comes along and helps his team, does everything he's supposed to do, puts up with a lot of foolishness. And what happens?"

He looked to me, puzzled. "S'posed to be the other way 'round, ain't it? I've been telling that boy to work hard, to do his best, to never give up…." Walter shook his head.

"You got to keep telling him," I said. "Every day, you got to remind him: He can't give up. Every time they yell, he's got to hit like Carl Furillo. Every time they make a stupid call, he's got to throw like Eddie Matthews. Every time they ridicule him, he's got to make a diving catch. Sooner or later they're going to start looking stupid. And the more they carry on, the quicker people are going to see the truth. You guys can't give up, Walter. If he keeps playing the way he is; if he keeps living right—if you guys can see this thing through—it's going to work out. It's got to."

He grinned at me as if I'd just bet a hundred dollars that the Washington Senators would win the World Series. "I don't know, Mr. Hall. I'd like to think you're right. But it ain't looking that way."

Chapter 20

Jeffersonville rolled into town Thursday. They had won seven of their last ten, narrowing our lead to three games and making us all more than a little nervous. Three of their guys were on blazing hitting streaks. Their pitching had been untouchable. And they'd committed only one error in the last five weeks. These guys were coiled and ready to strike. We, on the other hand, had dropped six of our last nine games. We were frustrated, and for the first time all season doubt eclipsed our swaggering self-confidence. We believed we could lose. And if there's one thing that is true about Charley Baxter, it is this: He hates to lose.

An hour before the game Charley went looking for Pete Fry. Somewhere within the bowels of Memorial Stadium, he'd pitched a withering fit, screaming that he didn't care about the all-star game. "If you're going to throw something, throw the election," he raged, "but let 'em play the games that matter." He ambushed the umps and scorers. One by one he cornered them, rebuking them for what they had done and demanding that they each make prompt amends. He stomped around the locker room like a wounded animal, alert and on guard for every threat. He called the team together. "It's us against them," he wailed, "all of 'em." He stood with his hands on his hips and looked around the room, his eyes coming to rest on each man. "No mistakes out there, and remember: Whatever they do, they do it to all of us."

The Bobcats straggled out to the field to limber up. Douglas slapped his mitt on Percy's butt as he passed. Andrews did the same, then Giles, and Smith, and Murphy.

Early on there were hopeful signs of repentance. In the bottom of the second Percy grounded out to short, and in the fourth he flied to center. But he'd gotten decent calls and seen a few good pitches.

In the seventh the Bobcats were down by a run. There were two men on and two outs when Percy came to the plate. A spark of hope ignited the crowd. They were on their feet stomping, filling the air with cheers, and doing all that a crowd can to reverse their team's misfortune. Charley climbed to the top of the steps. He stood there, as tenacious as Stonewall Jackson himself, arms crossed, scorching the ump with his eyes. With a 3-1 count Percy got a waist-high fastball and drove it deep into the left-field corner. Andrews scored. Billy Henderson was waved home; he scored. Just like that the Bobcats were on top, and Percy stood at second with what looked like the game-winning double.

Charley clapped his hands, he pumped a jubilant fist. "Nice work out there," he screamed. "Thatta way to go." The crowd thundered its delight, they hugged and screamed and stretched their arms toward heaven—while Pete Fry, sitting behind home plate, plunged his face into his hands, a snapshot of unconcealed anguish.

Friday morning, those who had missed the game had a hard time ignoring the headline that cheered: "Jackson's Clutch Double Lifts 'Cats."

◆ ◆ ◆ ◆

Late that afternoon I swung by the house for Rose Marie and Chris. We loved to spend Friday nights at the ballpark. We'd picnic in the stands, gorging ourselves on hot dogs and french fries, maybe some cotton candy for dessert, and a bag of peanuts for later. And we'd always get there early so Chris could pal around with the players, and Rose Marie could stroll by the river, spending an hour in the afternoon breeze.

I was near the on-deck circle; the sun was just giving way to the moon and the stars, and the cooling air magnified my senses, attuning each one to the irresistible lures around me. Denny Douglas was in the batting cage blasting one pitch after another, each swing booming like a shot from a twelve-pound cannon. I settled in behind him, still as a junked Rambler, marveling at the artistry and power. But the enchantment was soon broken. A pair of beefy hands slid up the cage beside mine and rested there. "Been meaning to call you," Pete Fry drawled.

"Ain't a lot of evidence of it," I replied.

"Yeah, well, been on the road a lot lately." Fry pulled a scroll from his back pocket and unraveled the sports section, to the story about last night's game. "You know what," he said, smoothing the paper against the fence, "you boys down there, you could've written this headline a thousand different ways." He tapped at the paper with his finger, as if I needed directions to the headline. "Can't help but wonder why you wanted the colored boy's name in there." He peered over the top of his glasses. "Got it up real big, too."

"You were here," I snapped. "It was a great play … a pressure situation. What else would we say?"

Pete cocked his head, as if he didn't quite grasp the question. "Well, I'd imagine just about anything." He stared at the paper, studying the layout and copy, and then he said, "Come on, Jack, with what we're going through right now—"

I spewed a long, sulky breath. "Look," I said, "it was a good play, and let's face it, this kid hasn't had a lot of chances lately." I rapped my knuckles against the paper. "This is no big deal—it's nothing to worry about."

"Well …" Pete stretched the word into three or four syllables "… I think you probably know better'n that."

Douglas dispatched three more balls to the left-field wall, and then Pete put his hand on my shoulder. "Just take it easy, will ya? That's all I'm asking. You've heard the crowds, you've seen the way they treat this boy." Fry smoothed over the paper again. "Let's just see if we can't sneak through the rest of this season without everybody getting stupid."

"That'd be nice," I scoffed quietly, "'cause the last couple of weeks, Pete—they've been about as stupid as I've seen."

Pete frowned. "You know something," he said, "I don't believe you got the memory of a just-hatched moth. Look around here, Jack; that boy makes the all-star team and more hell's gonna break loose than you got the stomach for."

Douglas fired two more salvos to deep center field.

"Look, you give him a chance to play and I'll turn down the volume."

Pete rescrolled the paper, nodding his agreement. Then he slapped me on the shoulder, and, turning to go, he said, "Fair enough. You take care now, you hear?"

I strayed out to left field where Chris was tossing the ball with Percy and Johnny Andrews. "You got to be on your game tonight." I smiled at Percy. His big eyes begged for elaboration. "Just talked to Pete Fry. I think he's called off the dogs for good; they're going to let you play."

His eyes burst wide. "For real?" he asked.

"About dad-gum time," Andrews said.

Percy's stare persisted, his eyes pleading for confirmation. "They gonna really call the game right?"

"Hey, that's what the man said, wasn't more than two minutes ago."

Still smiling, I turned to Chris. "Come on, pal, it's time to eat. Your mom's waiting.

"Good luck out there," I called to Percy.

Chris threw the ball to Andrews, then he ran over to Percy, gave him a quick slap on the rear end, and said, "No way they're gonna run your butt out of here."

The two of us headed for the concession stand. "Where'd you learn to talk like that?"

"That's what everybody's saying," he answered. "I hear it all the time now."

"Well, we don't need to repeat it, okay?"

"Yes, sir."

"And Chris …"

He glanced up.

"Let's pray they can't."

The two of us entered the grandstand juggling six hot dogs, three bags of fries, and three Cokes. I drooled with anticipation and wiggled into the seat beside Rose.

"Noticed you had quite a chat with Mr. Fry," she said.

I handed her a hot dog. "Yeah, I think they're going to give Percy a break tonight."

"You have something to do with that?" she asked.

"Might have.... A little anyway."

She wiped mustard from her lip. "The power of the press, huh, Hall?"

"Yep, that's what we do." I brushed at a spot she missed. "Watch out for the little guy, speak truth to power—all in a day's work."

"Well, I'm proud of you," Rose Marie said. "I know you're joking, but in a way, in our little town, that is what you did. And it couldn't have been easy."

She propped her feet on the seat in front of her and took another bite. "But it's complicated, isn't it, what one colored kid can do to people?" Her hands went to her lap. "I mean, it never occurred to these guys to cheat before now, before a colored kid came on the field." Rose dragged a napkin across her mouth, her mind still chewing on the thought. "It's just that nobody knows how to handle any of this, we don't know what to do, don't know how to get past it...."

"We'll get past it sooner or later," I said, "there's no way around that. And when we do, I hope we can say two things: that we saved baseball. And that we did the right thing; that you, me, Chris, the paper, the whole town—when this thing's finally settled, I hope we're proud of the way we acted."

Rose Marie wadded the hot-dog wrapper and tossed it aside, then glanced toward a pair of fans carrying signs. "Everybody's got their own idea about what's right. And what makes them proud may not be what you had in mind."

"Probably not," I said, "but this ..." I held up my hot dog "... families at the ballpark together, this is right. And giving a kid a fair shot, that's right too. Most everybody agrees on that."

"And they think we ought to be kind to one another too," Rose said.

"But all that—families and being fair and being kind—those aren't the burning issues here, are they?"

Sixty minutes later, in the second inning, Percy drilled a hanging curve-ball over the left-field wall and gave us the early lead. As he rounded the bases, Pete stomped out of the stands, his head bowed and his face pinched in throes of fresh pain. Two outs later he reemerged; he edged his way up the steps, a tall cup of Coke in hand, looking limp and frazzled.

Andrews grounded out to end the inning, and as the fans stood to stretch and wander, Pete strolled down near the field. Allen Brown, the base ump, strayed in Pete's direction. The two men never looked at one another, never openly acknowledged the other's presence. Brown leaned against the wall ten feet away from Fry, facing the diamond, but Pete's cup moved crisply with their conversation, and Brown's head dipped faintly in reply.

Out on the field Haddock finished his warm-up tosses. Brown pushed off the wall and headed back to his position. As the ball rounded the horn, the ump mumbled a few words to his home-plate partner, and the third inning was under way.

In the fifth Percy struck out looking at a pitch that was high. In the seventh an early pair of suspicious calls forced him to swing at a ball that was outside, and he grounded out to second. Before the eighth inning opened, Charley called Pete Fry down from the stands. Both men looked taut to the breaking point. Charley pointed and jabbed, and his face grew hot, while Fry, standing three feet higher, gazed out at the field, stone-faced, watching our infielders lap up the grounders that Taylor tossed their way.

In the ninth we were down a run. With two outs Giles was on second and Henderson stood at first. As Percy strolled to the plate, the ump turned toward the stands. He lifted his mask and sleeved the sweat from his eyes, cloaking a glance in Fry's direction. Pete folded his hands; he tented his index fingers and tapped at his chin. Charley flashed out of the dugout. He stared into the stands, his eyes glued on Fry, and he barked loudly, "You can do it, Perce. Good eye out there, good eye."

The ump lowered his mask and signaled the pitcher to play ball.

The first pitch swept outside, ball one.

The next pitch was outside too, but closer—a called strike.

Pitch number three looked high and away, but was called a strike. And Percy fell behind in the count.

The fourth pitch was a fastball, just out of the strike zone, but Percy knew he had to swing. He slapped at it, almost one handed, and sent the ball skidding down the first-base line, an inch inside the bag, grazing chalk on its way toward the bullpen.

Giles churned around third and barreled for home. He made the wide turn—the tying run dead in his sights—when the ump threw his hands into the air. He flagged both arms wildly to his right and screamed, "Foul ball!"

And at that instant—at 9:42 p.m.—two weeks of pent-up rage erupted.

Giles slammed his cap into the ground and charged the ump. They stood chest-to-chest, waltzing furiously around the plate, their noses nearly touching, as Jimmy screamed and stomped in protest.

Our dugout spewed rabid men. They shot out like starving lions who'd suddenly crossed paths with a herd of crippled wildebeests.

Faster than an echo, and triggered by an instinct that's bred into every ballplayer, the Patriots countercharged.

Punches flew. Players tackled one another. They clinched opposing players in headlocks. They screamed and cursed and kicked anybody they could reach. Within seconds white and gray uniforms clashed and piled into a heap of flailing men.

Chris stood on his seat, fully bewitched by the violence. His mother turned up to me in the press box, her eyes whiter than a pair of brand-new baseballs.

In left field the colored fans came unglued. Fifty, maybe sixty black men stormed the field. They trailed the Patriot players, fueled by the shameless trespass and frantic for justice. The white fans near my wife and son shot to their feet. They hurled ice and bottles into the black mob. Both crowds lobbed hostile threats into the other.

I waved at Rose Marie, frantically signaling her to rush up. She grabbed Chris by the hand and the two of them raced upstairs as I sped down to meet them.

"Jack," she gasped, "I've never seen anything like this. What in the world ...?"

Chris's voice trembled. "Everybody's screaming and cussing, they all want to fight," he said, "all of them."

We slipped into the press box. "Are we going to be able to get home?" Chris worried.

"Yeah," I told him. "We'll get home just fine."

Rose Marie stared out to the field.

Fury packed the next two minutes. And by the time it had burned itself out, blood trickled from the noses and mouths of most of the players. Police had broken up scattered fights among fans, and ten, maybe twelve colored boys had been cuffed and carted off to the Whitney city jail. My wife and son were beside me the whole time. Together, we had looked on—stunned by what we'd seen.

Then, in the season's most anticlimactic moment, Donny Jones pinch-hit for Percy. On the 1-2 count he hit a pop fly to shallow right field, and we dropped the seventh game in our last eleven tries.

"I've got to get downstairs," I told Rose Marie. "I'm going to be busy tonight, but you two can't stay here. I'm going to run you home and then hurry right back."

The ride was quiet, all of us burdened by what we'd seen.

"Don't worry about this," I told Chris. "A lot of people lost their temper—a close game, a couple of bad calls—it happens sometimes. But it's all over now, okay?"

"Yes, sir," he replied, his voice wavering, "I guess ..."

"What's on you mind, pal? You sound worried."

"They're going to win," he said. Our eyes met in the rearview mirror. "They're going to run Percy out of the league, aren't they?"

"I don't know, Chris. I don't know how much Percy and his family can take."

"I saw them," Rose whispered. "They were there. They saw the whole thing. His mother was holding on tight to that little girl, trying to shield her eyes, tears streaming down her face. I can't imagine what that's like, worrying all the time that somebody's trying to hurt your family."

We pulled into the driveway. I leaned over and kissed Rose good night. "I'll be home as soon as I can, but don't wait up." I looked back at Chris. "Sleep tight, pal. You're home now. You'll be tucked into your own bed soon, safe and sound as you can be."

Ten minutes later Joe was tramping from one end of Charley's office to the other, rubbing his head, muttering to himself. Burt sat backward in a gray folding chair, shell-shocked and drained. I pushed my way into the room. Joe turned and his eyes flashed. "Just the facts," he snapped. He reached for a handkerchief to blot his neck and forehead. "Talk to the players if you want, get some quotes, but don't go editorializing." He paced and turned, quickly reached the end of the room, and turned again. "Wouldn't believe it if I hadn't seen it," he muttered.

Burt cupped his hands over his face. He sighed and dropped his arms to his sides. "We got an announcement to make," he said. "You can consider this a one-man press conference."

"And you need to make this big," Joe added. "This has got to be as big as whatever we say about the brawl."

"Okay." I nodded. "So what's the big announcement?"

"We're gonna hold Percy out of the all-star game," Burt stated. "As of right now, he's out of the running. And if he gets more votes than the other third basemen, we won't let him play."

I reached for my notebook. "And you're doing this because …?"

"Two reasons," Joe began, "and you need to print 'em both. First, we're worried about the boy. He's a good player and we need him. And right now we got a bunch of folks who'd rather not see a colored all-star. We don't need anybody throwing at him or spiking him—we gotta protect our player."

"And the second thing," Burt added, "is we're worried about everybody else. We ain't gonna have any more of this. And if the league won't do the right thing, well then, we will. We're just gonna take the all-star game off the table—won't be anything to worry about anymore."

"Nat Quaid's coming off the ballot too," Charley chimed in from behind his desk. "So everybody can just relax."

I glanced at Charley, my lip curled in serious doubt. "Yeah," I said, "everybody who's white."

I flipped my book closed and wandered across the hall to the locker room. The mood was surly, the place was quieter than a library, and it reeked of sweat and bad humor. Rick Murphy, who's about as fierce as a month-old puppy, dabbed at a split lip with a damp towel. "We're tired of this," he snarled, slamming his locker shut, "and I'm telling you, Jack, we ain't gonna put up with it anymore. You need to print that. You need to let every idiot ump in the league know that we're done with this. You need to tell 'em…." His voice trailed away.

A strip of blood had crusted beneath Giles' nostrils, and his left eye had begun to go black. "I don't know what got into me," he groaned. "I saw the ump's hands go up and something snapped. I don't know, Jack, I couldn't help it. I'm telling you, I just couldn't help it."

Johnny Andrews pressed an ice bag to his black-and-blue thigh. "They can't get away with this," he griped. "They'd never pull this crap on Henderson or Douglas. We ain't gonna put up with it just 'cause the boy's colored—you know what I mean?"

Eddie Smith slouched in front of his locker, a towel wrapped around his waist. "This ain't Perce's fault," he said. "Boy's been minding his own business, he's been doing whatever anybody asks. This just ain't right."

Donny Jones sat on the bench beside Smith unlacing his shoes, smirking in disbelief. "I've been telling you all along," he sneered, "a nigger ain't gonna bring nothing but trouble." He sat up straight and looked around the room. "Well, take a good look around boys, and you just tell me: Whadda you see?"

◆ ◆ ◆ ◆

I reported the facts, just as Joe ordered, and revealed the Sunshine Circuit's worst-kept secret: The league had conspired to keep Percy out of the all-star game. By edict from the top, umpires and scorers were to neutralize the talent of the league's most gifted player, taking from him by force what God had freely and generously given, and thereby transforming him into something ordinary and indistinct—just one more country boy who'd namelessly vanish into the southern woodwork.

But what they had not foreseen, I wrote, was how their decisions would injure an entire team. The plot against Percy, I said, had fused a small band of men together, inspiring each one to defend and protect the others—regardless of their color.

I recounted how, one scheming call at a time, the umps and scorers had cut our lead to just two games. With play-by-play descriptions, taken from five games that had been played in three cities, I depicted how the strike against one man's genius had caused us to lose at least four games. And then, by playing back quotes from our town's favorite players, readers heard firsthand how, at 9:42 Thursday night, twenty men, with a single ear-splitting voice, had screamed: "No more!"

I wrote the story late Thursday night, alone at my desk, thinking that Pete Fry surely knew better. He had played the game, he'd been a member of good teams, and he knew, as fully as Charley Baxter did, that a wound to one man could cripple a whole team; that an attack on Percy would injure Henderson and Jones. And that Smith and Giles would inevitably bear the pain inflicted on Jackson.

But then I thought about Helen and Bud and Luther, my friend from the chicken plant. I recalled the sorrowful looks on my neighbors' faces as they imagined colored and white children mixed together in our own schools. Yes, Fry knew that twenty ballplayers would not stand for what he had done. But he also feared that thousands of people in seven nearby towns could not endure one more shock to the system that ordered their lives.

At the sound of the typewriter's bell, I slung back the carriage. I hated what Pete had done, but I wondered if I'd have chosen any better.

◆ ◆ ◆ ◆

Friday's paper, with its three-column-by-ten-inch photo of ballplayers stacked five deep, sparked gossip faster than Marilyn Monroe's love life. And the behind-the-curtains peek into Fry's conspiracy crammed more theater into our little town than the playhouse sees in a full season.

By lunchtime my report of twelve arrests had ballooned past any likeness to the truth. "Had to be at least twenty," some said, "and might've been nearer to thirty." The scrapes and bruises that I had described had escalated into twists and sprains, and at least one broken bone. The tales just grew taller, and the grapevine soon entangled the whole town.

By seven thirty that night an enormous crowd, colored and white, had been enticed to the scene of the spectacle. But this gathering came with more than curiosity. Agitation was in the stands as well—a restless anticipation—like race-car fans secretly longing for a five-car crash. Others came, I think, to decipher some meaning from it all, to see what a thing like this meant for life in our hometown. And a few came to make their feelings known; they carried a fresh batch of harshly worded signs ordering our colored neighbors back to the south side of town, where they would be out of view, and out of our lives.

But there was a bigger and more ominous surprise that night. For the first time colored fans carried signs too. In front of the stadium, near the Negro entrance, a dozen men and women waved hastily scrawled placards that read: "All-star game—Percy don't play, we won't pay." Leading the march, carrying a sign that must've been six feet long, was the reverend Phil Edwards. A tiny crowd looked on, lending support with nothing more than their presence. But slowly—one, and then another, and then another after that—they joined the march. Timidly, they began to chant, "Percy don't play, we won't pay." As the crowd grew, so did the volume. And as the volume swelled, the chant became more determined. Ultimately, fifty Negroes marched outside the stadium boldly shouting, "Percy don't play, we won't pay. Percy don't play, we won't pay."

The white crowd gawked at the demonstration. Some were amused; they laughed and shook their heads incredulously. Others were in no mood for a crowd of testy Negroes. "Y'all just get on outta here," they barked as they passed. But these commands, drowned out by the chorus, had no effect on the brazen crowd.

When Percy came to the plate in the second inning, insults rained down as heavily as they had twelve weeks before. He brushed them aside and lashed a double to left field, sparking applause from most of the white crowd and triggering glee in the left-field bleachers. Two pitches later Percy swiped third. And on the next pitch Murphy lifted a fly ball deep to right field. Percy tagged and scored, and the Negro crowd thundered its admiration. But then, quickly, and as methodically as thunder follows lightning, the joy took a malevolent turn. Signs stabbed the air, and the cheers mutated into a defiant chorus: "Percy don't play, we won't pay. Percy don't play, we won't pay."

White fans shifted skittishly, and a restless murmur ran a new lap through the crowd.

In the fourth Percy launched a hanging curveball 370 feet into the parking lot—just foul. But at the crack of the bat the colored fans rose and craned their necks, following the ball as it soared above them. Two pitches later he scalded a grounder past the shortstop for a single. He was 2 for 2. "Percy don't play, we won't pay," filled the air again, louder than it had before, and more insistent.

In the seventh Percy came to the plate for the third time. There was one out and Taylor was on second. The Jeffersonville catcher looked to his dugout; he then turned to the mound and held four fingers up in the air. As Percy settled into the batter's box, the catcher remained standing. He extended his right hand, signaling his pitcher—and the rest of the crowd—that they'd intentionally walk Percy Jackson.

Home crowds hate this play. They boo it emphatically every time—there is never an exception. Jeers declare their contempt for the visiting team's cowardice, for their refusal to face a dangerous hitter. The intentional walk is an admission of fear, but more than that, it is the ultimate sign of respect.

As the first pitch floated outside, the Negro crowd at Memorial Stadium did not boo. They came to their feet and cheered. They raised fists triumphantly. While Percy trotted to first, signs and slogans poured into the air again, louder and gutsier than they'd been just minutes before.

In the ninth the score was tied and Henderson was on first when Percy came to the plate for the fourth time. On the first pitch he sent a foul ball into the parking lot. Jeffersonville's relief pitcher watched it sail, unconsciously waving to his left, wishing the ball out of play. He turned and muttered a few words in Percy's direction. The catcher jawed at our hitter as well, both men hoping to rattle him.

Percy planted his feet firmly, he took two practice swings, and then sent the second pitch after the first—another foul ball with home-run distance. Percy backed away and tapped his shoes. The defensive chatter picked up steam, the third baseman joining in, then the shortstop, and then the other infielders. The pitcher looked in for the sign. He shook off the first one. Then the second. And then the third. The catcher hopped out of his crouch and paid a visit to the mound. And then, with the signals straight, the pitcher went into his stretch for the third time. He fired a fastball high and inside. Percy spun desperately, but the ball smacked him square between the shoulder blades. His knees buckled and he fell.

At the sound of ball against flesh, the Bobcats dugout exploded for the second time in two nights. Henderson, Andrews, and Giles led the pack—their faces twisted with rage—itching to exact revenge. More punches and blood and fury poured out. Negro fans stampeded onto the field. But the cops matched their speed, quickly outflanking them with nightsticks raised. Paddy wagons rushed to the scene, and bloodied and bruised Negroes—drenched in sweat, with their clothes tattered and stained—were roughly herded inside.

Those who had come hoping for violence got more than they imagined.

◆ ◆ ◆ ◆

Images of bloodied players and enraged fans fouled Sunday's paper, just as they had the day before. The sports page, crowded with descriptions of anger, arrests, and the fear that divided men of different colors, had been turned to a purpose for which it was never intended.

I labored through Saturday night's final hours, grieved by the work, and aching to write again about the beauty of athletes hitting, pitching, and fielding baseballs. I didn't know when, how—or even if—the game would ever get back to normal. But late Sunday morning there was a sliver of hope. As we pulled into the driveway after church, the phone was ringing.

"I'm real sorry to bother you on Sunday," Burt said, "but I need you in my office first thing tomorrow, maybe a few minutes before eight?"

"No problem," I answered. "What's going on?"

"Phil Edwards is coming by for a visit," the mayor replied. "Joe and I thought it might help to have you there."

◆ ◆ ◆ ◆

That morning I felt like a high-school kid before final exams. I had no idea what to expect, no clue about what was on Edwards' mind, or how he'd react to Burt's invitation. The others were uncertain too. On each man's face I found a furrowed brow, a hard-set jaw, or skeptical gaze. We made awkward small talk while Margaret poured coffee. Then, clumsily, we took a seat—all of us wary, but also hopeful.

"Appreciate you coming," Burt said to Edwards. "I know you're as concerned as I am about what's been going on around here. Thought we might work together to settle things down."

Edwards stroked his chin solemnly. "Yes, sir," he replied, "I'll do whatever I can to help."

"Reverend," Joe said, "I think you know we've been working on a couple of things lately. For one, we've been trying to keep this baseball team going.

We think it's good for the town, a nice thing for families. And ever since we signed Percy Jackson, we've drawn good Negro crowds. You all have pretty much kept the team alive." Joe paused. He slowly crossed his legs and then, more soberly, he said, "But we've also been trying to keep things peaceful. We've done our best to keep white folks and colored folks comfortable, we've tried to make sure nothing too drastic happens around here—nothing that's going to tear anybody's life apart, you know what I mean?"

"Yes," Edwards said, "I believe I do."

"We need your help, Phil," Burt said. "And all this business about the all-star game has gotten folks riled up. We need you to be patient right now, to help us keep everybody calm."

Edwards leaned forward, lacing his fingers together. "I believe I can help with that," he said, "and I'd be real happy to do it." He took a quick glance around the room. "But I'd need you all to pitch in. I couldn't do it on my own."

"I'm not following," Joe said.

"I can keep the colored folks calm, but only if Percy Jackson gets treated exactly like every other ballplayer. If you can see to that, then I can help you."

"Come on, Phil, if he was like every other player, we wouldn't be here," Burt grumbled.

"I understand," Edwards replied, "believe me, I understand that as well as anybody. But you got to start treating him as if he were." Edwards leaned back. "There's a lot of folks in my part of town who are tired. They need to see something change, they need to see something that gives them hope. If Percy gets treated right, if he gets what he's due, then I think we can get things calmed down. But if he doesn't …"

"Look, Phil, we need take one step at a time," Burt said. "We got this kid on the team for crying out loud—there's change for you. Think about it: A colored kid's the starting third baseman for the Whitney Bobcats—that right there is reason to hope." He gave the words a few seconds to sink in. "If we want to keep him there, we've got to be careful. One wrong move and I'm telling you, the whole thing unravels."

"We're on this boy's side," Joe added. "But all this trouble … it's giving people the wrong idea, it's turning folks against him."

Edwards moved a hand to his chin, rubbing thoughtfully. "With all due respect, Mr. Anderson, if you were on Percy's side, he'd be on the all-star team. If you were on his side, there might be a few white people in jail." He leaned in Joe's direction. "Let's be honest, you're on his side as long as he keeps colored folks coming to ball games. And for as long as he helps to keep them quiet."

"Phil, there aren't sides to this thing," Burt insisted, "that's the whole point of this conversation. We're trying to do what's best for everybody."

A frown slipped across Edwards' face. "Let me be clear," he said, "I want to help. I'm here to work with you on this. But folks down my way are tired of being the ones who have to pay the price, who have to accept the compromise, who have to be patient…." One by one Edwards eyed the white men who had gathered round him. "Every Negro in this town has got his eyes on Percy Jackson. We're all waiting to see what happens. And if you don't treat him right, there's not much I can do."

Joe was out of his seat now, pacing, running his hand over the top of his head. The man was perpetually drained these days, his emotional tank empty from trying to mend rifts that wouldn't heal. "It just ain't that cut-and-dry, Reverend, and it ain't anywhere near that simple. We've got to be realistic here."

"I'm being just as real as those riots, Mr. Anderson. And the way I see it, I might be the only one who is."

Joe paced on, silently. Burt propped his feet on the desk, wondering where to take the conversation.

"What do you mean?" I asked Edwards. "What's different about the way you see it?"

Edwards twisted around to face me. "Let me ask you something, Mr. Hall, why do you suppose I'm here? You broke the story about the umpires. You're the one who told the world how Pete Fry plotted to keep this boy out of the all-star game. Where are they? And while we're at it, where's the pitcher who plunked Percy yesterday? Why isn't he here?"

"We blew the whistle on those guys," Joe fired back. "We investigated the whole thing. We did what a good paper's supposed to do."

"Yes, sir, you did," Edwards replied. "And then you took Percy off the ballot. You blew the whistle, and then turned right around and gave the bad guys exactly what they wanted."

"Come on, Phil," Burt moaned, "we're trying to keep this place from blowing apart, you know that. And we could use your help."

"I want to help," Edwards replied, "but I've got to do the right thing." Edwards rubbed his eyes and forehead; he, too, felt the strain of the last two days. "We've never had problems with one another, and I mean to keep it that way. But I can't call something that's wrong, right." He turned to Joe. "I accused you of using Percy to get what you wanted … maybe I am too. But it's time we got a fair shake—at baseball and schooling and getting a seat on a city bus. It's not too much to ask."

Joe stood at the window looking into the square. "Yeah it is, Reverend. Right now it is too much to ask. And if you keep it up, if you keep marching and carrying on like you have been, I believe you'll tear this town in two."

Chapter 21

The brawls consumed the town's conversation. Every protagonist in every shop, store, and filling station blamed Percy for the troubles that beset us. And one truth was plain in every friend's tone: We were haunted by the thought of Negro kids in white schools. That image contaminated the town with a premonition that we were, slowly but inescapably, advancing on some inevitable point of no return.

But deep down, we all knew that Percy Jackson wasn't to blame; we knew he didn't have a spiteful bone in his body, and that he'd be the last man in Whitney to go looking for more trouble. We simply couldn't see straight. We were stumbling from one day to the next, unsure of where we were headed, and groping to find the way back to where we had been.

I drove to the hardware store Saturday morning, thinking back to the first day Percy appeared in the locker room. I could see the stunned stares that captured thirty faces. I heard the taunts. And I shuddered, recalling the horror that each man imagined as he envisioned a colored boy beside him in the shower.

On my way home I stopped for a cup of coffee. Helen had assumed the air of a prophetess predicting doom. "It's all coming to a head now," she warned. She grabbed a pot from the hotplate behind her, and her voice faded as she moved away. "There's just some things that ain't meant to be...."

I slurped at the coffee, drifting back to the first night Percy played. He rapped a pinch-hit double in the bottom of the ninth—the key play of the game—and as he trudged off the field, ignored by his teammates, Charley draped an arm over his shoulder. Near the dugout they faced a pack of menacing fans, and Charley pulled the colored boy close to his side, extending to him both comfort and consolation.

At work Monday morning I overheard Billy Bender, one of the sales guys, saying, "You gotta expect that kinda thing when niggers get to thinking they're as a good as white boys…." Before he finished the sentence my memory strayed to the day when, for the first time, Giles and Douglas sat behind Percy on the team bus. Their stomachs had once churned at the thought of a black man in their midst. Given a choice, they'd have preferred a malignant cancer to stepping foot on the same field with Percy Jackson. Giles and Douglas fully knew the indignity that Billy Bender only feared: A colored boy had been made their equal. But on that day, in that bus, they had both been kind, and they began the slow process of drawing Percy into the fold.

At lunchtime I listened to a radio announcer blame the town's troubles on Negroes in general, and on Percy in particular. Something sparked the memory of our trip home from Clayton. I pictured Johnny Andrews with Giles and Douglas—the three of them with their plates and glasses—searching for Percy in the back of the Big Chicken restaurant. They—unlike the radio announcer—knew what it was like to work side by side with a colored man. And they'd gone looking for him, refusing to accept his forced segregation.

Later that afternoon I'd been on the phone with the baseball coach at Jefferson Davis High. "Too bad about the other night," he mourned. "Guess it was bound to happen."

"Yeah, s'pose so," I replied, my mind roaming back to the stadium, to right field, where I'd heard Giles call his teammate "Perce" for the first time. Smith did it later, in the locker room after the brawl. Murphy did too. None of them had believed they could play with Percy Jackson. But now, just four months later, the kid who had been so thoroughly reviled sported a new and endearing nickname.

Anger and frustration swirled through town again. Salesmen, waitresses, radio announcers—they all knew that a colored boy had brought us trouble. Down deep they believed with all their hearts that Negro players could never be as good as whites. And the evidence that betrayed this knowledge spawned a citywide panic, forcing everyone to rummage for a truth that would bring comfort. The fruit of our restlessness—all the anger, insults, and worry—was attributed to the presence of one man: a bashful eighteen-year-old who was the best ballplayer most of us had ever seen.

The irony of all this still baffles me. On that day in March, when the Whitney Bobcats first laid eyes on Percy Jackson, their thoughts were no different than Helen's or Billy Bender's. If anything, their emotions were more inflamed by the flesh-and-blood threat that stood before them. And yet, 120 days later, with only a few exceptions, the people who should have hated Percy the most had rushed to his side.

The mere thought of mixing coloreds and whites was too revolting for the people to ponder. But for twenty-four white men it wasn't a possibility they had to imagine. It was the way they lived day to day, as ordinary as morning coffee. Andrews, Giles, Henderson, and Douglas—they and their teammates knew precisely what would happen when coloreds and whites were mingled together. And they were the only ones who did not tremble at the thought of Percy Jackson.

At the diner I nibbled at a ham-and-Swiss cheese sandwich, scanning the paper and figuring the *Whitney Herald* had earned a B+ for the day's effort. In sports we featured a fifteen-hundred-word interview with Sam Snead, done by a writer from *Time* magazine who had talked with the Slammer about his eighteen favorite holes from around the world. In entertainment we ran a likeable enough piece about Lucille Ball and the upcoming one-hundredth episode of *I Love Lucy.* And in national news a story about army and air force technicians stationed in IndoChina caught my eye. The five of them had gone swimming and disappeared, and now the higher-ups feared they'd been captured by communist soldiers.

We were, I thought, a pretty good small-town paper.

I was nearly through that last story, discovering that the missing technicians weren't the first American casualties in Viet Nam, when a sudden slap on the back sloshed coffee onto my favorite tie and into the lap of my just-cleaned suit. I lurched over the counter, raising the cup into the air, hoping to avoid any worse damage.

"Oh shoot. I-I-I'm sorry about that, Jack." Bud Parsons dropped onto the stool beside me; he plunged a napkin into my water glass. "Here you go," he said, handing it over. "I'm real sorry, Jack."

I mopped at the stains, annoyed at Bud's clumsiness, but figuring there'd been no irreversible damage.

"Hadn't seen you for a while," Bud said, "you been okay?"

"Yeah." I chuckled a little grimly. "All things considered, I'm all right."

We swapped a few lines about our wives and kids, and then, as that part of the conversation faded, Bud began to swerve on the bar stool. He twisted back and forth nervously. He thanked Helen for a glass of Coke. And as he pushed a straw through its wrapper, he said, "Hell of a thing out at the ballpark, huh?"

"Yeah," I replied, dragging the word out forlornly. "I s'pose that's the right way to put it."

Bud dropped his head. He poked at the ice with his straw. "Glad I missed it," he said. "I'd sure hate for my family to be around something like that."

I dipped the napkin into the water again and took a second swipe at the stains. "It wasn't the best night at the ballpark, that's for sure."

Bud was moored to the town—tied securely to it by every fond memory his mind could summon: his days at Jefferson Davis High, roaming streets and alleys that hadn't much changed in the past thirty years, baseball games in the park, his marriage and kids' baptisms, a thousand conversations at this very counter. Whitney was stitched into the man—as much a part of him as flesh and blood and veins—and like most of the people who lived here, Bud could not conceive of himself apart from this place. He's often graceless and awkward. He says what's on his mind, and his speech is rarely refined. He is uncomplicated, and he's certain that the good life is a quiet and simple one. "Everybody round here used to be real neighborly," he told me. "People looked out for one another, and everybody tried to steer clear of trouble…." He stabbed at the ice some more, confounded by the things that were on his mind. "Sure never had anybody go looking for it."

"Yeah," I agreed, an image of Phil Edwards suddenly conjured in my mind, "doesn't seem right. But things change, and we got to find ways to keep going."

Bud bowed his head silently and sipped his drink. "I've lived here all my life, and I ain't never seen or heard of anything like what happened out there."

"It was a first for all of us."

He scrunched up his nose and squinted, trying to think through the riddle. "We put that nigger on the team because we needed the crowd, ain't that right? I mean—we're inviting more colored folks to come out to the park ...."

"Yeah." I shrugged. "It's something like that."

"But it ain't working, is it? I mean—if this is what the niggers are going to do...?"

"There's plenty of blame to go around on this," I told him. "I don't think we can point the finger at one group, not this time."

Bud took another slurp through his straw. Then he got up and slapped me on the back, and as he turned to leave, he said, "You don't want to live in a town where there's race riots, do you, Jack?"

"No," I sighed, "I don't. But I'd sure like to live in one that's got baseball."

He let his hand rest on my shoulder, and he squeezed slightly—with affection I think—and then turned for the door.

This lunch meeting, I suspected, had not occurred by chance.

Back at the office I made a few calls and quickly discovered that the Whitney parks director had been busy. At eleven o'clock Friday night, after he'd gotten wind of the first brawl, Bud started calling other council members. He'd spent most of his day Saturday talking with city officials in Clayton, Jeffersonville, and Madison. He phoned the "baseball people" in five Sunshine Circuit towns—and had even tracked down Pete Fry after a Sunday-afternoon game in Fulton.

In less than fifty-four hours Bud had filled the town with a fresh batch of provocative rumors. And by eight o'clock Tuesday morning, a hungry crowd packed the city council room—all slavering for facts, and hoping to glean fresh news about where our town was headed. Phil Edwards and a dozen of his deacons were there. Reporters from every league city were in the gallery too, along with front-office men from three other teams.

When Burt came to new business, Bud's hand shot into the air. "I-I-I believe we got to repeal the exemption allowing niggers and whites to play together at Memorial Stadium," he declared. He turned and played to the crowd. "We've all seen what happens—it's tearing up our town; it's making this a pretty dad-gum sorry place to live. And I believe we got to do something right quick."

A fretful hum erupted around the platform, each councilman turning to the man beside him, gauging the other's reaction. And then, on cue, Bud's supporting cast played the parts they'd been given.

"I believe this business has just gotten everybody all riled up," Cale Warren announced. "Never used to see those folks carrying on like this—not 'til we put the colored boy on the team."

"I ran into Chief Leveret at church on Sunday," Jim Caldwell added. "He must've made twenty-five arrests over the weekend; told me they'd patched up twelve or fifteen people at the emergency room. None of that would've happened if we'd done the right thing. Looks to me like we're reaping what we've sowed."

Pete Fry was sitting two rows in front of me. He was bent forward, hands dangling between his knees, head down and grimacing at the floor. When Jim finished, Pete slowly came to his feet. He raised his right hand shoulder high, asking Burt for the floor. When it was granted, he said, "I'm the first to admit that the last few weeks haven't been good. They haven't been good for your town, and they sure enough haven't been good for Sunshine Circuit baseball. But, gentlemen, I've done some thinking on this, and here's what I believe: If you ban Negro players, you'll be taking a giant step in the wrong direction."

The audience burst into startled chatter, everyone wondering what in the world Pete Fry—the mastermind behind the all-star conspiracy—could possibly be thinking. Burt banged his gavel, demanding order. Pete slowly turned to the crowd. "Look," he said, "what I did was stupid. I didn't want anybody getting mad. I didn't want anybody thinking I was favoring one town over the other." He picked out a face in the crowd and explained. "If we'd have said colored boys could play in the all-star game, I'd have had every fan in Clayton screaming to high heaven." Then he turned to someone else. "And if we'd have said they couldn't, I'd have had my hands full with plenty of folks from around here. Keeping everybody happy just ain't possible," Pete said. He let his eyes pause on the colored crowd gathered in back. "And trying to make Percy Jackson look like a bad ballplayer—that's like trying to make Einstein look stupid." There were a few light chuckles and Pete looked down, rubbing his chin and gathering up his next few thoughts.

"Look," he said, swinging back toward the council, "what I did—what you fellas are about to do—it's like trying to dam Niagara Falls. This thing's coming at us too hard and too fast." He eyed the men around the dais. "I know this is tough, know it better'n anybody here. But there's no turning back. Colored boys are playing ball all over the place; they're playing right close to us, too, right here in the South. And for the most part they're getting along just fine." He raised his hand toward Bud. "I learned the hard way, it's too late. You ban these boys now and you'll be setting us back a good ten years."

Nobody moved. As far as I can remember, nobody sneezed, coughed, or spoke for thirty seconds, and Pete stood there, hands in his pockets, waiting for some kind of reply.

John Clark, the general manager of Kingstown, and the man who had signed Nat Quaid, stood. He held his hat in both hands, twisting it round and round nervously. "Pete's right," he said. "We got to have the colored crowd, there's no way around it. But on top of that, if the major-league teams keep signing these boys, we don't have a lot of choice in the matter—not if we're gonna keep any kind of big-league affiliation. We got to play the boys they sign. That's our job." He glanced at Pete and said, "There really ain't no turning back."

Bud seethed. From the dais he looked at both men as if God had just cursed them with the same festering boils that had once plagued Egypt. Several painful seconds passed, and then Bud replied, "Mr. Fry, I-I-I got to be honest with you, I don't much care about what's going on anywhere else. And you know something: Th-th-this was a nice place to live ten years ago. If this sets us back, well then, I'd be happy to go."

Cale Warren leaned back, folding his hands behind his head. "If what we saw out there last weekend is progress, then I gotta tell you, I'm with Bud. I'd rather go back. Right now we got folks who're scared to go to the ballpark—can you imagine that?" He shook his head sternly. "Didn't have anything like that ten years ago."

Burt rolled his chair back from the platform. He looked right then left, directly at each of his fellow council members. "You fellas got to hear what these men are saying. If we ban colored boys, we're killing professional baseball. We've talked about it before. We all know it." Burt narrowed in on Bud. "That what you want?"

Bud squirmed. He tapped his pen on the desk and bit his lip. Then, quietly, he said, "No. I'm just wantin' everybody to be happy, like they used to be."

From the other side of the platform, Hal Taylor cleared his throat. "Mr. Mayor, I wonder if you'd be willing to table this 'til we get back together next month. Now that we got this all-star business put to rest, and since the Bobcats'll be on the road for a while, I think we got a little time. I'd like to look into this, maybe talk to a few folks around town, get a feel—"

Before anybody had time to reply, Burt declared, "I don't hear any objection," and banged his gavel. "We'll talk about it next month."

◆ ◆ ◆ ◆

News of the Whitney riots spread like cancer. And it became more voracious as it traveled, feeding on the fears the Supreme Court had begotten, but never depleting them. Instead the rumors and gossip spawned a hardier form of this new disease, one that wouldn't be soothed with calming words or a politician's vague promise.

Phil Edwards had told the truth: White families weren't the only ones afflicted. Colored families anguished over these events as well. Many were angry, others were frightened, and nearly all were saddened by the sudden change in the way we lived together.

But none were more distressed than the Walter Jacksons.

After the game that Saturday, after the second riot, I had followed Percy to the armory. A pair of reluctant cops had hustled him across the street. With nightsticks drawn, and with their pistols in plain sight, they had rushed him past scattered packs of overwrought fans—their presence enough to discourage more trouble. But once they had delivered Percy unscathed, their duty was done. And they abandoned him there, leaving him to fend for himself for the rest of the night.

He was shaken and dejected. His eyes were flooded with tears that wouldn't stay dammed, and in a trembling voice he sniffed, "I hadn't done nothing. I'm just playing, that's all." He looked up at me—rattled and confused and frightened by what he had seen the past two nights. "That's the only thing I'm doing," he repeated softly. He flung the first tear from his cheek, then tossed a towel over his shoulder and trudged away toward the showers.

Walter Jackson had slipped into the room through the back door, twenty minutes later than usual. His jaw was clinched, his breath labored, and a film of anxious sweat glistened across his forehead. A crowd of white men had gathered at the street crossing, he explained. They were loud and blustering, and looked as though they "hankered to start more trouble." Walter had kept his distance, walked down the street a few blocks and come up to the armory from a different direction "just to be on the safe side."

"I'll tell you something," he said, his eyes wide, "life is mighty hard to figure. We're 'bout the only ones in all this who're minding our own business. The mayor's got something he wants to do; the Supreme Court's up to something; Mr. Parsons, he's got a plan; Pastor Edwards, he's got a plan too." Walter pushed his chin toward the shower room. "Boy's just doing his job … the only plan he's got is to play ball."

"Roberta holding up okay?" I asked.

Walter flinched at the mention of his wife's name. "She's pretty scared," he said. "All this fighting and carrying on ..." He stuck his hands in his back pockets and looked away. "Had a bunch drive by the house yesterday ... hollering and screaming, making all kinds of threats."

"Threats? Like what?"

Just then Percy strolled out of the shower room. Walter immediately turned to his son. "You all right?" Walter asked him.

"Yessir," Percy mumbled.

Walter went to the locker and began stuffing dirty clothes into Percy's bag. I sat quietly, watching, thankful that I'd never have to worry about Chris the way Walter was worried right now. We sat and talked awhile, waiting for the zealots outside to tire and drift away. Then, the two of them walked across the street to the parking lot. I hung back and watched. Walter draped an arm around his boy's shoulder.

Two decent guys, both feeling alone and stranded.

◆ ◆ ◆ ◆

After the riots the pressure on Percy mounted. Unrelated and unmanageable events conspired against him, brightening the spotlight that was already on him, and drawing more people—from every walk of life—into the fray.

Some of these things seemed inconsequential at the time; they were personal and occurred close to home. Others were public and visible; they involved well-known and powerful people. Yet, somehow, they all streamed together to make Percy Jackson the common symbol of opposing forces, and to cast him in roles he never wanted to play.

These things had, I suppose, been going on from the moment he stepped foot in the locker room. But after the riots, every move this kid made mattered to somebody. And every event that shaped this boy's life was—by one "force" or the other—assigned some new prophetic meaning.

I saw the first striking example on Tuesday night.

After the final game of the Jeffersonville series we were headed to

Chesterfield for three games with the Hawks. Sometime around eight o'clock—it was during the third inning, I think—a kid from the Greyhound office wandered into the press box.

"Who do I see about the team bus?" he asked.

"Depends," Jeff Harrison replied, "what about it?"

The kid looked down and pawed the floor. "It's broke down," he mumbled. "Can't get another one here 'til morning."

Jeff rushed the boy around the stadium to find Don Gordon, the equipment manager. Within seconds Don was on the phone, improvising, and patching Plan B together. This was Gordon in his element—thinking fast, making deals, coaxing last-minute favors. And sure enough, before the end of the sixth inning, he had rustled up enough tickets to put the team on the 11:35 train.

As the players showered and changed, a fleet of taxis arrived right on Don's schedule. At 10:50 Charley was herding everyone into the cabs; guys were piling in three or four to a car, while duffle bags and equipment were stuffed into waiting vehicles. And at eleven o'clock sharp, the Bobcats were rolling toward Whitney station.

I was in the cab just ahead of Charley and Don's, toward the back of the pack. The streets were wide open, and we moved smoothly down the road. In perfect formation the cars swept neatly into the final turn toward town, and it was there, at the apex of that curve, that we saw the burst of flashing red lights. A police car roared past and pulled alongside a cab that was four or five ahead of mine. The car slowly angled to the side of the road. I told our driver to pull in behind it; Charley's cab parked behind mine.

Two cops moseyed out of the black-and-white cruiser, flashlights in hand. I stepped outside and slammed the door. Charley rushed past me, marching toward one of the officers, shouting, "What's going on, Joe, we got a train to catch."

The cop flashed his light in Charley's eyes. "You got that colored kid riding with white boys in a white-only cab. That's what's going on!"

"Put that dad-gum light down," Charley snarled. He jammed his hands to his hips. "Right now this cab ain't white or colored. It's a team cab. You know that."

"I'm afraid it don't work that way," the cop said. He aimed his light at Percy. "He can't ride in there." Then, sliding the beam toward the driver, he added, "And I'm gonna have to issue this man a citation."

Charley held up his left hand, thumping his watch so hard I could hear it from ten yards away. "We got fifteen minutes," he hissed. "Write the ticket and let us go."

"You'll be on your way soon enough," Joe said, "everybody except the colored boy. I can't let him stay in there."

"But you're giving us the ticket," Charley hissed.

"That don't mean he can stay in the cab."

Charley glared at the cop. He cocked his head, a silent demand for more information.

The cop turned sheepish, like a schoolkid caught cheating. "I can't let this slide," he said quietly, "not tonight."

Charley stormed away, his lips pressed tight, shaking his head in disgust.

"I'll get the driver to call another cab," I hollered after him. "I'll go back and get my car and I'll drive him to Chesterfield. He know where he's staying?"

"Yeah," Charley growled, "boardinghouse right near the stadium; he's got directions."

"I'm sorry about this," the cop said.

"Who sent you?" Charley hissed. "Who put you up to this?"

Joe handed the cab driver the ticket. Then, looking back toward Charley, he said, "I'm real sorry."

Percy got out of the cab. "Why don't you wait over there," I told him, pointing to a Sinclair station. "I'll be back in a few minutes." Percy looked over to the gas station, then back to me. He looked up the road where three or four of the other cabs had pulled over, his teammates standing beside them, watching. And then, at ten minutes past eleven, in front of Charley and Don—and under the gaze of Murphy, Douglas, and Giles—Percy walked away, alone, caught in the glare of this irrepressible light, and bearing the burden of being different.

◆ ◆ ◆ ◆

In Chesterfield, Percy sparkled like diamonds in a jewelry store window. With the all-star conspiracy lifted, he returned to form, collecting five hits in twelve at bats. Defensively, he played without blemish.

The furor of the past few days had roused the home team's colored fans. Every night more than two thousand, none with much money to spare, shelled out hard-earned cash to watch Percy play. And while some gathered round Phil Edwards to march and shout, these crowds had come to laud Percy Jackson. They came to celebrate every hit, catch, and throw he made, as if they could all—through this shared experience—share his success.

But all his accomplishments, illumined as they were, grated hard against white fans, and they gave Percy a rough ride. Taunts and gibes flew freely around the stadium, and the anger—in a spot here, or a place there—occasionally boiled over. You could see it in a desperate face. And you could hear it in a cruel, sarcastic tone—the kind that can only come from a heart that's overrun with malice.

And it was, I think, as so many colored fans observed the white crowd's unconcealed anger, that they began to believe the once preposterous thought: that a Negro was more gifted than the white men around him. As that belief took root, they welled up with new-sprouted pride.

White fans, even the mildest mannered, wrestled with the same idea. And the truth of it made them vulnerable and exposed. It embarrassed them, humiliated them. And these were emotions they couldn't bear.

Both groups were on guard. The tension became more pervasive, affecting our lives at school and work, at church and clubs, and in barbershops and diners. And the problem, whatever it ultimately was, was personified by Percy Jackson.

That night, after the game, it was easier for me to worry than sleep, and so I spent the better part of that night awake and wondering what would happen.

When morning mercifully arrived, and long before you'd expect to see anybody who didn't have to be at work by dawn, I strolled into the motel coffee shop. Truck drivers and factory workers straggled in behind me. A construction crew, clad in T-shirts and speckled white painter's pants, waited at the cash register. And Charley Baxter, who didn't have to be anywhere for eleven more hours, sat in a red upholstered booth along the far wall. David Powers, the general manager of the Chesterfield Hawks, was with him.

And so was the mayor of my hometown.

You didn't have to be Ellery Queen to see that they'd been here awhile. Their plates, crusted with egg yolk and grits, had been shoved aside, melting ice floated in half-empty water glasses, and they were all fully absorbed by what looked to be a hefty conversation.

I waited at the hostess stand, fumbling through the newspaper, averting my eyes from them, and hoping to blend into the crowd. But when a waitress came to clear their table, Powers glanced up. He yanked his head in my direction, and like a nest full of curious young owls, they all turned. Burt waved me over, but I jabbed at a small table on the other side of the restaurant, signaling that I'd eat alone. He waved again, more insistently this time, and, warily, I trudged their way.

I slid into the booth beside Powers while the waitress poured fresh coffee. Charley, with no need for my consultation, told her I'd have a "number two." And as I stirred cream into the coffee, I learned from David Powers that we "seemed to be in quite a pickle."

"Is that right?" I said.

"Yeah," Powers answered, "'fraid so."

For the next sixty minutes the four of us talked about the Sunshine Circuit's desperate need for Negro players. "The fact is," Powers said, "if it weren't for the crowds you and Kingstown draw, I don't know that we'd be here." He took a long draw of fresh coffee. "We've got our eye on a couple of colored boys," he went on, "and we're ready to sign one of 'em. But the brass is keeping an eye on Whitney. If you guys ban colored players, the prospects ain't good."

Charley twisted at a toothpick that dangled between his lips. "I hear that Leesburg and Jeffersonville are ready to sign Negro players too. But they're in the same spot as David."

"And the big-league teams are edgy," Burt added. "There's been one or two kids in other leagues who've already been moved up north. They haven't been promoted, mind you, just moved to safer ground."

David Powers stared into his coffee cup. "So like I was saying, we're in a pickle."

The waitress delivered my breakfast and, as I stirred my eggs and grits together, I took a long look at the men around me. "I'm guessing you want me to follow up on this, to interview these people, report names and plans, give people the idea that nobody with a lick of sense would ban colored players now; let 'em know that the world's moving the other way—that my role here?"

"Yeah," Burt said, "I think that's about got it."

"We got to turn the tide on this thing," Powers added. "The other day, when Pete said that banning colored boys would set us back ten years—I believe he was wrong. I think it'll cost more like twenty."

◆ ◆ ◆ ◆

I went back to my room and started making calls. The general managers in Leesburg and Jeffersonville were quick to confirm what I'd heard at breakfast: Both were ready to add Negro players, but their plans hinged on the Whitney city council.

From his office in Leesburg, Paul Inman told me: "We got a kid from Florida, and honest to goodness, Jack, he might be as good as Jackson. He could draw the same kind of crowds." There was, I believe, a trace of desperation in Inman's voice. "This kid's the future of our franchise, and we gotta have him."

Bob Hamil, Jeffersonville's manager, said they were thinking about signing a pair of Negro players. "They're both good boys," he insisted, "and I've been hinting to a few of the colored folks around town that they might be coming. I believe the Negroes will get behind us on this, Jack. They'll buy tickets if we can get those boys in here."

I also talked to John Clark in Kingstown. "Look," he said bluntly, "if you guys ban Negro players, we're done. The big-league club, they'll yank Nat out of here the next day. We'll lose the colored crowd. And the last guy out … well, he'll be the one to turn out the lights."

I sat back in my chair and started arranging my notes, my mind beginning to churn on an angle. There was a polite rap on the door, and then a timid voice announced "housekeeping." The maid was in her midthirties, I'd guess, wearing a peach-colored uniform, white trimmed at the collar and sleeves. A nametag introduced her as Ruby. I drummed my pencil against a clipboard while she collected used towels and washcloths. I propped my feet on the desk chair beside me, scratching out an outline, mulling ideas over, and beginning the hard work of finding inspiration.

Between thoughts I glanced at Ruby and asked if she had any kids. "Oh yes," the maid said, "my little girl's ten and we got a boy, twelve."

As she spoke, I was easily infected by her bright, contagious smile. "Your boy's about the same age as mine," I said. "He like baseball?"

Her smile lit the room, "Oh, yessir," she said, "the boys in our neighborhood, they're playing out in the street all the time, they're out there past dark just about every night."

"Yeah," I said chuckling, "it's hard for us to get our boy to come in for supper."

Ruby returned a giant pair of up-and-down nods. "I know just what you mean," she said.

"Your boy play in a city league?"

"No, sir," Ruby replied, "there ain't nothing like that 'round here for the colored boys."

She began to strip the bed, and I looked down to my notes again, still laboring with an outline. "Hey, Ruby," I asked, "speaking of baseball, your family like the Hawks?"

Ruby nodded yes. "We can't afford it too often, but sometimes—you know—for a special treat.…" As she slipped my pillows into freshly starched cases, she said, "Saw 'em play last night."

"Looked like a lot of colored folks were out there, is it always like that?"

Ruby shook her head no this time. "A lot of folks 'round here like to keep up with Percy Jackson," she said. A glow came over her. "My little boy, he says when he grows up he wants to be just like Jackie and Percy—he's saying it all the time."

I looked up from my outline, startled. It had never occurred to me, not once, that the colored kids running around barefoot on the outskirts of small towns dreamed of playing ball like the Bobcats third baseman. I could not imagine, having been a witness to his life, that anyone aspired to the place he had been given in the world.

Ruby shifted her eyes right and left, nervous, and wondering why I stared. Finally, I looked away and said, "My kid wants to be pitcher. He throws a tennis ball against the side of the house and imagines he's Warren Spahn."

"Oh yeah," Ruby replied with a sympathetic grin, "we do the same thing." Then, with her work finished, she turned for the door. "Is there anything else I can do for you?" she asked.

"No," I said, "thanks."

"Well, you have a nice day." She pulled the door closed behind her.

"Hey, Ruby," I called after her. The door peeked open. "Before last night, when was the last time you saw the Hawks play?"

Ruby thought for a moment. "Must've been 'bout a month ago, when Kingstown was here."

Chapter 22

In the summer of 1954 we were surrounded by all kinds of threats to our health and happiness: the spread of communism, crippling disease, massive annihilation from terrible new weapons.... But that summer, in Whitney, when we lay awake at midnight, Phil Edwards worried us more than Nikita Khrushchev. When we kicked off the sheets at 1:00 a.m., it wasn't the threat of polio that haunted us, but possible exposure to the sons of nearby sharecroppers. And at three in the morning, when we stared at the ceiling, we imagined that our way of life would be destroyed, not by an atom bomb, but by an invasion of impoverished janitors, maids, and garbage collectors from the south side of our own city.

With those thoughts muddling my mind, I began piecing my story together. I knocked out a few words a day, still searching for nuggets of helpful information, and struggling to find the angle that would ease my readers' minds. I wanted to talk about peanuts and popcorn, and about fathers and sons at the ballpark together, inseparably bound by a common affection. I'd employ every word, phrase, and sentence to reroute my readers' minds away from thoughts of whites and blacks living blended lives in our schools and restaurants.

And that meant changing the way they viewed Percy Jackson. He had become the town's best-known Negro. He worked side by side with white men; he traveled with them, sat beside them, shared a water bucket with them, and in almost every visible way he lived with them as an equal. When our readers looked at Percy, many of them could only imagine colored boys standing beside their daughters in the school cafeteria, and the thought made them shudder. I had to bring a more wholesome picture to mind. I had to reveal the benign treasure that lay hidden behind the imagined threats. I had to help my readers focus on baseball, and to see that, in Percy Jackson, Whitney possessed a player who had been given portions of grace and talent that we had never seen with our own eyes. And that for as long as he was a Bobcat, Memorial Stadium would be a sanctuary—a place to retreat and enjoy the sheer beauty of the game, undefiled by the sins that beset the outside world. The task was better suited to the gifts of Hemmingway, Wolfe, or Rawlings. But it had, for reasons only God knows, fallen into my feeble hands.

As I pondered the work before me, Bud Parsons weighed his. As I drafted paragraphs and pages, he visited every church in town; he ate lunch at a different restaurant every day, and he called on every club, society, and guild our phone book listed. Wherever he went, he told frightened moms that there was no difference between the classroom and the playing field. "That's just the start," he warned them. "Who knows what's coming next."

◆ ◆ ◆ ◆

Every day I searched the town for soothing news, yet everywhere I looked, ugly things continued to unfold. Conniving men had distorted a pristine game for selfish ends. My town lived in a foul mood. And my neighbors, once content and carefree, had become suspicious, seeing a subversive threat in every dark face they encountered.

I might've learned to live with all that, might've adapted and given up the old ways. But one change I could not abide, and that was the one to Rose Marie. My wife did not digest the latest news well. And she—like Helen, Luther, Billy Bender, and every family who lived on every block in town—simply could not grasp what had happened. All of a sudden we lived in the midst of a grade-B movie. It was as if we'd all been transported to some thoroughly depraved world that looked exactly like ours, but was on a collision course with disaster. And the bewilderment was taking a toll. Every day I could see the ebb—in the brightness of Rose Marie's eyes, the bounce in her step, her easy, enchanting charm—they were all receding like sand with the tide.

On the front porch Friday morning, after I'd returned from Chesterfield, I tried to persuade her that it would all pass. She looked down at the paper and quietly turned the page. "That's your stock answer, Hall. You always think things'll work out if we just wait long enough. But Pete Fry was right, there's no turning back. This is it, Hall, this is how things are going to be." She ran her fingers through snarled brown hair, and the sunshine glanced off her cheeks. She looked down the street one way and then the other; she looked tired, and there were wrinkles around her eyes that I'd never seen before. They were not the product of age, but of fatigue and worry. "I don't know why we're surprised," she said, "you drop a rock in a pond you get ripples." She peeked down at the paper again. "Nothing you can do to stop 'em."

The saddest part of the whole mess, Rose Marie thought, was that our days at the ballpark were over, at least for as long as Percy played. "This'll settle down," I told her again. "This all happened because of the all-star game, because Pete Fry had the world's worst idea."

She returned a sober, you-just-don't-get-it frown. "We don't know that," she said. "And from now on, there's no telling what'll happen." She leaned her head back, tilting her face toward the sun. "Who'd have ever thought that watching a baseball game could be dangerous."

Rose Marie was hardly alone. The entire town was in suspense, everyone holding their breath, anticipating the episode that would surely follow the now famous riots. As a writer, as a man who worked for the town paper, it was my job to bring people together, to show them our common ground, and to rally them around the things we all shared. But when I looked at Rose Marie, when I watched her rock back and forth staring at the paper, my thoughts of civic duty faded. I began to think only about her. I longed to resurrect the girl who made me laugh out loud every day, who—for as long as I had known her—had never seen ten consecutive minutes of sorrow, and who—for the last fourteen years—had loved the life we shared.

The front section of the paper rested on my lap, opened to page three where a photo of Phil Edwards roared off the page. A snarl smeared his face as he and the colored crowd behind him barked, "Percy don't play, we won't pay." And for the first time since I'd stepped foot in Whitney, I wondered what life might be like in another town.

◆ ◆ ◆ ◆

That afternoon the Bobcats traveled to Fulton, where Percy provided further proof that his days in Class C ball were numbered. And where I, like a detective alert for evidence, discovered that his teammates had laid claim to the hidden treasure; that they had found the very thing I hoped to share with the Herald's readers.

In the seventh inning of the first game, with the score tied, the Rattlers had a man on third with two outs. The batter blistered a ground ball just inside the line. Percy lunged for it, rolling over the base into foul territory. He got to his feet and unloaded the ball faster than I had believed a mortal man could throw. As the team trotted off the field, Brent Davenport, our pitcher, stood beside the mound waiting for Percy. He reached up with his right hand and pawed the top of Percy's cap, shaking the third baseman's head playfully, thanking him for preserving the tie. And as the two of them climbed down the dugout steps, Davenport slapped Percy on the butt as the players parted ways.

The next night we were down a run in the sixth; Taylor was on first. Percy launched a fastball over the center-field wall, and I swear he hit the ball so hard it might have rolled to the Fulton town square. Andrews, Giles, and Murphy charged out to greet him as he crossed home plate; others waited outside the dugout. Without reservation or reserve almost every guy on the team hugged and slapped and pounded Percy. Even Taylor, after he'd scored the tying run, turned and waited to shake hands with his colored teammate.

These were otherworldly moments for Percy, times when he escaped to a place that moved in slow motion, where he was deaf to the crowd and blind to every ugly diversion, where there was no one on earth except Giles, Douglas, Smith, Andrews, Henderson, and Murphy; where the only sound was the sound of their praise, and where—for as long as the moment lasted—nothing could be better than playing ball with the Whitney Bobcats.

Percy's teammates, when they greeted him at home plate, embraced a now-prized part of their common cause … while those in the white-only stands saw a lurking threat to their well-ordered lives.

◆ ◆ ◆ ◆

In the days following the June council meeting, that threat was magnified by the work of Phil Edwards. He was unwavering, shadowing Percy from Whitney, to Kingstown, to Jeffersonville. By day he visited with pastors and colored businessmen, and with anyone else—from any station of life—who'd take ten minutes to hear what he had to say. Armed with an array of indisputable facts, he proved that Percy was the circuit's best player. "And now they're talking about banning Negroes," Edwards would say. "It ain't right, and it's time we all said so."

By night he and a small band of church members besieged the town's ballpark. At the Negro entrance they marched and chanted; they made their case to the Negro crowds, prodding them to join the cause. And in those days the pickings were good. Colored fans, quickened by the news out of Whitney, were eager to watch a colored boy play ball. Some nights they made up half the crowd, and as they watched and listened, as they grasped the cold, hard facts around them, the scales began to fall from more and more eyes. Businessmen, teachers, craftsmen, and laborers—along with sharecroppers and janitors—began to sense what team owners had already seen: the brute economic force of a colored crowd.

And so Percy, a young colored kid who had become a menace to a loud and powerful part of our population and a source of emerging pride to the meeker part of our community, gave them, for the first time, a faint voice in our town's affairs.

And I was the sportswriter who was hoping and praying, and using every ounce of talent I had to persuade both groups that this kid was just another ballplayer, one we could all enjoy together.

And so, because of the role I'd been given, I was in Joe's office early Monday morning to run my first draft by him.

◆ ◆ ◆ ◆

"This thing's gotta be on the money," Joe snarled, snatching the pages out of my hand. He dropped into his seat and grabbed a pen. "We're at a crossroads here, Jack, and I'll be honest with you, I don't know if we're going to get through it." He read carefully, making notes and edits, crossing out my words and inserting his. "That's good," he'd mumble as he made his way down the page. Then, "Yeah, I like that." Then, marking the page, "What if we tried this …?" And then, when he was about halfway through, he looked up and said, "Folks need to know this ain't some slippery slope." He paused for a second, thinking, then looked down again, crossing out another word or two, and saying, "They gotta see this as a step in the right direction."

When he had made his way through the story, he tossed the copy across the desk and leaned back, rubbing his head. "You know Bud's dead wrong about all this," he said, "we ban colored boys from playing baseball, it ain't gonna make anybody happy, 'least not for very long. It's gonna be front-page news in eight towns; that's gonna get all the Negroes stirred up, and that's the crack in the door Phil Edwards needs—won't be three months before he's got 'em wanting to get into the schools, and then it'll be the restaurants, and then they'll be wanting to share the drinking fountains." Joe shook his head, perhaps wondering why Bud was blind to something so plain. "I wish we'd have put that kid on the all-star team," he said. "Half the trouble we're facing right now would've vanished into thin air … wouldn't have cost us a thing. Jackie Robinson's been an all-star—what—four or five times now? Hasn't exactly brought on national calamity, has it?" He picked up the story again, marked another change or two, and then tossed it back across his desk. "That's nice work," he said. "I hope it does some good."

◆ ◆ ◆ ◆

Later that day the Clayton Cowboys arrived in town. And, for the first time in all the years I'd been in Whitney, more than two hundred of their faithful fans trekked 120 miles to watch them play. The sun had just perched on the horizon when the convoy arrived—forty or more cars—all of them spiraling up the red-clay road toward the stadium. One by one they pulled into the lot, and on the attendant's command each car made a crisp left turn into its assigned slot.

The Clayton fans crowded into the stands on the third-base side. They were loaded with signs and slogans, and every time Percy's name was called, they joined with locals, screaming the same hate-fueled lines we had all heard before. I kept an eye on them. And through the middle innings I thought to myself: If they had come to create a spectacle, this was a sorry performance. There was no creativity or passion. And they had failed to give birth to any unforgettable gesture—the kind of thing that grows momentous with time, and with each retelling of the story.

But I had come to a hasty conclusion. And as the ninth inning opened, I saw that our neighbors from the west had been sandbagging us all along, waiting until the end of the game to unveil their grand finale. As the first batter came to the plate, they all stood and, row by row, filed out of the stadium. Like soldiers in formation they kept good order and moved with precision. From the back of the press box I watched them exit. As they cleared the box office, they made a sharp right turn and marched for the Negro exit. A few broke ranks and rushed to the parking lot. They popped open the trunks of their cars and gathered up armfuls of freshly painted signs, then rushed back to resupply their waiting allies.

After the final out, as the home crowd began its retreat from the stadium, the Claytonites began to march and sing, and to make a deliberate mockery of Phil Edwards. They formed a gauntlet at the Negro exit, a hundred of them on each side, facing one another, creating a monstrous path that stretched twenty-five yards into the parking lot. They thrust their signs into the air and screamed, "Percy goes back, because he's black! Percy goes back, because he's black!"

The Negro crowd instantly recoiled. They bottlenecked at the exit, gaping at the white mob—frightened—and too cowed to think about a challenge. Phil Edwards pushed his way to the front. His eyes traveled up and down both rows slowly; he studied the white crowd, trying to read their intentions. He smiled and laughed. And though he showed no fear, he was careful to keep his distance.

A pair of Whitney cops stood nearby. "We could use a hand over here," Edwards called to them. But neither showed any sign that he'd heard. The colored crowd was growing restless. They chafed at the gate, growing more and more agitated, and bristling like a herd of frightened cattle.

Their panic inflamed the white mob. The gauntlet narrowed and the snarls grew louder, "Percy goes back because he's black! Percy goes back because he's black."

Edwards gave the cops another try. "How about a hand over here?" he cried again. This time the cops turned and slowly ambled away. Edwards studied the white crowd; he glanced back at the cops; he laced his fingers through the chain-link fence, weighing a list of very few options. And then he did the last thing anyone would have expected: He retreated. He abruptly turned and began shepherding the crowd back to the stands. "Everybody back to your seats," he called. "Come on now, let's get back to the bleachers." As he moved among his people, he picked out a handful of his closest disciples and issued new orders. They passed the word to others, who passed it on to still more. And they all scurried through the crowd, spreading the word.

The white crowd looked on, mystified. Their chant waned as they looked to one another, confused, and wondering what the Negroes were up to.

Edwards huddled with Moses Walsh, the choir director at New Hope Church. Walsh was at least six foot four; he wore a long, crinkly beard, and he must've outweighed Lou Groza by twenty pounds. The two men hatched their plan, and Walsh hurried to the bleachers. He took his position there, centered before the Negro crowd. He spoke to those who had congregated on those first few rows, and then he poised a hand in the air; he rocked gently, tilting his head to the side, he closed his eyes prayerfully, blocking out the tumult around him. And then, with the graceful movement of Walsh's arms, the Negro crowd began to sing.

I strained to hear them. Unconsciously, I leaned toward the Negro bleachers, bending my ear in their direction. And there it was—just faintly—a few tender voices, singing, "Swing low sweet chariot. Coming for to carry me home…."

This wasn't the response the Clayton crowd had expected. They had no reply, no plan for retaliation. A frustrated voice yelled, "Hey, niggers, time to go home." Another screamed, "What're you afraid of?"

New voices blended into the Negro choir. "I looked over Jordan and what did I see. Coming for to carry me home," and the sweet music became a spark to dry kindling. Puzzled white faces blazed. A fleshy, middle-aged businessman, sweat-soaked and burning with bad temper, broke formation. He ran to the fence and slammed his sign into it—two, three, four times. "Get your nigger butts out here," he screamed.

From the colored section of Memorial Stadium, a chorus of pure and reposeful voices swelled, bathing the air with calm. "A band of angels coming after me. Coming for to carry me home." One by one, and row by row, in domino fashion, men, women, and kids joined hands. They angled their faces heavenward and closed their eyes. They'd all been struck deaf to anything but the sound of their own sweet song.

The Clayton gauntlet couldn't hold. A gang of young men—guys who might have been nineteen or twenty—enraged and emboldened by too much beer, charged the fence. They pounded at it, wildly screaming, "Niggers are all chicken! You're all chicken!"

Three thousand colored baseball fans were on their feet, hand in hand and swaying to the music, their voices surging over the stadium walls. "If you get there before I do. Coming for to carry me home."

Twenty-five or thirty of the Clayton men began to mock the colored crowd's courage. They clucked and squawked, and flapped their arms like chickens. Others reprised the chant, screaming, "Percy goes back because he's black."

But the bedlam was no match for the innocent faith of the Negro song. "Tell all my friends I'm coming too. Coming for to carry me home. Sometimes I'm up and sometimes I'm down. Coming for to carry me home. But still my soul feels heavenly bound…."

As the song faded, the fury from outside rushed in—the chants and screams, the taunts and ridicule—but the serenity of the colored crowd couldn't be shaken. Moses Walsh, without pause, tendered a reply. His right hand bounced in the air, and on his signal the stadium filled with thousands of Negro voices, all faithfully affirming, "There is a balm in Gilead. To make the wounded whole. There is a balm in Gilead. To heal the sin-sick soul…."

Their voices flushed away the anger. And slowly, the Clayton crowd began to yield. The stocky businessman paced the fence line, head down and flustered, looking as though he'd been in a fistfight with Archie Moore. In a final act of contempt he picked up his battered sign and screamed, "You niggers stay where you belong." He hurled the sign over the fence where it fell harmlessly. And then, flushed and emotionally wasted, he withdrew from the battle.

The choir's voice soared higher and gained strength. The song charged across the field and into the parking lot. "If you can't preach like Peter, if you can't pray like Paul. Just tell the love of Jesus, and say he died for all…." The visiting crowd was no match for Walsh's choir. The Clayton women, clustered to one side, gradually lowered their signs. They became still and gazed inside, and I believe, for at least a moment, they were moved by the tenderness of the song. As the second verse came to a close, they, too, began a quiet retreat.

The outcome of the clash was no longer in question: Majestic songs had conquered the violence. Others began drifting away, and the mob's leaders now stood passively, hands pressed to the fence, their consternation the only testimony one needed to see that they'd been outmaneuvered.

Another sign flew over the fence, trailed by a feeble challenge, "Get your butts out here." Another followed. And one more after that. But the battle was over. And before the choir finished their second song, the rest of Clayton's overmatched crowd surrendered. They straggled back to the parking lot. This hadn't gone according to plan, and they didn't get all they'd come for. But they didn't leave empty-handed. They had, after all, not made the long drive merely to incite an embarrassing riot. They had come to cast their vote with the Whitney city council. And it had surely been counted.

I was thankful this had come to a peaceful end. I made a few notes, figuring I'd do a two-hundred-word box recapping what I'd just seen, then I made my way to the car. It was late and I was tired, and I wasn't in the mood for one more surprise. But from the stadium exit I could see someone lingering. And from the silhouette I knew it was Bud Parsons.

"It's late, Bud," I called from twenty yards away, "can't we talk tomorrow?"

"No," Bud said, "'f-f-fraid not."

"I'm tired," I whined, "and I've still got work to do."

"I-I-I hear there's more teams thinking of signing niggers," Bud said, ignoring my lament. "That true?"

"Yeah," I replied sourly. "That's what I hear."

"A-a-and I hear that you and Joe think it's a good idea."

"They need the crowds, Bud, that's all there is to it—pure economics."

Bud looked down, shaking his head. "No it ain't, Jack. The people around here, they don't think that way. And that bunch who drove here from Clayton, let me tell you something, they're not real concerned 'bout supply and demand." Bud looked up. "You guys got to get that through your heads. These people care about living the way we're supposed to live; they're out here protecting a way of life."

"Bud, I believe we have had this conversation before. I'm pretty sure we could pick it up here tomorrow."

"Yeah," Bud said, "m-m-maybe so. But that's not what I wanted to tell you." He sighed hard and clamped both arms around his chest. "Listen, I-I-I came to tell you to be careful. There's folks around here who're nervous. They don't like this kid playing, and they sure enough don't want to see three or four more. And, Jack, the folks I'm talking about, they ain't gonna work through the city council. You hear what I'm saying?"

◆ ◆ ◆ ◆

Tuesday morning the article appeared. I had never worked so hard to sculpt a thousand words, nor worried more about the effect they'd have. The story began on the left-hand column of page one and then continued on page three across all five columns, stretching eight inches deep.

My narrative took the expected course, talking about moms and dads and the altogether wholesome effect that baseball has on a town. But it also veered down a couple of dirt paths the *Whitney Herald* had never traveled. It contemplated the life of an eighteen-year-old colored boy and wondered aloud as to his goals and deep ambitions. I reminded my friends that while politicians and activists were "manipulating events to achieve social change," Percy Jackson never wanted to do anything except play ball. I pointed out that he had seen the demonstrations, but had never participated in them, or encouraged them, or even known they had been planned.

"If you're worried about Jackson's political agenda," I wrote, "look at the way he's lived for the past few months. The Bobcats have played thirty games on the road, and Jackson has spent each of those nights in a boardinghouse, a stranger's spare room, or a run-down hotel in the seediest part of town. But he has never complained.

"He has eaten more than fifty team meals in the back of a bus, in a noisy restaurant kitchen, or out of a vending machine—usually alone—while the rest of his team enjoyed good company and a decent meal in neighborly surroundings. Yet he has never asked anyone to change the rules.

"He has played thirty-two home games, and on every occasion he has dressed and showered at the armory, alone. Yet he has never hinted, suggested, or outright asked for anything to ever be altered.

"His one purpose in life," I wrote, "is to fully use the gifts God gave him. He wants to catch, throw, and hit. He wants to play at the highest level his talent will take him. And then, at the end of the day, he wants to go home.

"Is that too much for anyone to ask?"

I wrote about Whitney's colored population. They had, I said, never posed a threat to the structure of our society. The bus system, despite the bump Bea Washington had thrown in its path, operated peacefully. And after the Supreme Court's obscene intrusion, our Negro citizens had obligingly agreed to return to their own schools.

"At next month's city council meeting," I said, "we have another chance to work together to keep things calm. Our colored neighbors enjoy a night at the ballpark; they love to watch Jackson play, and their support has kept the team alive. Why, with all the more threatening circumstances churning around us, wouldn't we encourage them to have some harmless fun? And why, given the caliber of Jackson's play, couldn't the whole town revel in the thrills of a great game?"

I talked about the other Sunshine Circuit teams, their need for bigger crowds, and their plans to sign Negro players. And then I concluded with these words: "This is not the time to ban colored players. We need them to keep our team alive and to help keep peace in our town. Negro players will not destroy our way our life; they offer us the best chance we have to preserve it."

◆ ◆ ◆ ◆

In the days that followed, I saw two things that will always stay with me.

I saw again that words were a potent weapon in a battle for men's hearts, and that they could soothe as powerfully as they could inflame. And I also saw that a handful of men, seized by the fear of an uncontrollable future, could change the world in a single second; that they could, with a solitary act, create an image in men's minds, and with it, could sway a crowd as mightily as a full page of well-crafted words.

That morning I pushed my way into the diner feeling like a duck in a shooting gallery. Helen smirked, a bit coolly I thought, as she watched the coffee pour. "I see your point," she granted, "I really do. But Bud's right about this. We don't know what it'll be next…." She winked and turned. "Your breakfast'll be right up."

Mike the banker remained stoic. "You might be right," he said with a sigh, "who knows? At least with baseball we got a choice—I mean, nobody's forcing anybody to go to the ballpark, but the schools … like I've said before, if signing a few colored ballplayers will keep 'em out of the schools, well, I s'pose it's worth a try."

And even Luther seemed to warm to the prospect. He hunched his shoulders and grumbled, "We gotta do something, I guess. And there's some of those boys who can play, you gotta give 'em that. But it don't sit right, you know what I mean? Don't sit right at all."

When I got to the office, Joe and Burt were on the phones, calling around town to gauge reaction. They were discovering the same things that I'd found at the diner: Whether or not people agreed with the logic, not many questioned the motive. And by midmorning I felt a germ of hope that hearts were beginning to soften. By eleven o'clock I felt a timid wave of relief, and I could even feel the bubbling up of pride—not just in my work—but in the *Herald*. We had, in the midst of the clamor and competing claims, used our platform to calm fears and to tighten the bonds of our community. We had appealed to our neighbors' better nature and, I thought, our town would be better for it.

The more we talked with teachers, businessmen, accountants, and carpenters, the better I felt. They all yearned to preserve the good life, and yet, with so many threats pressing from every side, the town groped for ideas and answers. And perhaps—nobody could say for sure, but perhaps—colored ballplayers were the offering that would save us.

At home things had taken a more sinister turn. We'd had the expected crank calls. "Maybe four or five," Rose Marie told me, "nothing I haven't heard before." But on the phone I felt a tremor in her voice—a whiff of panic that conveyed more than her words.

"What else, Rose? Tell me what happened."

"Wait a minute," she snapped. "Hang on, Jack!" She slammed the phone down and stomped away.

"Rose!" I shouted. "Rose?"

She was back on the line a few seconds later. "There's a car, Jack. It's parked outside, a black convertible, a Pontiac, I think. There are four men inside, they're just sitting there, pointing at our house."

"I want you to lock the doors, Rose. And whatever you do, stay away from them, you hear?"

"Yeah," she said. "This is the third time I've seen them, Jack. Before, they'd slow down when they got close to the house—like they were looking for a lost dog or something.

"Hang on," she said again. Then, a moment later, "They just pulled away. I don't like this. It's four grown men, Jack. And they're not looking for the family dog … maybe the police should come by, what do you think? Could you call them?"

"Yeah, you said it's a Pontiac, right?"

"I think so. It's a two-door convertible, I know that. And it's black."

"I'll call Burt right now, and then I'll be home. Lock the doors, Rose, and stay where you are."

Chapter 23

I was relieved to see a police car parked at the curb. I sped into the driveway and back to the garage. Billy Fitzpatrick, a cop who'd been a fixture around town for twenty years, was fumbling through trash cans, foraging behind trees and bushes, searching for anything that looked suspicious. But mostly, I suspect, he was trying to ease my wife's mind.

"Find anything?" I asked out the car window.

"No," Fitz said, "nothing unusual." He thumbed toward Chris's swing set. "Clyde's 'round the corner checking things out over there." I saw Billy's partner. He was squatted down like a catcher, stroking his mustache and combing through Rose Marie's garden.

I slammed the car door, and Rose Marie stepped outside. "Everything all right?" she called.

Fitz tipped his cap to her and flashed a full head of Irish-orange hair. "Everything's fine," he assured her, "probably just a few boys out to scare you, I imagine." He looked back to me. "We'll keep an eye on things, Jack. Don't worry."

I reached to shake his hand. "Thanks, Fitz, that means a lot."

The cop returned a firm grip. "Gotta stop the bad guys, Jack. That's why we're here." Then he called to Clyde, and the two cops drove away.

For the next several hours I kept watch from my front-porch rocker. I didn't see any signs of a black convertible, but the Whitney police offered a consoling presence. And at four o'clock, comforted by Fitz's pledge that he'd keep his eyes open, I left for the stadium.

◆ ◆ ◆ ◆

That night, after the game, I visited with Walter at the armory. We talked baseball for fifteen or twenty minutes, and then I asked him about the threats he'd mentioned a couple of days before.

His brows peaked. "What about them?" he asked.

"Just curious," I said, "did anybody see the car?"

Walter returned a "beats me" shrug and turned to Percy.

"It was big and black," the boy said, "that's all I know."

"You remember if it was a two-door or four-door?" I asked.

Percy cocked his head, thinking. "Two-door," he recalled. "And it was a convertible, I remember the roof was slung kinda low in back."

"You remember anything else?"

"A big silver stripe," Percy said, "came right down the middle of the car."

◆ ◆ ◆ ◆

Just past midnight I swung my Ford down Pine Cove Lane. A car passed from the opposite direction. And given the hour, that alone was striking. But it was the chrome streak—"the big silver stripe"—that made me gasp. My eyes flashed up to the rearview mirror: a soft convertible top.

I wheeled into the driveway and hurried to the back of the house. I crept to the side yard and crouched in the shadows of three pines—and I waited. *Where is Fitz?* I wondered. *Where is Clyde? Where are all the cops who promised to be here?*

I heard tires on pavement. The Pontiac's lights had been doused. It slipped past the house, barely moving. The windows were down and I heard muffled voices. Brake lights flashed—on, then off, then on again—as the car inched by. After it cleared the house, it accelerated and disappeared.

In the next few seconds my mind repeated a single question over and over again, at least a thousand times: *Where are the cops?* I stayed where I was, crouched in the darkness. I didn't blink or twitch. I may not have even breathed. Then I heard it again. The black convertible stopped short. I slipped into the backyard, hurried across two neighbors' lawns, and then ducked behind a holly bush beside Caleb Baker's carport. The Pontiac sat across the street. I could see four shadowy forms inside—all sitting in perfect silence.

I hustled back to the house and called the police. The phone rang three, four, five times. Finally, Scott Hancock, a kid who was new to the force, picked up on the seventh ring. "Where are you guys?" I hissed. "You're supposed to be here. You promised!"

"Jack?" Hancock replied. "What's the problem? What's going on?"

"The Pontiac's here. Four men are inside. Where are you guys?"

"Things have been quiet at your place, Jack. We had a car patrolling 'til midnight, nobody had seen anything to worry about, so we sent 'em on another call."

I closed my eyes—crestfallen, furious, and scared. "Look, Scott, I need somebody over here."

"It may take awhile, Jack—I don't have anybody out that way right now."

"Do what you can, Scott. And do it right now!"

I ran upstairs and peeked through a thin slit in the bedroom curtains. The Pontiac had crawled forward and was directly across the street. Two men slipped out the front, the other pair followed. I watched as they huddled at the trunk of the car. Two of them slung burlap sacks over their shoulder. And two hoisted a heavy black footlocker. Then, quiet as a brood of cottonmouths, the four of them slithered closer.

With a strident whisper I commanded Rose Marie to get up.

She moaned in protest.

"Get up!" I ordered again. "We've got to get out of here!"

"Why?" she stammered. "What are you talking about?"

"I'll explain later. Get up, Rose, we got to go."

I ran to Chris's room. "Come on, pal, we're going on a little nighttime adventure." I picked up his slippers, then scooped him up out of bed and cradled him in my arms.

"What are we doing?" he asked. "I want to go back to sleep."

I set him down at the top of the stairs. "Wait here—I'll be right back."

"Rose," I hollered. She stumbled into the hallway.

"Please tell me what's going on," she pleaded, "Please."

"Later."

I picked up Chris and started down the stairs. Rose was a step behind, half-asleep and wobbly.

"Where are we going?" Chris moaned.

"It's going to be okay, pal, we're just—"

The front windows exploded. I heard a second crash. And then a third. Outside, a voice shrieked, "Nigger lovers!"

Chris erupted in tears.

"Oh no," Rose Marie screamed. "Jack, what's happening?"

Chris wailed uncontrollably. He grabbed me around the neck, clinging fiercely. "It's okay," I lied. "Everything's okay. You sit right here." I put him down and looked at Rose Marie. "Don't move!"

I flew downstairs and charged for the door. Through billowed curtains I saw the flash, and then—behind an instant of chilling calm—came an apocalyptic roar. The house shook. Rose Marie stumbled, just catching hold of the banister to avert a plunge down the stairs. More glass shattered. The air soured with the stench of gunpowder. And the Pontiac's engine roared away into the distance.

I raced back to the stairs. "Are you all right?" I screamed. "Chris, are you okay?"

"Help us, Dad," Chris cried. "Come help us."

"What happened, Jack?" Rose Marie burst into sobs. "What's going on?"

"I don't know," I said, trying to sound calm. "I don't know." Then, quietly, I muttered, "Thank God you're all right." I closed my eyes and pulled Chris to my side. And I whispered thanks for my wife and son's safety.

But the gratitude didn't linger. My home had been violated. My wife and son clung to one another on the stairs of their own home, sobbing, balled up together in fear—and both innocent as lambs. These were transgressions temporal men don't forgive. And I roiled in a blend of grief and rage.

"Stay where you are," I told Rose Marie, "I'll call Burt, we'll get somebody working on this." I marched toward the kitchen. "It was the Pontiac," I hollered up the stairs, "the same car you saw this morning."

I had just turned into the kitchen when I heard a bang on the front door. A voice hollered, "Is anybody home? Is anybody there?" I froze. The voice was familiar, but it wasn't Fitz or Clyde. It wasn't any of the cops I knew. I crept to the foyer, grabbing Chris's baseball bat on the way.

"Who is it?" I screamed. "Who's there?"

"It's me, Walter. Are you all right?"

"What the …?" I cracked the door open. "Walter, what are you doing here?"

"Is everybody all right?" he asked again, his eyes darting around the house frantically.

"Yeah," I said, "we're okay."

Walter looked down the street and waved urgently, signaling his wife and son who waited in a car parked at the end of the block.

"Who is it, Jack?" Rose called. "Who's there?"

"It's Walter Jackson," I said. "Everything's all right."

Roberta and Percy approached the house guardedly. At the end of the driveway Roberta paused, surveying the blown-out windows, the gunpowder stains that streaked the front wall, and the small flame that flickered beside our favorite rockers. Slowly, she walked to the door, kicking at the burning rubble and reducing it to embers. Then she joined Walter and Percy inside.

Glass was everywhere. Pictures, books, and family keepsakes littered the floor. The sunburst clock, once the centerpiece of the living room wall, lay on the floor in ruins—a fallen, impotent idol.

"What are you doing here?" I asked Walter. "How in the world did you know?"

"Percy spotted the car," Walter said, "he saw it at the stadium, and—I don't know—just felt like we ought to see what they were up to." Walter took off his hat and looked down, scuffing his toe across the floor. "I'm sorry," he said, "I'd have done something sooner, I-I-I just never thought anybody would ever do something like this."

Roberta Jackson's eyes roamed the house, lingering on the glass, the smashed vases, and family photos—and they welled up with tears. Then, with plain determination, she shrugged off her jacket, looked at me, and said, "Where's your broom and mop, we need to get at this."

"It's one o'clock in the morning," I protested, "we—"

Roberta Jackson threw up a hand, commanding me to hush. "Where's the broom?" she repeated.

"This way," I said, and led her to the kitchen.

As she gathered buckets and rags, I phoned Burt. "Somebody told the cops to leave," I told him. "I want to know who. And I want to know why."

"We'll find out," Burt promised. "I swear, Jack. We'll get to the bottom of this."

At one fifteen in the morning, standing in the kitchen beside Roberta Jackson, I broke. Grief overcame the contending emotions, swamping over anger, pride, revenge—even love. Sorrow became the one thing I couldn't contain, and like a five-year-old kid I burst into tears. "You wouldn't believe this," I blubbered to the town mayor, "you wouldn't believe it if you saw it with your own eyes."

"I'm real sorry, Jack," Burt replied. "And somebody's going to pay, I promise you, somebody's going to pay for what they did to you."

I raised my eyes toward Rose Marie and Chris. "Somebody already has."

A pair of police cars arrived five minutes later. Two cops combed the place for clues. The opening salvo, they quickly discovered, had come from three bricks; a hand-scrawled note had been tied around each of them. The first read "Nigger lovers." The second one, "We'll never mix with niggers." And the third demanded that we "Get the niggers off the field."

The third cop roamed the street, while the fourth, Sam Wright, asked me to tell him what happened.

"Where were you guys?" I railed. "You were supposed to be here. You promised."

"Yeah, I know," Sam moaned. "Me and Lewis had the last shift. We were riding by the place 'bout every ten minutes; didn't see anything out of the ordinary; nobody had seen anything all day, Jack. Just didn't make sense to stick around."

"You promised," I fumed. "You said you'd be here."

"We thought the trouble had passed. I'm sorry, Jack. Now listen, why don't you tell me what these guys looked like? Maybe we'll find these creeps."

I stared into the distance trying to remember what I'd seen. "One had a mustache, one might've had reddish hair," I said, "but it was hard to tell, he was wearing a baseball cap. And one," I thought, "was nearly bald." I glanced at Sam. "It was dark, I couldn't see much."

"You didn't see anything else? You couldn't make out their faces?"

"No," I said, "it was too dark."

Sam Wright, a cop I'd known for a decade, took a long look around my living room. He put his hands on his hips and studied me, as if he were trying to decide whether or not to trust me with a dark family secret. Neither of us spoke. And then a villainous smile squirmed to his lips. He fetched a handkerchief from his back pocket. Carefully, and with willful deliberation, Sam mopped the sweat from his face and neck. Then he slowly removed his cap, he leaned his head forward patting at the perspiration, making sure I got a very good look at his nearly bald head.

"I think I got it," he said, flipping his notebook closed, "but if you think of anything else ..." he slapped the notebook against my shoulder "... you be sure to let me know, you hear."

It was eighty degrees outside, and I suddenly shivered from an icy chill.

After the cops had gone, Rose Marie and Chris drifted downstairs. Roberta Jackson leaned her broom against the wall. She walked to my wife and son and took Rose Marie's hands into hers. "We're gonna get this all cleaned up," she said gently, "don't you worry."

Rose sniffed. "Thank you."

"You sit down," Roberta said, "and let me bring you something—some tea or water—or maybe a cup of coffee?"

"A glass of water." Rose nodded appreciatively. "That'd be nice."

"And what about you, honey?" she said to Chris. "Would you like something?"

Chris turned away, burying his head into his mother's side, still confused and whimpering.

"We'll find you something," Roberta said as she turned for the kitchen.

In a few minutes Rose Marie joined the work, and the five of us quietly swept and mopped and wiped away the awful mess that four of our neighbors had made. After a few minutes more, Percy walked over to Chris. He sat beside him on the couch and handed him a dust rag. Gently, and with a playful push on the shoulder, he said, "I could use a little help over there." Chris wiped his eyes and sniffed. He took the rag and held it in his lap. Then he pursed his lips and nodded okay and with his eyes still wet from the tears, he joined Percy in the foyer.

Joe and his wife came by and pitched in. Burt and Jean showed up too. And Mark Adair swung by with a photographer to find out what had happened. But my closest neighbors stayed home. They glimpsed through pulled curtains, or spied on us from the shadows of darkened porches. They knew why this calamity had fallen on us. And for them, the risks were too high.

The Jacksons were the last to leave that night. We stood at the door; it must have been 3:00 a.m. when Roberta reached for Rose Marie's hand. "It's gonna be all right," she said. "I know it don't look that way now, but it's in the Lord's hands." She closed her eyes, calling to mind a Bible verse she knew by heart. "He tells us that, 'We are troubled on every side, yet not distressed; we are perplexed, but not in despair; Persecuted, but not forsaken; cast down, but not destroyed.' He don't allow us to suffer more than we're able." She tightened her hold on Rose's hand. "It's gonna be okay," she said.

My wife mouthed, "Thank you," and reached around to hug Roberta. "Thank you," Rose whispered.

Roberta returned the embrace and then stepped away. She reached up and brushed a tear from Rose Marie's cheek. "Sweetheart," she said, "it'd take me a thousand years to repay you for what y'all have done for us." Her dark fingers lingered on Rose's face. "I'll be back tomorrow and we'll finish this up, okay?"

Rose squeezed Roberta's hand and nodded.

I stepped out to the front porch with them. "Thanks again," I said, "you've been a big help, all of you. We're sure grateful."

Walter bowed his head. "I'm awful sorry," he said, "just as sorry as I can be."

"Me, too." I placed a hand on Walter's shoulder. "Listen, I know it's late, but could I have a word with you? It'll just take a second."

"Sure," Walter replied. "What's on your mind?"

I guided him down the front steps and we stood in the driveway, our backs to Roberta and Percy. "Walter, you need to be careful. These guys are coming after you—tomorrow, the next day, next week—I don't know. But they're coming; I'd put a thousand bucks on it."

Walter rubbed at the back of his neck and head. "I know," he said. "And after this," he swept his hand back toward the house, "I'm surprised they hadn't come already. Can't figure out why they'd come here first."

I tightened my grip on his shoulder. "You need a plan—one that doesn't include the cops. This is all up to you. You've got to protect your family."

My friend glanced up coldly. "Yessir," he replied, "I understand."

◆ ◆ ◆ ◆

Rose Marie, Chris, and I spent the next three nights at the Whitney Inn, and it was there, over those seventy-two hours, that we began to feel like strangers in our own hometown. The first of the aftershocks came early Thursday morning. We were on our way to the coffee shop and I stopped to buy a paper. I had reached into my pocket and was fumbling for a dime when I caught my first glimpse of the front-page photo. I had expected it; there was no reason for me to be surprised. But that first glance … the shock, the sudden and crushing weight of sorrow…. I reached for the paper and spread it open before of me. There was our home—assaulted and defiled—and splayed across three columns above the fold. Had I not been in a public place, restrained by the dread of humiliation, I'd have bawled like a jilted bride.

At the table I tossed the sports section to Chris. "Let me know what happened in the National League, will you?" I asked. Then Rose Marie and I took turns reading Mark Adair's story. We were relieved that Chris wasn't in school, that he wouldn't be forced to the awkward end of puzzled stares, or pestered by meddlesome teachers, or embarrassed by a flood of blundering questions from parents, and coldhearted kids.

All over Whitney, as soon as rubber bands popped off newspapers, that photo began to play on people's minds. I saw it at the diner and on the streets—and even at the office: People averted their eyes from mine; friends whispered to one another when I passed; conversations, even with people I'd known for years, were inexplicably stilted. And suddenly, we all felt awkward, everywhere.

I strained for an explanation. This was the place where I'd lived for the past ten years, where I had led the fruitful part of life—as a husband, father, and reporter—and where I made a contribution to the world, using whatever gifts I'd been given to keep my friends engaged in the life of our town. And it wasn't as if Rose Marie had been a spectator. While I was at work, she'd been all over the place—at the Garden Club, at church, playing bridge with friends. She was the secretary of the PTA, and hadn't missed a single game in her son's entire Little League career. And Chris—for the past six years he'd been every teacher's favorite kid.

But now it felt as if we'd been cast outside the pale, as if—subconsciously, and perhaps even reluctantly—we'd been forced to the fringe of town. The desolate act of four men, breathed to life on the front page of Thursday's paper, stirred up men's imaginations, provoking them to wonder—if even faintly—whether I had been the spark that ignited the town's troubles.

◆ ◆ ◆ ◆

Later that night the Bobcats fell to Leesburg, 5-3, but Percy continued to pile up imposing stats: a pair of hits and an RBI, a walk in the fourth—and in the top of the sixth he snagged a sharply hit ground ball to rob a

Generals hitter of a sure double. Over the course of nine innings, while the whole town wondered about the future of colored players, Percy proved again that he had no peer.

◆ ◆ ◆ ◆

We didn't get back to our room until after midnight. Chris was too tired to bother with pajamas. He waved a toothbrush in the vicinity of a few molars, then fell into the rollaway bed and was dreaming sweetly before I had a chance to say good night.

Rose Marie took her turn in the bathroom, and I flipped to the Steve Allen show, hoping that he and Gene Rayburn would ease the load that weighed us down. We enjoyed a song by Steve Lawrence and Eydie Gorme. We laughed at a stand-up routine by Lenny Bruce. And then, at about twelve thirty, I kissed Rose good night. We were exhausted and emotionally drained, and despite the hundreds of reasons we had to lie awake and worry, we were both dead to the world five minutes later.

But the respite wouldn't last. And our sleep was rudely pared by the shrill sound of an impatient phone. Through a bleary, half-opened eye, I checked the clock: Only an hour had passed, and I groaned, certain that my life was about to take another painful turn. I reached for the phone. "Yeah," I said cringing.

"You were right," a voice trembled.

"What? Who is this?" I mumbled.

"It's Walter. There was an explosion, just like at your place." His voice quivered. "Everything, the house—it's all a mess."

"I'll be right there," I said. Wide awake, and with my own voice wavering, I asked, "Is everybody all right?"

"Yessir." Walter sighed. "I took your advice. Roberta and the kids, they been sleeping at my brother's house. He and I been trying to keep an eye on things here…." Walter's voice ebbed away. "My house—they've bombed my house."

"I'll be right there," I said.

I threw off the covers and stepped into the slacks that I'd tossed over a chair. "It's the Jacksons," I told Rose Marie.

"What is it?" she asked. "What's wrong?"

"Their house was bombed. It's the same guys, Rose, the same guys who got us. I'm heading over there."

"Wait," she insisted, "I'm coming with you."

While Rose dressed, I called Joe and told him to get a photographer over there right away. I called Charley to let him know that his best player had just been attacked. And then, with a heart that felt more like a bowling ball, I shook Chris awake and broke the news: It was time for another late-night adventure.

We pulled up to Walter's place at two o'clock. A fire truck was angled into his lawn. Its red light pulsed for a hundred feet in every direction—steadily and with an eerie rhythm. Through each beat I could see smoke rising. Crumbs of glass glistened in the bushes and grass. The whole scene was wrapped in the scent of burning wood.

The family watched from across the dirt road—their neighbors gathered around them—everyone afraid and struggling to make sense of what was before them.

I slammed the car door behind me and watched as firefighters packed their gear. Rose got out of the car slowly. She gazed at the house, the family, the fire truck—at the rising smoke. She couldn't reckon this assault of confounding images. There was no frame of reference, no means for measuring the depth of this depravity.

Chris was shaken and scared. "Why did they do this?" he asked. "Why do they want to hurt us?" I picked him up and hugged him.

"They got to get through me before they can hurt you, pal. And that's not going to happen." Chris put his arms around my neck and hugged back. I nestled him closer, caressing his back and head, and I whispered in his ear, "Nobody's going to hurt you. I won't let anybody hurt you or Mom."

The three of us walked over to the Jacksons. "Did you see who did it?" I asked Walter.

He stared straight ahead. Firemen brushed by us. "No," he said blankly, "but I saw the car—black convertible, chrome stripe. I was right up there," Walter said, flinging a hand to the side, "was just a few houses down; saw a burst of light, the explosion came right behind … went off about a quarter to one."

"Police been here?"

"No." Walter sneered. He glanced at his watch. "And I called them before I called you."

Rose Marie went to Roberta. "I'm so sorry," she said. Roberta clung to Rose's hand and the two women stood together, watching the smoke climb.

Chris edged alongside Percy. The ballplayer put his hand on the boy's shoulder, and Chris leaned into Percy's side. They stood quietly too. And then, after Chris had absorbed all his mind could hold, he said, "I'll come over tomorrow with some rags. We'll work together, okay? Just like at my house."

A car rushed up beside mine; Jimmy Giles charged out of the driver's side. He put his hands on top of his head. "Oh no," Giles groaned. "Oh no." He reeled toward his teammate's home, "This is unbelievable." He cried, "unbelievable."

Denny Douglas emerged from the passenger side. He stood beside the car, motionless and silent, taking a full inventory of the damage. He stared straight ahead—at the burned house, the broken glass, the water-stained curtains. And then Denny hollered, "This ain't gonna stand, Perce. We'll find who did this. We're gonna see some justice here, I promise you."

It was twenty past two when a police car finally showed. Fitz and Clyde were the cops on duty; neither seemed to be in much of a hurry. They talked to Walter for ten minutes. And then Fitz searched the house while Clyde canvassed the onlooking crowd, asking the frightened neighbors what they'd seen. A half hour later they climbed back into their car, and as I watched from Walter's front yard, I inspected each man's features. I saw them in precise detail—as if through a telescopic lens—as if both men moved in slow motion. A chill ran through me. And then I heard an echo of my own voice from the night before: "One had reddish hair," I had told Sam Wright, "and one wore a mustache."

A fireman approached Walter. "That's about all we can do," he said.

Walter thanked him. Then he turned to his family and said, "Come on, let's see what's left."

While they were inside, Charley's Buick arrived. Johnny Andrews was sitting shotgun, Henderson and Murphy were in back. As the car slowed, the players jumped out, their eyes bulging in horror.

"This is scary," Henderson said. "I can't believe one human being would do this to another."

"Holy—why would anybody do this?" Murphy asked.

Percy's teammates clustered together in the front lawn.

"This is sick," Giles said, "I don't understand…."

"No, it's evil," Andrews said, "this right here ain't sick; it's pure evil."

"We'll find these guys," Douglas vowed. "We got to make this right."

Percy and Walter stepped out of the house, each with an armload of family valuables.

"When you get that stashed away, could you step over here?" Charley called. "Both of you."

We huddled around the Buick. Charley looked at Percy and Walter. "Listen," he said, "I'm sorry we weren't here. We just weren't thinking. We should've known. We should've had somebody with you." The lines in Charley's face tightened. "Nobody's gonna get near you guys again, okay, Perce? We missed 'em the first time, but it ain't going to happen again."

He went to the trunk of the car, signaling his players to follow. "I've talked to the guys," he told Percy, "that's why I was a little late." He yanked out a big canvas bag and slammed it to the ground. He pulled a bat out of it and handed it to Henderson. "Start passing these around," he said. He pulled out another one, and then another, and then two more after that. "Everybody's on their way over here," he said. "Just about everybody. Wherever you go, whatever you do—you're gonna have three guys with you. And every one of 'em's gonna have a thirty-six-ounce Louisville Slugger." He slung the bag against his car. "I don't know who did this, but if they want to take on the Whitney Bobcats, well then, bring it on."

Another car pulled up. Tommy Lewis, Galen West, and Sam Fowler hurried out. A third car was right behind. Haddock, Davenport, and Schaeffer were inside. They all grabbed their bats, and with a nod, a glance, a look, or touch—they all let Percy know that he had nothing more to fear.

Charley eyed the players who had gathered. "All right," he said, "me, Giles, and Davenport, we'll take the first shift; after that—"

"Uncle Charley," a callow voice intruded. Charley looked down at Chris. "Yeah, buddy, what is it?"

Chris pushed his chin toward the canvas bag. "You forgot me."

The Jackson family had piled into Walter's car. Rose Marie hurried to the passenger side, to where Roberta sat. "We'll meet here in the morning," she said. "I'll bring a mop and plenty of rags."

They pulled away, but the rest of us lingered, struggling through the events of the past few days. Charley tossed the canvas bag back into the trunk. "Dad-gum shame," he said. "Kid was really getting good."

"What are you going to do?" I asked. "The thing with the bats—that's a powerful gesture—but what are you going to really do?"

Charley slammed the trunk closed. "You know exactly what I'm going to do." He groaned. "It's not like I got a lot of options here." I turned and looked at him—startled at first—and then, silently, I groaned, too. I'd seen this look before. It was the burst of anguish that comes with the last out of a tough loss, when there are no more options, when defeat must finally be accepted. "I'll be on the phone first thing tomorrow," he said. He looked up and his eyes were damp. "We got to get this kid out of here."

Early the next morning Charley met with Joe and Burt, and together they all came to the inescapable conclusion: It was time for Percy to move on. Twenty minutes later Charley was on the phone, and by noon the deal was done. By the end of the week the Sunshine Circuit's best player would take the field for the Terre Haute Huts. And that night, just before game time, we got word that Nat Quaid was on a bus and headed to the Decatur Commodores.

Nobody was willing to bring it up that morning, but we all knew where this would lead. And that afternoon, when the rest of the Bobcats heard the news, they understood too: None of them would be in Whitney next year.

Chapter 24

Friday morning the train station bustled with harried passengers and overtaxed porters. It teemed with the sounds of hissing engines and the fading whistles of departing trains. The place brimmed with the climactic thrill of reunion—and with the heartbreak of unbearable parting. And we would soon add our own emotions to the mix.

In the main terminal I spotted Haddock and Andrews. Both players stood guard at the entrance to the platforms, each with a Louisville Slugger in plain view, the bat resting on his shoulder, fingers twitching on the handle.

"You expecting a baseball game to break out?" I said with a smile to Johnny.

He managed a grin in reply. "No," he said, "but nobody's going to mess with Percy today, not around here anyway."

"Anybody's got a problem with Perce," Haddock chimed in, "they're gonna have a problem with us first."

The Jackson family waited at gate three. I had to smile at Percy, decked out in a new suit and a pair of gleaming black shoes. Charley stood beside him; Giles, Douglas, and the others, they were there too—each with a bat at the ready and willing to make sure that nothing spoiled Percy Jackson's farewell.

"Kid's going to make us proud," I said to Charley as I reached to shake Percy's hand.

"Yeah." Charley beamed. He slapped his third baseman on the back. "I can't wait to see what you do up there, Perce."

Percy looked down, grinning bashfully.

Rose Marie raced for Roberta Jackson and hugged her neck. "Are you scared?" she asked.

Roberta's eyes sprung wide and she bit her lip nervously. "Yes, ma'am, a little," she said. "But we're excited for him too."

"It's going to be great up there," I told Percy. "No distractions. No nonsense. You can just play ball."

"They already got three Negro players in that league." Walter smiled. "Don't seem to be having any problems at all."

The fateful call came. "All aboard!" the conductor screamed. Percy looked around and sighed. He traded a long hug with mother, father, and sister. He reached for my hand, and for the first time in his life, Percy looked me in the eye. "Appreciate what you done," he said. Then he grabbed his duffle bag.

One by one his teammates approached him. Each player slapped him on the back. They grabbed hold of his hand; some hugged him. Each one wished him good luck, and Percy knew, without doubt or misgiving, that these men would miss him—not just because he hit like Musial—but because they had become friends.

Douglas was next to last in the line. He grabbed Percy's hand and yanked him forward, wrapping him up like a love-starved bear. "I'm gonna miss you," he growled. He pushed Percy away, still holding him by both shoulders. He looked him up and down and with a massive grin he said, "Having you around here, I tell you what, it's been a blast." Denny reached for a bat that rested against the pillar behind him. "I want you to have this," he said. "I hit thirty-two home runs with it last year, heaven only knows what you'll do with it." A tear slid across Denny's cheek. "You break it and I'll kill you."

Percy reached for the bat. "That's real nice," he replied. Then he looked down and stood there silently.

Douglas winked at him. "Go on," he said, "you keep jabbering away like this and you'll miss your train."

Giles was the last man to say good-bye. "I'm sorry all this happened," he said. "If it hadn't been for you, none of us would be here. You saved us all, Perce. We all owe you."

Percy couldn't muster an audible reply. He put his hand on Jimmy's shoulder and then glanced back at the team. Tears streamed down

Percy's face. Embarrassed, and on the verge of losing control, he turned for the train.

"Hey, Perce," Giles yelled. "There's one more thing."

Percy stopped and turned.

Jimmy reached into his jacket pocket. "You remember the first night you played? You pinch-hit, remember, ripped a double into center field." He held up his hand. "This is the ball. I've been holding it for you, been waiting for the right time to give it to you." Jimmy handed the ball to Percy. "We all signed it. We want you to remember what happened here, want you to remember that there was a time when we were all on the same team."

Chris ran up beside Jimmy. "I signed it too, Perce. Right there, see?"

Percy pulled Chris to his side. "Yeah," he sniffed, "I see."

"And I did too," I called from the back of the platform. Percy lifted the ball in my direction. "Thanks," he said.

Then he looked at his team for the last time. Every eye had reached its dew point. Nobody could summon the composure to utter one more word.

The conductor called again, for the third time, "All aboard."

Percy heaved a sad, shuddering breath, and disappeared.

We watched the train pull away. And when it had finally vanished, Douglas said, "Now there's irony for you."

I shoved him away. "Didn't know you knew the term," I joked.

"There's plenty you don't know." Douglas grinned.

"So tell me, where's the irony?"

"Perce," Denny said, still gazing down the tracks. "He's the one folks don't want playing. And now, because of what they've done, he's probably the only of us who will."

◆ ◆ ◆ ◆

Two weeks later the city council repealed the Memorial Stadium exemption, thereby forbidding whites and Negroes to ever be on the same field at the same time within our city limits. There was no angst in the council room that day—no outrage, no astonished gasps when the final vote was taken. With Percy gone there was nothing to fight for. The principle of the thing had lost its face and voice. And without the physical presence of Percy Jackson, the opposition lost heart, leaving a clear path for Bud Parsons.

Though it passed in relative calm, the vote's effects would reach far into the future. With no hope for another Percy Jackson, the fate of the Bobcats was sealed. That morning, with the closing bang of Burt's gavel, the final chapter of the Sunshine Circuit's illustrious story neared its end.

◆ ◆ ◆ ◆

OCTOBER 1954

Since that day life has raced in the wrong direction. Mistrust and resentment now darken the most common affairs between men of different races. Phil Edwards charges around town inventing new ways to cast doubt on white men's motives. Colored leaders have banded together. They meet weekly to pool their strengths; the protests have become louder and longer, and the anger—long seething but kept under cover—boils over and is vented in plain view.

Rumors entangle the town. Doctors, lawyers, and plumbers all worry out loud about the prospect of mobs and marches. And if the whispers are true, the agitators won't stop until they've forced the school doors open.

The covenant between Dick Reeves and Chester LaBarr fractured into more pieces than Humpty Dumpty. The radio station, along with the *South Side News,* now stands with Edwards, demanding unobstructed access to schools, buses, and lunch counters. Their editorials, news reports, articles, and announcements are all written to nourish the strife. And in Whitney's southernmost neighborhood, forbearance is no longer a virtue.

◆ ◆ ◆ ◆

After the Sunshine Circuit died, Rose Marie and I were forced to confront another unavoidable truth: It was time for us to move on too. And at the end of the year I took a job with the *Atlanta Constitution.* As I write this, we've been in our new city for several weeks, and I'd be lying if I didn't confess that we long for home. We yearn for Whitney the way mourners ache for the presence of a loved one who's been unexpectedly taken. We are incomplete, all of us lacking an essential ingredient that makes men whole: the place where we belong.

We are sad but hopeful. And the three of us share the sense that in this city—even if in fits and starts—Negroes and whites will figure out how to move forward.

The Crackers, Atlanta's double-A team, has its own fleeting and checkered past with Negro players. And there are, for now, none on the roster. Last year Nat Peeples appeared in their first two games—both on the road—and then was shipped to Jacksonville before the team played a regular season game in Ponce de Leon Park. But Earl Mann, the Crackers' owner, has always had a knack for making the right move. And when it comes to ballplayers, Whit Wyatt, the Crackers' manager, reminds me of Charley: He's got a heart that's softer than Santa Claus.

I'm already in love with Ponce de Leon Ball Park. A magnolia tree stands in center field—it's actually in play—and it's given birth to the queerest set of ground rules I've ever seen. Only two players have hit a home run into the tree, Babe Ruth and Eddie Matthews. Just close your eyes and imagine that. And last year, in this very park, Bob Montag hit the world's longest home run. This is—I swear on every Bible in the First Baptist Church—absolutely true: At the moment of Montag's swing, a train rolled along the tracks that parallel the first-base line. The ball rocketed four hundred and fifty feet over the wall, splashing down into one of the three coal cars. A week later the train's fireman appeared at the locker-room door. He found Montag and tossed him the ball. On it he'd scrawled: "Atlanta to Nashville to Atlanta—518 miles." Montag signed the ball and lobbed it back to the trainman, laughing 'til he had to wipe away the tears.

How can you not love this game? These gems, these far-fetched tales.

Without baseball we'd laugh too little, and life would be dreary. On the day I draw my last breath, these stories will come to mind. I'll think of Charley Baxter and Jimmy Giles; I'll remember Montag's improbable home run … and smile. I'll be delighted that these were the things I shared with Chris and Rose Marie. And I'll know, as surely as I know where the A, S, D, and F keys are on this typewriter, that they were the gifts of an extravagant God.

On a few cold, blustery afternoons I've wandered into the stands. I've sat there alone and imagined the action. Montag, along with Chuck Tanner, Pete Whisenant, Billie Porter, and Frank Torre—these are the team's current stars. I can see them out there. I can hear the crowd. And even on gray, wintry days, I catch a whiff of springtime. As much as I miss Charley—as often as I think about Giles, Douglas, and Henderson—I'm grateful that I'll be a part of a new season. I sit in the stands and my heart's heavier than a bag full of bats, but I'm glad that baseball is a part of my life for one more year.

Furman Bisher's my new boss. He's been the sports editor here going on five years, and the guy's so good it scares me. In his hands baseball, football, basketball—even golf—become wondrous parts of the life we've been given, things provided to give us joy, and to foreshadow the splendor of the world to come. With every phrase he writes, readers are drawn into the sheer pleasure of the great games man has created. I am hoping, through proximity and coaching, to become half as good as he is.

We've been warmly welcomed. Rose Marie has been invited to play bridge and to have coffee. And the moving van hadn't been gone for sixty minutes before our icebox was full of casseroles, pies, and homemade cookies—all the kind gifts of hospitable neighbors. Chris has found a kid his own age just a few doors down. And a creek runs behind our new house, begging to be explored by adventurous boys and their trusty dogs.

It's hardly home, but we all share a dash of hope.

As I've sifted through the events that have brought us here, I've often thought about the editorial I'd sculpted so carefully. Looking back, I wish I had done it differently. I wish I had introduced readers to Walter and Roberta Jackson, that I'd brought them into the presence of a father and mother who loved their son, who worked hard, who were honest, and who did their best to live decent lives—just like most of them. With the tools at my disposal, I should have brought readers face-to-face with Horace the sharecropper and Ruby the maid. With my help they might have seen for themselves that these were gentle people who couldn't possibly do them harm.

At the time I was intent on detouring minds around any thought of coloreds and whites mingled together, and I squandered the only chance I'd ever have. Now I can't help but to think that the *Herald's* readers, if they had known what I did, would have granted Horace and Ruby the simple pleasure of watching colored kids play ball. If I had done things another way, who knows how much grief we might have been spared.

On our way out of town we stopped by the Jacksons' house. It had been repaired and rebuilt, but still showed scars. We stood out front, the four of them and the three of us, and we wished one another well. My wife held hands with a colored maid, and in her eyes and by her smile, you could see that she loved Roberta Jackson. Walter and I shook hands; we clasped one another's shoulder and looked each other in the eye, man to man. I told him how glad I was that our paths had crossed; he thanked me for being his friend, and we both meant it from the heart kindred souls now bound together by something more than baseball.

When we look back on our time in Whitney, there will always be much that we miss. But I suspect, as the years go by, the thing we'll miss most is the Walter Jackson family.

◆ ◆ ◆ ◆

These days, when I sit in the stands at Ponce de Leon Ball Park, I shake my head and wonder why all this happened. On my way to the office, when I turn off Marietta and on to Forsyth, I grieve, wondering what good can possibly come from the destruction of a peaceful life in a beautiful town. Every day I ask myself: What's the purpose in all that pain?

Hints appear here and there: Percy finished the season hitting .315 for

Terre Haute. Next year Charley takes the reigns of a triple-A team in Florida. And I'm at a big-city paper working alongside a guy who's destined to become a legend.

When I ponder those things for more than a few seconds, I drift back to the first day I saw Percy play, to the day that Walter Jackson nearly ran me over. I had never been to South City High, and I had no need to be there then; I was just killing time on a slow day. Yet that day became a turning point for an entire town. Walter Jackson stormed out of his classroom, and because he turned right instead of left, his family would never be the same.

Because Walter Jackson turned right, Rose Marie and I suffered more than I thought any couple could bear. Yet we are closer now than we've ever been before, bound together tighter than I knew was possible, giving the phrase "one flesh" altogether new meaning.

Because Walter Jackson turned right, the trajectory of Chris's life changed forever.

Joe's life changed too. Burt and Bud and Helen and Phil Edwards and Chester LaBarr—nothing will ever be the same for any of them—all because a colored schoolteacher, during the course of an uneventful day, made a right-hand turn.

One day. One game. A chance collision with one man. And so many lives irreversibly altered.

Next year I suspect that Percy will follow in Jackie Robinson's footsteps. We'll watch him play on national television. Chris and I will be glued to the set. Our new neighbors will be gathered round and Jack Buck or Harry Caray will announce to the whole world that Percy Jackson has stepped to the plate. Chris will turn to the crowd and say, "I know him. That's our friend."

What's the point of it all? I don't know. I catch a glimpse here and there—a clue, a suggestion, an inkling of what may come. I see the unlikely role that baseball plays in America's new drama. I see many things dimly, and I trust, one day they will become clear. I see enough to give me hope.

And when I think back to the day that Walter Jackson nearly knocked me down, I am certain of this: It is hard to have faith in chance.

... a little more ...

When a delightful concert comes to an end,
the orchestra might offer an encore.
When a fine meal comes to an end,
it's always nice to savor a bit of dessert.
When a great story comes to an end,
we think you may want to linger.
And so, we offer ...
AfterWords—just a little something more after you
have finished a David C. Cook novel.
We invite you to stay awhile in the story.
Thanks for reading!

Turn the page for ...

- **Fiction That Rings True**
- **Discussion Questions**
- **Resources**
- **A Conversation with Richard Doster**

Fiction That Rings True

Safe at Home is fiction. The characters are the author's invention, but the events in their lives were inspired by the flesh-and-blood South of the 1950s. Many of the events in this novel happened … to somebody. The oppression and humiliation, the anger, sadness, and frustration—even the moments of grace—were real.

The Bus Boycott

The bus boycott that's described in *Safe at Home* is roughly modeled on the Baton Rouge Boycott of 1953 (not the famous Montgomery Bus Boycott that began two years later).

In February of that year the city of Baton Rouge raised the bus fare from 10 to 15 cents. Black passengers, who made up 80 percent of the system's riders, objected. Although they paid full fare, African Americans were required to sit or stand in the back of Baton Rouge buses while the front ten seats, always reserved for white passengers, often went unoccupied.

Reverend T. J. Jemison, pastor of Mt. Zion Baptist Church, condemned the fare increase and asked the city to amend this seating policy. The parish council complied, unanimously passing Ordinance 222, which abolished reserved seating. The ordinance, however, was not enforced. In the ensuing months a series of events provoked the successful boycott: A black woman was mistreated—verbally and physically—for refusing to give up her seat. African Americans protested her treatment; as a result, drivers were forced to comply with the ordinance. In defiance they launched a strike, prompting the Louisiana attorney general to nullify Ordinance 222, stating that it violated existing segregation laws.

In response black leaders formed the United Defense League (UDL). On June 19, 1953, Jemison and Raymond Scott, a black tailor, went to WLCS radio and announced that a boycott of the bus system would begin the next morning.

Several months later T. J. Jemison would advise Martin Luther King Jr. concerning another bus boycott in Montgomery, Ala. *(Source: Louisiana State University: http://www.lib.lsu.edu.)*

Several of the events in Percy Jackson's life are fictionalized accounts of actual experiences. These stories come from articles, newspaper accounts, biographies, and other books. The best single source chronicling the black minor-league experience is Bruce Adelson's study: *Brushing Back Jim Crow: The Integration of Minor-League Baseball in the American South.* Adelson gathered hundreds of first-person accounts. Here are a few that inspired events in the life of the fictional Percy Jackson.

Reaction of White Teammates

Percy Jackson is named in honor of Percy Miller, who, Adelson reports, was the first player to break the minor-league color line. Miller played in 1950 for the Danville Leafs of the Carolina League. "The most outstanding thing that summer," Miller told the author, "was when it got so the players would play catch with me. At first, they'd be throwing the ball to each other, and I'd be standing on the side. I started rolling the ball up on the wire behind home plate and catching it when it came off. Then one day, they said, 'Get a bat. We'll play some pepper.' I grabbed a bat and started to pepper them.... After that, they seemed to warm up to me. But I only felt accepted by a few...."

In the Locker Room

In *Safe at Home* when Percy first joins the Bobcats, he's forced to dress in the armory across the street from Memorial Stadium. This is based on an event that occurred in 1952, to Jim Clarkson. According to the April 2, 1952, edition of the *Sporting News:* "A local city ordinance barring Negroes from being in the clubhouse at Municipal Stadium served to prove how popular Jim (Buster) Clarkson, veteran Negro infielder, is with his Milwaukee teammates. When the Brewers arrived here for an exhibition with the Buffalo Bisons, Jack Tighe, manager of the International League club, explained apologetically that there was a sign, 'White Only,'

on the clubhouse door, but that Clarkson could dress—alone—in the National Guard armory across the street."

Unlike Percy Jackson's teammates, "the other Brewers … chorused in unison: We dress where [Jim] dresses."

Segregated Dining

One of the more touching scenes in *Safe at Home* is when Percy is joined in the back of the Big Chicken Restaurant by three of his teammates. Nat Peeples, who played briefly for the Atlanta Crackers, inspired this scene. Peeples told Adelson: "We stopped one time in Douglas. They told us they'd fix me a plate in the kitchen. So I ate in the kitchen. I looked up, and [Chuck] Tanner, Dick Donovan, and three or four more guys came back there and ate with me. [Usually] the guys had to bring food to me on the bus. I couldn't go into the restaurants. Chuck Tanner was one of the nicest guys on the team. He sat with me on the bus. He sat with me on the airplane…."

The Reaction of the Crowds

In the novel the reaction of the crowds—black and white—may appear extreme. However, black minor leaguers, almost universally, commented on the hostility of whites and the exuberance of blacks. Willie Tasby, who played a couple of seasons in the Piedmont League, put his experience succinctly. He told Adelson, "Shreveport was the worst. The black people sat down the right field line in the bleachers. It was so bad that if the black guys popped up, the black fans would jump up and applaud us, trying to make us feel good. If we got a hit, oh, man, they would just go crazy. If we hit a home run, they got drastic. They would wait for us outside the ballpark. The whites would try and drown them out, but they couldn't, even though there were more whites. Those people really tried to make us feel good." Further into the interview, he said, "I regretted going to that ballpark. Those people could think of more derogatory names than I had heard in my life. They wouldn't let up. You had a feeling those people would come out there and shoot you….The police were standing right there, but you got the impression that they'd be the leaders if something happened…."

Discussion Questions

Gather your friends together to talk about the themes and characters in *Safe at Home.* Use these questions to spark a lively discussion.

From the very first sentence this story asserts that baseball played (and still plays) a significant role in shaping our culture. What was your immediate response to this claim? Did your response change as you read the story? Explain.

What surprised you most about this depiction of the South in the 1950s?

There is a lot of talk about keeping the "status quo" late in the story. How is this sort of thinking still prevalent today?

What were your initial impressions of Jack Hall? How did they change over the course of the novel?

How is the relationship between Jack and his son, Chris, like that between Walter and his son, Percy?

What did you like most about Rose Marie? Least?

What role does Roberta's relationship with her son, Percy, play in the growth of Rose Marie's character?

Why were so many people in Whitney reluctant to change with the times?

Which scenes in the novel prompted your most visceral reactions? Which scenes broke your heart? Which scenes gave you hope?

What do you think was Jack Hall's greatest struggle in this story?

How does Jack's faith play into the decisions he makes?

Are there redeeming qualities beneath the overt racist surface in characters like Bud? What are those qualities?

What role do you think baseball, and sports in general, played in the civil rights movement that followed the time period depicted in this book?

All of the characters in this story (as in life) are flawed people. Describe some of the good/bad traits of the main characters. How are you like and unlike these people?

Which character did you relate to the most? The least?

How is the church depicted in this story? What are the similarities between Jack's pastor, Alan Spencer, and the Jacksons' pastor, Phil Edwards?

What was your emotional response to Pastor Spencer's sermon on the "Good Samaritan"? Why do you think a message like this didn't have a greater measurable impact on the issue of racism in America?

What will you remember most about *Safe at Home?*

The character growth in Percy's teammates is significant. Why do you think they were more readily able to embrace equality than the rest of the townspeople? What does this say about the factors that most significantly prompt necessary change in society?

What was your reaction to the way the story ended? In what ways is it a sad ending? In what ways is it hopeful?

Resources

Want to learn more about the inspiration for *Safe at Home?* Check out some of these books, many of which provided helpful background information for the novel.

Robinson, Jackie and Alfred Duckett. *I Never Had it Made: an Autobiography of Jackie Robinson*. New York: HarperCollins, 1995.

Adelson, Bruce. *Brushing Back Jim Crow: The Integration of Minor-League Baseball in the American South*. Charlottesville, VA: University of Virginia Press, 1999.

Snyder, Brad. *Beyond the Shadow of the Senators: The Untold Story of the Homestead Grays and the Integration of Baseball.* Chicago: McGraw-Hill, 2003.

Moore, Joseph Thomas. *Pride Against Prejudice: The Biography of Larry Doby.* New York: Praeger, 1988.

Aaron, Hank. *I Had a Hammer: The Hank Aaron Story*. New York: HarperCollins, 1991.

Dittmer, John. *Local People: The Struggle for Civil Rights in Mississippi.* Urbana, IL: University of Illinois Press, 1995.

McAdam Doug. *Freedom Summer*. New York: Oxford University Press, 1988.

Roberts, Gene and Hank Klibanoff. *The Race Beat: The Press, the Civil Rights Struggle, and the Awakening of a Nation*. New York: Knopf, 2006.

Raines, Howell. *My Soul Is Rested: The Story of the Civil Rights Movement in the Deep South*. New York: Penguin Books, 1977.

Jeter Naslund, Sena. *Four Spirits*. New York: William Morrow, 2003.

Author Interview

1. What was the inspiration for *Safe at Home?*

It was an accumulation of three things, really. First of all, a few years ago, Major League Baseball celebrated an anniversary of Jackie Robinson's life. I don't remember if it was his birth or death or signing with the Dodgers, but it piqued my interest and motivated me to explore what he'd gone through.

Second, every summer my wife, Sally, and I take a minor league baseball trip. We usually catch three or four games in Greenville, South Carolina; Asheville, North Carolina; Columbus, Georgia; or Lexington, Kentucky. We love the Atlanta Braves, but there's something especially charming about minor league baseball. You're close to the players, the people, the promotions, sometimes even the food is homier than you find in the big leagues. It's a much more intimate experience—the kind baseball fans truly savor.

The third piece of the puzzle fell into place during one of these swings. About five or six years ago we were at an arts festival in Asheville, North Carolina. At one of the vender stations, a young African American couple there was selling items commemorating the Negro leagues—photographs, plaques, T-shirts, and more. Some of the items displayed the logos for the Detroit Stars, the Homestead Grays, Indianapolis Clowns, Kansas City Monarchs … and it all was signed with the vendor's tagline: "For the brothers who played, but didn't get paid." If I recall, a portion of the profits went to a group who provided for Negro league players and their families.

Those things came together and got me thinking about black players breaking the color line, and about what that might have been like in the more intimate venues of minor league baseball. And then, once I came across a few good source materials, I became fascinated with writing a story about this volatile time in history.

2. Tell us about your relationship with baseball when you were growing up. Are there any similarities between you and the characters in *Safe at Home?*

Actually, I didn't become a baseball fan until I was an adult. When Sally and I moved to Atlanta in 1989, neither of us was a knowledgeable fan. But being in a major-league city for the first time (the Braves barely qualified then; they were 63-97 that year and finished last in the division), we thought we ought to have the experience. We went to a few games and started listening to the Braves broadcasters: Don Sutton, Pete Van Wieren, Skip Caray, and then, a season later, Joe Simpson. The chemistry between these guys was infectious. They were likeable, and play by play, situation by situation they taught us all about the game.

Then, in 1991, the Braves made their improbable charge from worst to first. They were one game behind the Dodgers (the Braves were in the West Division back then) going into the last week of the season, and hysteria gripped the city. We were glued to the TV every night. The iconic tomahawks could be found everywhere—on mailboxes, attached to skyscrapers, dangling from car antennas. The whole city stayed up late waiting for scores from L.A.

Sally and I went to the next-to-last game of the season. It was October 5. David Justice, our right fielder, caught the final out in a 5-2 win over Houston. Nobody in Atlanta will ever forget Greg Olson, our catcher, leaping into John Smoltz's arms. The Braves had clinched a tie for the N.L. West. But then the strangest thing happened: The players stayed on the field. The fans stayed in their seats. The coaches, the vendors, the announcers—everybody stayed. Together we watched the end of the Dodgers/Giants game on the JumboTron (or whatever it was called then) in center field. When the Giants beat the Dodgers, there was jubilation at the old Fulton County Stadium.

We've been serious fans since that day, but our affection for baseball is a direct result of the Braves announcers. Pete Van Wieren, the professor; Skip Caray, the crusty curmudgeon; Don Sutton, the patient teacher who has something nice to say about everybody; Joe Simpson,

the average player who relates to every man. They were always welcome guests in our home. Before the 2007 season the television networks busted up this team. We're still grieving.

3. What surprised you most as you did research for this book?

Here's the first and least surprising answer: Anybody, from the perspective of the early twenty-first century, is shocked by the fervency of segregationist attitudes. Looking back to this time, you have to be astonished by the fear of white southerners, by the apprehension and paranoia following the *Brown v. Board of Education* decision. The language, attitudes, and anger—is beyond our imagination today.

The other thing that surprised me was the patience and good nature of the black players of the era. Many of them consciously and deliberately modeled Jackie Robinson. I believe they had some vague notion that they were engaged in something bigger, something that transcended baseball. They persevered for unselfish reasons. They persisted, not only for their love of the game, but for the greater good of society.

A third thing that surprises me is how far we've come. The segregationist attitudes that existed just fifty-plus years ago were so extreme, so rabid, that it's hard to look at that time and compare it to now. Today I walk my dog through our Atlanta neighborhood and pass and wave to black neighbors and think nothing of it. But not so, fifty years ago. Some of those who read early versions of the manuscript commented on how hard the story was to read. They had forgotten (or had never known) what things were like in that era. We've got a long way to go in race relations; it is still, perhaps, the defining issue of our country, and we remain, largely, a segregated society. But we've come a very long way, and I think that gives us reason to hope for the future.

4. How would you describe the intersection of faith and life in this story?

In the course of the story, Jack reflects on his situation and surmises, "It's hard to have faith in chance." He's acknowledging the fact that there's always more to a situation than meets the eye. Throughout this

story Jack and the other characters are wrestling with the truth that all things, even those we don't understand, those that have no hint of redemptive purpose, must ultimately work for good. And the working out of that good takes place in and through the lives of ordinary men and women.

Another thing we see in the story is the corruption, not just of people, but of the "powers and authorities" of the world. Jack and Rose Marie and Bud and Burt—all the characters in the story, and all the people who grew up in that time—none of them knew a society that wasn't segregated, that wasn't, fundamentally and essentially, unjust. The culture and society were flawed, and the people were a product of that impersonal, cold, inflexible system.

As we're doing this interview, I'm working on a sequel to the story. In the next book Jack befriends Martin Luther King Jr. During the Montgomery bus boycott, Jack asks King about timing. He wants to know "why now?" Why, when the buses have always been segregated, is this the time to take action? King explains (and the dialogue is based on his actual words) that when the system itself is flawed, when institutions have veered from the path of righteousness, we're compelled to act. He tells Jack that Christians, when they see powers and authorities behaving in ways God didn't intend, have a duty to respond.

That's what's going on in *Safe at Home*—ordinary men and women are coming to grips for the first time with a crooked system, and slowly, through the actions of their ordinary lives, transforming it, realigning it, making things as they ought to be. In this story we get a glimpse, I hope, that it is our relationships, our mundane interactions, our conduct—with teachers, repairmen, checkout cashiers—that are the means by which the world is transformed, renewed, and redeemed. In this make-believe story we also discover the truth that no-name players in anonymous cities have been an intricate part of God's plan to redeem the world.

And by the way, I love the fact that this is still occurring in baseball. Look at the starting lineup of most teams today. You'll find white guys,

black guys, Asians, and Latinos playing side by side. In a spot here and there, you'll also find Australians and Canadians. Baseball, at least this facet of it, is a great example of healthy, productive diversity—of one (team) from many (ethnicities and nationalities).

5. What do you hope readers will take away from reading *Safe at Home*?

Most importantly I hope that when they come to the final page, they'll be able to honestly say, "Now *that* was a good story." I want readers to care about Jack and Rose Marie and Chris. I want them to pull for Percy and empathize with Walter and Roberta. I hope, in some vicarious way, readers struggle alongside Burt and Joe. And I even hope they understand what's going on in Bud's mind.

It would thrill me to know that readers were anxious to pick up the book and continue from the last turned-down corner, eager to see what happens next, and then, when they came to the end, to be disappointed that it was over.

Beyond that I hope they come away with some appreciation for what anonymous people living regular lives accomplished through the sport of baseball ... one small town at a time.

6. What has been the most rewarding aspect of writing? The most challenging?

The most challenging part is, to the extent of my limited ability, to make full and beautiful use of the English language; to take the twenty-six letters of the alphabet and sculpt them, word by word, sentence by sentence, paragraph by paragraph, into a narrative that's delightful to read, that might, if I'm extraordinarily lucky, cause someone to read a sentence twice just because it's so darn pretty. You can't have a good story without strong characters. You can't have a compelling narrative without an engaging plot. But what I love most is our language, the sound of the words rolling off the tongue, a rhythm and cadence that ensnares the reader; that's enchanting and addictive.

And the most rewarding thing? To go back and read a paragraph for the fiftieth time and still think to myself, *Not bad ... not bad at all.*

7. What can you tell us about any current or upcoming writing projects?

A sequel is scheduled for release in March 2009. When we pick up the story, Jack and his family are in Atlanta. They befriend restaurateur and future segregationist governor Lester Maddox, the civil rights crusading newspaper editor Ralph McGill, and Martin Luther King Jr. Jack takes a deeper and more pervasive view of life in the South. He becomes more engaged in its culture, wanting the world to see and appreciate the region's writers, musicians, artists, and businessmen—the South's contribution to the world. More and more he laments the predominate picture the world has—of burned-out buses, snarling German shepherds, and blasting firehouses. We'll see more of Chris, a young man whose life was changed the night his home was bombed, whose attitudes are shaped by an early friendship with a black baseball player. And whose mother has grave misgivings about the direction his life is taking.